EPITOME OF EVIL

EPITOME OF EVIL

MICHAEL J. BROCHERT

gatekeeper press
Tampa, Florida

Epitome of Evil

Published by Gatekeeper Press
7853 Gunn Hwy, Suite 209
Tampa, FL 33626
www.GatekeeperPress.com

Library of Congress Control Number: 2022940831

ISBN: 9781662929359
eISBN: 9781662929366

Table of Contents

DEDICATION

If everyone is truly unique, what a sad day for mankind—
the world will only know one Margie.

ACKNOWLEDGMENTS

My heartfelt thanks to the staff and volunteers at Recovery International, Inc., a non-profit assisting people to cope with their nervous symptoms. Their main office is located just outside of Chicago, but meetings are held all across the country. The best part isn't just that it's free, but that it works. I have practiced their system all my life.

Many thanks to my son, Paul. As my personal computer nerd, he tolerated Dear Old Dad's outlandish outbursts regarding disappearing cursors, struggles with auto-correct and format foibles.

To my wife, Margie: for me, it's been forty wonderful years; for her, it's been eleven or twelve, not necessarily consecutive.

Ron Mazanka, for his assistance in poker terminology. Ron is the new old face of comedy in Vegas.

CHAPTER

1

Tuesday, July 25, 1967

Disgusted by the unexpected wad of phlegm deposited in his right palm while attempting to thwart a gag reflex, Sgt. Dolan ransacked the front seat of the unmarked police cruiser, frantically searching for an improvised towelette, finally settling on his stain riddled dark blue pant leg.

"Why the hell not?" His partner scoffed, catching a glimpse of the social faux pas.

"It's this goddamned smoke," the veteran cop complained, waving his freshly wiped hand in front of his face in a vain attempt to circulate air.

"And the heat. It's so damned hot, it's a miracle that our perp back there hadn't already melted into the asphalt before we picked him up," the rotund dimwit smirked at his well-timed racial slur, as his outsized head jabbed toward the rear seat.

The third day of Detroit's riots and overcast skies trapped heat in a thermal inversion, slow roasting residents, tricking weary minds into believing the sporadic explosions of local businesses the result of spontaneous combustion, rather than the work of vandals and looters. The entire police force slogged through twenty-four-hour days since Sunday, crashing for only minutes at a time in makeshift precinct houses, straining to maintain a modicum of control in a Kafkaesque nightmare.

"You'd think the city could spring for air conditioners in these buckets," Dolan bitched, tugging at the neck of his stiffly starched, half size too small powder blue shirt, struggling to peel the soaked garment from his irritated skin.

"Wouldn't that be sweet?"

"But that would make our jobs too cushy. Before you know it, cops would refuse to get out of their cars and enforce the laws," the sergeant reasoned.

"Hell, if it wasn't for these people, we wouldn't be getting out of our cars half the time anyway," the driver concluded with an arch of his brow and a slight jerk of his head to the rear seat.

Robert Thayer, known as Bobbie to his friends, decided to keep his mouth shut. Prevented by the civil disturbance from reaching his accounting firm in downtown Detroit, the twenty-six-year-old professional spent three days coddling his two children, Nina, age five and Robbie, age three. A telephone call from his diabetic mother four blocks away, prompted an illegal midday excursion. Relinquishing his usual button-down Italian cut suit and spit polished wingtips for jeans, tee shirt and scuffed ankle high tennis shoes, the dutiful son traversed the deserted Boston-Edison neighborhood of past their prime mansions, cutting through the alley until hailed by the occupants of the telltale municipal car. Obeying the concealed loud speaker's instruction to stop, Thayer waited until the two white officers in the slow rolling sedan exited to flash a disarming smile and proffer his patented business schmoozing greeting.

"Shut up and put your hands where I can see them," Dolan yelled as he drew his weapon while approaching the suspect from the right.

"I got him covered, Sarge," the driver hollered while shielding himself with the open door.

"Look, I was just…"

"Shut up! Not another word," Dolan commanded, grabbing Thayer by the upper arm, throwing him forward onto the hood of the car, splitting his legs with a brisk kick and patting him down for weapons. Reassured, the veteran pulled Thayer off the vehicle and requested identification.

Reaching toward his back pocket, Thayer shook his head in dismay. "I left my wallet at home in my other pants."

"Yeah, right," the rookie called out from behind the door.

"What were you doing in this alley?"

"Just going to my Mother's house."

"Oh, that's a beaut Sarge. Looks like we got us a big bad wolf on his way to grandma's."

"No ID and in violation of curfew, you're going in bud." Dolan holstered his thirty-eight and ratcheted on the cuffs, escorting Thayer to the rear seat.

Bobbie decided to remain calm; no need to exacerbate a troubling situation. "*Stay cool and the numbers eventually fall into place in a balanced bottom line.*" Thayer found Dolan's constant bitching disquieting: the heat; a rash; the garbage fast food; indigestion; the defensive posture assumed by the police; the nerve of people to blow up and loot businesses in the city of his birth; his wife's constant nagging about his drinking; anxiety over the safety of his family. The apparent worsening of Dolan's condition on the way to the station sounded a sensory alarm in Thayer: irritable; sweating profusely; darkened, sunken eyes reminiscent of the villains in Saturday afternoon monster movies he watched as a kid; exaggerated movements; abnormally loud voice, almost as if exhibiting a hearing difficulty; and the steady stream of complaints. The slightest comment certain to draw the ire of the pudgy racist behind the wheel, Thayer elected to play it safe, continuing his vigil of silence. Barely tolerating the stifling ninety-degree heat, Bobbie experienced intense neck pain as a result of his hands cuffed behind his back, thrusting his shoulders forward. As Thayer squirmed to adjust to the discomfort, Dolan's passenger side window exploded in a hailstorm of glass fragments, spraying the occupants as they instinctively ducked for cover.

"We're under fire!" Dolan screamed, while simultaneously stabbing for the radio handset, as the rookie veered off to the left, bouncing up the curb and strafing the front fender on the limestone exterior of the corner bank building, screeching to a halt.

"Central! This is car 5420 on Linwood, just south of Clairmount. We're taking fire. Snipers! Location unknown. Send backup now!"

"Roger, 5420. No units available for assist. Advise you extricate yourself from the situation immediately. Ten four."

"Extricate! What the hell is extricate? Did you hear me? We're under attack, you idiot. Send the damned cavalry!" Dolan screamed, as he threw the microphone against the dash from his crumpled position.

"Christ Sarge, I can't get the door open," the panicked novice yelled as he bashed his massive upper body against the frame. "We're too close to the building."

"Roger, 5420. I say again. No units available. Suggest you retreat from the area. Ten four," the response squawked from the floor.

"Get us the hell out of here Reichert. I don't care if you have to get out and pick this crate up and put it on your back."

"Yes sir," the frantic trainee replied, twisting the ignition key while hunching down, his ample midsection hovering over Dolan's head. Dropping the gearshift into drive and stomping on the accelerator, the big block Ford sedan screamed, as the tires stripped off a trail of rubber struggling for traction across the sidewalk, side swiping a utility pole on the right as they bounded down the curb and sped away along Linwood, blowing by blocks of burned-out hulks of once thriving businesses.

"Some of your brothers just tried to kill us."

Thayer uprighted himself, shook to shed shards of glass stuck to the sweat of his face and neck, again electing to keep quiet. Dolan's agitation concerned Bobbie, but he assessed the fat cracker as truly dangerous.

"Maybe we should teach your brothers a lesson," the shaken wheelman blurted out in an obvious attempt to restore his self-confidence.

Thayer remained on his muted vigil while he surveyed the cops. The visibly trembling driver courted a complete breakdown, while Dolan displayed an uncharacteristic calm that Bobbie attributed to his front-line experience; certainly a refreshing break from the litany of earlier complaints.

"You know Sarge, it must be something in the gene pool. When I get frustrated, I don't feel the need to loot an appliance store. Only an asshole would want to drag a fucking refrigerator down the alley. No sirree. When I get pissed, I like to pound on something. What do you say we take this dip shit out and shoot his ass? That'd show his brothers we're through clowning around," trainee Reichert reasoned, the creaky voice a dead giveaway of his fear.

A tremendous concussion pushed the police car sideways, the width of an entire lane, as the Cunningham Drug store on the northwest corner of Linwood and W. Grand Boulevard, exploded into a ball of flames.

"Jesus H. Christ," the rookie screamed, hunching down on the steering wheel.

"One of my favorite places to eat lunch," Dolan whispered to himself while staring at the destruction out the window. "I loved their butter toasted hot dog buns."

Reichert recovered and maneuvered a left turn onto West Grand Boulevard, squealing the tires in a continuation of the needless high-speed getaway.

Thayer pondered his predicament, allowing himself to relax somewhat as they neared the temporary Third Street precinct house located a stone's throw from the General Motors world headquarters building. As the rotund wheelman glided across the deserted boulevard to negotiate his turn onto the John C. Lodge service drive, his plotted course changed with an abrupt instruction from Dolan.

"Go!" The reflective Sergeant ordered, pointing his arm straight, similar to an Old West wagon train leader.

"Finally decided we're gonna teach our perp here a lesson, eh Sarge? Where to?"

"Head over to the old Packard Industrial Complex, up the way there."

"You gonna get it now, asshole; a lesson in the school of hard knocks."

"Shut up and drive, Reichert," Dolan ordered, picking up the mike. "Central, this is 5420. We're escorting a Canadian to the border. We'll be out of service for about an hour."

"That's a roger, 5420. Glad to see everything worked out okay for you guys. Tell our neighbors to the north we said hello."

Ten-four. 5420 out.

Bobbie struggled to contain a wave of nausea while frantically collecting his thoughts.

"Excuse me, sir." The polite tone reminiscent of an Eddie Haskell remark on *Leave It to Beaver*. "But you don't really want to do this. Please. I'm an accountant. I was just going over to my Mother's house…"

"Can it, dickhead. Don't need your mouth flapping like a whip-poor-will's ass."

"Please, I have a wife and two children," Thayer pleaded.

"Shut up."

"But this isn't right. You can't be doing this."

"Button it up, or I'll do it for you."

"But you've got it all wrong."

"Enough!" The driver screamed.

"Pull in over there," Dolan instructed, pointing to a break in the battered cyclone fence. The cruiser slowly motored around to the rear of the sprawling abandoned auto plant, halting close to a garbage strewn loading dock.

Thayer felt an intense shiver ripple from his head to his feet, as the cold sweat drenching his body combined with his nervous trembling.

"Get out," the trainee ordered, reaching in and clamping onto Bobbie's upper arm to expedite the command, while Dolan pried a side access door loose.

"Over here," the matter-of-fact monotone directed.

As the trio entered the cavernous monument to Detroit's manufacturing past, the striated light filtering through fractured panes presented barely adequate illumination to maneuver around the maze of machinery and assorted scrap metal, as well as, casting a surreal pall on the unfolding nightmare. Thayer prepared himself psychologically for a beating, leaning on his strict Baptist upbringing for strength. Following Dolan's exact pace to ward off unnecessary criticism from the Nazi chunk behind him, Bobbie winced as his left knee buckled under the sharp thwack of a leather-coated blackjack between his shoulder blades.

"Just giving you a preview of things to come, my man. Now keep your ass moving," the paunchy sadist blurted with recovering bravado, accenting his instruction with a solid shove to the mid-back.

"Shut up!" Dolan commanded.

"Just giving the asshole a heads up on…"

"Zip it, both of you. Let's just get this done," Dolan recited in a detached timbre as he grabbed the tube railing of the metal staircase in the northeast corner of the plant. Ascending in what seemed a never-ending workout on a stair master stuck on maximum incline, Thayer found the reverberating metal clunk of the officers' feet on the perforated aluminum steps in sharp contrast to the nearly silent ascent of his gym shoes. Forcing his mind to focus, Bobbie ruled out overpowering the officers, resigning himself to beg, if necessary, to avoid serious injury.

Finally reaching a landing just under ceiling height four stories above ground, Dolan fussed with a rusted lock assembly while Reichert spun Thayer around, sucker punching him with an upper cut to the chin. Gnashing teeth ignited electric jolts short circuiting brain synapses, while his torso propelled back, smashing his skull into the exposed cinder block wall, sounding a dull thud. A lukewarm sensation filled Bobbie's mouth simultaneously as a spray of blood escaped through reverberating lips, showering his assailant's face. Sinking down the concrete backboard, Reichert crashed his elbow into Thayer's right collarbone. Associating the crack with a fracture, a puzzled prey pondered the two unusual metallic clicks as he sank into a half-conscious state. Thayer glanced at the steps.

The rookie remarked, "Them's your teeth bouncing down the steps, asshole. You got to be more careful. Hanging around in a dangerous place like this could be hazardous to your health."

"Bring him out here," Dolan commanded.

"You got it, Sarge," the eager tormentor replied, grabbing the sunken carcass and lifting it with the ease of a stage prop barbell.

Dolan repeatedly slapped Thayer's swollen face to revive the suspected perp. "You brought this on yourself, you know," the cop calmly explained to Bobbie as the rookie propped him up from behind with his blackjack wedged against his throat.

"Please! I'm an accountant. I have a wife and kids," Bobbie pleaded through distended lips.

"Yeah, right! And I'm the king of... what's that desert place, Sarge? Oh yeah... Siam," Reichert regaled, tightening his chokehold.

"No really, please..." Thayer managed to whisper.

"No, that's enough. I don't want to hear another word. You and your kind are guilty of ruining my city. I love this place. We get rid of a few of you animals and we'll all be better off for it."

"Please, God, I have a wife and..."

The butt end of Dolan's Billy club jabbed into Thayer's left eye, exploding the socket in a gush of blood; the scream muted to a high-pitched gurgle by Reichert's paralyzing grip. Kneeing Bobbie firmly in the buttocks and simultaneously releasing his chokehold, the semi-comatose, battered frame collapsed to the flat-tarred roof. Dolan fiddled with the cover of a giant cooling system, as his rabid underling unleashed a barrage of kicks to Thayer's head and chest.

"Drag his sorry ass over here," Dolan yelled, as he lifted an immense circular aluminum exhaust fan off a square metal box, exposing a deep ventilation shaft. "Drop his ass in here."

"Outstanding, Sarge," the eager assistant commented as he hoisted Thayer, dropping him headfirst into the abyss.

"Shit! Would you look at that? What are the chances?"

As Bobbie started his descent, his restrained arms flew out in a wishbone pattern, catching the cuffs on a protruding metal flange, providing the impression of a high diver suspended in a flying V pattern.

"Well, don't that beat all? Lookie here Sarge. We got us an acrobat."

"Damned nice of you, Canook. I would have forgot my cuffs. Damned things cost twelve dollars wholesale," Dolan remarked, unlocking the blood-soaked bonds, propelling Thayer into the darkness.

CHAPTER

2

December 22, 1980

Lucinda Walker stomped her imitation black leather spiked heeled boots on the concrete and cradled her flopping breasts with crisscrossed bare forearms, while huddled in the entrance of the burned-out furniture store with the enthusiasm of a *Soul Train* dance contestant, to fend off the cold. The nineteen-year-old hooker hated the toe contorting knee high lace-ups, but the seasoned veteran learned quickly that pleasing a john's fantasies garnered more profits. She joined the human wave of competitors dashing out of steel grated storefronts and abandoned tenements to flag down passing motorists in a whimsical routine reminiscent of an Ewok celebration in the *Star Wars* epic.

The epitome of urban decay by day, Twelfth Street transformed into a dynamic marketplace of sex after sundown: testosterone touting teens wailing and flailing to plant their first seed; seemingly happy suburban husbands breaking the strain of boredom, tolerating the same bumper to bumper traffic that only hours earlier they labeled irritating, to peruse the smorgasbord of flesh; perverts of every persuasion salivating at the potential to partially placate insatiable appetites for the unimaginable. Extending north and south, the three lanes wide, one-way avenue provided a habitat for lust virtually undisturbed by the police. Anything goes, for a mutually agreed upon price.

Lucinda recognized the rusted '72 Chevy Nova cruising by for a second sweep. Determined to best her rivals, the aggressive whore stepped into the street, causing the distracted driver to jam on the brakes.

"That's right! That's right! Least your beat-up old ride knows to stop for a beautiful thing like me." Lucinda teased, sliding her hands down curvaceous hips.

"Get the hell out of the way!" The nervous john demanded.

"You got a lot of attitude for a man being in a heap of trouble. I could sue your ass. I watch them lawyers on TV: 1-800-CALL SAM. I know my rights."

"What the hell are you talking about?"

"My severe emotional distress. If you smart, we work out an out of court settlement. I'm talking ten dollars for the time of your life baby. Unless you some weird assed white boy with one of them fetish things for dead girls and really means to hurt me."

"Shut up and get in."

"Oh, you just a sweet talker, ain't ya?" Lucinda laughed, struggling to open the creaky door. Extending her left leg into the vehicle, her stiletto heel caught in the floorboard, torquing her body, causing her to plop onto the plastic covered seat. Glancing down, Lucinda squealed, "You know you gots all kinda holes in da floor?"

"Used to be a racecar," the john responded.

"Reminds me of one dem waffle irons," the hooker remarked, still starring down, mouth agape.

"Can we please get going?"

Adjusting her position with a scooch, Lucinda inquired, "What's this?" As she tried to pinch the clear seat cover. "My Momma got this shit on her couch. Cockroaches slidin' all over like they was in the ice capades."

Lucinda chuckled. Her story drawing a 'shut the fuck up look', the teen directed, "Turn into the alley, over there."

Giving the narrow lane the once over, the john balked, "I don't know about this."

"Where the man flappin' his mouth? He disappear? I works this alley all the time. Sept for catchin' the clap, it be safe as this trashed out city can be."

The Nova eased into the opening, sandwiched between two burned out high rises. Inching along, fighting the competing interest of a cautionary mental tic and surging primal instincts, the john continued his advance.

"Somethin' botherin' your foot?"

The comment jolting the intense concentration of a man possessed, the john awkwardly responded, "My foot. What? What are you talking about?"

"Then, why don't you mash on the gas so we can get on with it and poor Lucinda can get back to makin' a livin'?"

Hunching down, bobbing his head back and forth to view up the sides of the buildings, the john remarked, "Now who's runnin' their mouth?"

"It ain't but a ways more, but I got one dem premonitions dat I done lost my good looks and charm before we gets there. Now can you speed it on up, please?"

Exhibiting the cervical rotation of an owl, the john continued his nervous surveillance: straining to peek under the driver's door header; a forearm swipe to wipe condensation off the window, followed by a quick glance forward into blackness; checking the windshield mounted mirror to foil an attack from the rear; ducking toward his antsy passenger to view the opposite wall of worry as the Nova slowly rolled forward.

"There! I ain't been jerkin' you off," the hooker flinging her wrist forward to extend her index finger. "Not yet, anyways. But we gonna get to that," she smiled.

Fifty years earlier, the stunning courtyard of garden park apartments, the tunnel broadened to a lot of cheap lust.

"Slide in over there," Lucinda pointed, directing the john in between a silver Fairlane and a two-tone GMC pickup.

"Now, let's see what you got!"

The john arched his back and unzipped his pants.

"No, no, no. We ain't there yet honey. I means the green that makes me make you shoot the jizz."

"Oh, yeah, I forgot. I'm a little nervous," the john responded while fumbling to reach his ankle high pant pocket.

"You more than that, sweet thing; you got the bug."

"No, I'm clean. I swear."

"No honey. I meant you been without so long, you thinking with your little head," Lucinda smiled.

"Yeah, your right about that," the john agreed, scooting to the middle of the seat. "What was that?" The startled customer asked just as Lucinda began fondling his sack.

"That be Yolanda, squattin' to pee in the bucket. Now you got to concentrate so we get done with the business."

"What's she doing that for?"

"She be avoidin' the clap."

"What does that do?"

"You writin' one dem dummy books, or somethin'. Now let's get to business. I gots to make a livin' here and you runnin' your mouth again."

As Lucinda worked her magic, the john came to life. "You big for a white boy. Can't believe the ladies don't fuss all over you when you let them see something like this. Oooh, that's it, baby."

"Sit on me, please."

"Oooh, you be so polite. Can't be refusin' you, now can I? But first, we got to laminate you."

"You gotta do what?" The chest heaving john questioned.

The streetwalker reached into her boot top, removing a foil packet. Gripping the Trojan between her thumb and index finger, she raised it to her mouth and tore it open with her teeth while continuing to stroke with the opposite hand.

"Oh yeah, right," the john nodded.

As Lucinda eased down on his lap, the john flipped up her bra and torqued her around to suckle her nipple.

"Oh baby, that feel good. Old Lucinda gonna work you some extra for wakin' up her points."

The john buried his head into the streetwalker's breast, dramatically increasing the intensity of his quest, now biting the erect tip.

"Careful there, baby! You be clamping down too hard, you gonna snip off that snack and put Lucinda in da 'ployment line."

Biting down with the ferocity of an escaped pit bull on an unsuspecting neighbor child, the excruciating breast pain masked the initial penetration of a sharpened number two lead pencil into the base of the prostitute's skull, short circuiting her scream. Lucinda slumped sideways to the passenger seat. Her post mortem convulsions reminiscent of a flopping fish in the bottom of a boat. With the giggle of a child, the assailant stared at the anomaly until all motion ceased. *"I just love this part."*

Firing up the engine and rolling out of the drive-in den of iniquity without headlights, the john circled around to Fourteenth Street and merged in with northbound traffic, then headed east to dump the body.

While flooding the interior of the Nova with the high-powered, sudsy water after a generous application of tri-sodium phosphate, the predator watched in amazement as the forensic evidence disappeared down the drain. Holes drilled throughout the floorboards and rocker panels facilitated the endeavor. *"True genius often requires adaptation of the simplest concepts to foil an adversary. Who would ever guess a quarter carwash would be a sociopath's best friend?"* The john reflected. Tapping his index finger on top of the steering wheel while waiting the mandatory twenty minutes for the wiring to dry out, the killer fired up the engine and exited the wash singing, "Hi-ho! Hi-ho! It's off to school we go!"

CHAPTER

3

Late Spring, 1987

THIS WAS THE PART he really dreaded; merging onto the expressway in his little rattle-trap. The American Motors salesman kept stressing the mileage; that should have set off the first warning, but whittling him down from $1,400 to $385 just made the deal too good to walk away.

"C'mon, you piece of crap!" Jack pleaded as he tightened his grip on the wheel, as if that would help to increase the speed. "We're going downhill and you still can't get it moving? I can walk faster than this," Jack admonished as he glanced over his left shoulder to view oncoming traffic in the right lane of southbound I-75. "Holy crap!" He screamed as he viewed the bumper-to-bumper line of tractor-trailers, whizzing along at sixty miles per hour. Sweat gushed off his forehead as he glanced at the speedometer, "Thirty-two miles an hour; that's all you've got?" Jack screeched as he jammed the floor shift into fourth gear. Flicking on his left blinker, a faint smile formed at the relief the signal actually worked. The ear-splitting blare of an air horn interrupted his glee as a solid steel front bumper filled his rearview mirror. A quick peek to check his speed, "Damn, forty-seven miles per hour?" Jack stomped on the accelerator so hard he swore the tassels on his maroon loafers curled. Realizing no noticeable result, the 1976 Renault Le Car struggled like the little engine that could, its' four-cylinders reeling from the effort. A glance into the side mirror took a second to register, "Smoke? What's that trailer doing sliding into the center lane? Oh, Lord!" Jack squealed as he realized the truck brakes locked up and its trailer jackknifing. Finally, hitting fifty-five miles per hour; the truck stabilized and now followed five car lengths behind. "Oh man, that was close," Jack commented as he finally got up to speed with traffic, releasing his death grip on the wheel and moving with the flow of morning rush hour to downtown Detroit.

Having spent the night at his girlfriend's Royal Oak townhouse, he meant to sneak out without waking her. Stubbing his toe on the console table leg, sounded like a train derailment in the quiet dark room. Jack's left loafer flipped out of his hand and splashed into the fish tank.

"Jack," Sarah moaned. "What's going on?"

"Just going fishing, Babe," Jack chuffed, reaching into water to retrieve his footwear.

"Come back to bed."

"I'd love to, but I don't want to miss Mink's lecture this morning."

"We're gonna see him later in the day, aren't we?"

"Depending on his schedule."

"So, come on back to bed."

"How about we meet at my place for lunch?"

"Sounds good."

"Can't wait. Love you," Jack whispered as he exited the door, shaking the water from his shoe.

Although an ungodly hour, Jack Zechariah Michaels would rather soak his naked body in liquid heat and storm the gates of hell than miss one nanosecond of a lecture by Joe Mink. He was voted Wayne State University's most popular professor for the last five years in a row. No simple feat, since he only taught in Monteith College, a four-hundred student honors school located within the University. The vibrant pedagogue injects life into otherwise drab material with an unparalleled dramatic flair, leaving the indelible mark of that one influential teacher that no one ever forgets. Assembled in State Hall with six-hundred fellow insomniacs, J.Z. marveled at the sellout crowd. The only professor to display universal appeal, Mink drew attendance from every cross section of the student body for his 7:30 a.m. social science analysis of the 1967 Detroit riots. Attendees hung on every word; the pervasive quiet reminiscent of a requested moment of silence in a memorial service, as the eloquent raconteur paced the aisles in a well-choreographed marriage of sound and motion.

"Any questions?"

"Sir, are you insinuating that the conduct of looting and pillaging is an acceptable form of civil disobedience?" A shaky high-pitched voice from the back of the auditorium inquired.

"No, not at all. What I am saying is that the conduct is understandable. People get swept up in a mob psychology, akin to the stereotype liquored up cowboys forming a lynch mob on *Gunsmoke*. Years of repressed feelings, whether legitimate or not, explode in rage as the event seems to take on a life of its own; the safety in numbers axiom, if you will."

"Professor, how can you summarily dismiss the official estimates of death as recorded in the findings of the Kerner Commission?" The representative from the *Southern Edge* asked, as he readied his pen atop the stenographer's pad.

"I was there. I saw it. I don't give a tinker's damn what the Federal Government says. I was trapped at Henry Ford Hospital for five days. We had forty-three DOAs at Ford alone, and we were only a satellite triage station."

"Why would the government lie about something so easily detectable?" The student journalist pressed.

"No one seems to have taken the time to uncover evidence to dispute their figures, including news organizations with significantly more resources than your publication. I'm only telling you what I know from firsthand experience," Mink relayed with a sincerity evidenced in his eyes, as well as, his tone.

"Professor Mink," the reporter continued, "Do you have an estimate of the true figure of deaths?"

"You're a persistent fellow, Mr.?"

"Shaloub. Mamoud Shaloub," the reporter responded.

"Well, Mr. Shaloub, I conservatively estimate somewhere in the area of 150 to 200 people missing and/or killed."

"How could you possibly arrive at that figure?" The reporter pressed.

"Rumors mostly," Mink replied.

Mamoud prepared to pounce on what he perceived as the Professor's Achilles heel, but Professor Mink raised his arms, palms in a pushing motion, "Hear me out, please."

The reporter settled back as Mink explained.

"When you hear one rumor, you discount it. When you hear that same rumor through several different sources, that should make you stop and think."

"So, you think there is a government cover up?"

"Yes, I do," Mink stated, while checking his watch.

"Sorry, but that's all the time we have. I want to thank you for coming out this early." A rousing applause drowned out his final comment, "Remember, be a voice in your community at every opportunity. Class dismissed."

CHAPTER

4

A HIDDEN GEM IN THE rapidly declining downtown, the Detroit Athletic Club, or, the DAC, as its shareholders referred to it, provided the privacy the Group of Five required. Deteriorating membership and a lackluster chef contributed to a slide, allowing existing patrons to skirt strict enforcement of the rules. Reserving a residence suite on the top floor of the Renaissance style building, a waif of cigar smoke hung shoulder high in room 712, providing the impression of an executive session with their heads literally in the clouds. The well-dressed group met informally once a month at different locations to partake in a friendly game of poker and aid each other in the advancement of their careers, wherever and whenever possible, since they shared a secret impenetrable bond; a tontine of evil.

Chief of Detectives, Tony Marzoli strutted into the room sporting an original Anthony Riminelli designed black linen suit with faint gray pinstriping, matching Santoni calf leather shoes and freshly coiffed, jet black hair. Extending his right hand to Judge O'Hara revealed a forty-thousand-dollar Patek Philippe watch.

"Tony, great to see you, as always," the Judge professed, while vigorously shaking his hand. "How's the best dressed cop on the force doing?"

"Outstanding. Great to see you to, Jim. It's been way too long." After a brief pause, Marzoli leaned into the Judge as though his next remark was a secret and inquired, "One of the guys downtown heard a rumor that Judge Columbo goes commando under his robes. Any truth to that?"

Flummoxed, O'Hara shrugged and replied, "I wouldn't have any idea. If he does, he certainly has never mentioned it."

A gentle acknowledging head-bob the only response. Glancing to the table on his right and nodding, "Comish, always a pleasure."

"You too, Tony."

"Mr. Prosecutor."

"Enough already," a dismissive Riley Evans ordered. Scanning Marzoli as though absorbing every detail, "You don't have any idea what kind of problems your fancy wardrobe poses, do you? I can't believe Internal Affairs isn't all over you."

"Look who's talking?"

"Big difference. I'm the prosecuting attorney. People expect me to dress appropriately."

"Everyone just thinks I'm a clothes horse."

"With a watch that costs a years' pay."

Judge O'Hara stepped in between them. "That is quite enough."

Glancing around the room, Tony inquired, "Where's Butchie?"

Dolan chimed in, "Take a guess."

"In the crapper. The man spends most of his life in there," Marzoli chuckled.

"Gentlemen, before we get down to discussing business, I'd like to remind you all how boring this game has become. Each of you bring a wad of dough and contribute it to my retirement fund by the end of the weekend." Judge O'Hara smiled, exhaling a plume of smoke from his Monte Christo cigar, while the other three groaned. "We've talked about new blood to keep the game interesting, but never seem to act on it. What do you think about inviting the guy that Butchie talks about all the time?

Granted, he always seems to end every mention with wanting to kill the guy, but it sounds like he's a real player."

"Could spice things up, but there may be a lot of private matters he could overhear," Commissioner Dolan interjected.

"We'll discuss business before, or, after," the Judge explained. "If he happens to hear something he shouldn't, we'll have to rely on his discretion."

"Or, we could just have Butchie break his neck," Chief of Detectives Marzoli chuckled. "But then, we'd be right back where we started."

"Is everyone in agreement?" The Judge glanced around the table. "So ordered."

Evans tapping toe, to a beat only he heard, sped up. Judge O'Hara noticed his impatience.

"Riley, something on your mind?"

"How in the hell did we allow this thing to hit the papers?" The irate prosecuting attorney grilled, taking immediate command of the meeting.

"Who was to know? The article appeared in that college rag at Wayne State. It was just a summary of the views of that professor who was poking around the tombs," the defensive Police Commissioner responded.

"Eliminate the problem!" Prosecutor Evans ordered.

"We can't go around killing everyone," Judge O'Hara pleaded.

"Of course we can, you moron, we're the police," The prosecutor responded with a sickening smirk.

"Now wait just a goddamned minute here. This is getting out of control," O'Hara complained, his striking head of silver hair and squared jaw providing the distinguished look of the perfect jurist.

"Going soft on us, Your Honor?" The Prosecutor chided with a vicious stare. "That robe finally enshrouding you with a true sense of wisdom and justice?"

Closing his eyes and bowing his head, the Judge took a moment to collect his thoughts. "We can't follow the ridiculous course of killing everyone. These things pop up every now and then. People are enraptured for a while and then it fizzles out. Just let it be and it will work out. There's no way anyone can trace anything back to us."

"We'll just call this an insurance policy," Prosecutor Evans concluded, extinguishing his cigar with entirely too much force, effort and enjoyment. Arching his brow at Marzoli, "Take care of it?"

"Consider it done," the Chief of Detectives responded.

Dolan leaned over to the only member who remained silent the entire meeting, "Butchie, what'd ya say we take that new Caddie out for a spin?"

CHAPTER

5

Elated at surviving another episode of the Joey Chitwood Thrill Show, as he described every outing in the Le Car, Jack thought that if this was the best France had to offer, no wonder they got crushed in two World Wars. As he turned from southbound Epworth onto westbound Joy Road, he caught his first glimpse of Dearborn Beer Distributors, three short blocks on the southside. Observing an open overhead door, Jack cruised up the front drive, confronting the coterminous blare of a horn and the screech of brakes. Veering right, the Tasmanian Devil landed on the six-foot wide mini-strip of grass between the building and the public sidewalk.

"Jesus H. Christ, almost bought the farm on that one," Jack grumbled as he slammed the door of the Renault, stretched his aching back and sucked in a deep breath. *"Nothing like a good impression on the first day,"* he mumbled to himself while rounding the corner into the warehouse.

"Better look where you're going, asshole."

The admonishment brought Jack to a halt. Perusing the long line of red and white beer trucks with nary a sole in sight, Jack shook off the comment and continued further into the building, hoping to find some direction. On his third step, a dingy yellow forklift shot out from an archway, its' solid rubber wheels sliding to a halt inches from Jack's left side. Michaels jumped to his right.

"Damn, you scared the crap out of me!" The loud idle of the propane gas machine caused Jack to raise his voice.

"You blind, College Boy?" The hi-lo driver scolded, the bulge in his jaw evidencing his chew.

"No sir," Jack responded. "Just looking for the office."

"Them steel toed boots?" The driver questioned, while leaning to the opposite side to spit.

"What?"

"Jeez, you deaf, too?" The squint of his dark eyes displaying his impatience.

"I'm sorry. I didn't under…"

"Your boots! Are they steel toed?"

Jack glanced down, "Aw, yeah."

"Gonna get your toes cut off."

"What?"

"Through the arch and turn left; can't miss it."

"Can't miss what?" But the hi-lo shot off between two trucks.

Jack shook his head and continued through the arch. The amount of activity startled him: directly ahead, a huge steel door, reminiscent of a bank vault, disclosed a hi-lo inside a cooler, lifting up pallets laden with four half barrels of beer; to his left, another archway, beyond which were hundreds of free standing pallets, each stacked with seven layers of twelve ounce bottles for a total of forty-nine cases per pallet, moved in what seemed to Jack as a helter-skelter motion; to his right, two young men hand stacking pallets with an odd assortment of various sizes of beers in bottles and cans. Scooting through the randomly placed pallets, Jack noticed a small windowed office. Approaching the scarred wood door with an upper glass panel, Jack knocked.

"What the hell is it now?" The scraggly tobacco laden voice demanded.

The obvious lack of ventilation blurred the ten-foot square room with a hanging cloud, so Jack inhaled a deep breath as he pushed open the door. Immediately overcome with cigar smoke, Jack coughed into his folded left hand, cleared his throat, then squeaked out between gasps, "I'm looking for Jimmy Pepatino."

Exhaling enough smoke to warrant a smog advisory, the disguised figure behind the desk responded, "That'd be me. Whatever you're sellin', I ain't buyin', so pack it up and hit the road. I've got a shit ton to do."

"Mo Futz, over at the Raven Lounge told me you were short a man or two in the warehouse…"

"How is Old Mo?" The voice inquired in an almost pleasant timbre, as the image of a short, stocky man in his late fifties with gray curly hair emerged from the cloud. Before Jack could respond, Pepatino rose from his chair, squinted to get a better look at Jack. "Never cared for that dumb son-of-a-bitch."

Jack cringed, but shot for the gold. "Funny, he said the exact same thing about you. Told me you'd be wearing the same number 9 Red Wings jersey you stole from Gordy Howe's locker thirty-years ago. Then something about lacking the talent to make the big time."

Bracing himself for the screw up, Jack let out a slow quiet exhale as Jimmy broke out into a raucous laugh, displaying a perfect set of glistening white teeth.

"God, I miss that crazy old son-of-a-bitch. Never could play hockey worth a damn. Had to cover for him his entire career. But I still can't hire you. You're too skinny. You could never do this work. What are you, maybe 130 soaking wet? A half barrel of beer weighs 165. No way!" Jimmy shoved the stogie into his mouth, clinched it between his teeth, fell back into his chair and hoisted his feet up onto the desk.

Distracted by the sight, Jack fanned his hand to clear his smoke blurred vision and asked, "Are you wearing roller-blades?"

"Yeah, what about it?"

"Nothing. Just sort of unusual, isn't it?"

"Lot easier to get around the warehouse and keeps me fit, don't you think?"

"Cutting back on the rum-soaked cigars would probably help too."

"A real smartass. Generally, I admire a smartass. Been called that many a time in my day. But a skinny smartass just won't cut it."

"I can do it!" Jack's deep voice resonating off the tiny room's walls. "I'll work twice as hard as anybody you have in this place, for the same pay."

"So, you say!" Pepatino questioned while gritting the cigar. "Tell me, what did Mo see in you anyway? He generally wouldn't give a skinny runt like you the time of day."

"Helped him break up a brawl between four guys at the Raven. Put two in the hospital. Pissed me off they interrupted the music. Thought I'd being going to jail. Mo covered for me. We got to talkin' and I told him I needed a better paying job. He told me you would be just the guy to talk to."

"Really? Well, you must be a lot tougher than you look," Pepatino jested, shaking his head, breaking the one-inch cigar ash bond, causing it to fall to his desktop. An entire thirty second pause. "When could you start?"

"How about right now?"

Pepatino scanned the candidate up and down. "Them steel toed boots?"

"Yeah, they are."

"Get rid of 'em. Hi-lo runs over your foot, gonna cut your toes off."

CHAPTER

6

Aɴxɪoᴜs ᴛo ᴇᴍʙᴀʀᴋ oɴ a new career at union wages, Jack triple pumped the accelerator, turned the key, waiting for the firecracker pop that would bring the Tasmanian Devil to life. As he shoved the beast into first gear, he realized he had no idea where to go.

Located on the south side of Joy Road, Michaels edged out into the westbound lane, just east of Livernois Avenue. He immediately noticed a railroad spur running along the west side of the single story, sixty-thousand square foot cinderblock structure, with a locked gate at the far corner. *"How the hell do you get in this place?"* Jack mumbled to himself. A quick U-turn, Jack traversed the hundred feet of frontage, turning up an apron cut leading into an abandoned alley running along the easternmost edge of the building. Three-foot high weeds and enough broken glass to make the purchasing manager at Waterford Crystal cry, Jack knew that wouldn't work. Stumped, he gleaned a truck pull out of the warehouse, turn right onto Joy Road, then another quick right on to Howell St. *"Follow that truck,"* Michaels decided. A third right at the dead-end of the residential street opened into a fenced lot the approximate size of the warehouse. The beer truck peeled off to the left and backed against the wall of an identical building, but only a quarter the size. Jack coasted the Devil to the far-right corner, adjacent to a row of ten older vehicles that would be a good start for a cut-rate used car lot.

Approaching the rear of the building, a weather-beaten white boxcar with a red, "Miller High Life" moniker sat on the spur, just inside the locked gate on the southwest corner; identical 12' x 15' roll-up doors on each end of the building; in the center, three tractor-trailers, side by side, in a well; a generic gas pump that you would see in any self-serve station, flanked by concrete-filled thirty-six inch high, four-inch diameter pipes; a three-inch thick solid steel framed entry door between the fuel dispenser and easternmost garage door. Visibly lacking, security lighting and cameras.

Jack tracked behind the trotting truck driver, passing a lane of seven delivery vehicles backed against the east wall in various states of repair to his right and perpendicular to a long line of city delivery trucks extending to the front entrance, on his left. The sudden slam of a steel plate to the concrete floor never interrupted the gait of the driver, while Jack attempted to dive for cover. Two seconds later, the roar of a hi-lo motor from the area of the loading dock revealed the source. Jack relaxed, continuing his trek, but losing site of the employee. Passing the mechanic's bay, the area in front of him opened into a flurry of activity; the driver Jack followed ran around the sides of the three trucks closest to him and threw open the five bay doors, allowing a fork-lift operator to unload pallets of empties, while another followed right behind, loading each bay with fresh cases. Once loaded, the worker reached for the strap, yanked down and secured the doors, then moved the vehicle out onto Joy Road, around the corner to the back lot. Jack immediately appreciated the well-orchestrated flow.

Grabbing the attention of the same hi-lo driver who initially commented on Jack's boots required an above the din, "Yo!"

Sliding his beat-up yellow steed to a halt, the driver chortled while pulling off his stained mustard colored leather gloves and tossing his right leg up onto the manifold, "College Boy, what can I do for you?"

"Jack Michaels," the response louder than necessary since his ears were still adjusting, while holding out his right hand.

"Roy Blue," gripping Jack's hand. "You the new guy?"

"You bet!"

"I do, on a regular basis, but not on you," Roy smiled. "Follow me, College Boy." Roy drove between two trucks to the other side of the loading line, disclosing several pallets of jumbled empties. "Your job, should you choose to accept it, Jim…"

"Jack."

"Don't be a dick!" Roy's smile disappeared. "…is to stack the same empties onto one pallet. Quarts get stacked seven rows high; twelve-ounce returnable bottles eight high; cans fourteen rows high. Each row is laid out the same; three cases side by side overhanging about four inches; four cases perpendicular, again, hanging four inches over the edge. Got it!"

"Got it."

"Get rid of those boots before you lose your toes and invest in a good pair of leather work gloves. I don't want to lose time driving you to the clinic."

"I'm good, thanks."

"College boys," Roy snorted as he jumped up on his hi-lo.

Jack surveyed his 15' x 25' work area. Bordered on two sides by cinder block walls, with an open area facing the truck line, filled with a forest of empties. Tossing out three 4' x 4' wood pallets from a stack twenty high, Jack stuck both hands into separate quart cases and immediately felt the stabbing pain in his right middle finger. "Son-of-a-bitch!" He screamed. Tossing the case in his left hand onto the empty pallet, he tenderly lifted the lid on the offending case. A broken bottle neck penetrated the left side of his middle finger, between the first and second digits, digging deep into the bone. Concentrating on the contour of the glass, Jack gently pulled his finger back. Each millimeter spawned a hundred-fold beads of sweat.

Noticing the attention on one particular case of empties, Roy Blue shot back on his yellow steed, "Hey College Boy, this ain't rocket science! You can't take the time to study every bottle."

Without breaking his concentration, Jack calmly replied, "Just trying to un-shish kabob my finger."

"You fuck up already? Damn, that's gotta be a record. And believe me, we got some real dumbasses working here," Roy grinned. "Looks like a bad one. Go in and see Pepatino. He's gonna love this!" Roy gripped the suicide knob on his steering wheel and whipped the hi-lo in a quick U-turn to resume loading.

Jack kept his right arm up and squeezed the finger with his left hand. Blood streamed down his arm. As he pushed open the office door, Pepatino immediately recognized the problem and exploded.

"You dumb fuck! I told you, you couldn't do this job," He screamed, his face beet red, as spittle flew with the intensity of steam from a pressure cooker. "Now you've screwed up our work comp loss ratio," The rant continued. "Screw it, you're fired! Get the hell out of here!" The Boss ordered.

Flustered, Jack eyed Pepatino, "Are you through?"

"You really are a smart ass."

"No sir, but I think you're over reacting. You're gonna give yourself a heart attack, you keep that up." Jack's calm demeanor annoying Jimmy. "I just came in to see if you had any duct tape."

"Duct tape?"

"Yeah. If I could just duct tape this finger, I'll be good to go. Don't need a clinic. I'll take care of it when I get home. No need to miss any work."

"Duct tape? You sure?"

"Hundred and one uses," Jack smiled.

"Go to the mechanic shop. Half the equipment in this place is held together with that stuff. Don't think the guy can actually fix anything." Pepatino's face returning to its natural color.

"Thanks, boss," Jack tossed out as he exited the office.

"I like that kid," Jimmy mentioned to himself, as he grabbed the inventory clip-board off his desk.

CHAPTER

7

As Jack hustled through the warehouse on his way to the locker room, Roy Blue coasted alongside. "Bet that finger hurts like a bitch," the foreman chuckled.

"It's throbbing, but I cleaned it up and put six stitches in it last night, so it should be alright."

"You put the stitches in, you say?"

"No health insurance. Besides, it just like sewing on a button. Why pay all that money for something you can do yourself."

"Ah huh!" Roy remarked, nodding his chin. "See you put the duct tape back on."

"Use number 87."

"Better be careful around here with use 87. Some of these idiots may think you're flipping them off."

"Got that covered," Jack replied, "Both literally and figuratively," as he slipped on a pair of extra-large leather work gloves. "Picked them up at Monkey Wards on the way to class this morning."

"You just might survive, College Boy," Roy prophesied as he darted off.

Jack sucked in a deep breath to stymie his gag reflex, as he yanked open the locker room door. "Damn, it's like being back in high school," he complained as he plunked down on the single six-foot long wood bench in the center of the room. "Smells worse than a bag of smashed assholes," Jack yelled.

A belly laugh erupted from the attached shower room. Seconds later, a bent back head with a ruddy face appeared in the archway, "Dammit, College Boy, don't you know it's impolite to crack a funny ass remark when a man of my age is trying to piss?" Pepatino screamed. "After standing here ten minutes, I finally get a stream and you come along and make me piss all over myself. Got anything to say?"

"Yeah. Don't you ever just speak in normal conversational tones?"

"No. I'm Italian. That's all we do is scream."

"Family dinners must be a hoot!" Jack snickered.

"Watch it, College Boy. I'm still your boss."

"And a good and kind one you are, Sir."

Rolling toward the door, Jimmy took a wide swipe over Jack's head, prompting him to duck.

"You're on rollerblades in the john?" Jack asked.

"Gets me here fast. You'll appreciate that when you get to be my age."

"Uh huh."

"Take care of that finger, College Boy!"

CHAPTER

8

Preparing for the first city trucks to roll in, Jack pulled a stack of pallets from the corner of his work station and slid them to the center, logistically a much better location once things started flying. Returning to the corner to clean up debris, he felt a blow to his back, slamming him into the corner wall. Shaking his head to recover, Jack's ears split from the roar of an engine. He found himself engulfed in propane exhaust fumes spewing from the rear of Torpo's six-thousand-pound cast-iron forklift. While Jack twisted around, struggling to breathe, Max kept the gas pedal to the floor.

"Max, Max, what the hell are you doing? You're gonna kill me. I can't breathe!" Michaels screamed.

With a sickly-looking grin, Max kept the pedal down, while Jack struggled to control his thoughts. Choking, he realized he had only seconds to extricate himself before passing out. Jack grabbed for the top rim of the propane tank mounted behind the driver's seat and hoisted himself up and around to the side of the machine. Taking a second to clear his throat, Michaels slugged Max in the shoulder. "Are you nuts? You could have killed me, asshole," Jack fumed.

Hunched at the shoulders and clutching his hands together against his chest, Max giggled, "Just funnin' with ya!"

"That's some sick ass fun," Jack scolded.

Roy Blue whipped his hi-lo next to the feuding workers. "Whenever you ladies are ready to work, just let me know."

After an hour of stacking empties, Jack calculated he had a few minutes of down time before the next wave of trucks advanced for unloading. Sneaking off to the mechanic's bay, he scoured the disheveled work bench and found a spool of twine. Cutting off a twenty-foot length, he casually approached the passenger side bays of the nearest truck in line. Raising each door until he found one with an empty bay on his side, but a full bay on the driver's side. Jack hopped up into the truck. He attached one end of the delicate rope to the vertical aluminum center poles that act as a faux wall to stabilize the load and tied off the other end after running it through the handles of three cases of twelve-ounce empties in the center of the full pallet.

As the trucks advanced in line, Jack maintained a steady clip stacking empties, while keeping an anxious eye on his proposed stunt. Max deftly demonstrated his skill, operating the fork-lift with all the aplomb of a symphony orchestra conductor in a sold-out summer concert. Sliding off a full pallet of twelve-ounce returnable bottles, the load suddenly collapsed. Cases crashed to the aluminum floor of the truck bed, then cascaded to the warehouse floor. Stymied, Max jumped off his steed, with the remaining cases still suspended, to inspect the bay. Three cases of empties were dangling in mid-air. Scratching his head, a still perplexed Max exclaimed, "What the fu…" as he noticed Jack doubled over in laughter, falling backward onto a partially filled pallet of empties.

Righting himself, Jack exclaimed, "Now that's a great joke!"

Max remounted the hi-lo, jammed it into reverse to clear the truck, then forward while lowering the rack and depositing the remaining unbroken empties for Jack to stack. As Michaels approached, wiping tears from his eyes, Max leapt from his seat, landing on Jack, knocking him to the concrete floor, while unleashing a barrage of punches.

"Are you fucking crazy?" Jack screamed while wrapping his elbows around his head for protective cover. "Get off me, asshole!" Jack ordered, but Torpo kept pounding.

Jack felt a tinge of relief as he gleaned the distinctive yellow color of Roy Blue's hi-lo appear. "Can you get this asshole off me?" He yelled.

"No can do, College Boy," Roy stated matter-of-factly. "Gotta fight your own battles."

Not one to solicit trouble, but plagued with a determination few people understood, once provoked, Jack indulges a Machiavellian strategy of anything goes. He consciously slowed his breathing and assessed his position; no serious injury to date, but his out-of-control opponent seemed hell bent on eventually correcting that deficiency. Sensing Max straddling him, Jack hoisted his right knee up for two rapid succession blows to the groin. Torpo screamed and rolled off, chuffing for breath and cupping the boys as though he expected them to fall off.

Jack, sensing the danger had passed, regained his footing and glared down at Max, "Will you please knock it off? I can't afford to lose this job." Jack mentally worked on calming down; again, slowing his breathing and changing his thoughts. Turning from his adversary and tossing empties two-handed onto the top row to complete a full pallet, Jack felt the smash of a beer bottle to the bridge of his nose, accompanied by the simultaneous crack of bone, then collapsed to the floor.

Roy Blue ripped the empty from Torpo's hand and scolded, "Why in the hell did you have to go and do that? You could have killed him!"

"He called me an asshole."

"You are an asshole, asshole!"

"Yeah, you know that, but that doesn't give him the right to call me an asshole."

"Are you listening to yourself, asshole? You're not making the least bit of sense," Roy Blue's frustration clearly evident as he turned to assist Jack. "Now the two of you shake hands and let's get back to work. We've got trucks to load."

As Max reached out to shake Jack's hand, Jack whipped his right elbow around, striking Max squarely in the mouth, knocking out an upper front tooth. As Max reacted to the blow, Michaels tore the leather glove from his injured hand, grabbed hold of his taped finger and attempted to flex it several times into a fist.

"Holy shit! This is gonna get real ugly, real fast." Roy Blue stepped back, refusing to act as referee.

Max swung a hard blow to the left side of Michaels head, knocking him backward over a partial pallet of empties, but it was Max who cried out. "Mother Scratcher, you broke my fucking finger. You got a cement head, or somethin'?"

Still bleeding profusely from his nose, Jack regained his footing and inched closer to his opponent, as Max circled around, anticipating a punch. Jack unexpectedly charged, collapsing Max's midsection with a brutal shoulder butt, forcing Max to fly backward into the bastards' room. The two employees assembling the pallets of odd assortments of beer, scattered to a safer location. Now, with a clear view of the commotion from the drivers' room, as well as, Pepatino's office, a sizeable crowd gathered quickly.

Noticing Jack's blood-soaked shirt and divining a serious injury, one driver yelled out, "5 to 1 Torpo kicks the kid's ass."

Roy Blue called out, "I'll take a hundred of that."

Jimmy Pepatino skated in, nudging by-standers aside with his hockey stick, winding up next to Roy Blue, "Do you think the kid has it in him?"

"Something about him. Not your average college boy."

"I'll take that bet for a hundred," Pepatino yelled to the driver.

The crowd moved in lockstep with the combatants. Max swung multiple successive closed fist-punches, only landing a serious hit every tenth time. Jack, considerably more measured, waited for openings, then hammered Max with the palm of his open hand, an elbow, or a vicious kick. Jack, now clearly the aggressor. Torpo stepped back, catching the heel of his boot on a stray pallet, tumbled backward and crashed his head against the conference room wall. Jack lunged, landing on Max and grabbed hold of his broken finger, giving it a quick twist. Max cried out in pain, as Jack seized hold of another finger and bent it back until it snapped. The crowd collectively cringed.

Max shook his head, exhaled a painful breath and mouthed, "No more."

"You sure? 'Cause the last time I thought we were done, it didn't end so well for me," Jack sputtered angrily. Michaels separated another finger, "Now you're sure we're through, cause if we aren't, I gonna rip this finger right off."

"We're done. We're good," Max mumbled through rapid breaths.

As the two prone combatants collected themselves, an approaching voice inquired, "Hey guys, whad I miss?"

"What the fuck is he doing?" Jack's blurred vision preventing a clear focus. "What's that he's twirling?" A dumbfounded Michaels asked, "Is that what I think it is?"

"Why do you think we call him Rodeo?" Roy Blue cracked a rare smile.

"I'm caught in the *Twilight Zone*," an exasperated Jack declared.

"No. No you're not. You're at Dearborn Beer," Max huffed.

CHAPTER

9

LUDELLA FELT A TINGE of trepidation every time she fired up the black-on-black 1967 Cadillac DeVille convertible. Purchased by her husband on the afternoon of his promotion to partner, Bobbie called and insisted she meet him out front in exactly thirty minutes.

"Oh, you too good to come to the door and get me? Now I have to run down to the street? Mister high and mighty partner." Ludella huffed, slighted by his first lack of manners in eight years.

Losing track of time talking to her Momma, Ludella snapped to attention at the hail from outside.

"Baby, look out the window?" Bobbie pleaded.

"Mister Bigshot is givin' me all kinds of orders," Ludella relayed to Momma.

"Baby, please! Just look out the window."

As Ludella stretched the spiral wall phone cord toward the living room, she realized her predicament; she returned and hung the receiver on the side of the phone, crossed the front room and pulled aside the drape. Bobbie, with a full tooth grin, was perched behind the wheel of a shining convertible the size of an 1800's Erie Canal barge.

A twist of the key and the 429 cubic inch motor rumbled, snapping Ludella from the remembrance she experienced every year before her trip to the Livernois precinct. A tear trickled down her cheek. Unable to report his disappearance until after the 1967 riots concluded, the polite white police lieutenant wrote it off as just another black man walking away from his responsibility, as they were so prone to do. Trying to explain that Bobbie wasn't like that; he was a professional, just having been promoted to partner at a prestigious Downtown Detroit accounting firm, met with a condescending wink and nod.

Turning into the Livernois Precinct lot and navigating the freighter to a spot at least three spaces away from the nearest vehicle to avoid dents, both the cherry Caddie, as well as, Ludella, dressed in her Sunday finest in a closed neck, white chiffon dress, a modest two inches below the knee, turned heads.

Entering the non-descript, modern, single story structure, a world of turmoil instantly halted. The Desk Sergeant, unaccustomed to the silence, raised his head and immediately abandoned his normal surly attitude and smiled at the caramel complexioned beauty approaching the counter as though gliding across a New York fashion stage.

"Why Mrs. Thayer, so good to see you again," the Watch Commander remarked, extending his right arm across the counter. "Has it been a year already?"

"Sergeant," Ludella nodded her head and reached her white gloved hand and gripped with a firm two second shake. "It's been twenty-years since my Bobbie disappeared," her smile fading to a solemn expression, as the normal pandemonium erupted around her.

"So sorry that we haven't been able to help," the Sergeant's voice drifting off in an apologetic cadence, "But if you'll take a seat over on the bench, I'll call down Detective Goodson. He's been assigned a few random unsolved cases recently, so let's see if he can help you."

With the uproarious background, the five-minute wait graded on Ludella, both temples thumping to a blistering beat, to a point where she actually considered surrendering to her frustration. Adjusting her clutch under her left arm, Ludella stood as a voice inquired, "Mrs. Thayer, is it?"

Ludella rotated left, viewing a comical figure sporting an off the rack, crumpled suit two sizes too large, that instantly reminded her of the TV character, Columbo. Dark, sunken eyes supported by puffs indicative of a week overdue for a dialysis treatment and a forlorn expression that instantly elicited pity. "Detective Goodson," she hesitantly inquired.

"If you'll follow me, please?" The plainclothes officer shuffled off in a stunted stride reminiscent of a death row inmate to the electric chair.

"*Oh my,*" Ludella silently intoned, "*this poor creature can't possibly help.*"

As they passed through an off-white cinder block corridor, the space opened to a smoke-filled bull-pen set-up with two scuffed gunmetal gray desks side by side, abutting two identical desks. The pattern of eight four desk groups formed the aisleways, with offices lining the two exterior walls. Each desk contained stacks of bulging manila folders, a five-line black punch dial telephone atop an 18" x 24" table top monthly calendar, most scribbled full of indecipherable notes pasted over with coffee stains and embellished with the stench of over-flowing ashtrays.

Detective Goodson guided Ludella into the lunchroom, immediately apologizing for the mess as one would to an unexpected guest. Bunching several ripped sheets of paper towel from the under the top cabinet dispenser, Eric zipped them once under the faucet. Quickly picking up empty food containers with one hand, he wiped coffee stains, sandwich remnants and a cornucopia of crumbs with the other.

It reminded Ludella of her dorm room at Michigan State University years ago: pasty white semi-gloss cinder block walls; scratched pale green and cream floor tile; recycled kitchen cabinets salvaged from someone's remodel; a mini-fridge jammed under a tan Formica countertop, missing the front trim strip; and a $29.00 microwave with an ill fitted door that released the equivalent radiation of a chest x-ray while re-heating a cup of tea.

"Please have a seat, Mrs. Thayer."

Ludella glanced at the orange fiberglass chair. Determining her Sunday best would remain unscathed, she sat.

"Can I get you something to drink? We have several different sodas in the fridge. I wouldn't recommend the coffee; one cup could cause permanent liver damage and possible loss of eyesight," Eric smiled.

"I bet he doesn't do that very often," Ludella thought. "No, but thank you for offering."

As Detective Goodson reached inside his right breast pocket, extracting a 3"x 5" notebook with a black pen wedged into the wire spiral, Ludella noticed his hand tremor. As he pinched his index finger to his thumb to lift a page, the shaking intensified. *"Oh my! This young man is troubled way beyond his years."*

Witnessing his indecipherable scribbles as he logged onto a fresh page, Ludella felt compelled to interrupt. "Shouldn't you have all this information already in a file?" She questioned in the same soft tone a grandmother would use soothing a sleepy child. "I've come here every year for twenty years. Surely we don't have to go over all this again."

Quickly turning his head and raising his hand to his mouth, Eric cleared his throat, "Mrs. Thayer, I'm going to level with you." Again, raising his cupped hand to catch a cough. "The Desk Sergeant informed me you would be in today, so I started to look through our records of previous detectives who may have been assigned the case." The raspy voice finally started to smooth. "I couldn't find a thing. So, I called downtown to the main records department. Unlike us, they actually have computers with all this stuff on it. No one could find anything under, Bobbie, or, Robert Thayer. No missing persons file; no investigative file; nothing."

Ludella willed herself to catch a breath; her heart raced, each beat pounding against the inside of her chest like a sledgehammer; dots of perspiration drenched her forehead; and her cool chiffon dress stuck to her skin. "But, but, that can't be," she stuttered. "No one has really looked for my Bobbie in twenty years?" Ludella's throat felt parched; her voice crackling. "How could this be?"

Clearing the phlegm, Eric continued, "I'm not saying no one has looked for him. What I'm saying is, we can't find any paperwork."

As Ludella sat shaking her head repeating a hushed mantra of, "Oh Lord! Oh Lord! Oh Lord!" The Detective continued. "A lot of terrible things happened in the '67 riots. I personally have never believed the official numbers of people injured or missing. Most of the experienced detectives know a lot of reports never got filed the way they should have. So, they probably reached the same dead end I did, then just gave up."

Stunned, Ludella felt as though someone finally admitted her beloved Bobbie was dead.

"Mrs. Thayer, Mrs. Thayer," the detective uttered tenderly, sensing her distress. Lifting her gaze to the Detective, Eric asked, "If you could provide me with some details, I promise you, I will look into it. I can't promise results, but whenever I have some free time, I'll try to follow up on any leads I develop."

After conveying the details of the last contact with her husband, Ludella's confident stroll diminished to a sleep walking gait similar to the tormented detective.

CHAPTER

10

T HE EXTRA SECOND EXPENDED to tug on the tarnished brass handle, insuring the weathered solid core door securely latched, even though the initial resounding click left no doubt, bordered on obsession. The mental quirk registered, prompting a smile, but failed to alter the practice. The modest three-bedroom brick bungalow on Detroit's Upper East Side contained a refuge, purging Eric Goodson's psyche of the mind-numbing refuse of his career as a detective in the on again, off again murder capital of the world.

Disregarding the wishes of his guardian to attend college, Eric followed a childhood dream and enrolled in the police academy the day after high school graduation in 1966. Exhibiting a talent for mediocrity, the rookie comfortably settled into an uneventful routine, resisting any attempts at alteration, until his exposure to the following summer's race riots. Although no significant outward changes other than finally rising through the ranks on sheer seniority and premature graying around the temples, the experience forever transformed an unusually tranquil mindset to a constant subliminal barrage of grisly random flashbacks.

As Eric traversed the six limestone steps, a familiar voice called out, "I see you've made great strides in controlling the OCD."

"Uncle Lenny!" Eric blurted. "I may be a bit on the compulsive side, but you exude all the ostentatious extremes of a personal injury plaintiff's lawyer."

"You mean the car?" Leonard responded, his arm resting on the window frame of the two-seat, two-tone, silver over black 1979 Stutz Bearcat convertible. "Your Auntie Mims loves this car."

"I'm pretty sure Aunt Mims loves you even though you drive that showboat. Do you need a captains' license to pilot that thing?" The question prompting an infectious chuckle. "So, what's on your mind, Unc?"

Concerned about Eric's long festering conflict, Uncle Leonard, concocted a sure-fire cure. "There's a young lady your Auntie Mims and I would like to introduce you to."

"Ah Unc, another blind date?"

"This girl is a stunner. She was a runner up in the Miss Michigan contest last year, Erie," Leonard applying the term of endearment to his hands down favorite nephew along with the typical tripe, as though selling a phony whiplash to a jury.

"If she's so good looking, why can't she get her own date?"

"She's a little shy, but I'm telling you, she's a real looker. Why if I were ten…okay, twenty… so you caught me, thirty years younger, I'd be after her myself; that's if your Aunt Mims wasn't so darned cute at seventy."

"C'mon Uncle Lenny. Don't make me do this. These set ups are the worst."

"May God make the unfortunate decision to take me tonight in my sleep if I have exaggerated in the slightest."

"You better watch yourself, Unc. Remember, you're a lawyer. If God takes you, it's not because he needs your legal representation in a rear-ender. It'll be to atone for your greed and that of your clients'."

"I'll take that as a yes."

"Okay, but this is definitely the last time."

"After Angie, you won't ever think of another woman. Trust me."

CHAPTER

11

Eric grudgingly agreed to meet the beauty contest also ran on the roof of the Woodbridge Tavern, in Detroit's old riverfront warehouse district, to view the Fourth of July fireworks display on the Detroit River. The unique click with each step on the worn cobblestone street previewed a journey back in time. Entering the turn of the century wooden saloon, the crackle of peanut shells littering the creaky soiled oak plank floors provided a distinct accompaniment to the blaring honky-tonk piano.

Addressing a middle aged, heavily mascaraed hostess in a notch above lethargic, but friendly manner, Eric stated, "I have a reservation for 7:00 p.m. under the name of Goodson."

"Oh yes sir. Your guest is already seated. If you'll follow me?"

"Just a second. Can you point her out to me?"

"She's over there in the far corner with her back to us; the one with the black satin hot pants, spiked heels and white cotton tank top," the hostess commented as though critiquing a layout in *Vogue*, her lower lip curled under the bite of her upper teeth.

"There must be some mistake?" Eric questioned, a spark of life in his voice.

"No mistake. A bit too tart for me, but obviously effective when trolling for men."

"I meant the woman, not the wardrobe."

"Oh, of course." The maître d' paused, snapping back to reality. "She distinctly asked for Goodson. I seated her myself."

"And some people don't believe in miracles," Eric huffed, uncharacteristically whipping out a ten spot, raising the lass' cupped right hand, depositing the tip in and closing her fingers over the bill, accompanied with a high pitched, "Thank You!"

"Hope she doesn't catch cold in that outfit once the sun goes down," the hostess snipped as Eric approached the table with a noticeable swagger in his step, his eyes fixated on the seemingly unending legs extending from the cheap plastic chair out into the aisle way.

"Hello, I'm…" Eric stood dumbfounded, unable to recall his name.

"If you check your driver's license, I wouldn't be surprised if it said 'Eric Goodson,'" the mellifluous voice complemented with an endearing smile.

"I'm sorry. You're just not what I expected."

"Are you disappointed?"

"Disappointed? How could I be disappointed? No, no. You're a very pleasant surprise, believe me."

"Are you going to sit down?"

"Oh yes, sure. I'm sorry," Eric stumbled as he backed into the chair across the table.

"Catholic?"

"Pardon me."

"From your penitent nature, I assume you're Catholic."

"Tortured by Felician nuns from an early age."

"You could move your chair around next to me if you like."

Eric's eyes bulged, prevented from popping clear out of his head by taut veins vibrating from the strain, "Sure."

"Otherwise it will be difficult for you to see the fireworks with your back to the river."

"Oh, right."

"You thought I had an ulterior motive in mind?"

"*One can only hope,*" the floundering clown muttered to himself while signaling the waitress to place their order.

The ice-cold draft beer and deep-dish pizza tasted exceptional; an ideal complement to the easy flowing conversation.

"So, what do you do for a living?"

"I'm in my first semester of a Master's Program at Wayne State. I just took a job in the mail room for a schlock lawyer in the Asner Building downtown. The pay is really good for what I consider busy work and he says I can stagger my hours around my class schedule, so it should work out okay. Lenny and Mims tell me you're a detective? That sounds exciting."

"Nothing like you see on TV; its no *Magnum P.I.*, that's for sure. Since I've already got my twenty years in, they had to do something with me. They bumped me up to a detective 2nd grade, working primarily cold cases."

"The cases no one solved."

"That's it. Most of my days are actually spent sitting in a bullpen with seven other detectives drinking stale coffee and reviewing old files, that's if we can actually find them."

"Are you originally from the Detroit area?" Eric inquired, actually wanting to know everything imaginable about the goddess next to him.

"I grew up at Schoenherr and Eight Mile. I attended Trix Elementary School. Now I live in Bloomfield Hills. I moved back in with my parents for a while."

"You have got to be kidding?" So, you must know about Chicho's Pizza on Eight Mile Road?"

"Know about it. I grew up on the stuff. Those curly little spicy pepperoni and the oil just oozing out with every bite. My Dad would give me a dollar to get two of their personal pizzas. We'd sneak out to the garage and have one almost every Saturday afternoon."

"Weren't they great? I mean, this pizza is really good, but Chicho's is a whole 'nother level."

"Are you a native Detroiter?"

"Born and bred. Spent my entire life within the city limits. We moved to Gratiot and Eight Mile when I was a kid. I inherited the house from my parents. I live on Eastburn. I go by Trix School every day on my exercise run."

"See there. We grew up in each other's back yard. Some things are just meant to be," the dark-haired vixen smiled, leaning over and placing her right hand on Eric's left thigh, her sagging tank top allowing a clear view of its spectacular contents. As Angie raised her head to look up at Eric, she caught him staring, "Enjoy the view?"

"Outstanding," the voyeur replied. "Oh jeez, I'm sorry," Eric stumbled, then continued. "No, I'm not. I could stare at every inch of you for the rest of my life and never tire of you. You are by far the most beautiful woman I have ever seen. I can't believe we're sitting here next to each other and I feel like I've known you forever," Eric explained, chattering like a child deflecting blame.

"That has got to be the greatest recovery of all time. What am I going to do with you?"

"Anything you please, for as long as you desire."

"My goodness. I may be in over my head."

"I hope so, because I know I am."

With the backdrop of a spectacular pyrotechnic display, Angie gently leaned her head onto Eric's shoulder. The couple quietly exchanged whispers until the grand finale.

"I'd love to see your home."

CHAPTER

12

THE PARKING GOD SMILED on Eric, awarding him a year's worth of luck in downtown Detroit in a single evening with a spot directly across from the tavern entrance. As they strolled across the cobblestone street, Eric gently rested his left forearm on the natural curve of Angie's lower back. Rounding the rear of the vintage black 1978 Pontiac Grand Prix, Eric felt a tug empty his arm with a simultaneous high-pitched shriek.

"Shut up bitch, or I'll cut you," the assailant yelled, spinning Angie around into a choke hold and rendering a glistening thin steel blade to her throat.

"Just hold on a second, fella," Eric pleaded with his left arm extended, while slowly reaching his right arm behind his back for his service revolver.

"Shut the fuck up, honky. And gives me your wallet before I carve this bitch up."

"There's no need for anyone to get hurt here. Look, here's my wallet," Eric calmly offered as he whipped up the 9mm Ruger and cocked the hammer eighteen inches from the mugger's face. "Now I'm breaking regulations pulling my gun after I've had a few beers, but I don't give a rat's ass. What does that tell you?"

Stunned, the attacker instinctively tightened his grip and pushed the blade to within a millimeter of Angie's carotid, "Puts the gun down now, or I slit dis bitch."

"Dream on, cowboy. A cop never drops his gun."

"You a pig?"

"That's right."

"Ah shit. Makes no never mind to me. Drops your gun and gives me da money."

"You heard me, asshole. I'm a cop and I'm not dropping my gun. You only see that in the movies. I'll tell you what I'm going to do. If you mess up another hair on her head, I'm going to permanently part your afro. If you drop the knife, you can leave, no questions asked."

"I drops my blade and you gonna shoot me."

"No, I'm not. I'm with the most gorgeous woman of my life and you're screwing it up. I'm not hanging around here all night playing with you. Drop the knife and haul ass, or I'll drop you. Your choice."

Taking a moment to mull over his options, the thug dropped the stiletto and ran.

"God, you were great," Angie squealed in her throaty voice, grabbing Eric around the neck and planting a kiss on his lips, as he fumbled to holster his weapon. "Thank you."

"I'm just glad you're okay," Eric commented as he opened the car door.

Angie flipped up the armrest, scooched next to Eric and nestled her head on his shoulder.

"Are these seats leather or vinyl," Angie inquired as Eric pulled from the curb.

"Vinyl."

"Oh good."

"Why do you ask?"

"Because I think I peed my pants."

CHAPTER

13

THE SWEAT OF PASSION long since cooled, replaced by a ritual lather of torment induced anguished REM sleep. "No!" Eric screamed, springing upright in bed. "Please don't shoot. You can't do this! Please. No!"

"Eric, it's alright. It's just a bad dream," Angie, initially startled, then gently planting her palms on Eric's moist shoulders and reassuring him in a comforting voice.

"Oh God, I'm am so sorry."

"Was it about what happened at the restaurant?"

"No, it's from a long time ago. It's the same thing night after night," Eric relayed, his chest heaving to keep up with his staggered breathing.

"What happened to you, Eric?"

"I can't talk about it."

"You've got to talk about it. It's the only way to stop it."

"Don't tell me, a psychology degree?" Eric lightly scoffed, but entertaining the thought of the perfect woman may as well include an advanced degree.

"No, I majored in social work. But this is just plain common sense. Now tell me what's bothering you?" Angie persisted with a tender caress of his cheek and the patience of an ideal parent.

"Isn't this a little heavy for a first date?"

"You and I both know it's more than that. We're soul mates. There's no getting around that. Now tell me what's bothering you."

"But you're so young. I could have a daughter your age."

"Do you?"

"No, of course not," Eric sighed. "I'm trying to tell you that I'm almost twice your age. It's not natural for someone as young as you to have such insight."

"That's not relevant. What matters is that God provides someone for everyone. It's just a matter of them realizing it at the time and acting on it."

"Why would He send someone so perfect to me?"

"Maybe you've done something He recognizes as deserving."

"I can't think of a thing."

"Then, perhaps, I really screwed up," the bare vixen concluded, doubling over and planting her face in the bed sheet to stifle her laughter.

"Oh, thanks a lot," Eric chortled, gently smacking the side of her covered head with his pillow.

Collecting herself, Angie insisted, "Now, tell me about the nightmare."

"I can't. I just can't," Eric sobbed.

Angie wrapped her arms around Eric and whispered in his ear, "In time, you will, my love. Once you truly realize we are now a team."

Although the lingering effects of the nightmare dissipated, Eric's mind continued to race.

"What's on your mind now?"

"I've only known you for a matter of hours, really. Not the months and years of most couples. But I find myself fretting…"

"Let it out."

"I'm already afraid of losing you."

"There is nothing to fear. I'm not going anywhere, other than with you. This is just the beginning of what is going to be a long journey. I intend to stand back-to-back with you and fend off the world, if need be."

"This is going to sound ridiculous and I can't believe I'm going to say this. You'll probably jump out of bed and head for the hills, but I love you."

"I love you too."

CHAPTER

14

Arriving fifteen minutes early, Jack hustled through the warehouse and into Pepatino's office to collect his first paycheck; double the hourly rate at his last job.

"Jesus H. Christ, Michaels, you look like hell," Jimmy screamed while still chomping on his cigar. "Would your Mother even recognize you? Goddamn! Broken nose, black eye, busted lip and a cut-up hand. Jeez, and this is only the first week."

"And you thought I couldn't handle it," Michaels chuckled.

"You're still on probation. And there's always next week," Pepatino laughed, handing a check to Jack. "Nice show you put on with Torpo, by the way. No one, and I mean no one, has ever gone the distance with him before. Guess I should have warned you to be careful around him; he is crazy, you know?"

"This coming from a guy who wears the same hockey jersey every day and runs around this place on roller blades, with an actual hockey stick?"

"Watch it, College Boy!"

"Sorry, am I on thin ice? No pun intended," Jack smirked.

"Oh, you're gonna be a handful," Jimmy shook his head. "And I really don't need another jackass in the zoo."

Then why is Max still here?"

"Started here right out of high school, then got drafted. Mr. Mayer, promised all the guys who served that their jobs would be here when they got back. Everyone saw the change in him, but he continued to be a great worker. Never missed a day in fifteen-years; never late; never complains; he's the poster boy for the perfect warehouse employee."

"Except he's crazy?"

"Look, I'm not making excuses for him, but he was a tunnel rat in 'Nam. You couldn't have a clue what he went through."

"Sure do. Handed him a .45 and a flashlight and sent him in the tunnels after the Viet Cong. Wow! Amazing he survived. The death rate for those guys was worse than bubonic plague."

"You catch on fast, College Boy. It's not so much crazy, as it's a hazing; his way of establishing dominance, I guess."

"Could have warned me. Wouldn't it be safer to teach him to lift his leg every once in a while?"

Pepatino chuckled. "My bad. If it's any consolation, he's done it to every new employee, except Roy Blue. Only guy I think Max is really afraid of. Now, go on, get out of here. I have work to do. Go next door to the drivers' room and they'll cash the check for you." Pepatino leaned back in his wooden swivel executive chair, cupped his hands behind his head, threw his feet up onto his desk and exhaled a cloud of rum-soaked cigar smoke that should have set off the fire suppression system, had he not removed the overhead nozzle.

Just as Jack threw the last case of empty twelve-ounce returnable bottles on the stack to complete his shift, a hi-lo screeched to a halt, pinning him between the machine and the loaded pallet. Michaels twisted his sweat drenched head, "Torpo! I'm dog tired and I don't have time for this. Now get the hell outta my way."

"Now is that any way to treat your new best friend?" Max's smile revealing a newly missing upper front tooth.

"What's the old proverb; with friends like you, yada, yada, yada…" Jack felt his heart pumping and his temples beating against his skull. With a slight shake of the head, he finally resigned himself, "Okay, Torpo. Bring it on! But this time I'm really gonna hurt you."

"Whoa, whoa, whoa, my man. I'm not here to fight you again. I may be stupid, but I ain't bent over."

"What? What the fuck does that even mean?" Jack's voice rising in his frustration.

"That's for me to know and for you to find out," Max chuckled.

"Are we in kindergarten now?"

Ignoring the slight, Max mellowed his tone, "Two things: wanted you to sign my cast," pulling back his long-sleeved powder blue work shirt and sticking his broken hand out along with a pen in the other; and, me and the guys want you to come out with us tonight."

"For real?"

"Yeah man. You're one of us now."

Jack thought to himself, *"Terrific, I've just been admitted to the schlub club."* "Outstanding!"

Max shot off, the smell of propane exhaust melding nicely with the odor of rancid beer.

CHAPTER

15

THE CARAVAN OF MISFITS motored past the burned out and abandoned hulks of decaying buildings along northbound Livernois, through the once thriving area of boutiques and custom tailor shops called the Avenue of Fashion, now known as the Avenue of Trash On, turning right onto eastbound Eight Mile Road, the northernmost border of Detroit. *"Where in the hell are we going?"* Jack mumbled to himself, as he coached the Tasmanian Devil up to the fifty-mile-per-hour limit. Ten minutes later, his question answered as Torpo turned into the drive of the *Booby Trap Lounge.* As if the mammoth twenty-five-foot neon sign of gargantuan flashing breasts adjacent to the roadway was inadequate, their painted motto covering the entire north side of the one-story building, summed it up nicely, "A Businessman's Paradise."

"You have got to be kidding me," Jack grumbled as they each fought for parking space in the jam-packed lot. Jack slipped in between an off-road Ford Bronco and a rusted out dark blue Chevy Nova. Shouldering the driver's door with just enough umph to open it, but not enough to rip it from its tender hinges, Jack straightened to find himself face to face with Max.

"We have to stop meeting like this," Jack chided.

"I can't believe you drive that piece of shit." Max examining the Renault as though studying the carcass of a long thought extinct species of fish that washed up onto the shores of the Detroit River.

"I got a great deal."

"The only way that could be a great deal is if they paid you to take it. What the heck is a Lecar, anyway?"

"It's Le Car. That's French."

"I feel sorry for you."

"Why would you feel sorry for me?"

"Because driving a Lecar, you ain't ever gettin' laid," Max laughed and turned to enter the club.

Following close behind, Jack exploded, "It's Le Car. Le Car dammit. It's French."

"Yeah, French this," Max raised his right hand, shoulder height, extending his middle finger.

The powder blue work shirts emblazoned with beer emblems proved enough credentials to not only breeze past the bouncer stationed at the building's center entrance, but also adequate currency to avoid the ten-dollar cover charge. As the three-inch thick, solid wood door slid from its' frame, the group was instantaneously blasted with Rod Stewart asking, *Do You Think I'm Sexy?*

Deafened by enough woofers, tweeters and base speakers to support the Rolling Stones in an outdoor rock concert, Jack easily surmised the warehouse gang as regulars from the maître d's waving them to a posh red leather step-up horseshoe booth, just left of center stage, hosting dueling strippers, cheek to cheek, polishing a chrome pole with their thongs. Jack felt his face flush and quickly glanced away.

Flummoxed by the contradiction to their slogan, as well as, the overall upscale customer base, Jack leaned into Max, shouting above the din, "You come here often?"

"Only when I get a lap-dance," the skinny degenerate smirked, while shaking his head. Both Rodeo and Pepatino exploded in laughter.

Jack just stared at Torpo, until Max collected himself, then responded, "No," cupping his hand to the corner of his mouth for a megaphone effect, "I can't afford it, you know that; we're making the same union wage. No, I helped them out the first time I was here years ago. They were short on their keg order and about to run out of draft beer in the middle of the weekend. Their distributor wouldn't deliver after hours. The manager saw my uniform shirt and asked me if I could do him a favor. I jumped in my car, shot back to the warehouse and loaded up the panel van with six half barrels of beer. Done it a number of times since. Seems to happen almost every time they train a new assistant manager. It's out of our territory, but as long as our competitor and the Liquor Control Commission don't find out, we're golden."

Jack nodded his understanding, failing to notice the well-endowed waitress clad only in a fine selection of jewelry, black with rhinestone studded stiletto pumps and a G-string.

"Rough day at the office? You boys really look like you could use a drink, or two, or three," her perfect smile undetected, as Jack turned his head, startled at the sight and let loose with a stutter reminiscent of a love-struck woodpecker digging for his favorite insect to share with his mate.

With a cigar butt clenched between his teeth, Pepatino chimed in, "The College Boy will have a beer. Better yet, bring us a couple of pitchers."

Max announced, "The new kid is buying!"

"Wait! What?" Jack exclaimed, stunned at the proclamation.

"Yep, that's the rule, kid," Rodeo drawled in his southern twang.

"Hold on now! I can't afford this," Jack pleaded.

"Sure you can, College Boy. You're making big money now." Pepatino declared with all the certainty of a Circuit Court Judge issuing a final verdict.

"But, but…" Jack stammered.

"You know, College Boy, I'm getting the impression that you've never been to a titty bar before." Pepatino gloating at his fine deductive skills.

Jack shook his head, "Never have."

"Well boy, we gonna break your cherry tonight," Rodeo proclaimed, jumping out of his end booth seat and reentering on the other side, prompting everyone to scooch over, pushing Jack to the other end. "Send over Trish the Dish," Rodeo demanded with a raised arm.

Pepatino leaned into Rodeo, "You whip that thing out tonight like the last time we were here, I'm gonna wrap it around your throat and choke you to death. Got it!"

"But Boss, the women love it. Can I help it if I'm hung like a horse?"

"Don't say I didn't warn you."

"Trish for table two," the disc jockey announced over the PA system while dropping the turntable needle on Donna Summer's *Hot Stuff.* Within seconds, a fully glittered, six-foot four-inch tall, curvaceous, blue eyed, long curly red-haired vixen arrived tableside. All heads bobbed toward Jack. Observing his awkward reaction and ruby red face, Trish took the lead and grasped both hands on Jack's knees and spun him toward her. Instantly recognizing him through his facial bruises, Trish maintained her giddy expression with the aplomb of a seasoned CIA operative stationed behind enemy lines. *"My God, is he acting like this because he recognizes me?"* Then she realized, *"No, I think he is genuinely embarrassed."* Gyrating to the blaring music, Trish rubbed several tender body parts against her blushing customer, while Pepatino, Rodeo and Max reached over, under and around Jack to stuff dollar bills into the performer's G-string. *"He certainly isn't my usual ass grabbing patron,"* Trish thought, *"lucky for him,"* while she shimmied and twirled to the music. Timing the end of the song, Trish leaned in and kissed Jack on the cheek.

"Thank you," Jack managed to whisper.

Confident in her deception, Trish rubbed the back of her hand on Jack's chin, but raised her voice to a fake falsetto, "That's so sweet."

As the stripper turned to sashay to another table, Rodeo twisted at the waist, calling out, "Hey baby, what about me?"

Trish stopped, turned and drew her inverted hand down the side of her lithe frame and declared, "Not on your best day, cowboy!"

As the table erupted in laughter, Rodeo yanked out his upper four tooth bridge and wiggled his tongue through the gap at the fleeing dancer.

"Jeez, that's disgusting," Jack rebuked.

"Someday, she'll beg to have this," Rodeo proffered, grabbing his package.

"Yeah, and some day you'll actually learn how to repair one of our trucks," Pepatino castigating the hillbilly lothario.

CHAPTER

16

NURSING THE FIRST OF two required drinks, the Professor bristled at the ten-dollar charge for a bottle of Evian. Slouched with his back facing the southeast corner of the lounge, he immediately perked up at the announcer's call for Trish the Dish. Reticent to call her over, he privately ogled her from afar. Tracking her movements to various clubs over the last several years, Trish was tied in first place for the enviable position of his class president. The other candidate was a college student with remarkably similar physical attributes, so much so, he thought they could be related.

As Trish arrived tableside, the Professor hung on her every movement. Aghast, as the rowdy peons pawed at his prize, one patron acted decidedly different. As the lap dance ground on, the Professor observed the recipient's reluctance. *"Well, at least he displays some decorum; unlike the animals with him. If they violate my prize, I will deal with them. Every one of them will pay dearly."* As the song continued, he thought, *"My, but she seems to be exhibiting an unusual amount of effort on the young lad. Much more than the typical patron. No matter; she is still the perfect candidate."*

Interrupted by his waitress as she plunked down a second Evian, "That'll be ten dollars, please."

"What? What's that again?" The Professor responded with a rapid shake of his head.

"Ten dollars, sir." The odd look prompting, "Two drink minimum."

"Oh, yes, of course," the customer rummaged through a roll of bills.

In an effort to secure her tip, the server commented, "Sorry that I startled you. Our manager really gets on us about collecting the minimums."

"Ah, yes. No problem," as he anxiously attempted to look around the server.

"I see you're really into Trish. She's a real stunner. From the minute she started here, she became the most popular of our girls. Would you like me to call her over?"

Clearing his throat, "No, that won't be necessary."

"She wouldn't mind, you being a regular and all."

With cranial pressure building, the throbbing behind his eyes intensified to an unbearable level, prompting a curt, "No."

Sensing his disdain, the server flipped the ten spot onto her tray, covering it with an empty glass and stuffed the dollar tip into her G-string. "Thanks, Big Boy."

Anxious to return to his surveillance, the lap dance just concluded with Trish planting a gentle kiss on the customer's cheek, before sashaying away. Although the low lighting prevented the Professor from seeing it, he knew the young lad blushed.

The lap dance beneficiary hopped down from the booth and headed for the restroom. The Professor waited a few seconds before following him. As Jack hunched up to the urinal, his stalker headed for the sink, feigning a hand wash, as he glanced in the mirror. The sudden recognition infuriated him. Struggling for control, he turned off the tap and pulled two paper towels from the dispenser. A few quick swipes to continue the ruse before exiting back to his corner.

"That bitch! I can't believe what she would see in that obnoxious little prick. I'm going to see to it that they pay dearly for their misdeeds."

CHAPTER

17

THREE HOURS LATER, ALL their singles spent, the warehouse gang departed, just as the valet pulled a car up along the front of the building.

"Whoa, check out the Vette," Max shouted.

Admiring the custom machine, Jack mentioned, "My girlfriend has one just like it. Man, will she be surprised there's another one cruising around town."

"Candy apple red, like this?" Pepatino questioned.

"Yep. She loves fast cars."

"So, when you go out on a date, does she let you drive this beauty?" Max grinned.

"Are you kidding? She loves the Le Car."

"You're so full of horseshit, you're starting to draw flies." Max heaved with laughter at his own joke.

"Dats a good one Max," Rodeo chuckled, then yelled, "Ah, crap!"

"Now what?" Pepatino complained.

"Forgot my teeth on the table," Rodeo exclaimed, dashing back into the building.

"Won't see him again tonight," Max declared.

"Why's that?" Jack asked.

"His excuse to get a free lap dance. His bridge is in his pocket, but he'll tell the staff he left it on the table. Then suggest, instead of the demeaning task of searching through the garbage, he'll settle for a lap dance," Pepatino explained.

"Must be a new assistant manager," Max says. "Otherwise he'll be out in two minutes."

Jack just shook his head as he yanked the door on the Tasmanian Devil.

Pepatino inquired, "So College Boy, whad ya think?"

Without missing a beat, Jack responded, "Foods not bad."

A fake punch to Jack's shoulder and Pepatino roared, "Go on, get outta here!"

CHAPTER

18

Towering over his nephew in a faux Ichabod Crane pose, the trial attorney lifted his left hand to his face and gently swiped his curled index finger under his nostril, while conterminously clearing his throat, "Erie, I don't mean to pry, but isn't this all a little sudden? You just met her a few days ago and she's already moved in."

Eric nonchalantly shifted to his right in the powder blue patterned Queen Ann wing chair, glanced up and into Leonard's striking blue eyes. "What can I say, Unc? It was love at first sight. Besides, wasn't it you who said, 'If only I were a few years younger…'"

Repeatedly nodding his head, Leonard responded, "I did, I did, but I never imagined things would progress this quickly."

"Neither did I. As far as I was concerned, I was a confirmed bachelor."

Leonard instantly recognized that Erie's voice abandoned its usual melancholy and morphed into a joyous cadence and timbre, as he nodded for his nephew to continue.

"In the short time we've been together, I can't imagine my life without her. Isn't that how you feel about Auntie Mims?"

"Sure, it is."

"Well, there you go. I rest my case, as you ambulance chasers would say."

"Please understand Erie, your Aunt Mims and I look at you as our own. We just don't want to see you get hurt. We would never stand in the way of your happiness. But when you leave a telephone message asking if I could get a judge on short notice to perform your wedding ceremony, we got concerned."

"I certainly didn't mean to cause you guys any discomfort."

"That's an understatement. Your Aunt Mims replayed that message at least ten times with tears streaming down her cheeks. I didn't know whether she was overjoyed, or, distraught. In hindsight, I'm sure it was a combination of both."

"So, you'll do it?"

"Of course, I'll do it, Erie. As a matter of fact, I know just the judge to ask. I'm sure Jim O'Hara would squeeze us in whenever we want."

"How about tomorrow?"

Leonard's eyes bulged.

"Is that too soon?"

"No, no, no. But there's a lot to do."

"Such as?"

"Blood tests for one; finding the appropriate clothes, for another."

"Done and done." Eric nodded his head and smiled.

"Well alright then." Leonard agreed, bobbing his head. "I'll call the judge from the car on my way home."

"From the Stutz?" Eric questioned incredulously.

"Certainly. Why?"

"Because that things roars like a locomotive. Whenever you call me from that monstrosity, I can't make out a word you're saying. Am I the only one who thinks that?"

"Honestly, no. Everyone complains about it. They all ask, what is that noise? My answer is always the same; that's the sweet hum of success."

Both men chuckled. Collecting himself, Eric commented, "Wow Unc, that's pretty brash, don't you think?"

"Comes with being a plaintiff attorney. People expect it. You've always got to be on."

Eric just shook his head.

"What?" Lenny inquired.

"You are one of a kind, Unc. After you, they broke the mold."

"That's what I keep telling your Aunt Mims. I'm sure, on occasion, she wishes the mold had been broken before I was made," Leonard responded, while extending his arms and motioning with his fingers for Eric to stand for a hug. Wrapping his arms around his shorter nephew, the old lawyer patted him briskly on the back. "I love you so much! Anything for my Erie."

As Leonard turned to leave, Eric blurted, "Damn, I almost forgot. One more thing, Unc. We want you and Auntie Mims to stand up with us."

"We'd be honored."

CHAPTER

19

Eric UNCHARACTERISTICALLY SOFTLY WHISTLED The Rascals tune, *It's a Beautiful Morning*, as he sauntered into the jam-packed coffee room. Coming to an abrupt halt, he tapped his right foot on the scared asbestos green and cream tile floor to the melody, while sixth in line for the sludge the City passed off as coffee.

Accustomed to his presence stifling the normal interactions of his underlings, Captain Bart Bigelow clutched a Styrofoam cup in his right hand, while collecting four empty sugar packets and a stir stick in his left. He moved sideways to allow the next-in-line access to the pot, as he discarded the refuse in the swing top metal canister. Moving toward the exit, he caught site of Goodson. "My, but aren't we in a good mood today, Detective. And look at those duds! Not your typical Arlan's special. I don't recall you being scheduled for Court today?"

A collective silent sigh of relief enveloped the remaining group, once they realized they escaped the Captain's inquiry.

Eric raised his head to look up at the six-foot, five-inch Commander, decked in his heavily starched dress blues, "Good morning, Sir and no, Sir."

"If you're bucking for promotion to detective first grade, it's gonna take more than a slick suit. Gonna have to crack a few of your cold case files."

Staring directly into his Boss' eyes, the normally subdued Detective proffered an energetic response, "Nothing like that, Sir. Although I certainly wouldn't turn down a promotion. I've got a real special engagement sometime today."

"So special, you don't even know the time?" The Captain's head askew with pursed lips, clearly relaying his skepticism.

"Oh, that's not it at all, Sir. I'm just waiting for a call from the Court."

"But you just told me you're not on the Court schedule."

A subtle, awkward shuffle emanated from the onlookers, their crinkled faces evidence of their discomfort.

"No sir, I'm not."

"I've had teeth extracted that didn't take this amount of time. Just spit it out, Goodson."

"Oh shit," Dibble muttered, prompting a glance and shaking fist from his partner.

A full-face grin accompanied Eric's reply, "I'm waiting for the clerk to call, because I'm getting married today."

"Well, now we're pissing through tall cotton." The Commander's unusual comment drew skeptical looks from the entire room, while his ear-to-ear smile signaled relief.

"Sir?"

"Just an expression," the Captain relayed, while shifting his cup to his left hand and reaching out with his right. "Let me be the first to congratulate you."

The breakroom came alive, as all his comrades did an about face, wrangling to position themselves within earshot to catch the latest office gossip.

"Way to go, Goodson. Never thought you had it in ya," Detective Netzel remarked, as he reached up and palmed Eric's shoulder with a mild squeeze.

"Is this the broad with the unusually long face you met at the 4-H exhibit at the State Fair?" Detective Dibble chuckled, until he caught the backhand closed fist to his gonads from his partner, Diana Sobel.

"You're such a dick, Dibble," Sobel remarked, glancing down to her left as Dibble gasped for air. Redirecting her attention to Goodson, "She's a lucky girl, Eric. You're one of the good ones. And if she ever needs any advice on how to keep you in line, just have her call me."

"Well, I hope it never comes to that," Eric answered as he stole a glance at a groaning Dibble.

"Are you kidding? Angie's a real class act. Gorgeous too. She's the complete package. If I were you, I'd be at that courthouse three weeks in advance," Eric's partner opined.

"Thanks, Quentin," Eric blushed.

Feigning concentration on a cold case, Eric literally jumped out of his lopsided roller-chair at the first ring of his phone. Colliding with Dibble, the Detective's fourth cup of the morning sloshed onto Goodson's white shirt and tie. Grabbing for the receiver, Eric announced, "Hello, this is Detective Goodson."

"Detective, this is Judge O'Hara's clerk. We are ready for you. Can you be here in the next fifteen minutes? The Judge would like to fit you in before we leave for lunch."

"No problem. I'll be there." Slamming the receiver down, Goodson screamed, "Un-fucking believable! I've got to be in court in fifteen minutes and look at this mess."

Detective Sobel buzzed around the row of scuffed metal desks. In a defensive move, Dibble covered his crotch. "Always thinking of yourself, asshole. Move aside. You've already caused enough damage."

"But I…"

"Can it, Big Boy." Turning to Eric and inspecting his shirt, "That'll never clean up in time." Taking a moment to think, Sobel called out, "Quentin, you guys are basically the same size and your tie goes pretty well with his suit. You guys hit the men's room and exchange shirts. Problem solved."

Frozen in place, staring down at the massive brown stain, the solution failed to register. Quentin gripped Eric's left arm, just above the elbow, "Come on, partner, we gotta get you to courthouse." Directing his attention to Captain Bigelow's office, Quentin yelled over the din, "Lights and sirens, Cap?"

"Lights and siren are a go!" The Captain replied, with an exaggerated salute.

CHAPTER

20

Just as Quentin brought the battered brown 1982 Ford Fairmont to a screeching halt at the northeast corner of Jefferson and Woodward, Eric jumped out the passenger side, while his partner yelled, "Good luck!"

Usually enamored with the quality of the Spirit of Detroit sculpture mounted in the front of the building and its brother statue, The Joe Lewis Fist, directly across Jefferson Avenue in Hart Plaza, Goodson ignored the landmarks and hustled to the main entrance of the City-County building. The aluminum and glass rectangular structure housed the Wayne Circuit Court, with Judge O'Hara's courtroom on the twelfth floor. A shoulder-to-shoulder crowd of several hundred anxiously awaited one of the eight elevators. Realizing the time constraints, Goodson opted for the stairs. Half-way up the twelve flights, Eric's chest heaved. He paused to catch his breath and wipe the sweat off his brow.

"Jeez, I've got to start working out," Eric huffed as he bent down with his hands on his knees. Looking up, he pleaded, "Lord, it just wouldn't be right to take me before the ceremony." One additional deep breath, he continued his trek, bounding the steps two at a time. Exploding through the twelfth-floor door, a bustling crowd lingered about, awaiting their turn in one of the four courtrooms. Perspiring as though caught in an unexpected cloud burst, Eric sucked in a deep breath and scanned the solid sea of heads. At the far west end, standing an average head taller than the rest of the horde, Eric observed an elegant white hat perched upon glistening black hair. Propelling himself through the throng, as though a full-back dodging tacklers for his last attempt at a record-breaking season, Eric tripped over an unattended briefcase. Lunging forward, arms extended, his hands caught something soft, curbing his forward momentum. Eric looked up into glistening emerald green eyes.

"My, but you sure know how to make an entrance," the sultry voice announced, accented with blinding white teeth and bracketing dimples. "Are you alright? My God, you're ringing wet and breathing so hard."

Huffing, Eric spit out, "Twelve flights. May have to take a nap after we're done here."

"Darling, that's the last thing you'll be doing when we leave here."

As the solid mahogany wood door swung open, Judge O'Hara stood in front of his bench, flanked on one side by his clerk and on the other by Leonard and Mims Goodson. Two counsel tables were shoved aside to allow Angie and Eric to stand centered, three feet in front of the Judge.

As they approached up the side isle, Aunt Mims leaned in to Lenny and whispered, "My goodness, she's so beautiful; so tall and slender. That woman could drape her body in rags and still put most runway models to shame."

Leonard cocked his head, "Reminds me of you when we were young."

"Hmph. Age, alcohol and reefer have taken a serious toll on you, my love. Not on my best day could I hold a candle to her. Striking is the only word that comes to mind every time I see her."

"You're as gorgeous today as you were the day we first met."

"Good answer, you silver tongued devil. I can't believe my heart still flutters at your same old B.S."

After a brief introduction and exchange of handshakes, Judge O'Hara clasped his hands behind his back and glanced down over the top of his wire rim glasses and nodded to the groom; an identical acknowledgement to the bride required His Honor redirect his eyes upward.

"This is, without a doubt, the most rewarding part of my job. As I stand before you, I'm struck by the similarity of my black robe to that of a priest's cassock, sans the collar. It reminds me that performing a wedding ceremony is a sacred duty." Looking down, "I see you've followed my clerk's advice and already exchanged rings. My apologies, but we always have to squeeze these things in. Please don't read anything into that, other than we're pressed for time."

Turning to the groom, "Eric, do you take Angie to be your lawful wedded spouse; promise to love and cherish her for the rest of your natural life?"

"I do."

Turning to the bride, "Angie, do you take Eric to be your lawful wedded spouse; promise to love and cherish him for the rest of your natural life?"

"I do."

"By the authority vested in me by the State of Michigan, I pronounce you legally married. I recommend sealing the deal with a kiss."

Eric rose on his tiptoes, while Angie bent her knees ever so slightly. As their lips met, Eric felt the distinct touch of tongue. Seconds later, Angie moved her lips to Eric's left ear, "There's a garter belt as high up as it could possibly go, just waiting for your nimble fingers."

Eric felt the rush of blood, hoping it was only to blushing cheeks.

CHAPTER

21

T HE UNUSUAL SOUND EMANATED from the rear of the auditorium, at recurring acceptable intervals of approximately two minutes, the tone and timbre reminiscent of the elusive Sasquatch. Initially mildly irritating, the groans increased as the morning social science lecture progressed, the odd reverberation accelerating to downright disruptive.

"Jeez Jack, you look like ten miles of bad road," Sarah scoffed.

"Great to see you too," Jack winked and plopped into the raging orange fiber glass chair beside her.

The hot flash streaming through her body rapidly diminished as his head dipped to his chest. A lateral nod while biting her lower lip, the only overt sign of incredulity, as she gently patted his knee. *"Must be a record. Asleep in thirty seconds. Amazing! What is it about this guy that drives me crazy? Ordinarily, I would never have given him a second look, but that voice; so deep and reassuring."* Sarah scribbled notes at a furious pace. Although she had an incredible memory, the writing reinforced her confidence. Glancing at her slumbering classmate, she allowed her mind to drift. *"So predictable. He shows up every day in his Dockers, denim shirt, loafers and argyle socks. He's definitely the hardest working guy I've ever met. Never complains. You can tell immediately what position he'll take; the morally right choice. And look at him now; snorting like a hog wallowing in a new bucket of slop. What can it be? He's not my type. I always go for the bad boys.*" Sarah's digression interrupted by the booming voice through the sound system.

"Would someone please determine who it is causing all that racket," the exasperated professor demanded, adding a dramatic flair to an otherwise boring topic.

As the student body scoured the hall in unison, Sarah Garvey jabbed Jack in the ribs while verbally summonsing him through stiffened smiling lips in a sad impression of ventriloquism. "Jack, wake up! You're disturbing the entire class." The polite nudge prompting the slumbering pupil to tilt back in his folding chair, striking his head against the light switch, plunging the room into darkness. "What the... Jack, wake up! You've really done it now!" Sarah's muffled holler accented by significantly increasing the velocity of a second poke. "C'mon Michaels, you idiot, wake up. Mr. Rasmussen realizes it's you and you're done like dinner. Snap out of it, will you," Garvey pleaded.

"That's it. That's all I can take. Class dismissed," the instructor terminating the discourse fifteen minutes into the scheduled hour program.

Sarah raced across the back row to the side exit to avoid guilt by association, before the attendants filed past the grotesque sight of the mouth agape, exhausted, snoring student. Their barrage of derogatory comments failed to inflict the intended rancor, the slumbering pupil expending all his energy struggling to suck air through obviously blocked passages.

"Asshole."

"What a jerk?"

"Idiot!"

No way he's passin' this class."

"At least you got that right, Mr. Agnelli," the professor derided as he shook his head at the unbelievable sight.

"Where the heck did everybody go?" Michaels inquired as he approached Sarah Garvey mainlining caffeine in the cafeteria at Mackenzie Hall. Decked in a Ralph Lauren pleated skirt, silk blouse and Ferragamo pumps, the stunning coed could easily be mistaken for the CEO of a Fortune 500 company, rather than a commuting undergraduate. Her presence radiated through the dingy old converted office building that remained a favorite meeting place of upper classmen; an escape from the clamor of the popular ultra-modern student union.

"I certainly hope you enjoyed your nap, because I'll bet it costs you four credit hours," the sizzling hot blond chided with a mesmerizing flash of enamel reminiscent of a winter storm white out, but lacking the tension.

"Augh, come on, you really think he'd flunk me because I fell asleep?" Jack questioned, weak kneed and fighting off a churning stomach that he assumed the result of a combination of nervousness over his predicament and the presence of the woman he loved.

"Fell asleep is a complete understatement," Garvey scoffed, her elegant one-carat diamond earrings glistening in Jack's eyes as he memorized the movement of her lips with every syllable. "I bruised an elbow, I jabbed you so hard. You were in some kind of hibernative coma."

"Hey, I was whacked from unloading box cars of beer all night. I just dozed off, is all. I'm sure he'll understand if I make an appointment to go see him and explain the circumstances," Jack remarked confidently, but inwardly doubting his ability to sell the excuse.

"Listen Jack, plenty of people fall asleep in lecture hall and escape completely unnoticed. But no, not J.Z. Michaels; everything is always larger than life. Your snore disrupted four hundred students. Then to top it off, you accidentally cut the lights on a professor who, not two weeks before, you accuse of wasting your valuable time so why doesn't he get it in gear and teach the material he's paid to cover. I really don't think you have a prayer," Sarah concluded.

"You really ought to try law school. But remind me, if I'm accused of murder, not to hire you. What a pessimist!"

"Jack, you get out of this one relatively unscathed and I'll never doubt you again," Sarah chuckled, leaning back while brushing aside a golden wave of hair, exposing her royal blue eyes.

"Doll, I love it when you talk dirty to me. Meet me at my place around noon?"

Always brimming with self-confidence, Sarah initially tolerated Jack's chauvinistic references, eventually considering them terms of endearment, but resented the all too frequent sexual innuendo; it reminded her of a well-kept secret. "Bug off."

"Is that a 'maybe'?" Jack pressed.

"Men are dogs!" Sarah thought, but responded, "Couldn't if I wanted to; Aunt Martha is visiting."

"Didn't know you had an Aunt Martha?"

"She visits every month."

"Really? And I've never met her?" I can't believe it!"

"Jack?"

"What?"

"I really don't have an Aunt Martha."

"Then why would you say you did?"

"Just give it some thought."

"Don't have a clue."

"No kidding?" Sarah shook her head in disbelief. "Why don't you go see if you can catch up with Rasmussen?"

"What a great idea. Why didn't I think of that?"

CHAPTER

22

Clipping along in the confident gait of a successful professional, John Z. Michaels, considered all the angles, finally deciding to grovel, but only as a last resort, to salvage his social sciences credit; the only remaining required course for graduation from Monteith College, an elite honors school within the forty thousand-student Wayne State University. The unique program provided an incredible educational experience allowing the young Turk the opportunity to forgo all basic college curriculum, signing up for any class he desired, without restriction, including all graduate level courses, as long as he achieved the timely completion of six credit hours per semester of Monteith social and natural sciences through the first three years. Flunking Rasmussen's class jeopardized smooth scheduling for his senior thesis, which encompassed a twelve-month research project.

Ascending the rickety wooden stairs of the dilapidated Victorian home serving as the temporary faculty offices of Monteith for the past ten years, Michaels decided to dazzle Rasmussen with his smooth flowing bull. Entering the bulging screened door, Jack sauntered to the first-floor rear bedroom now serving as an office and knocked gingerly on the entry frame to the tune of the Rolling Stones, *Satisfaction*.

"Is that you creating all that racket, Michaels?" The voice from across the narrow hall interrupted in the middle of the second riff.

"Hey Mr. Mink, what gave me away?"

"The melodic rap. Only you could play name that tune while your future heads for the dumper," Mink responded as he entered the narrow hallway. "Damn Jack, you look worse than Ali after fourteen rounds of rope-a-doping."

"It's the new job."

"As a punching bag?"

"Pretty much," Jack chuckled as he shook his head, then continued, "This thing with Rasmussen can't be that bad?"

"No, it's worse. Rasmussen left instructions for his secretary to call security and have you physically removed from the building, if you showed up. Lucky for you, I think she's in the rest room at the moment. He e-mailed the faculty requesting an emergency meeting for tomorrow to vote on expelling you from Monteith."

"Man, that's a bit of an over-reaction, wouldn't you say? I mean, come on, all I did was fall asleep during his lecture, which was incredibly boring, by the way."

"You mean, all you did today, don't you?"

"Hey, I never said anything to the guy that wasn't true."

"I understand that. Sometimes people don't want to hear the truth; or, you could sugar coat it a bit. It's called tact. Something you should work on."

Today you allegedly fall asleep and snore so loud you interrupt the lecture and then you turn the lights out?"

"I didn't do it on purpose. I fell asleep."

"He'll never believe you."

"The guys a putz!"

"Everyone, including Rasmussen, knows that. He doesn't have to be told. It's called what?"

"Tact."

"Besides, he's a tenured professor. That putz will be here long after you're gone. He can only be discharged for immoral acts."

"You mean I'm gonna have to run all over town interviewing farm animals to build my defense?"

"Cute. I'll try to run interference for you, but no promises."

"Thanks Joe."

"No thanks necessary. I haven't done anything yet. I just happen to harbor this weird opinion that you could be an intellectual bright spot with just a little polishing."

"Thanks again. I gotta run."

"Maybe faster than you think."

"Dare I ask?"

"It's the *Southern Edge*. They've already been here interviewing. They think they have a hilarious story to run in the next edition.

"That communist rag? Why would they even consider something this mundane?"

"I don't know. But if you make the front page, I probably can't help you. It would be seen as an embarrassment to the entire faculty."

"Gotcha. Thanks again Mr. Mink."

"You bet."

CHAPTER

23

In the mid-sixties, The *Southern Edge* transformed from an award-winning journalistic masterpiece to a festering bed sore on the backside of the University. Overrun with a zealous staff of Black Panthers proselytizing the propaganda of every nascent left-wing political offshoot imaginable, the twice-weekly publication continues to employ rag tag militant misfits, pushing First Amendment boundaries to their outer limits. Located in the same ramshackle retail storefront on Cass Avenue, just north of Forest, for the past forty years, the once inflammatory décor of Che Guevara, H. Rap Brown and Students for A Democratic Society posters peeling from the walls fail to incite reactionary comments, as much for the occasional visitor's lack of historical perspective, as the current mood of civic indifference.

"What a dump!" J.Z. let escape a bit too loud as he balanced in a sardine can sized foyer walled by scarred metal desks, as the closing door brushed his backside.

"Looks like your smart mouth has got your ass kicked at least once already."

"What? Oh, this," Jack responded as he touched his bruised face. "No, it's just work related."

"Other than your pompous assed interior design opinions that no one here gives a shit about, there must be something I can do for you, cause we didn't call for no plumber in plaid?" The lanky, handsome, black man inquired as he approached the business casual dressed visitor.

"Hi, I'm Jack Michaels," the embarrassed student exclaimed, extending his hand.

"Ah! Tomorrow's front-page story," the well-spoken inquisitor concluded, allowing Jack's hand to hang midair.

"That's what I wanted to talk to you about."

"Do tell. And here I thought we were being graced with the presence of the C.E.O. of the House of Michaels to revamp our outdated image."

"I'm sorry about that. This place is just not what I expected."

"You thought something along the lines of The Daily Planet from the *Superman* series?"

"I don't know. I don't know what I expected. Whatever it was, it certainly wasn't this."

The interrogator let Jack sweat.

"Look, I apologize. I'm sorry. Can we get by this and start over?"

A piercing stare that suspended time preceded a response. "Agreed. But I must tell you, you look nothing like you do in the photo."

"The photo? You photographed me in the class?"

"An interesting pose. You apparently do fall into that slim margin of people who truly have no good side. From what I know of you thus far, it seems to match your personality."

"Slow down there, Lois Lane."

"I beg your pardon."

"It was meant to be humorous. You never gave me your name, so I improvised. You know, you being a reporter and all."

"Mamoud Shaloub."

"Pardon me."

"My name is Mamoud Shaloub."

"You're kidding, right?"

"Do I look like I'm funnin' with you? Why don't you just haul your preppy little ass out of here? We don't have anything to discuss."

"Look, I am sorry. You just didn't strike me as Muslim."

"Oh! Exactly what is a Muslim supposed to look like in your mind?"

"You know: a bearded towel head wearing a skanky white sheet, carrying a gasoline can while smoking a lit cigar on the way back to his party store."

"Did you actually graduate from Cotillion?"

"I was held back a few years. Something about grades."

"You mean, grating."

"Oh yeah, that could have been it," Jack snickered. "Now can we discuss my predicament?"

"You mean beside your tacky manner?"

"Not more than twenty minutes ago someone told me I had absolutely no tact."

"Now I know how I must have frustrated my Momma when I was a kid."

"Me too."

"Yes, but I grew out of it at the age of eight."

"Ouch!"

"Let's get on with it. What's on your sick little mind?"

"The story."

"What about it?"

"I need you to kill it."

"Not a chance."

"What's the big deal anyway? This is not the kind of thing that generally interests the *Southern Edge*."

"Slow news day."

"You even have a photo of me?"

"In living color."

"How could you possibly have found out about the incident and got someone there that quickly?"

"Actually, a stroke of luck. One of our photographers attends Monteith. He thought it was a news worthy sight, so he snapped a few shots. We have a great view of you leaning back with your mouth wide open, eyes closed and sleeping like a baby."

"Are you sure you can't deep six it?"

"No way."

A metallic tap on the storefront glass door interrupted the exchange. Jack turned and observed an obvious vagrant waving and exposing a fractured tooth smile.

Opening the door, Jack asked, "Can I help you?"

"'Youse could if youse could spare some change," the panhandler responded in an indecipherable mumble, but the extended hand an unmistakable universal sign. Jack dug into his khaki pocket and handed the drifter seventy-five cents. "Thank you, sir," was Jack's interpretation as the beggar bowed and ducked down the street.

"You're welcome. Hope it helps," Jack replied, pulling the door closed.

"Now why'd you go and do that?" Mamoud barked.

"What?"

"Give that dirty old bastard money."

"From the looks of him, he could use it. Why?"

"'Cause it gives our people a bad name and you're only encouraging him."

"I guess I always figured that if I ever wound up like that someday, maybe somebody would help me out. I meant no offense. Now can we get back to the point? Who cares about some guy who dozes off in a lecture hall? That'll put your readers right to sleep."

"Ordinarily, I'd agree with you, but when the same student told the professor off two weeks earlier, then disturbed the class to the point of causing an early dismissal, I'd say this borders on civil disobedience."

"You have got to be kidding!"

"Do I look like I'm playing with you?"

"The simple truth is, I was exhausted from work last night. I fell asleep. I have a terrible snoring problem. When I leaned back, my head must have banged the light switch. It's as simple as that."

"That's not quite the story we're going to print."

"Now that you know the truth, anything less would be a lie."

"Really?"

"Yes, really. Where's your journalistic integrity? God knows, looking around here, that's about all you have."

"You a catty assed bitch."

"Does it show? It's always been one of those well-kept family secrets. Look, I'll make you a deal. You don't have to kill the story; just postpone it until Friday's issue. They're trying to kick me out of Monteith. You're only assisting them by writing the article now. I never thought you would want to help out the administration. Wait until I'm past tomorrow's hearing date. I promise you, it'll be a much more interesting piece by that time."

"How so?"

"I haven't quite figured it all out yet, but I never seem to do things the easy way. If you cut me some slack on this, I promise that when I run across something interesting, I'll give you the scoop."

"There isn't anything I like about you, but I'm not out to break your balls. Let me think it over. I'm not making any promises. The editing committee has to agree."

"Thanks."

"Yeah. Whatever!"

CHAPTER

24

JACK RESUMED A BRISK pace back to his studio apartment on Palmer, just east of Cass Avenue on the northeast corner of the urban campus. A short block east and his building qualified as a ghetto rat trap; located a mere fifty feet from the university boundary, the description mysteriously upgrades to student housing. Advertised as a furnished garden terrace apartment, Michaels jumped at the opportunity, sight unseen. The porch turned out to be a two-foot-wide overflow drain with a solid brick wall obstructing the million-dollar view of a hanging dead potted fern swinging in the breeze of a broken window in the adjacent abandoned building. Jack chalked up the powder blue '85 K-car blocking the front walkway to just another of the millions of abandoned vehicles littering the city.

The distinct vocals of Van Morrison emanating from his room prompted him to cautiously open the door. "What the...?" J.Z. reared back in disbelief. Allowing two seconds to survey the strange sight, he finally cocked his head to one side. "Gramps?"

"Mongo!" The wrinkled hand strained to reach the spinner to take the next turn.

"Please don't call me that."

"Green." Albert craned his neck to locate the appropriate circle, his vision obstructed by an ample tush encased in fine woolen slacks.

"Over to your left," the familiar sultry voice offered.

"Sarah?"

The high cheek boned, blond beauty torqued her torso to secure a view of the door. "Hi Jack. Your Grandfather's a hoot. How many men travel with their own twister board?"

"He's a dirty old man."

"Lighten up, Mongo."

"Don't go there," Jack insisted. Sarah flipped him a look.

The game ended with the two participants tumbling to the floor in hysterical laughter. The apparent age disparity a common sight on the streets of Naples, Florida, struck a chord of disbelief in a studio apartment in Detroit's inner city. Sarah reached out to help Albert up.

"Good woman. You should marry her. Reminds me of your Grandmother. She so beautiful." The senior Michaels clasped his hands, raising them to his lips and kissed his thumbs.

"Gramps, that's enough."

"He's so cute."

"Like a python." Turning to his grandfather, Jack remarked, "Gramps, you've got to learn to properly park your car, or they're going to pull your license."

"No provide space for handicapped."

"You were just wound up like a pretzel. What disability do you have?"

"When you old, like me, you park like crazy person. Police understand. No ticket me." Albert folded up the plastic tarp and packed it in the box, "Time to go." He reached out and pulled his Grandson to his chest, wrapped his arms around him and hugged tight, briskly patting him on the back and then guided him aside. His attention focused on Sarah. As he peered into her blue eyes, he instinctively lifted her hand and gently kissed the back, "I no have debt and I drive good at night." As he reached the doorway, he turned and winked at Sarah.

"What a heartbreaker," Sarah swooned. "I see where you get your occasional charm."

Jack took a step toward the couch and stopped. His tiny fold out table was decorated with a white lace tablecloth, single lit candle and medium sized vase of a half dozen yellow roses.

"Well, if this isn't a sight to behold…"

Transporting two plates with sandwiches, Sarah threatened, "Knock it off J.Z., or you'll be wearing this tuna."

"…A picture of domestication."

Sarah wiped her hands on the bath towel doubling as an apron, "I'm warning you; don't take it any further."

"To what do I owe this honor?"

"I felt bad about raking you over the coals this morning. I wanted to make it up to you."

"Who are you trying to kid? I saw the look in your eyes. You loved every second of it."

"You're right. I don't often get the opportunity to gloat. But it was selfish of me. Truce?"

"And you think a tuna sandwich will do the trick?"

"*All men are dogs,*" Sarah thought to herself, sighing inside, "*but this little pup is downright irresistible.*" "You've got to eat. You only have an hour before you start work."

Jack overtly surveyed Sarah's legs, rolling his eyes down to her ankles, then up to her ass. The silent, lecherous look aroused her.

"*I love it when he does that!*" Sarah thought, then relented, "*God, I'm such a hypocrite.*" Finally rationalizing his remarks as simply playful, she acquiesced, "Oh, I get it. You're a sweets freak," the six-foot vixen groaned as she pushed herself against his hard, lanky body, allowing J.Z. the opportunity to nuzzle his head in her chest.

"Yep."

"Didn't your Mother ever tell you that too much candy can rot your teeth?" The taunting temptress smiled as she shoved him backward onto the bed, turned, leaned over and grabbed her purse off a chair and walked out.

"Many times, Snooks," Jack shot back just as the door closed. "But Dad had the foresight to explain the wisdom in dental plans."

CHAPTER

25

In the few serious romantic interludes in Eric's life, things tended to proceed with an air of caution; slowly building an attraction that led to intermittent sex. Now, wild animal lust in an anything goes scenario was the order of the day, every day. Eric replaced the nick-knacks on his nightstand with a Brita water pitcher and two glasses. "You're incredible," Eric mumbled at the conclusion of an hour session.

"And you are an insatiable lover. The perfect combination of man and machine. That's the mark of a confident man."

The two embraced. Just as Eric dozed off, he felt her hand move down beneath the covers and gently start stroking.

"Officer, I've got to admit, I've been a bad girl."

As they completed another round, both collapsed and fell into a deep sleep.

At roughly 2 a.m., Eric sat up in bed, yelling, "Please no! Stop shooting! Stop shooting!"

"Eric, darling, wake up. Wake up."

Eric tossed the sweat drenched sheet aside. Cupping his face in his hands, "I'm so sorry you have to put up with this."

"It's okay," she whispered. "It's really okay. We're partners. It's time to talk it out. Tell me the story."

Eric discussed vague generalities at first, refusing to fill in gruesome details. The lanky brunette persisted, finally triggering a complete emotional breakdown in the tormented cop.

"We were on patrol," Eric sobbed. "Two cars going east on Bethune, two blocks north of Henry Ford Hospital. Everyone was on edge. I hadn't slept in three days. I had no business being out there; none of us did. Christ, we were hallucinating half the time we were so tired and stressed." Eric paused, his chest heaving while his lungs gasped for air.

"Take your time," the calming instruction as the angel cupped his cheeks in her steady palms.

"It was pitch dark. Half the streetlights in the city never worked anyway, and the rest were busted from the rioting. We couldn't see a thing clearly. It was about ten thirty. The guys in the first car contacted us on the walkie-talkie that they saw movement on a front porch to our left. Both cars stopped. We all got out on the passenger side, using the vehicles for protection," Eric relayed, his breathing again more labored after initially settling down and the excessive mucous buildup requiring a gross backhand. "It looked like someone was sitting on the porch. You could see the shape of a head above the railing. Then, the outline of what appeared to be a standing person holding something suddenly emerged right by the steps, followed within a second or two by a loud thwack." Tears again swelled in Eric's eyes. "Someone yelled gun," Eric blubbered. "And all hell broke loose. Shots rang out; one round after another. I hadn't even drawn my weapon." Eric sobbed, shaking his head back and forth. "I couldn't believe what was happening. I thought the noise was too hollow for a gunshot. I kept yelling for everyone to stop, but no one heard me," the anguished cop bawled, hoisting his hands up to bury his face. "Must have been a hundred rounds exploding. The figure in the center of the porch collapsed and fell down the stairs. When the shooting finally stopped, all of us moved toward the house," the confessing detective continued, his mood changing to an almost robotic tone. "Laying on the walkway at the base of the stairs was a woman about sixty years old, still clutching a broom in her hands, her body riddled with bullets of several different calibers. She had just come out of the house. It was the wooden storm door snapping shut behind her that touched off the melee. On the porch was what we assumed to be her husband, literally cut in half from a direct shotgun blast, his upper body still balanced perfectly in his lawn chair. Next to him was a young girl, about eight or nine, her arm blown off. I felt her neck; she was still alive. The sergeant told me to leave her be. I told him I couldn't do that. He asked me if I wanted to wind up like these assholes who were harboring snipers. I just looked at him and kept my mouth shut. I knew the right thing to do. I just couldn't raise the courage to follow through," the contrite cop wailed in convulsive gasps. "We just let her bleed to death while we got the stories straight. We were two blocks from the damn hospital and we let her die. No one mentioned it again. Can you believe it?"

The sensuous mentor reached around Eric's bare waist and placed her head on his shoulder.

"I've seen her face every night for the last twenty years."

Angie turned her lips to his ear and whispered, "It's time."

Taking a moment to collect himself, Erie responded, "Time for what?"

"To confront your demons."

"How do I go about doing that?"

"Right the wrong," the soft confident tone conveyed, "No matter what it takes."

"I don't have the strength."

"You're stronger than you think."

"You overestimate me."

"But you have a secret weapon."

"I do?"

"Yes."

"What is it?"

"Me," Angie whispered as she tenderly pulled Erie down and snuggled him.

26

Eric spent a restless night. Rather than tussle with old demons, the discussion with Angie gnawed at him. He knew he lacked the necessary confidence, but if he didn't start now, he'd keep putting it off. Why not start laying the groundwork to right the wrongs? *"That's it. It's time,"* Eric convinced himself while rolling over to get comfortable and pursue elusive sleep. His mind raced; thoughts on fast forward; a nonsensical jumble. *"Slow down, detective. Take it one step at a time. Where would a good investigator start? Well, police have to file reports on everything. Every second of our time has to be accounted for somehow. There are logbooks, incident reports and duty rosters. That's it! The records bureau."*

Bounding up the crumbling slate front steps of a dilapidated Detroit Police headquarters at 1300 Beaubien, on the fringe of downtown's decaying business district, Eric shook his head at the ring of double parked dinged and battered patrol cars encircling the four-story crumbling Greek Classic meets Motown designed soot-stained structure. *"Damn, it looks like intermission at a demolition derby. No wonder people don't feel like there are enough police on the streets---they're all here."*

Eric stopped at the lobby candy booth and purchased a Snickers from Rudy, a blind merchant operating his stand for the past thirty-two years.

"Here you go, son," Rudy computing the exact change for a ten spot from the metal cash box and handing it to Eric.

"How did you know?"

"You get a feel for the sick humor of you cops over the years."

"But a ten was all I had, really."

"I know son. I could tell you were one of the good ones," the merchant smiled.

"Sure is a mess outside. Why don't they clean this place up?"

"I wouldn't know. It all smells like heavenly chocolate to me."

"See you around."

"Come back anytime, you hear; with or without the correct change."

The second-floor clerk directed Eric to the tombs, three stories below ground level. As the elevator door opened, he stepped out into a pool of standing water and surveyed the dark cavernous room. "Hello! Is anyone here," Eric called. "Excuse me, is there anybody around?"

"Yeah, whad'aya want?" Came the gravelly response from around the side of the elevator.

Eric turned to his right and negotiated through the slop to a fenced cage housing a bulbous purple nosed attendant reeking of booze and stale urine. "I'm here to find some reports from July, 1967."

"What the hell you wanna do that for?" The gruff reply.

"I'm looking into some things that might have happened in the riots."

"Oh yeah. What kind of things?"

"I don't exactly know."

"Well then, I can't exactly help you, can I officer?"

"That's detective to you," Eric snapped, then collected himself. "Is the mold down here affecting you, or are you always this surly?"

"That and my old lady refuses to munch on the baloney pony. She thinks I'm a pig. Can you imagine that?"

"Yeah I can, actually."

The disheveled guard broke into a combination raucous laughter and phlegm spewing cough as he rose to unlock the gate. "You'd think the do-gooder assholes would eventually give up when they see the condition of this place, but I guess I got no such fucking luck."

"Why, has someone else been down here looking for the same material?"

"How the hell would I know whether it was the same crap?"

"Who was it?"

"Some cutesy professor or some shit."

"Did you get a name?"

"I look like a fucking receptionist?"

"None that I'd want to date."

"You're a pretty fucking funny cop; a regular Bob fucking Hope. The crap from the '60's should be down a hundred feet or so, then turn to your left. Then down ten or fifteen stacks and that should be in the general vicinity."

"Thanks for your help."

"You can wait to thank me when you find 'em. Ain't gonna be easy. I ain't no fuckin librarian. I don't got no dewey fuckin decimal system here."

"Understood."

As Eric attempted to navigate the aisles, he realized what a formidable task lies ahead. Files strewn everywhere; wet, soggy papers soaking up the dampness of the earthen floor providing a squishy, slippery mat; empty manila folders hanging off corroded steel shelves as though hurricane force winds ripped their contents from the metal prongs; and absolutely no semblance of order, whether alphabetical, by category of crime, or calendar year. "*Hmph, this could take a lifetime,*" Eric shrugged, simultaneously releasing a controlled exhale.

CHAPTER

27

THE ADMINISTRATIVE ASSISTANT PICKED up the handset, "Hello."

"Yeah, this is Zekens, down in the tombs," the raspy voice sounding like an intentional distortion to thwart identification. "The Commissioner told me to check in if anybody ever came snooping around for records on the riots."

"Has there been someone there?"

"No, I'm just fucking lonely and thought I'd double check to see my phone was still working cause I ain't had no calls this month. Of course, there's been someone here, asshole. He's here right now."

"And who would that be?" The defensive tone unmistakable.

"A precinct plain clothes cop by the name of Goodson."

"Okay, thank you for your help, officer Zekens."

"You better be getting' your punk ass down here with another fifth of scotch as promised. Some of the good stuff this time; Glenlivet 12-year single malt. I don't wanna be waitin' a week like the last time either, or, I'll be comin' up there to pound on your faggotty ass. You hear me, Mr. administrative assistant?"

"I'm sure the Commissioner won't forget."

"Damn straight," Zekens scowled as he slammed down the receiver.

"Yeah," the only comment from the voice on the other end of the line.

"We got another snoop from the sixties."

"Yeah?"

"Goodson, a precinct dick."

"Well take it from here." Click.

CHAPTER

28

J.Z. HEARD THE SCREECH of tires, but disregarded the noise as an echo from the road. By the time he sensed danger, the speeding vehicle clipped his pant leg, forcing him to dive between two out of service delivery trucks in the mechanic's bay. As he collected himself, Michaels caught the unmistakable avulsion of shredding steel from the accelerating car as it plowed into a metal support brace protecting the corner of the brick arch separating the docking area from the loading zone. Slamming into a seven-row high stack of empty twelve-ounce returnable bottles, the Coup de Ville propelled glass projectiles with the frequency and intensity of a Viet Cong mortar attack, while skidding to a stop inches from a group of employees playing poker on a makeshift table.

The driver squeezed out, his gold chains sloshing across the lapels of his thousand-dollar cashmere sport coat, as he shouted, "Take this piece of crap back to the dealer and tell them to give me a new one." He pushed back his shoulder length black hair and tucked the Omega watch back under the sleeve of his custom silk shirt. His dark eyes bulged as he uncomfortably awaited a reply. "Anyone fucking hear me?"

"Screw you. What do we look like, your man servants?"

Butch wrenched his neck left, toward the familiar voice. "*I knew it! I knew it! That skinny little Hispanic shit. Gonna have to seriously hurt him someday. David always said he was the toughest little bastard he ever met. Told stories about Roy Blue this and Roy Blue that. He's a fucking hi-lo driver with no respect for his betters. Really looking forward to seriously fucking him up. I really, really am."* "Hey bud, you work for me. You do what I tell you to, or else."

"Or else what, you fat assed bastard?"

"I'll can your ass."

"You wish. I work for your Mother, not for you."

"You keep Momma out of this, you hear?"

Roy moved with the precision of a stalking cat, now within five feet of Mayer. "You come in here all liquored up and damned near kill us, then start barking orders like you think you own the place. You're lucky I'm more interested in this game, so I don't come kick your candy ass all over this warehouse."

"You better hope I don't tell Momma about your attitude."

"Oh boy, I'm scared shitless. Your late stepfather hired me to run this place and that's exactly what I'm doing. Putting up with the likes of you is not in my job description, Butchie."

Blue's calmness unnerved Mayer. *"What's with this guy? Doesn't he ever sweat? It's fucking eighty degrees in here and the Spic never sweats."* "The name is Butch, not Butchie. My friends call me Harrold. You can call me Mr. Mayer."

"I wouldn't call you if you were late for dinner, you…"

"Roy Blue! What's going on?"

"Is that you, College Boy?"

"The one and only. Glad to see your smiling face." Michaels re-tucking his plaid shirt tail into his Dockers, then bent down to brush off the debris from his recent dive.

"Do I look like I'm smiling dealing with dip shit here?"

"You better watch your mouth, Roy."

"What are you…"

"Mr. Mayer, is that a keg of beer sticking in your sun roof?" Michaels interrupted. "New advertising gimmick?" Jack chuckled. Everyone's attention now drawn to the Caddy. "You know, for a few bucks extra, I'll bet they could custom fit that baby. Certainly, would eliminate a problem on rainy days."

"Who the fuck are you?" An incensed Mayer questioned, as spittle flew across Jack's face.

"I'm the new guy," Jack calmly replied, while retrieving a handkerchief to clear the slaver. "Don't you recall? In my interview, you thought I'd be the perfect fit to balance out all these assholes," Michaels replied with all the assurance of a corporate lawyer closing a million-dollar deal.

"I didn't interview you," Butch slurred, scratching his head.

"Wow, I must not have left a lasting impression," Jack pondered. "Well, no matter, certainly a man of your stature has significantly more important things to do than waste his time exchanging barbs with the hired help. Why don't you go make yourself comfortable while we get the trucks loaded."

"Well now, maybe you ain't as stupid as you look. Get my clubs out of the conference room closet and throw all my stuff in the trunk. You can park it out back," Mayer gnarled as he tossed the keys to Michaels.

"You got it, Butch."

"That's Mr. Mayer. Don't you people get it?" The pompous managerial imposter wailed as he turned and waddled away.

"We certainly do, Mr. Mayer."

"I never thought I'd see the day," a conciliatory Blue proffered, shaking his head in amazement.

"You didn't. It's just a ruse. The guy's a complete dumb ass. He's never held a job in his life. It's simply an accident of birth. If his stepfather had dropped dead two weeks earlier, there wouldn't have been a quickie marriage to Mrs. Mayer and the kid wouldn't have a pot to piss in. It's nothing more than luck. As an accomplished gambler, you should know that."

"I know, but he grinds me."

"Good, then you won't mind messing with his pea brain. Let me get the clubs, then you follow me out to the back lot."

J.Z.'s imitation gangster lean prevented him from smashing his head against the bottom of the half-barrel, while he fired up the battered month-old Caddy. As he inched down the driveway to Joy Road, he observed Max and Rodeo approach from his left side. "Hey Max, how you doing?"

"Anybody I can. Want to be done?" Max squealed with delight.

Michaels shook his head. "I don't have a clue what that means. Sorry I asked."

As Torpo pulled himself together, he placed both hands on the roof, just beyond the top of the driver's side door and leaned in the open window, "Hey, I see you found the sixth half barrel. Man, Pepatino was really pissed. Me and Rodeo lost it last night on I-75, going over that big bridge at the Rouge Plant. Found the other five, but just couldn't figure where the last one went."

"Max, I really don't want to know," Jack countered, as he swung the car around and parked in the far corner of the twelve-acre property, flipping the keys into the trunk and slamming the lid.

"He said throw everything into the trunk, didn't he?"

"No question about it."

"Sure hope he has AAA," Jack chuckled as he hopped on the hi-lo forks.

As Michaels reflexively winced anticipating the irritating clang of the steel plate straddling the fissure between the rear of the trailer and the dock as the lift truck bounded out of the semi with a pallet of bottles, he gently applied the brakes. The forward edge of the metal berm slid off the end of the trailer, suspending the front wheels of the forklift over the crevasse. Jack stared in amazement as the stack spilt, toppling forty-nine cases of long necks to the floor in a nightmarish domino effect, triggering a geyser of rank smelling random arches of fizz.

Just as the load split, Pepatino rolled up, skidding sideways to a halt. "Goddamn Jack, how many times do I have to tell you to slow down?" The afternoon shift foreman screamed, as he repeatedly flicked his stick, sending the errant bottles back to a fictitious center ice.

"Speed had nothing to do with it, Jimmy. The damn plate slid out from under me."

"Yeah, yeah. Always in a hurry. You don't listen is your problem," the beet red face accenting the scolding.

"Pepatino, can you actually talk in normal conversational tones?"

"Sure I can, but you don't listen to me when I holler, so why would I quiet down?"

"It must be some sort of carryover from your professional hockey days, yelling at refs and stuff."

"Well, are you gonna get down and clean this mess up or do I have to stand here and scream at you till you do?"

"They started wearing helmets in hockey after your retirement, didn't they?"

"If you don't get moving I'm gonna dock your pay."

"You know, it could be that hair growing out of your ears."

"That's it. At eight dollars a case times forty-nine, that's, that's… help me out here J.Z."

"Oh, I see now. You comb it down for sideburns. Very inventive."

"Jesus Christ, you must raise my blood pressure three-hundred points," the lunatic supervisor ranted as he turned and skated away.

CHAPTER

29

BALANCING A WANDERING MIND with the reality of a road full of dim wit drivers required much more luck than skill: cruising gang bangers in upchuck bouncing low riders block the thoroughfare while soliciting scantily clad temptresses with their silky tongued barrage of expletive deletives; homeless winos hobble out with grime infested rags to smear a perfectly clear windshield for a buck; and, avoiding eye contact at all costs, the lecherous suburban element descends under cover of darkness to fulfill licentious fantasies. Losing the challenge, J.Z. swerved to miss a lavender '63 Chevy Impala loaded with young toughs.

"Damn, that was close!" His thoughts quickly drifted to Sarah Garvey. Her affect unmistakable; complete unguarded comfort without the gamesmanship he experienced in previous relationships. She was truly one of the great ones.

Whipping into his thirty dollar a month parking spot in the crushed stone lot of the adjacent print shop, Jack dragged his aching carcass from his 1976 Renault Le Car and stretched. *God it would be so nice to see Sarah.* A quick pull opening the key entry only front steel framed security door with a burned-out flood light overhead, reaffirmed Jack's belief that no portion of his three-hundred dollar a month rent ever touched a rainy-day repair fund. Catching his toe on a worn piece of hallway carpet ten paces in, propelled him to his apartment.

"And how was your day at the office, dear?"

The welcome voice sparked new life into the exhausted warehouse worker. "Well, I was run over by a hit and run drunken boss inside the warehouse and I've been docked a week's pay for breakage; otherwise just another boring afternoon. How about you, Snooks?"

"My substitute teaching assignment fell through, so I spent a quiet day here outlining my senior thesis?"

"Wow, not only a vision of loveliness, but organized too."

"You know smart women turn you on," Sarah growled.

"Oh right. It was the Vulcan mind meld that cranked up the Governor."

"You know what I mean, Jack."

"I certainly do. What do you say we perform an experiment in alternative energy sources? Rumor has it, this rambling one, one-thousandth of an acre of heaven just happens to be sitting on a geothermal hot spot similar to Yellowstone National Park."

"Yes, but here there is only one little hot spring," the teenage giggle a sensuous emphasis.

"Ouch, that hurt."

"Well, you don't have time for treatment. You've got to get busy and give serious thought to your defense against Rasmussen."

"Hey, that was just an accident. What more should I have to say?"

"Sticking with that argument will get you kicked out of Monteith. I can't believe you're taking this so lightly?"

"It bothers the hell out of me. I'm a wreck over this. Is that what you want to hear? Unlike most of the students here, riding on the family meal ticket, I've had to scratch for every nickel. You really think I want to throw all that away? It's not like he's discriminating against me. He's just pissed. I can understand that. I also think I can explain it."

"Think about it as you drive me home."

"The Vette in the shop?"

"New rear tires."

"It's no wonder the way you fly around in that thing. I can't believe you've still got your license."

Sarah pursed her lips. "If you were a cop, would you give this face a ticket?"

Jack arched a brow. "Speaking about the Bear, we saw one the other night identical to yours."

A wave of nausea swept over Sarah. "Where did..." A slight cough interrupted her. "Who's we?"

"The guys from work."

"Where were you?"

"Oh, just out bar hopping, you know. Say, why don't you stay here tonight? It's a long way to the burbs. And you said it yourself, I've got a lot of work to do. You could help."

"We wouldn't get the right kind of work done."

Jack's mouth ran before his brain kicked in, "My place not good enough for you?" The snide reference to her three story, fifteen hundred dollar a month townhouse in Royal Oak sucked the color out of her face. He didn't even know why he said something so stupid. Wishing he could take it back, Jack fumbled for an apology.

"I thought we were past that. My life style is no one's business, including yours. I like nice things, yes. Have I ever complained once about anything in the last year?"

"I'm so sorry. I don't know where that even came from."

"Forget it. I'll call a cab." Sarah reached for the wall-mounted phone, hoping Jack would stop her.

"I can't think of anything I'd rather do than drive you. Please forgive me. I'm just a bit frazzled."

Sarah leaned over and gently kissed him on the lips. "By the way, Professor Mink called. He wants us to meet him tomorrow night at the Jam for drinks. He says it'll either be a celebration, or, a wake, depending on the outcome of your hearing. He also suggested you put together a more convincing argument."

"The truth shall set you free!" Jack sang out as a humorous retort, as well as, a vain attempt to rebuild his own self-confidence as the door closed behind them.

"In your case it certainly will; right out of school."

Entering the morning semi-formal hearing chaired by the dean of Monteith, Jack pulled open the door, waited a full five seconds for effect, then strutted into the room with a well-dressed mousy little character in tow.

"Jeez, I can't wait to hear this," Joe Mink whispered, leaning into Sarah with his hand covering his mouth.

"Dean Avery, before we get started, I'd like to introduce Van Mackleprange, my attorney from the A.C.L.U."

"This is gonna be better than I ever imagined," Mink chuckled loud enough to be heard by everyone within his immediate vicinity.

"Dean Avery, if I could take a moment, perhaps we can shorten these proceedings by outlining our position," counselor Mackleprange squeaked in a comical impression of Mighty Mouse. "We contend this is nothing more than outright discrimination. Professor Rasmussen has singled out my client due to his affiliation in a protected class; namely, a gay Native American Christian Scientist."

"Un-fucking believable!" Mink snorted.

"This is outrageous! Why any idiot can see he's not an Indian," Professor Rasmussen ranted.

Michaels turned and winked at Mamoud, the representative from the *Southern Edge*.

"Therein, gentlemen and ladies, lies the problem," Mackleprange waxing eloquent. "I offer as defense exhibit one, Mr. Michaels' student declaration form clearly indicating under the statistical data section: Race-Native American; Sexual Preference-homosexual; Religion-Church of Scientology. Is there any possibility of working out an amicable solution to this problem?"

"Professor Rasmussen?" the Dean inquired.

"Why this is preposterous! I've never seen any evidence that he's religious, or gay, or a so-called Native American. He could have wrote down anything on that form at any time."

Reaching into his leather valise, the circus midget lawyer extracted a formal looking document, waving it in the air above his head. "I have here a sworn affidavit from the admissions director that states the student declarations form is genuine and taken directly from the administrator's locked file cabinet." Mackleprange manifesting growing confidence, "It is Professor Rasmussen's blatant profiling that fosters prejudice…"

"Excuse me, Mr. Mackleprange," Jack interrupted. "Dean, can I say something here?"

"Why not?"

"First, I'd like to publicly apologize to Professor Rasmussen. I lost my temper at the start of the semester when he spent what I considered an inordinate amount of time telling jokes. That was wrong of me. I realize now that he was probably just loosening the class up. The sleeping incident was the result of me being over tired. When I leaned back, my head hit the light switch. I'm sorry."

"Well then, I think this matter is resolved. Mr. Michaels, you drop the discrimination claim and your status in Monteith is unaffected. Dismissed," the Dean ordered.

As the room emptied, Rasmussen waited behind to corner Michaels. Leaning into his ear, the pedagogue whispered, "You and that Madison Fifth Avenue pirouetting teacher of yours' are a disgrace to this institution."

Jack looked at him like he had two heads and left.

CHAPTER

31

PUNCHING OUT AT 10:30 p.m., Jack hustled to the Traffic Jam, a cozy little college pub on Second Avenue on the south side of campus. Laden with heavy woods, private booths and low lighting, the Jam catered to the faculty and students in their early twenties.

Sarah's unmistakable golden locks served as a homing beacon for the triumphant defendant.

"What are the chances L. Ron Hubbard's legions will deposit a rattlesnake in Mackleprange's mailbox?" The vixen chuckled.

"I don't know how you did it, but I must admit, it was unique," Mink laughed.

"I'm just glad no one had the foresight, or, for that matter now, the hindsight, to search the other student declaration forms. Two semesters ago, I checked the boxes indicating a transvestite Nordic Mormon; before that, a female African American agnostic. I never envisioned my efforts at screwing up the college stats would ever come in handy."

"Where did you ever come up with that idea," the raspy voiced vision questioned, leaning forward and clasping onto Jack's taut muscled upper arm.

"From our little tête-à-tête last night. I called the A.C.L.U. office this morning on a whim. I told the secretary my predicament and what I had filled out on the form, and the next thing I know, Mackleprange was all over this like white on rice. He never even questioned my veracity. All I told him to do was check the form."

"You better hope no one looks beyond last semester," Mink chuckled as they hoisted glasses in a toast to freedom. "There is one little lingering detail I think I should mention. After you left, the Dean felt it necessary to separate you and Rasmussen permanently."

"Great!" Jack interrupted. "That guy is totally strange. Pulls me aside and calls me an embarrassment to the school and refers to Sarah as some kind of dancer."

Garvey choked on her drink, spitting back into her glass.

"My sentiments exactly. I think the guys' a half bubble off plumb."

Sarah fought to catch her breath while forcing a smile.

"I could see why he'd feel that way about me, but what could he possibly hold against you? Go figure."

"Forget about that now. The Dean reassigned you to a position of research assistant; sort of an *Animal House* double secret probation instead of completing the remainder of your social science credits."

"Oh crap, that's just great. What putz did he stick me with now?"

"Me. I'm also your new senior advisor."

Sarah continued to eke out a smile, still struggling to maintain her composure. The sweat fell in what felt like torrents, permanently staining her silk blouse.

"Joe, you wouldn't bullshit me about this would you?" J.Z. questioned.

"Boy Scout's honor," Mink responded, holding up a three-finger salute. You are now the new research assistant on my pet project."

"Which is?"

"An investigation into the alleged atrocities by police during the '67 riots."

"Cool."

CHAPTER

32

THE CRUMPLED YELLOW LEGAL pad page hit the top of the overflowing trash can, rolled back and fell to the floor. After thirty-six straight hours, not even a coherent opening sentence. Rasmussen slammed the blue Bic pen onto the desk. It bounced up and into his three-quarter full coffee mug, splashing the remnants across the rosewood antique in a pattern eerily similar to a Rorschach test.

"Un-fu…" The tirade interrupted by a phone call. "Yes," Rasmussen answered.

"This is Dean Avery."

"Dean, how very nice to hear from you," Rasmussen responded, while searching for something to clean up the mess.

"I hope I'm not disturbing you, Frank."

"No, not at all. What can I do for you, Sir?"

"Well, this was something I wanted to discuss in person, but your secretary informs me that you've been sequestered in your office for the last day and a half. Is everything okay?"

"Just putting the finishing touches on a rather interesting research paper."

"Well, that's great to hear. That happens to be partially the reason I called."

"Oh."

"Your last three articles were rejected by the Peer Review Committee as unprofessional. That, coupled with the fact that as the Social Sciences Department Head, you have failed to publish in five years, causes me some concern."

Rasmussen's entire body trembled; bile rushed up into his throat. "Sir, I'm not saying all, but a lot of the past rejections are political. There is a certain amount of jealousy involved."

Shaking his head, "Now Frank, the other professors in your department don't seem to suffer the same fate. Take Mink, for instance. He's a publishing machine."

"That's because I assigned the two best research assistants to him. The people I have are barely able to write, much less do proper analysis."

"This is an honors college. Every student should be more than capable to assist you."

"You would think so, but I'm finding out that's not true."

"Frank, I've got to be honest with you. I'm getting a tremendous amount of pressure from the department faculty to replace you."

Rasmussen's mind raced; sweat gushed from every pore. *"Those ungrateful fucking bastards. I gave them their fucking jobs!"*

"Are you there, Frank?"

"Yes, yes I'm here. Dean, I built the Monteith Social Sciences Department. I put it all together for you. I hired the faculty. I set up the curriculum."

"I know you did, Frank. And I appreciate everything you've done. But you've got to realize the mentality we're dealing with in today's environment. It's all about what have you done for me lately. A committee of faculty members is pushing for Mink to head up the department. They made quite a case: wildly popular with the students and faculty; nationally recognized as a leader in the field; and, fearless in pushing the boundaries of investigative research."

"But sir…"

"Listen to me, Frank. You're my guy. You have been from the start. But I have to do what's right for the school. If your recent project gets published, that's a start. In the meantime, I suggest you get back down in the trenches and schmooze with the faculty and change your attitude with the student body. This recent incident with Jack Michaels made you look foolish."

"Yes sir, I'll get right on it."

"I knew you would rise to the occasion. Thanks, Frank."

As Rasmussen heard the click of the receiver on the other end, he slammed his earpiece into the cradle, grabbed hold of the base of the phone and threw it across the room, crashing it into the bookcase.

His inner office door unexpectedly opened and his secretary peeked in. "Is everything alright, Professor?"

"Peachy. Just got a little carried away is all. Thank you."

CHAPTER

33

THE VAGRANT SHUFFLED ALONG Livernois Avenue with all his worldly possessions slung across his shoulder in a tattered black plastic heavy-duty trash bag. Playing a hunch that a more industrialized area promoted a safer environment for the homeless, he lumbered east at Joy Road. Standing before him in the driveway of the very first building he encountered, a glistening, just out of the showroom, lavender Cadillac Coup de Ville.

"*My, my, my,*" the wanderer thought to himself. "*Now there's a real gentleman's car. Yesiree!*" As he got closer, he pretended to rub the soiled sleeve of his ragtag coat along the side as though wiping off atmospheric dust particles. Stopping to glance in the mirror, he adjusted his cap and smiled, exposing his rotted and fractured teeth while imaging himself behind the wheel. Captivated in his dream, the drifter failed to hear the overhead warehouse door opening.

"Hey you, slime bag, get your grubby paws off my car," the male voice screamed.

The congenial old man gently tilted his head up and pictured an enormous inflated suit with a monstrous face atop, running toward him. Attributing the incident to his vast repertoire of hallucinogenic experiences over the years, the panhandler dipped his head back down to continue his enjoyable vision as a satisfied luxury car owner. Just as the smile returned, a tremendous jolt struck his entire body, propelling him six feet back and slamming him onto the public sidewalk. Within a second, a maniacal man straddled the defenseless bum, grabbing his stained pea coat, pulling him a foot up off the ground with one hand and repeatedly punching him in the face with the other. "You worthless piece of crap, I told you to get away from my car, didn't I?" Blood burst from his lips; several of his remaining teeth cracked under the barrage; his nose exploded in a gusher of red. Beside the pain, he encountered a bizarre glint of telescoping gold similar to a bright star appearing, then disappearing into the night. "You fucking puke, I'm going to pound you 'till there's nothing left," the insane ranting a jumbled garble to the mendicant.

The foreman caught Mayer's mad dash out the front from a distance. Abandoning his lunch hour impromptu card game, Roy Blue mounted his hi-lo, threw it in gear and raced across the warehouse floor. Screeching to a halt inches from the fracas, Blue jumped off the machine. "Hey, what the hell are you doing, you dumb bastard? You're going to kill him. Now get off him before you piss me off," Roy Blue yelled, grabbing the demented boss from behind in a full nelson, pulling him backward while the crazed assailant continued to swing.

"Get off me, you son of a bitch," Mayer yelled, twisting to get free to resume the attack. "I'm gonna kill him. You hear?" He ranted, "I'm gonna kill this fucking asshole! He touched my car."

"The only thing you'll be doing for a long time is cooling your wimpy ass in jail if you don't leave this poor guy alone," Blue relayed with a sense of authority.

"But he dragged his filthy mitts across my car! This cocksucker had the balls to lay his grimy paws on my new Caddie," Butch continued, the spittle spraying like a leaking garden hose.

"College Boy, where the hell are you?"

"Right behind you, Roy," Jack responded.

"You're a big help."

"Hey, you looked like you had it all under control. Besides, a guy with glasses ain't supposed to fight."

"Those are safety glasses you're wearing, College Boy."

"Hey, did anyone call for an official ruling? Glasses are glasses. Should I call the police?"

"You call the cops and you're fucking fired," Mayer wresting now to get at Michaels. Jack reared back as Roy Blue tightened his grip. "On second thought pretty boy, call the cops. I've got more juice on the force than you'll ever know."

"J.Z., take this guy inside and clean him up," Roy ordered, nodding toward the bum. "Butchie, if I let you go are you going to be a good boy and get in your car and get the hell out of here?" Blue inquired, tightening his hold to an almost unbearable torque.

"Fuck you!"

"Wrong answer." Roy Blue shoved Butchie forward, while simultaneously imitating a professional place kicker going for the game winning three-point field goal. Mayer sucked in a deep breath and collapsed.

"Now you ready, Boss?"

"Yeah," the contrite response.

As he started his engine, the venomous sadist stuck his head out the window and screamed, "By the way, asshole, you're fired."

"Up yours', you prick," Blue responded with the appropriate salute.

"Roy, this guy is really busted up. I think we should get him to a hospital," Jack conveyed.

The foreman surveyed the lacerations. "When I ran with the gangs, we used to get a lot worse than this. He'll be okay. When you put on the bandage, squeeze the cuts together real tight; it'll heal faster and leave less of a scar."

'What'll we do with him then? We just can't throw him back onto the street."

"He's a lot tougher than he looks. My guess is, he's a real survivor," Roy commented as he surveyed the vagrant. "Blind in one eye; screwed up shoulder; slash marks on his wrists; my guess is this guy will outlive us both."

"Whad'ya go by?" Blue asked, his comforting tone accented with a gentle touch to the shoulder.

"Ahbi," the faint, mumbled reply.

"What's that you say?"

"Ahbi," the strained jumble reverberated over cracked teeth without the slightest jaw movement.

Roy and Jack exchanged confused glances.

"Did he say, Ahbi? Unusual name," Blue shrugged. "Hard to tell what he really means, but Ahbi's fine by me."

"I think I know this guy. I've seen him around school. Yeah, that's it. He hustles on campus. Man, he's a long way from home."

"Da! For a college boy, you sure can say some dumb things. This guy has lived on the streets for years. That's his home; it's where he belongs."

"But it's not right to throw him out. If that's what we have to do, I'm going to find him a good lawyer to sue that sick bastard."

"Maybe we won't have to. We need a part-time custodian. Maybe just a call from an attorney would spook them enough to hire him to avoid a lawsuit."

"Great idea. I know just the guy; Van Mackleprange."

CHAPTER

34

Hustling back to his apartment to hit the books, Jack decided to detour and grab a quick bite at the Palmer Bar, directly across the street. The dark, seedy, roach infested tavern a wino favorite, J.Z. reasoned the sizzling grille sufficiently stymied the spread of salmonella, creating a relatively safe bet in a burger.

"You done collecting your academy award?" The deep voice resounded in a low boom from behind, striking an air of familiarity.

Uncertain of the intended recipient, Michaels turned on his stool at the bar and encountered a set of glistening pearl teeth floating below two evenly spaced white orbs, providing the effect of a theatrical black light pantomime production. Still attempting to assimilate the baritone overture, a tall figure emerged from the shadows of the booth.

"Mikey, my man. How the heck are you?"

The reporter leaned into Michaels, "Name's Mamoud."

"Yeah, whatever."

"A man who disrespects others has no respect for himself."

"Can I buy you a drink?"

You've got some real chutzpah, I'll say that about you."

"Don't your Muslim buddies get upset when you use those Yiddish terms?"

"Probably, but in this case it's the only word that describes what you did."

"I often find that about Jewish phrases; an incredibly unique language. Now what is it you think I've done?"

"Perpetrated a fraud on the Administration."

"Whoop-de-doo! I'll be sure to turn myself in."

"I checked the records after your little display. You've made a mockery of the minority statistical analysis; a bi-sexual Polynesian Buddhist one semester, or an Incan hermaphrodite Shaker the next. What is it with you?"

"Multiple personality disorder. Did you ever see *Sybil?*"

"We're going to expose you in our next issue."

"It must really be a slow news week. Don't you have anything better to do than pick on some poor heterosexual Caucasian Catholic kid? Lighten up. Come on, have a drink."

"No thanks. Don't drink."

"That's exactly my predicament."

"What are you running your mouth about now?"

"No one appreciates a good sense of humor anymore, much less a decent practical joke. A simple thank you for the entertainment would do. But no, now I'm the subject of a *Southern Edge* exposé. Nobody is interested in me. I told you before, if you drop this nonsense, I'll give you a scoop if I ever run across one."

"What could you ever come up with?"

"I don't know. Maybe nothing. Whatever it is will certainly be a heck of a lot more interesting than smart-ass entries on some obscure student form."

"They're important to tally the minority stats for the school."

"You don't think you Black guys stand out? Just count the number of brothers in a typical class and within a point or two, there are your raw percentages; no muss, no fuss."

"You're a racist."

"No, I'm a pragmatist. And you're a whinny asshole. Now if we're through with the name-calling, chill out. Sit down and let me buy you a soda, or let me eat my ptomaine burger in peace."

Mamoud paused, tortured at the prospect of one more second of exposure to the irritating prick, but yet found himself somehow intrigued.

"You are trouble looking to happen. For some inexplicable reason, I'm curious about what makes you tick?" Mamoud inquired while mounting the stool next to J.Z.

"I have no idea. I'm just an average guy trying to get by; working and going to school. I'm hoping that someday I can get into law school."

"Nothing average about you, including your mouth. You'd probably make a good lawyer."

"Hey, I just speak my mind. More often than not, it gets me in trouble."

"Imagine that."

"What about you? What's your story?"

"Came here on an athletic scholarship. Hurt my knee, end of scholarship."

"Probably for the best. It saves you the embarrassment to admit you played for Wayne State."

"There you go with the loose mouth again."

"Sorry, force of habit. Go on, I'll keep quiet."

"Got a job on the *Southern Edge* and found out I had a knack for journalism. I hope to catch on with a major paper eventually."

"Well, hang in there. You'll make it. You're tenacious and that's important in your field. So, any other Shaloub's running around?"

"What's it to you?"

"Jeez! There's the hostility again. Just when things were progressing so smoothly. It's an innocent comment. I'm just trying to make small talk. Evidently, I'm not very good at it."

"No, you're fine. I'm not used to exchanging pleasantries with your kind."

"Now who's the racist?"

"You know what I meant."

"Yes, I do. Nothing more than I did a few minutes ago when you bit my head off."

"Just my Mother and Sister."

"What?"

"Family. You asked about family."

"Where is she?"

"She still lives with me in the house I grew up in."

"Where's that?"

"The Westside ghetto."

"I'm from the Lower East Side; about two miles from here."

"Your family still there?"

"Only my Grandfather, but he lives on the Upper East Side now. Lost my Dad when I was a kid. Mom died four years ago. Been on my own ever since."

"Dad disappeared during the '67 riots. My Momma raised me and my sister."

"Damn. This is like some afternoon soap opera or something. Too strange."

"This don't mean we're friends, or nothing."

"Of course not. We both have reputations to consider."

"Look man, I got to go. Remember, whatever it is, you owe me a story someday."

"I don't know whether it will ever amount to anything, but I have been assigned to work as a research assistant to Joe Mink. He really intends to pursue the rumors of police atrocities during the riots.

Mamoud just shook his head, "Humph."

"Some kind of analysis of what he calls KIA's and MIA's. The same harebrained notion he discussed in his lecture about the body count being significantly higher than the government reported."

"You really think there's something there?"

"Don't have a clue. But Mink is hell-bent on looking into it."

Mamoud responded as though he took a contender's unexpected right hand to the solar plexus, stopping dead in his tracks; his color camouflaging the rapid loss of blood from his head. "Yeah, that might be interesting. Let me know if anything comes of it. See you around."

CHAPTER

35

Forsaking the desk mounted podium for a gentle back and forth stroll through the three short classroom isles, the Professor relished the undivided attention of his hand-picked students as they hung on his every word. Unlike the public university lecture halls, filled with what former disgraced Vice-President Spiro Agnew described as an elite corps of impudent snobs, this forum provided a pedagogical sanctuary; rejuvenating a lust for imparting knowledge to truly worthy pupils. Void of the angst of microphones, telephones, video-taping, coughs, sneezes, whispers, snores and whores. Yes, whores! Those scantily clad temptresses without an iota of respect for an institution of higher learning. Tank-topped, black rooted blonds, sporting spandex encased ass cheeks, spray painted faces and accessorized with come fuck-me pumps.

No, this is what it was; what it should be; what he created. The perfect classroom. Three rows, ten-deep, of old-fashioned flip-top wood desks with scrolled iron side supports and a half inch thick knee knocker board, forcing students to sit ramrod straight. Neatly arranged diagrams of *Dante's Inferno Nine Circles of Hell* printed clearly on the chalkboard. Bulletin boards with notices of coming events, extra credit reading, lesson plans and test results.

In the first seat, center row is Nadine, a mid-thirties cosmetologist decked in a knee-length Lilly Pulitzer apple green and peony pink patterned summer dress, accented with an imitation single strand pearl necklace and unobtrusive earth-tone flats.

Directly behind, Rolanda's transformation from chubby street walker to cotillion quality bearing distinguished her as the recruit of which he was particularly fond. Of course, slitting the throat of her pimp with a razor-sharp ten-inch stiletto, while he increased his fringe benefit package at her expense, probably contributed to the surprised look. Oh, what a look it was! Adding a whole new paradigm of pleasure to the conscription program.

Ann Marie's abduction proved the most brazen. Spirited from the Novi Hilton on her wedding night, the Professor's timing remained impeccable. Entering the penthouse suite and removing the ice bucket, left three options: a call to room service; a chivalrous act on the part of the groom; or, his predicted move, the selfless act of the new bride. Surveilling Ann Marie for weeks, he constructed a psychological profile that allowed him to anticipate her every move, including the removal of her wedding garments. She must be taken intact; nary a spot on the virginal attire.

The original plan included the kidnapping of the entire female wedding party over the course of several months, but observing one of the bridesmaids hauling all six of her sisters' dresses to the resale shop altered his agenda. Now he was able to substitute any number of victims, but the same visual effect remains.

Twenty-eight in all. The search continues for number twenty-nine, but number thirty, the most exciting and challenging, has already been selected. Tracking her for years, the Professor suppressed his urge to expedite the time table. She embodied the angel atop the tree. The call for assistance at the most opportune of times. The class will now be complete.

"Hi-ho, Hi-ho, it's off to school we go!"

CHAPTER

36

SARAH TWIRLED WITH ARMS flailing in a spastic ballerina impression, stumbling into Jack as she attempted to extricate herself from a giant cobweb. "Yuck! I can't get this crap off me," Sarah groaned.

Steadying Sarah with a gentle hold on her delicate shoulders, J.Z. offered, "Here, let me help you with that." While brushing the sticky fibers off, Jack turned to Mink. "Remind me once again what we're doing in this hell hole at 8:00 a.m. on a Saturday."

"When I was in the tombs, I found an incident report dated July 25, 1967, where a Sergeant Dolan and an Officer Reichert accompanied 'C' to the border…"

A dull thud, "Ouch! Damn, that hurt," Michaels fussed, bending down in the dark to rub his knee after bumping into a protruding pipe. "Couldn't you at least scrounge up a couple more flashlights?"

"We're a long way from the border," Sarah observed.

"Exactly!"

"I think you just won the grand prize, babe," Jack chided.

Ignoring the interruption, "It didn't say anything about picking someone up. What do you recall about your studies of the riots?" Mink questioned while continuing his foray into the urban jungle.

"Well, for four to five days the city was virtually shut down. There was a curfew in effect. No one was allowed on the streets except in the outlying areas," Sarah recited with precision.

"Right again. Both the tunnel and the bridge to Canada were closed. It got me to thinking. What good would it do to drop somebody off at the border?"

"They lied in the report," Jack popped in, his interest peaked.

"I always knew you had it in you, Michaels." Mink exuded excitement through the darkness. "If there's one complaint cops make, what is it? They even make a big deal of it on all the TV shows."

"Paperwork!" Sarah blurted, disclosing her competitive nature.

"You guys are really picking up the scent now. Cops have to record virtually every second of every day. I literally stumbled on Reichert's '67 personal log. The spiral end was sticking up in a pile of mush on the floor and the wire caught on my pant leg. Out of curiosity, I opened it and recalled his name. All I could make of his shorthand was '7/25 3:21 p.m. stopped in Boston-Edison to investigate possible suspect'. The rest was all water damaged."

"But that doesn't prove a thing," Jack injected.

"No, but then I really got lucky and found the precinct mileage logs and checked for car 5420 as indicated on the incident report. There's no way they traveled to the tunnel or the bridge. They have a total of four miles unaccounted for; that's two miles from the precinct house on Third and the Boulevard. This is exactly two miles from the station house."

"So are thousands of other locations. This is a city that had almost two million people at that time," Sarah proffered.

"Yes, but when you tie it in with the rumors of police that dumped bodies down ventilation shafts and off the roofs of abandoned factories, this one fits the bill."

"Oh, I see now. It's wild goose chase time," Michaels scoffed.

"That's pretty thin even for you, Mink," Sarah chimed in. "Don't you have a little more to go on?"

"No, not really. And there's another problem. After all the urban renewal, this is one of the last remaining possibilities."

"Go fish!" Sarah instructed.

"Got any sevens?" Jack chuckled as they reached a metal staircase along the far wall.

"Augh come on, Mr. Mink, this doesn't look good to me," Jack pleaded, wiping the sweat from his forehead as they stepped onto the roof.

"At the first sign of danger, we'll turn back. I promise. I just want to check out a few of these ventilation…"

A sudden crack and Sarah screamed, "Jack!" The rotted flat roof gave way directly under her. An instinctive lunge caught a massive clump of Sarah's blond hair in one hand, eliciting a scathing howl of pain. Jack twisted around to gain solid footing and thrust his free arm for her raised hand while Mink grabbed hold of Jack's belt from behind.

"Mink, on two, pull back as hard as you can," Jack instructed, the crackling of boards beneath his feet ripping away his confidence. "Ready, one, two!"

Sharp shards of wood underlayment tore at Sarah's armpit and all along her side, shredding her blouse and exposing her undergarment, as the yank propelled the trio back several feet. Mink and Jack landed on their backsides and Sarah plopped face down, reminiscent of eager early season ice fishermen rescuing a dimwitted buddy.

"Can we go now?" Jack pleaded, his chest heaving to catch a breath.

"We're so close. Just stay here and let me get to this one unit," Mink nodding his head in the direction of the vent now twenty feet away.

"Are guys incapable of keeping even one promise?" Sarah asked, rolling onto her side to survey her injuries.

Backing up three feet to a tile covered rise in the roofline that marked the outer wall of the original structure, Mink located the rusted remnants of an antenna. Breaking off one arm, he substituted the device for a walking stick to test the strength of the roof before advancing with much the same hesitancy as a soldier crossing a minefield.

"Look! It came off easily," Mink called out holding a massive aluminum ball in his arms. "And the shaft is more than adequate to fit a grown man."

"Good. Can we go now, Mr. Holmes?" Jack huffed, thoroughly fed up with the escapade, "Sarah needs medical attention."

"I'm okay. They're just scratches and probably several slivers. I'm fine, really guys."

"Jack, just hang in there with me. My last request, and you have my word on it, let's just check at the bottom of the shaft down in the basement," Mink pleaded.

"What was that?" Sarah asked as something scurried across her foot.

"Probably a rat," Jack responded. "This place should be loaded with them."

"Oh god," the usually unflappable beauty squeaked.

"And if we don't get out of this putrid smelling cellar shortly, we'll most likely be on today's brunch menu."

"Here it is!" Mink called out, shinning his light fifteen feet up. "See there. The access panel is even open. I've got to get up there."

After five minutes of stumbling in the darkness, Jack returned with a coil of thin steel cable. Tossing the wire up and over a support beam, Jack instructed Mink to tie the tag end around his waist.

Struggling to maintain leverage as rusted metal slivers sliced their palms, Jack called out to Mink, "We can't hold you much longer."

"Just a second more. Let me take a quick scraping of this strange colored mold." Joe scrambled to balance his pocketknife in one hand and open a clear plastic sandwich bag in the other. "Got it!"

Sarah and J.Z. strained to steadily lower the line. As he touched down, Joe flipped the loop over his head with one hand, as he anxiously displayed his booty with the other.

"An old shoe and some goop," Michaels growled as he bit at the metal slivers in his hand.

"I must admit, I would have preferred a bag of bones. But this is better than nothing."

"Hardly," Sarah smirked.

Their arrival to the first-floor black maze of decaying machinery, trash and spider webs a welcome relief, the trio stopped to get their bearings.

"What was that?" Jack questioned, as he brushed his hand across his right ear and heard a simultaneous sharp metal crack all the way across the warehouse.

"It's probably hornets," Mink surmised.

A second snap startled Jack. "Hornets hell! Someone's shooting at us," J.Z. screamed, grabbing Sarah by the hand. "Mink! Put the light out! Let's get the hell out of here."

Scrambling through the labyrinth of factory remnants, the threesome tripped repeatedly in the dark, bouncing off awkward shaped hardened objects in their race to safety. Stopping momentarily to catch a breath and determine their progress, another shot rang out, ricocheting off a foul-smelling tank directly above Mink's head.

"How in the hell can they see us when we can't see a thing?" Jack's scream forced into a constrained whisper.

"No time to figure that out now. Let's just keep moving," Mink implored.

"We're right behind you professor. Just hope you're heading toward the door."

With a glint of light ahead, they accelerated their pace to a mad dash for the parking lot, abandoning all thought of their vulnerability in the open space. Piling into Mink's British racing green VW Beetle, cranking the key to ignite the engine's less than enthusiastic roar, they silently prayed no one followed as the Bug executed its spirited putter through the lot and onto the roadway.

"Well, that was invigorating," Mink sighed, the ethereal comment that only an academic could make.

"You damned near got us killed," Michaels growled.

"Who do you think was shooting at us?" Sarah asked, attempting to keep the discussion on track.

"Could have been almost anyone; vagrants, drug dealers, security guards. I have absolutely no idea."

"Those guys had some sort of advanced technology. They could see in the dark, for Christ's sake," Jack reasoned, his senses on overload.

"Well, no matter. We made it. And I have a size eleven gym shoe and some goop."

"Whoop-di-doo!" Jack replied. "I'll be overjoyed if we live through this."

"You really suspect someone is after us?" Sarah queried.

"Sherlock here, is investigating police corruption and someone takes several pot shots at us in the pitch dark. Do I think we're in danger? Naw, it just one big coincidence." Jack sarcastically remarked, feigning indifference.

CHAPTER

37

SHAKING OFF THE MORNING melee as a coincidence rather than an ambush, Mink retreated to the comfort of his office. He savored the mid-day Saturday solitude. An urban university known as a commuter's college, Wayne State's campus transformed from a bustling nationally top ten ranked school by enrollment during the week, to a virtual ghost town on the weekend. Unencumbered by the incessant demands of students and the tiring political shenanigans of the administration, Joe poured a steaming mug of fresh extra strong coffee and gently dropped his middle-aged expanding tush into his pillow backed couch, sinking to within twelve inches of the floor. The overall fit of a fine Italian soft leather shoe, the sofa exemplified his sole extravagance upon receiving his doctorate and first teaching position at Monteith. The subtle loss of hair, body shape and steadily creeping age disappeared when encased in that single piece of furniture, transforming the pedagogue's mindset back two decades; the beckoning call of nature the only rift in the smooth flowing illusion, when a forty-two-year-old consumes his second mug of the stimulating elixir.

The restroom door only opened halfway as Mink, fidgety from the urge, reached across his body with his right hand to turn on the light switch. "Damned janitor, always leaving that waste basket behind the door. You'd think he'd finally…"

The rebuke cut short by a vice-like grip across his face, blocking his vision and forcefully pulling and spinning him backward into the tiny half bath. No time to react, the smell of leather from a suffocating glove his last clear recollection as a sharp pain penetrated the base of his skull, instantly exploding up into his brain, erasing all memory of falling in a heap to the floor.

CHAPTER

38

A HIGHLY UNUSUAL SATURDAY AFTERNOON routine for a twenty-year old, Jack continued a legacy of the altruistic spirit engrained in him by his deceased Mother. Plagued by illusory demons her entire adult life, Heidi Michaels search for peace finally ended with the discovery of Recovery, Inc., a non-profit self-help organization to assist nervous patients to overcome their symptoms and lead productive lives. J.Z.'s Mom embraced the system and eventually served as a volunteer group leader, allowing Jack to witness first-hand the miraculous results.

The inspired progeny approached the weekly sessions as reinforcement for his well-balanced psyche and perhaps, a positive buffer on the abacus of souls, if indeed heaven exists, while at the same time leading those less fortunate from the depths of despair to that fictional plane titled normalcy. The cross-town drive a minor inconvenience in comparison to the personal satisfaction experienced as the catalyst for the emotional cathartic purge when participants realize that sustained inner calm called progress.

Jack fumbled with the key to unlock the side door to the basement entrance of the crumbling Lutheran church while juggling a briefcase and the fifty-cup coffee urn.

"Here, let me help you with that," the kindly voice offered, as the wrinkled hands reached out for the key. "It's a tricky old thing. Sometimes I have to jigger it for minutes at a time before it decides to open."

"Why thank you, Rose."

"I'm always here fifteen minutes early to make the coffee anyway…" the grandmother feeling compelled to explain, "…Especially after the pot you made at your first meeting as leader."

"Thank you for recalling."

"My, but it was god awful, wasn't it?" The chuckle simultaneous with the tumbler click.

"Rose?"

"Never seen coffee quite that thick."

"Rose?" The reprimand significantly sterner, accompanied with a devilish smile.

"Oh, yes, well I can see why you'd like to forget it. But you did make a lasting impression," the portly matron exclaimed, while gently pushing the door inward.

With the intensity of a hungry hawk eyeing a field mouse scurrying along a road side ditch, Rose watched as J.Z. filled the coffee maker approximately one third with water and set it on the card table. She immediately stepped in to add the appropriate proportion of ingredients while instructing Jack to take a seat.

As the other participants arrived and finished exchanging pleasantries, Michaels opened the meeting with the customary voluntary reading by each attendee of an excerpt from *Mental Health Through Will Training*, the definitive work by Abraham A. Low, M.D., the founder of Recovery, Inc.

"Would someone care to give the first example of an experience in which they practiced the Recovery method this past week?"

Each member scanned the others.

"I think I could start," the soft tone of the strawberry blond traveled across the table, while she covered her right arm in a protective coddle.

"That's great Tracey. Please tell us about your experience."

"Well, I was sitting in our upper flat and the heat was stifling. I went to open one of the front windows and quickly realized that it was painted shut."

"How did that make you feel?"

"Angry. I wanted to lash out and smash the glass."

"Tracey, try to keep to a description of exactly what happened. Describe your symptoms."

"Well, my stomach knotted up; I felt a rage building; I began to curse out loud even though my baby was sleeping; and I had a feeling of light headedness. Then I got down on myself because I thought I'd wake the baby; I had feelings of being an inadequate mother."

"Tell us how you handled the situation."

"First off, I told myself that this is just a triviality. I could easily remedy the situation by grabbing a knife and working around the window frame to break the paint seal, or open another window."

"So, you began to spot your symptoms?"

"Yes. I also convinced myself to control my muscles and the feelings of light headedness and stomach knots were distressing, but not dangerous."

"And how would you have reacted before your Recovery training?"

"I would have picked up the telephone and swore at my landlord until he would have hung up on me. Then, I would have continued my rage until I woke the baby. At that point, feelings of low self-esteem would overtake me when I realized what I had done and I would have crawled into bed and stayed there all day until my husband got home."

"Thank you, Tracey. Does anyone have a comment on Tracey's example? John?"

"She could have spotted that she had the will to bear the discomfort of her symptoms."

"A good comment. Anyone else? Abbot?"

"She should have endorsed herself for spotting and dealing with her symptoms."

"Good point. An extremely important part of the program is to pat ourselves on the back when we try to combat our symptoms. As Abbot appropriately called it, endorsing our good behavior. It's often overlooked, but a crucial part of the method."

"I always try to see humor in everything," a graying, mid-fifties member advised. "I would wonder whether the landlord had to pay extra to have the window painted shut, or if it was included in the original quote."

"Very good point, Neil. Dr. Low teaches us that humor is essential to recovery."

The meeting progressed until each member provided an example, concluding with a brief social interaction along with coffee and sweets. Rose wrapped up four of the treats in a napkin and handed them to Jack. "For your grandfather. Tell him I made the German nut cookies just for him."

"Now Rose, you know we're not supposed to fraternize outside the meetings."

"But he's such a handsome man," the widow blushed. "You go on now. Don't forget to tell him I said hello."

"Will do."

As Jack walked toward the door, Rose commented, "Such a nice boy."

CHAPTER

39

J.Z. CRINGED AT THE sight of the open front door as he pulled up the drive to the Depression era, three bedroom, used brick bungalow on State Fair, just west of Gratiot. The only home on the bustling half mile road without the security grates lovingly referred to by residents as ghetto curtains, Jack repeatedly scolded Albert Michaels on his lax attitude for personal safety. Bounding up the porch two steps at a time, Jack paused to knock on the screen door. "Gramps, you in there?" The ten seconds of quiet afforded the dutiful offspring the opportunity to enter. From the tiny arched foyer, another summons. "Grandpa!" Nothing. Jack edged into the sparsely furnished living room, the silence rapidly lapsing to concern. "C'mon Gramps, this isn't funny!" Cautiously advancing through the modest dining room and into the kitchen, Jack glanced down the short hall to the bathroom. Empty. Calling up the stairs. Nothing. As he turned toward the entry to the basement, an earsplitting metallic bang resonated through the house, noticeably vibrating through the floor under his feet. A split second later, a tremendous crash accompanied by unintelligible screams sent Jack hurtling into the basement. His vision obscured by the lingering dust, J.Z. coughed as he called out, "Gramps?"

"Mongo?" Jack despised the moniker borrowed from Alex Karras' role in the movie *Blazing Saddles*. Who would have guessed the old Russian immigrant and his son, Jack's father Peter, would develop an affinity for all things Mel Brooks? They swore Jack's infant waggle reminded them of their favorite character. The day Albert Mistrotovich landed at Ellis Island, he declared himself an American, forsaking his homeland, language and name. As the cloud settled, the indefatigable seventy-eight-year-old, retired, self-employed window washer stood hefting a ten-pound sledgehammer and a smile. "Brought that som-a-bitch down, no?"

"What are you doing, Gramps?"

"Iron furnace no heat good no more. Put in new boiler, yes?"

"Yeah, okay." Jack scratched his head. "No, it's not alright. You're way too old to be tackling a job like this. You could get hurt."

Albert nodded in satisfaction, ignoring his grandson's admonition. "Split right down middle. Just like plan."

Jack swiped his index finger across his arm. "What's this white powder from?"

"Pipes."

Jack scanned the aging ductwork of the converted coal fired furnace. "Jeez Gramps, this has got to be asbestos."

Albert brushed himself off. "We go." The old man tossed the hammer onto the debris. Jack jumped at the deafening impact. His grandfather didn't even blink. As the septuagenarian climbed the stairs with the ease of a twenty-year old, Jack just shook his head, hustling to keep up.

Albert retrieved two twelve-ounce cans of beer from the fridge and flipped one to Jack. "Natty Lite. My brand." Snapping the tab top, J.Z. took a healthy swig. "Gramps, you left the front door open again. That's dangerous in this area."

"You have key?"

"You know I don't."

"Every time you done with nut class, you come here. How you get in, if door locked when working?"

Unable to score a point as usual, Jack switched gears. "They're not nuts, gramps. They're just nervous people. Mom practiced the method for years."

"She no die from feelings. Cancer kill her."

"How can you argue with that logic?" "Gramps, you remember Rose from the meetings? She wanted me to give these to you."

Albert's eyes lit up as he bit into the first cookie. "Nuts." The old man smiled and put his arm around his only living relative.

CHAPTER

40

Lᴙᴅɪᴀ Sᴛᴀɴᴋᴏᴡsᴋɪ's sᴄʀᴇᴀᴍ ʀᴇᴠᴇʀʙᴇʀᴀᴛᴇᴅ across campus, arousing a usually apathetic student body to scramble en masse to the nearest emergency phones to alert authorities. The responding hoard of bright flashing police lights in front of Monteith Center attracted gawkers in droves, reminiscent of a K-mart blue light special.

"What do we have here?" Marzoli droned in his standard detective murmur as he entered the foyer, turning to the wall mounted mirror, adjusting his tie and primping his slicked back jet black hair with a saliva-soaked Boy Scout salute. An undetectable chuff acknowledged his personal satisfaction as unsuspecting subordinates snapped to attention.

A medium height, nondescript plain clothed officer stepped forward. "What brings you down here, sir?"

"I'm the Chief of D's. I can go any damn place I please. Now give me the short version."

"Yes sir. College professor, named Mink, stabbed once in the back of the neck with a pencil. His secretary found him this morning on the bathroom floor. We caught the call and were the first on the scene. I checked the deceased while my partner secured the area," the tense cop relayed.

To quell further curiosity as to his presence, Marzoli leaned forward to check the nametag. "Nice going, Goodson." Sensing the need for an additional stroke, "And congratulations on the detective second grade exam. I reviewed the list this morning and recall seeing your name on it."

"Thank you, sir," Eric beamed, wishing he could call Angie immediately, but calming himself down to get the job done.

"This the one who found the vic?" Nodding his head toward the matronly sobbing woman.

"Yes sir. Name's Stankowski."

"Ma'am, was the door locked when you arrived?"

"Yes."

"Anything missing?"

"I didn't look closely, but I don't think so."

"Did the professor have any enemies?"

"He was such a sweet man. I worked for him since he started here. What kind of monster would do this?" Lydia sobbed.

Marzoli stood motionless, prodding the grieving secretary with his silence.

With a delicate sniffle into her white lace handkerchief, Lydia collected herself. "No one comes to mind?" Pausing a second, as though a thought escaped her, the old maid reluctantly recalled, "Well, there was this student last week that we tried to expel. But he certainly wouldn't do something like this. Besides, that really involved Mr. Rasmussen, not Mr. Mink. And it was all resolved."

"Do you remember his name?"

CHAPTER

41

THE UNMISTAKABLE ENGINE RUMBLE initially attracted passerby attention, but capturing a glimpse of the driver brought one to an immediate standstill. The impeccably restored candy apple red, tri-power, 1967 Corvette convertible kicked out 435 HP, as the big block sucked in gulps of air through the white striped hood scoop. The corrugated stainless-steel lake pipes burnished to a faint pale blue hue with the accelerated heat from the exhaust. One paper thin black leather glove gripped the wheel, while the other rammed through the floor mounted Hurst four speed shifter.

Pushed back in his seat from the increase of speed while descended halfway down the Trumbull entrance ramp onto westbound I-94, Jack glanced over at the instrument panel. "Seventy? Really?"

The quick head jerk said all that was needed, but the smirk concerned Jack.

"Hold on, Buckaroo!" Sarah yelled as she smashed the gas pedal to the floor and power shifted into fourth gear. Jack shut his eyes and grabbed hold of his three-point safety harness, as Sarah headed straight for the cement bridge support at the base of the entrance. At the last second, she veered left and shot into oncoming traffic, braking and downshifting to bring Bear into sync with the flow of commuters.

"You drive like you're in a dead heat with Richard Petty for the finish line at the Daytona 500," Jack grumbled, as perspiration dripped from his underarms, caught by the jumble of shirt at his waist.

"Wow, never figured you for a wuss," Sarah grinned. "I'll have you know that I am a licensed race car driver through the Sports Car Club of America and the Bear here, meets all the specifications of the Super Touring Ultimate class." Zipping in and out of lanes, while brushing wind whipped hair from her face, Sarah continued, "Notice the three-point harness holding you in place; the roll cage; and, a fire extinguisher."

"You really are licensed?" Jack smirked.

"Smart ass. Yes, I'm licensed. I was actually looking forward to inviting you to my next race at Waterford Hills, but now I'm having second thoughts."

"No, no, no, I'd love to go," Jack pleaded, "As long as I'm a spectator." He managed to mumble.

Coasting into the lot at Dearborn Beer, Jack motioned with his finger, "Pull over there, next to the Tasmanian Devil."

"I don't know, Jack. I don't think it's a good idea for Bear to see what happens to a car when it becomes a total loss," Sarah grinned.

"Make fun! Go ahead, I can handle it. But the Devil is good for another hundred thousand miles."

"Then why is it sitting there with the hood up?" Sarah scoffed.

"Oh, one of the guys is doing a little routine maintenance for me."

As they parked, Ahbi slammed the hood of the Renault, popping off the right front amber reflector, the wire connector allowing it to dangle against the tire.

Sarah gagged as she chuffed, "That things a soup can on wheels!"

"Are you through?" Jack huffed as he fumbled to undo his harness.

"You know Jack, I'm not too cool for a lot of things," Sarah now breathing deep to hold back her laughter, "But, I am too cool to ride in that thing."

"Insulting a guy's wheels is like insulting his manhood," Jack stated matter-of-factly, while exiting the Vette.

"No, no it's not. I can vouch for your manhood. I can even vouch for your great taste in women. What I can't understand is your love affair with a car called a Lecar?"

"It's a Le Car. It's French. Why can't anybody get that straight?"

"She's all tuned up, Mister Jack," Ahbi relayed in his jumbled language.

Jack placed his hand on Ahbi's shoulder and with the gentleness of handling a newborn, mentioned, "It's Jack. Mister was my Father. Thanks for taking care of her for me. Let me know how much I owe you."

"No, no, sir. Can't takes nothin' from y'all. You been so good to me." Tears welled in Ahbi's eyes.

"Won't hear of it. You're an incredibly talented guy and I thank you for taking the time to do it," Jack explained, while removing his hand from Ahbi's shoulder and directing him toward Sarah

"Sarah, this is Ahbi. The best probationary janitor and, I hope, engine tuner on the planet." Turning to Ahbi, "Ahbi, this is Sarah."

As Jack took Sarah by the arm, they headed toward the overhead warehouse door. In a totally uncharacteristic move, Ahbi stepped in front of them, head bowed and mumbled "I woundn't take da lady in there today, Mr. Jack"

Tired of correcting Ahbi for the mister remark, Jack asked, "What's going on?"

"Nothin unusual for this place, it seems," Ahbi responded, shuffling his feet.

"Spit it out, Ahbi."

"Well sir, this time, they got guns."

"What?" Jack stammered. "Whose got guns?"

"They fixin' to hurt a burglar."

"Oh, crap. This can't end well." Jack looked at Sarah, "Stay here with Ahbi while I get this straightened out."

"Are you kidding?" Sarah gushed, "After all the stories you've told me about this place? No way! I'm going in. Wouldn't miss this for anything."

A rhythmic pounding accompanied the trio as they passed the fourth disabled rig along the warehouse easternmost wall and spotted Rodeo and Max, both sporting guns. "What in the hell is going on this time?" Jack demanded.

"There comin' through the wall. In broad daylight," Max flailing his arms while clutching a .357 magnum with an ear-to-ear grin.

"Crumblin' the cinder block with a sledge like they was smashing crackers. So, when they stick their heads through, we gonna blow them off," Rodeo drooled, his tongue sticking out between his missing upper four-tooth bridge.

"Does Roy Blue know about this?"

"He tol' us to have at it," Max's manic state building with glossy eyes and rapid breathing.

"He must have thought you guys were just kidding. Did you tell Pepatino?"

"Jimmy told us to call the cops, but we said we'd take care of it," Rodeo waving the gun as though a baton.

"He must have thought you called the cops." Jack exhaled a deep breath and shook his head, "Look, you just can't wait till they come through and shoot them."

"That's right. That's right," Max agreed, then directed Rodeo, "Go grab a couple of tire irons. We'll pound the piss out of 'em first."

"This really is the circus Jack talks about," Sarah thought. *"I never believed a word of it, until now."*

As Rodeo turned to bolt for the mechanic's shop, he froze while eyeing Sarah, "Whoa Momma! You one sexy bitch," the mechanic blared while reaching down to lift his shirt tail with one hand and rub his crotch with the other. "Gonna have ta show y'all why dey call me Rodeo."

Just as Jack stepped squarely in front of the lecherous mechanic, Sarah flashed a blinding grin and groaned, "The man of my dreams; an unkempt, slithery, nimrod."

Rodeo stood still, mouth agape, digesting the comment, while Max declared, "I don't understand what she said, but I think she likes you. No offense Jack."

Michaels blew off the comment with an eye roll. As a cascade of larger cinder chips crashed to the floor, evidencing the intruder's progress, Sarah responded, "You bet I do. Now why don't you boys hand those guns over to Jack?" Just as the nitwits agreed to comply, the head of a eight-pound sledge hammer pushed through the wall, wiggling side to side, then retreated.

"Oh baby, we got 'em now," Max yelled, extending his gun hand to the hole and repeatedly stroking his mustache with the other. Rodeo lined up opposite Max, both hands trembling as he aimed his six-shot Colt 45.

"Sarah, run to the front of the building and get Pepatino," Jack instructed, recognizing the escalating situation.

With a significantly heavier blow, an entire 8"x 8"x16" block crashed to the floor. Realizing the tunnel vision of his two cohorts, Jack turned, wrapped his arms around Ahbi and yelled, "Down!" As a rain of bullets blasted the brick wall opening. Shots ricocheted throughout the warehouse, bouncing off the brick wall, the concrete floor, pinging off aluminum truck bodies, ripping through entire rows of stacked cases of beer and exploding tires. Jack and Ahbi managed to crawl under the nearest disabled vehicle, cover their heads, while screaming from the repetitive explosions.

Just as both magazines emptied, Pepatino sprang out from behind a pallet of cans, as if jumping over the boards and onto the ice after a two-minute penalty, racing to the mechanic's bay. Roy Blue broke cover, jumped up onto his hi-lo and hustled to the scene, while Max and Rodeo fumbled to reload.

"What the fuck is going on here?" The stumpy Italian screamed. Quivering hands impeding their progress, Jimmy reached out and ripped both guns away. "Are you crazy? Do you have any idea of the damage you two have caused?"

Roy Blue slipped off his leather driving gloves, sat quietly, sidesaddle, dangling his legs and firing up a Camel. A discreet grin evidencing his enjoyment.

"But they was breakin' through the wall in broad daylight," Rodeo pleaded, his thumbs imbedded in a leather strap.

"Is that a fucking cowboy holster you're wearing? You come to work in your Halloween costume?" Pepatino's face alternating various shades of red.

"But you got the hockey thing," Rodeo pleaded, allowing his shoulders to hunch, while dropping his lower lip.

"Don't but me!" Jimmy screamed. "You're taking this Rodeo nickname way too serious. I told you dumbasses to call the police, didn't I?"

Heads hung low and shuffling their feet in a slow-motion comical dance, Max responded, "Well, we told you we'd take care of it."

"And this is what you do?" The Boss screamed.

Sarah ran to the group, "Where's Jack?"

"Down here," the deep voice unmistakable, as Jack rolled out from under the nearest truck, turned, and took hold of Ahbi's arm.

Pepatino stormed off, repeatedly slamming his stick at an invisible puck, while continuing his rant. "You two doorknobs go check the alley and make sure no one's bleeding to death out there. And if they are, you come back in here and get me. Got it!"

As Jack and Ahbi were dusting themselves off, Roy Blue slid on his leather gloves and fired up his forklift, "I tell ya, College Boy, where else can you get this kind of entertainment and get paid for it? I love this place."

Wrapping their arms around each other's waist to walk out of the warehouse, Sarah inquired, "What is that under Max's nose?"

Jack chuckled, "I asked the same thing my first day. Apparently, he's been trying to grow a mustache for the last twenty-years. Looks kind of like a bird's nest ripped apart in a wind storm, doesn't it?"

"Yeah, that's a good analogy. And Rodeo, is it really true?"

"One hundred percent." Jack, in his finest announcer's voice, intoned, "Welcome to Dearborn Beer! Not the most efficiently run business, but we are the most exciting."

CHAPTER

42

THE RAPID POUND ON the ill fitted door rousted Jack from a dead sleep, but failed to stir Sarah.

"Hold your horses," Jack called, swinging his legs to the floor from the rock-hard couch. Sitting up, still half-dazed, J.Z. shivered. Taking a moment to decide if he should hit the head, a second round of knocks changed his mind. On his fourth step, the groggy collegiate reached out and slid back the deadbolt and turned the knob, allowing the out of plumb door to the cramped studio apartment to glide open effortlessly.

A cheap suited officer flipped a badge. "Are you John Z. Michaels?"

"Jack?" Sarah called, rolling over, "What's going on?"

"Nothing babe. Just put the pillow over your head." Turning back to the detective, "Yeah, that's right, but everyone just calls me Jack, or J.Z. Why? What's the problem? If it's about the shooting, you got it all wrong. We were the ones they shot at." The faint tilt of the head and arched brow, prompted Michaels to pause.

"That's not why I'm here. Where were you early Saturday afternoon?" Officer Goodson inquired.

"That's easy, I was at my Recovery meeting on the eastside of town."

"What are you recovering from?"

"No, you don't understand. I act as a leader for a non-profit group that helps out people with nervous symptoms. We meet every Saturday in the basement of Our Blessed Savior Lutheran Church."

"Can you give us the names of people who could verify your story?"

"We only use first names in the group. I don't have any personal information on anyone. You're welcome to attend next Saturday's meeting, but you'll have to lose the badge. You mind telling me what this is all about?"

"A professor Mink was found dead."

In the millisecond it took for his brain to process the statement, Jack's legs turned to mush. Dropping in a heap, an onslaught of dry heaves sucked every ounce of air from his lungs. As he gasped to catch a breath, the detective leaned down and patted him on the back.

"You gonna be okay?'

"Yeah," the muddled reply as he wiped spittle off his mouth with a backhand.

"Come on, let me help you up," the sincere tone complimented with a gentle hand clasp onto Jack's upper arm.

"You certainly don't think I had something to do with it?" The sniveling collegiate responded.

Purposefully abstaining from a verbal reply, Goodson shrugged his shoulders.

"What are you doing, Jack?" Sarah groaned without uncovering her head.

"Hang on just a second, l," Jack pleaded mildly and then returned his attention to Officer Goodson, "We were up all night studying."

"Uh huh," the officer responded, slightly bouncing his head. "Does the name Lorraine Window Cleaning Company mean anything to you?"

"I don't... I can't... No," Jack mumbled as his stomach knotted up.

"Well sir, we are just checking all the possibilities. Thank you."

As the plainclothes cop turned to walk out, he hesitated and turned back, "You mentioned a shooting?"

"Oh, it was nothing. Just some kid with a BB gun."

"Right. Thanks again.

CHAPTER

43

As THE RICKETY APARTMENT door lock telegraphed its distinctive click, J.Z. backed up to the edge of the couch and plopped down.

"What's going on, Jack?" The muzzy coed muttered.

"I just lied to the police."

"What?" Sarah bellowed, hoisting herself to a sitting position. "Why would you?"

"Someone's trying to frame me in a murder. They must have used one of my Granddad's old marketing pencils."

"What are we going to do?"

"I don't know."

"Who did they kill?"

"That's the worst part," Jack's voice trailed off as he reached over to hug Sarah. "It was Joe Mink."

The scream reverberated through the decrepit building without a trace of concern from the other residents. Jack cuddled Sarah for hours; her exhaustive wailing eventually dissipating to a mild sniffle, then fitful sleep.

44

THE WIND OFF THE river propelled the scent of sludge and rotting fish inland, scattering the lunchtime crowd off the Hart Plaza boardwalk, providing the ideal isolated meeting place. No secret codes, handshakes or signals; the participants realized their familiarity a brilliant cover.

"Nice job icing the professor," Evans exhibiting a rare smile.

Dolan hung his head, fearful of the anticipated wrath. "Wasn't us."

"What do you mean?" The Commissioner maintained a hunched position for what seemed an inordinate amount of time. "If we didn't, who did?" Prosecutor Evans ranted. "And why?"

"Our guy didn't get to him in time. Somebody just did us a favor," Dolan reasoned.

"But who?"

"Don't know."

"You're the top cop in this city. It's your job to know. No one falls on the wire without expecting something in return. Now we've got another player to worry about and we have no idea who he is."

"It's not as bad as it looks. It'll all work out," Commissioner Dolan assured.

"You're awfully fucking confident. It's our necks on the line here."

"You're not going to believe our dumb luck. The pencil jammed into the back of the vic's head positively traces back to a student. It's the same M.O. as the hooker murders. We'd have to give a free pass to an unknown, but we can make the kid look good for it. The publicity alone would destroy his credibility."

"I like it. Frame the kid, or kill him." Evans now deep in thought.

"There's more. The geek was a research assistant for Mink. Gotta dump him anyway; this gives us a backup."

"Where's the down side?"

Dolan glanced down at his shoes. "Goodson caught the radio call on the homicide and interviewed the kid."

"You're shitting me?"

"No, but that's not bad. He's going to be out of the way in a short while."

"That's what you keep telling me, but he's still around, meddling in our business."

"He's a fucking moron. He couldn't find his ass with both hands. He'll never be a real problem for us."

"Then get rid of him."

"What we're planning takes time. You just can't kill a cop. Even if he's an asshole, all the troops rally. What we have planned is truly a work of art. This way, we can keep an eye on him in the meantime."

"I guess nothing's perfect."

CHAPTER

45

DETECTIVE SECOND GRADE GOODSON plopped on the couch, dumping a pile of manila folders from under his arm. For the first time in his life, he experienced real self-confidence; not the occasional flirtation with a short-lived satisfaction for a job well done; or, the instant jolt of chutzpah automatically triggered by a confrontational event; but a lasting, grounded, god I feel good about myself, calmness. The sensation fueled an urge to excel, allowing him to stretch his limited talents to the max, unleashing a determination to compliment his achievements at home with advancement at work. Eric devoured anything remotely resembling a police manual, or training aid, studying the contents until he understood every word.

Angie nestled her lithe, curvaceous body into the living room upholstered Queen Ann wing chair, draping the historic recreation as an original Louis Vuitton clings to a world renown model on a French fashion show runway.

"Hitting the books again, professor?"

"They assigned me an old serial killer case."

"Really? I'm proud of you."

"Don't get too pumped up. It's a career ender; nothing but busy work. No one expects results. It just keeps me out of everyone's hair."

"What's it about?"

"A string of old prostitute murders that no one cares about. The perp hasn't left a body in years. Originally killed four girls by shoving a lead pencil up the base of their skulls. Then he just seemed to quit, but girls keep disappearing, so we assume it's the same guy."

Angie slid her legs around from the arm of the chair to sit upright. "Sounds gruesome."

"I think now he's decided to do something with the bodies. The frequency of disappearances has picked up over the years, but this guy just doesn't leave clues. The only people that could help are hookers and they're reluctant to talk, much less file a timely report."

"But you can understand why."

"Sure, but it makes our job tough. Trails are stone cold. Most times we don't even find out a girl's missing until her roommate is picked up for one thing, or another. And then it's, 'oh, by the way' and she only has a street name to go on. Now what do you say?"

"I think I'm a lucky girl to have such a wonderful guy. It's your opinion that's important."

"I think I can solve it, if I catch a break."

"That sounds awfully tentative."

"You never let up, do you?"

"No, and neither should you."

"I won't. I can't tell you how great I feel. It's as if I'm getting mentally stronger, the more I study and learn. I feel more even keeled. I can't recall the last time I had the nightmares."

"It's called keeping busy. When you're thinking about other things, you don't have time to dwell on dark thoughts. It's a simple concept that shrinks have made a fortune off of for years."

"Well, thank you doctor."

"You really want to thank me?"

"I'm right in the middle of something now. Could it wait about twenty minutes?"

"Men really have a one-track mind, don't they?"

"What?"

"Everything revolves around sex in your mind."

"Pretty much, yeah. Is that unusual?"

"For a guy, not at all. But I was talking about something completely different."

"Really?"

"Really. I thought that since your fire was lit, why not take advantage of it. And no, it has nothing to do with sex. Although, I must admit, now that we're talking about it, I'm finding it stimulating."

"What in the heck are we talking about?"

"Tracking down your demons and stomping on them, once and for all."

"I told you, I've been to the tombs. There's no way to find any hard evidence in that rat hole. And cops aren't going to talk."

"Have you asked them?"

"You've got to understand a cop's mentality. You don't rock the boat. You don't turn on your own. I'm almost forty years old. It's too late to start over. I'll just have to live with it."

"And I'm twenty-three, gainfully employed and years away from biological deadlines. I'm willing to risk it all to help you. What's stopping you?"

"I'm finally at peace with myself. That will have to do."

"What about the lives that have been destroyed?"

Eric ignored Angie's question. Dropping his head, he continued to read the open file. His concentration askew, he knew she was right, but his strength waned at such a daunting task. Angie sensed the emotional turmoil and decided to let it go.

CHAPTER

46

"Are the cuffs really necessary?" Jack inquired as Detective Marzoli instructed the patrolman to ratchet them up an additional notch. "Jeez, these things are cutting into my wrist."

"Shut the fuck up, or you'll find out how it feels to have a billy club shoved up your ass," the Chief of Detectives scowled. Then turning to the officer, "Take this piece of crap to 1300 Beaubien and throw him in the bullpen until I get there."

"But sir, protocol demands we take him to the precinct."

"You hard of hearing," Marzoli leaned in to read the name tag, "Officer Taylor?"

"No sir."

"Then do what you're told, or I'll see to it that you spend the rest of your career as an elementary school crossing guard. Got it?"

"Yes sir!"

Marzoli bounded up the steps to police headquarters and attempted to time his entry into the revolving door. "Son of a bi…" he screamed, as the door caught his left heel. Pounding on the push rail to force the mechanism to speed up, he finally exited, then trotted through the lobby.

"Detective Marzoli," Rudy hailed from behind the candy stand.

"Rudy, how do you always know it's me? You are blind, right?"

"Yes I am. It's your distinctive aura."

"Really?"

"No, I'm just funning with ya."

"Then, how do you know?"

"You're the only one who gets tied up in that door every time you use it."

As Marzoli headed toward the elevators, he flipped Rudy the bird.

"That's not nice, Detective."

As the elevator door closed, Marzoli just shook his head.

"Chief…"

"Not now, Denise," the Detective glowered as he hustled past and threw open his office door. An impeccably dressed little man scooched forward to propel himself off the couch as Marzoli demanded, "Who the hell are you?"

Handing a business card to the Detective with his left hand, the interloper reached out to shake with the other, "Van Mackleprange, attorney for Mr. Michaels."

"How in the world would you even get here before me?"

"I specialize in police misconduct cases for the American Civil Liberties Union. As soon as I heard you showed up at the scene, I knew something was amiss. I assumed you would break protocol and usher him down here to your home turf."

"Sneaky little bastard," Marzoli mumbled.

"What's that you say?"

"Oh, nothing." The Detective scratched his head. "I assume you want to see your client?"

"I've already informed your secretary to begin processing him out, since he won't be answering any questions."

"You what? Why you little…"

"You heard me. And by the way, here is a little gift for you, the Commissioner and Prosecutor Evans." Mackleprange reached into his suit coat pocket and removed a stack of papers.

"What's this?"

"It's a seven-million-dollar lawsuit for police misconduct, false arrest, false imprisonment and prosecutorial misconduct. I have phrased everything in terms of intentional acts to purposefully negate your insurance coverage."

"What does the Commissioner and Prosecutor Evans have to do with this?"

"You know, that's a real interesting point. I've been in civil litigation for the ACLU in this region for almost thirty years. In that time, I've noticed your little cabal rise through the ranks in tandem. Oh, and if the suit happens to get assigned to Judge O'Hara, I'll move to have it reassigned. Please make sure to bring Mr. Michaels around to the lobby. You have a nice day now, hear?

As the attorney exited, Marzoli flung the papers across the room.

CHAPTER

47

Preoccupied with the outlandish events of the past twenty-four hours, Jack stepped in front of Jimmy Pepatino's hi-lo, causing the Italian volcano to erupt.

"What the hell's the matter with you? Don't you ever look where you're going? I could have run your ass down," Jimmy screamed at the top of his lungs, his head as red as a Hockeytown jersey.

"Can't you talk like a normal person just once?" Jack asked as he shrugged his shoulders and continued on.

"Goddammit, don't you walk away when I'm talking to you," the manager yelled.

"Give me a break. I haven't even punched in yet."

As Jack kicked open the hollow core wood door to the armpit the warehouse workers called a locker room, he fought to keep from collapsing. Suddenly, his senses overloaded with a fresh pine scent, sparking the ridiculous reaction reminiscent of a cheesy cleanser commercial; the off-white linoleum floor sparkled; the usual piles of rank beer-stained clothes were washed and somehow found hangers; the urinal, commode and sink glistened; and a neatly made recycled army cot stood opposite the row of new wooden lockers occupied by the afternoon shift.

"Roy Blue!" Michaels screamed, "Call 911, I'm hallucinating."

The door opened just enough for the hi-lo driver to stick his head in. "Isn't it cool?"

"What the hell happened?"

"Ahbi, the black tornado," Roy smiled, "The man's a cleaning fool."

"Where is he?"

"Right behind me." Roy relayed, withdrawing his head and allowing the door to close as he shuffled Ahbi in front of him and entered the room, "This man won't stay down. I ever get him driving a forklift and watch out; I won't need half the crew."

"Well, look at you," Jack smiled. "An official uniform shirt and everything."

The old man grinned, revealing his orthodontic nightmare. "Thank you," he mumbled without jaw movement.

"Man, you look like twelve miles of bad road. What happened to you?"

"Don't remember," Ahbi's gibberish extremely difficult to understand. "I try hard, but it just don't come to me. I know it should, but it don't," the custodian explained, shaking his head and sinking down to his cot.

"So we got the okay from Mrs. Mayer to keep him on?"

"She witnessed her son's display in the driveway. She's more than happy to keep him, especially now that she's seen what a hard worker he is. Wondered whether she could trade him for her son, but then realized only a mother could love someone like Butch."

A faint knock drew their attention. Roy pushed the door open. "Oh, I completely forgot," the foreman remarked in an uncharacteristic apologetic tone. "Hold on a sec." Blue whipped out a paycheck from his shirt pocket and while leaning onto a locker, held his hand out to Michaels. "Give me your pen." With a quick scribble, Roy handed the paper to the slight built woman in the modest print dress with two infants in tow.

"Enjoy the game, hon," the soft voice relayed.

"Always," the gambler remarked, withholding any term of endearment.

Jack marveled at the weekly ritual, but followed the lead of all the other employees, ignoring comment on the episode. Roy Blue's apparent aloofness to his two little girls really amazed him.

"*God, couldn't you just grab them and kiss their cheeks off,*" Michaels thought, then returned his attention to the official new janitor. "Glad to have you on board, Ahbi. Remember, there are only two important rules to surviving around here: one, avoid Harrold Mayer at all costs; and two, never play poker with this guy."

"I'll pay you back someday, I promise," Ahbi muttered, as tears streamed down his cheek.

CHAPTER

48

Pepatino struggled to balance the cheap plastic hand-held calculator sitting atop his clip-board, while entering figures with fingers disfigured from years of professional hockey injuries. "Goddammit," the dispatcher screamed as his arthritic digits refused to comply.

An orange fork-lift with a full roll cage and one out of round wheel, thumped to a halt alongside, "Jimmy, its' six o'clock, so we're heading over to Lou's for lunch. Care to join us?" Jack inquired, a smile gracing his face for the anticipated diatribe.

"Can't you see I'm busy, College Boy?" His boss bellowed, his face reddening by the second. "Fucking inventory! Fucking adding machine! They can't make the numbers big enough for a guy's fingers," Jimmy ranted, as Ahbi cautiously approached, hugging the interior warehouse wall, reminiscent of a mouse scooting along a kitchen baseboard. "Gotta fucking count this crap every goddammed day, like I'm some kind of fucking bean counter, or something," the rage intensifying.

From behind, a cautious quivering voice, inquired, "can I help you sir?"

Pepatino twisted at the waist to confront the interloper, while Jack prepared to jump off his machine to protect Ahbi. In a totally uncharacteristic move, Jimmy smiled and calmly stated, "I appreciate the offer, but I don't really think you can help."

Relieved, Jack fell back into his seat, while Ahbi quietly rattled off numbers.

"What's that you said, Abhi?" Jack asked.

"Well, sir, des 7 cases per row, 7 rows high, dats 49 cases," Abhi rattled off, then took a quick glance to the side. "Looks like, 54 deep, stacked two high is 5,292 cases." Tilting his head so his good eye glimpsed the aisleway, "Des 36 rows, dats 190,512."

Stunned, Jack and Jimmy both hunched their shoulders with quizzical facial expressions. It took a moment, then Pepatino asked, "You one of them rain men, or something?"

Abhi smiled, displaying an orthodontic nightmare of fractured yellow teeth, "No sir. Just comes easy, is all. Like des 4,572,288 bottles in dem cases too, if you needs to know."

"No, just the case count is fine," Pepatino responded, gently taking hold of Ahbi's arm and walking him through the warehouse.

"Eleven minutes!" Jimmy screamed, extending his right leg straight out and circling twice around Ahbi, as though celebrating a successful shot on goal. "That's got to be some kind of world record!" Rotating his head to make sure no one listened in, Pepatino wrapped his arm around Ahbi's neck, pulling him in close, "Now, lets' keep this between you and me. Mrs. Mayer finds out, I could be looking for another job. You've already replaced an entire janitorial crew."

"Dats fine, sir. Won't say nothin' to nobody."

"But I will," Jack bellowed from the hallway leading into the locker room."

"Careful, College Boy! I can train a chimp to do your job," Jimmy laughed.

A full tooth grin graced Eleanor's face as the "beer boys" piled into Lou's on Livernois. She spent her entire adult life as a diner waitress; the last thirteen years at Lou's, directly across the Avenue of Fashion from Dearborn Beer. Every Friday at 6pm, she withheld six seats in the tiny eatery for the warehouse crew, their powder blue work shirts with various patches distinguishing their product mix, the only group that consistently made her laugh. Overhearing their conversations, a bi-product of the thirteen-seat restaurant, reminded her of an episode of the *Bowery Boys*, especially the last few months since the addition of a young man they nicknamed, "College Boy".

"Well, if it ain't the men of my dreams," Eleanor chuckled as the men in blue crammed in around the horseshoe counter. Slipping a razor-sharp yellow number two lead pencil from her bleach blond Bouffant hairdo, accented with black roots, with one hand and holding the order pad in the other, she inquired, "What can I get for you gentlemen?"

"Who came in?" Max questioned, looking around.

"Ain't you the cutest," Eleanor teased. "Like I haven't heard that three-thousand times in my illustrious career."

Smiling with his missing upper four-tooth bridge, Rodeo quipped, "Forget 'bout dese chumps and let me take y'all away from here, darlin'."

The scrunched-up face alone drew guffaws, but Eleanor added, "Why, so we can travel the world living in your Ford camper, sleeping on that ratty stained mattress in the back? No thanks. And don't get any ideas about whippin' that disgusting thing out in here again," Eleanor ranted with a stabbing motion of her pencil toward Rodeo, "Or, I'm gonna tie it in a knot and stick this through it to kill it, once and for all."

Uproarious laughter prevented all but Ahbi noticing Max, in the midst of chugging a sixteen-ounce plastic glass of ice-water, suck in a cube, blocking his windpipe, fall backwards off his stool, gasping for breath. Paralyzed, the janitor failed to draw attention to Max's predicament, until

Jack noticed Ahbi's Barney Google sized eyes and glanced down. "Holy crap!" Jack yelled, jumping off his seat. "I don't think he's breathing."

"Wait, what?" Pepatino muttered, puzzled. The stocky Italian wiped his mouth with a swipe of his work shirt, looked back over his shoulder and caught sight of a prone Torpo with an eggplant purple face. Swiveling a half turn on his stool, the ex-hockey player hoisted his size ten EEE roller-blade and slammed it into Max's mid-section. With a poof, the frozen projectile arched up and over the counter, snatched with Eleanor's nonchalant grab and promptly deflected into the trash.

"Now if you boys are through clowning around, how 'bout you order before I lose my good looks," she deadpanned. Nodding toward Ahbi, Eleanor stated, "Your usual, Hon?"

"Uh-huh."

"You a regular here, Ahb?" Jack inquired.

Before he could respond, Eleanor jumped in, "Has been for years, but now it's three squares a day, inside."

As the rest of the crew scarfed down Lou burgers, Ahbi mashed his apart with a fork. Picking up the pieces with his fingers, he forced small bits into his mouth. Not allowing the door chime to interrupt their feast, the beer boys failed to notice the arrival of eight young toughs. As they piled in, Ahbi glanced with his one good eye and immediately began to tremble. Just as Jack was about to ask what was wrong, Ahbi was hoisted up off his stool and tossed aside. The crash into the wall mounted ice cream cooler, caught everyone's attention.

"Get da fuck outta my seat," the thug ordered, glancing at Ahbi, "And go crawlin' in da alley, where's you belong." Straddling the stool, the gangster plopped down. Eyeballing Jack, "Youse guys are done. Moves your ass for my boys."

Without breaking his gaze, Jack calmly stated, "Max, you sit this one out. Don't want you to screw up your hand again."

"Uh-uh. Why should you have all the fun?"

"Rodeo, you okay with this?"

"Gonna be like a dog with two dicks. Ain't no more fun than that."

"Jimmy, you wanna sit this one out?"

"What? Now I'm too old? College Boy, sometimes you grind me."

"You guys are the best," Jack nodded, then swung his right elbow, striking the goon squarely in the throat, knocking him backwards off the seat.

As the ruffian rolled back and forth, holding his throat, the warehouse crew jumped up. Pepatino's hockey stick, number 9 jersey and in-line skates gave the impression of a game day face-off.

Jack eyeballed the remaining group, "We can finish this right here, right now, or you can pick up your buddy and get him the medical treatment he needs. Your choice."

Just as it appeared the jackals were positioning themselves in the confined space, the door jingled.

"College Boy!" Roy Blue called out. "You gettin inta trouble again?"

"Roy Blue, we were just discussing the options available to these gentlemen after they hurt our friend Ahbi."

Roy turned and gazed at Ahbi, still crumpled on the floor with his back resting against the cooler. "You hurt bad?"

"Kay," Ahbi responded while shaking his head affirmatively.

"And who is this gentleman rolling on the floor over here?" As Roy Blue bent over to take a closer look, "Yo-yo, is that you?"

As the face in front of him came into full view, Yo-yo's eyes bugged out as he counted the teardrop tats; four tears, with the last one sporting a cluster of three. "Youse really Roy Blue?"

"In the flesh."

As Roy Blue reached out and took hold of the gangster's hands, pulling him up to a sitting position, Yo-yo noticed the spider web tattoo on his left hand, between his thumb and forefinger.

"My Daddy use ta tell stories 'bout cha," Yo-yo, a head taller and eighty pounds heavier than Roy Blue, stared up at the sinewy, middle-aged, Hispanic man.

"Good, then you know I'm not clowning around." Roy Blue looked down and locked stares. "I find this place somehow mysteriously goes up in flames, or there's a drive by shooting, or if Eleanor or Lou are being harassed, I come looking for you and your boys. Got it?"

"Yeah."

"Good. Now beat it."

As the gang bangers filed out, Roy Blue commented, "Keeping you boys out of trouble is a full-time job. Now, can you sit quiet for the next fifteen minutes so I can eat my lunch in peace."

"Wow, never heard Roy Blue say more than two or three words at a time," Jack truly amazed.

"Here's another one for ya, College Boy," as Roy Blue flipped him the bird.

CHAPTER

49

Butchie sensed the same rare atmospheric disturbance that drives animals wild moments before an earthquake as he approached the door marked, "Mrs. Mayer". Reaching for the knob, he paused, raising his hand to mid-chest and rubbed his thumb across his fingers, perplexed at the accumulation of moisture. The urge to barge in restrained by years of conditioning from condescending tirades, he decided to knock.

"What is it now?" The raspy voice of a three pack a day habit barked.

"Momma? It's me, Momma," the hesitant sociopath squeaked in an uncharacteristic whine as he slinked into the room.

"Well of course it's you. Who else would call me Momma? I still can't believe the Good Lord saddled me with someone so short on brains as you."

Harrold stood still, two steps into the office, accepting the anticipated rebuke, refusing eye contact. Her brief pause a sign to respond.

"You wanted to see me, Momma?"

"Yeah, in the same way my ample ass wants to be jabbed by a needle for a flu shot; it ain't nothing I've ever looked forward to." The iron maiden primped her shoulder length bleach blond hair and scooched down her black leather mini skirt as she stood up and rounded the desk. "Your little scuffle could cost me this business. I've put up with your crap long enough.

If it wasn't for being tied down with you, I would have been ahead years ago. It's amazing how a one-night stand can continue to screw up your life. When I roped your Dad into marrying me, I thought it would be clear sailing. But no, you were like a fucking anchor around my neck."

Harrold stood silent. *"If it wasn't for me, bitch, you wouldn't have all this. Who do you think induced his heart attack? Taped him to a chair and made him watch as I tortured his little pooch. He croaked when I threw the mutt on his twenty-thousand-dollar stainless steel barbeque grill. Fried him up extra crispy, I did. Still recall that awful smell from the burning fur."*

"Now, I'm trying real hard to make a new life with the Grosse Pointe crowd, but it ain't easy with the likes of you running around kicking the crap out of innocent people. So, I want you to see a shrink. Maybe they can help. Go see that broad who's on all the talk shows lately, touting her book. What's it called? Something about helping anybody. You better damn well make the appointment. I want you to straighten up, for Christ sakes, and try to do something right for a change. Now, get out of here! You make me sick."

"Yes, Momma." Harrold continued his penitent hunch as he turned, closing his eyes and sucking up a deep breath of second-hand cigarette smoke. A sinister smile emerged as he pulled the door shut behind him. *"She still loves me."*

CHAPTER

50

DETERMINED TO EMULATE THE finest investigators in his department, Eric noticed one common denominator; i.e., work habits that ignored the clock. He opted to use his Saturday free time to check out Michaels' alibi. Located just minutes from his house, in a declining neighborhood at Outer Drive and Van Dyke, the aspiring sleuth arrived at Our Blessed Savior Lutheran Church clad in Levi's and a tee shirt. Formally listed as an enclave of white city workers according to official records, the seediness of the area exposed the charade as nothing more than a mail drop for Caucasian cops to skirt residency requirements.

Pulling the weathered wooden door open, Eric paused and glanced back assuring himself he locked the Grand Prix. Quiet conversation emanated from the basement as the curious investigator descended the steps, careful to duck to avoid smacking his skull on the low overhead. A group of eight adults sat around two adjoining square tables on metal folding chairs, under faulty fluorescent lights straining to kindle within the sagging molded suspended ceiling.

Jack spent the entire morning tussling with his emotions, ignoring all the rote phrases routinely tossed about by the group. Realizing the futility of his insincerity, he decided to seriously practice what he preached. By meeting time, he had pulled himself together enough to bluff his way through. As Eric entered the room, the leader announced enthusiastically, "Well, we have a new recruit today. Please sit down anywhere you like. We were just about to get started."

Eric selected the exact spot Jack had predicted; between Rose, the charming grandmotherly image and disarming smile a natural magnet; and John, the fastidiously dressed, silver haired business type who couldn't possibly be as crazy as the rest.

"We use only first names," Jack instructed as each participant recited their names, "and a first timer is not allowed to speak, other than to introduce himself, so he has an opportunity to learn the Recovery method."

Abbot drew the attention of all attendants, fidgeting at the table as though overdue for a fix.

"May I give the first example?" The bespectacled accountant inquired, swiping sweat from an extended brow.

"Please," Jack offered with a nod of his head.

"Thanks. This has been bugging me all week," the uncharacteristically agitated middle-aged C.P.A. fired off.

"Excuse me, Abbot," Jack chimed in, "Stick to a description of the facts."

"Oh, right. It's just that I get so gall darned burned up…"

"Abbot, you've got to concentrate on the proper manner to state your example," Jack patiently directed.

"Let me start again," Abbot requested, sucking in a deep breath. "Last Monday, two old buddies invite me out to watch a ball game. I haven't been out in months. They kept at me until I said yes. When we finally get there, the place is packed and we have to stand there all jammed together in the lounge area like a bunch of sardines stuffed in a can. I couldn't believe it!"

"Abbot, stick to a description of how you felt and what you experienced."

"Right. My heart began to race; my hands were trembling; I felt pressure in my head; I felt like I was going to pass out; I obsessed that this could cause me to spiral into another black hole of depression."

"Did you attempt to use your Recovery training?"

"Yes, I told myself to calm down and started spotting that my symptoms were distressing, but not dangerous; that I had the will to bear the discomfort; that my friends meant no harm and how nice of them it was to invite me out; I was able to change my thoughts and concentrate on the game."

"How would you have reacted before your Recovery training?"

"I would have thought up some excuse as to why I couldn't go and then, climb back into bed. Then I would get down on myself for missing the opportunity; slip into crying jags about how empty my life is."

"Anyone care to comment, or assist Abbot in his analysis?"

"He sure did a heck of a job!" Neil responded, kinking the starched creases in his custodial uniform as he leaned forward.

"Can you put that in Recovery language?"

"He maintained control of his muscles and forced them to work for him instead of being a prisoner to his feelings?"

"Well put, Neil. What else can you say about it?"

"Ah, that he spotted the sabotage and could overcome his fears."

"Very good. Anyone else?"

"Uneasy feelings are just average," Rose chimed in, glancing at Jack with her patented head-bobbing smile.

"It's important to endorse our accomplishments," Gloria mumbled with her hand covering her mouth.

As the discussions continued, Eric found himself enthralled and decided to stay until the meeting ended.

"You're welcome back anytime Eric. The system really does work. You can ask any of these people what their lives were like six months ago," Jack offered.

"No thanks. There's nothing I can't handle."

CHAPTER

51

Angie sashayed from the kitchen in her tight-fitting jeans and halter top wiping an ice cold can of Stroh's across her forehead. Eric sat on the couch, feigning sleep, while his playful partner plopped her firm, ample butt on his lap, wrapping one arm around his neck and handing him the beer with the other.

Without opening his eyes, Eric pictured every inch of Angie's six-foot frame, taut with the kindness of youth and exhibiting a cum hither aura.

"Well, my little junior G-man, how did your first undercover operation go this afternoon?" The playful seductress questioned in a throaty tone, stroking her free hand through his thinning hair.

"The kid's clean," Eric replied in a matter-of-fact drone, hoisting the beer to his lips.

"Three hours on the job and you develop the instincts of a twenty-year veteran?" The vixen teased, nudging her nose into his right ear.

"That hurts! How can such a beautiful creature be so vicious?" Goodson whispered through labored breaths. "You know I've already got enough time in to retire."

"Yes," Angie whispered, tickling Eric's neck with the tip of her moist tongue, "But you'd be such a young retiree in so many ways."

Unable to tear his mind from the day's events, Eric cratered the mood, "You had to see him. He's volunteering his time and really doing some good. Unless he's an academy award winning actor, he's not involved."

Sensing the importance, Angie pursued the change. "Did you tell him he was being dropped from the suspect list?"

"That's not my call, but anybody with half a brain can tell he doesn't have what it takes to kill someone. But the Chief of D's really wants to go after this kid. Besides, the killer used a pencil."

"Isn't that the same M.O. as the serial killer we talked about?"

"Very observant. So, you really do listen to me once in a while?"

"Of course. I love to hear about your cases."

"We never released the detail of the murder weapon, so the only ones who knew are the killer and the police."

"And this student isn't old enough…"

"Exactly!"

"Do you think I'm being too hasty?"

"It's what you think that's important."

"What troubles me is, why is Marzoli so hell bent on hanging this kid?"

"Time to change your thoughts and your mood," Angie whispered in his ear. "Have I ever shown you how I can tie a Maraschino cherry stem in a knot with just my tongue?"

CHAPTER

52

THE FOURTH-FLOOR CORNER OFFICE, traditionally reserved for the Commissioner, escaped the political whims and management philosophies of various administrations over the past fifty years. Maintaining the architectural integrity of the 1930's public works design with wood pegged oak plank flooring, sculptured wet plaster ceilings sporting elaborate fans with highly polished brass accessories and arched stone encased windows that provided a panoramic view of adjacent parking lot below. Dolan loved his office; an oasis from a bitter marriage and a reminder of his professional success. It defined the parameters of his comfort zone, allowing him to completely relax. Taking a jolt of Irish coffee from his favorite mug, with his feet perched along the edge of his desk, his office door flew open and slammed shut with such force that Dolan jumped, slopping hot coffee on his freshly laundered white shirt.

"Damn it, Dolan, when I tell you to take care of a problem, I expect it to be done immediately," Evans screamed.

"Screw you, asshole. Look what you did to my shirt. Lucky for you I don't carry no more, cause I'd shoot your ass," Dolan bitched, wiping the remnants of liquid with a handkerchief. "Don't you ever relax? You're a fucking stroke looking to happen."

"Not when my career's at stake," the Prosecutor responded without hesitation.

"It's not only your ass on the line, hot shot. You tend to forget that. Why don't you get in the habit of getting a morning blow job from one of those law school tarts you been banging, so you mellow out a bit."

The attorney's tone loosened dramatically. "Well, where do we stand?"

"Goodson will be done like dinner shortly. What we have set in motion is nothing short of spectacular."

"See to it, would you?" Evans turned to exit, but abruptly halted, as Dolan continued.

"But we do have a slight problem with the kid."

"Throw him in the system and lose him," Evans instructed without a hint of remorse.

"He's got this A.C.L.U. lawyer that's like a scrawny stray dog on a bone. We couldn't hold him. Then there's the lawsuit, yada, yada, yada."

"Send that sadistic asshole buddy of yours to take care of him. And knock off the colloquialisms; they don't become you."

"We'll have to think of something so it doesn't look too coincidental."

"Whatever it takes!"

CHAPTER

53

ABIGAIL THURSFIELD, PHD, CLICKED the eject button on her Dictaphone and removed the tape, concluding her 6pm session. Jotting a quick note on the cassette, she slipped it into a 7"x 5" envelope and stapled it to the inside cover of the patient's file. Taking a moment to refresh herself before heading out to catch the last hour of the P-Jazz concert on the outdoor mezzanine floor of the Pontchartrain Hotel, Abigail hustled out of her Penobscot Building office, through the waiting room, directly into the arms of Harrold Mayer.

Startled by the collision, she glanced up at the smiling face, "Oh, I'm so sorry. I was in such a hurry, I didn't see you."

"No problem whatsoever. As a matter of fact, I was just coming to see you, Doctor."

"Well, my visiting hours are over. You'll have to call my secretary in the morning." A tinge of discomfort rattled Abigail, as she realized she was still caught in his embrace.

Attempting to step back, the hug tightened. "There now, are you tryin' to end this romantic interlude? Seems to me, this might be one of them once in a lifetime encounters. A love at first sight thing."

"What? I don't understand," Abigail blurted, twisting to break the clasp. "Let me…"

"Whoa, darlin'! Is that any way to treat a new patient and the love of your life?"

"Who are you?"

"My, my, my. For an educated woman, you're a little slow at the switch. Ain't you one of them PhD's? Oh, maybe they gave you a pass cause you're a woman, is that it?"

"Please!"

"Oh, we're gonna get to that, but first Momma says we got to have a session on the couch." Mayer hoisted the psychologist with one hand, while covering her mouth with the other. Entering the office, he kicked the door closed behind him. "Locks automatically, don't it?"

Astounded by his strength, Abigail just nodded, tears streaming down her cheeks. Mayer lugged her into the inner-office, slammed the door and tossed her like a ragdoll across her desk and into her executive chair. Glancing over her head, Mayer exclaimed, "Man, I had no idea you had this kind of river view from, what is it, the forty-fourth floor?" Craning his neck, "Where's the couch?" Looking back at Abigail, "Don't all you shrinks have a couch?"

"No..." she eked out.

"Lucky for you I'm an accommodating type of guy. Wow, that's a million-dollar word, ain't it? I've been takin' one of them self-improvement courses and they tell ya to increase your vocabulary. I think it's working. What do you think?"

Searing back pain ripped through her body. "I don...I don..."

"What's the matter? Cat got your tongue? I used to love those little critters; douse 'em with lighter fluid and toss a match on 'em. Man would they howl."

Abigail struggled to recall all the relevant data on sociopaths, but her mind was fogged in pain.

"Well, can't disappoint Momma. She read your book, *No One is Beyond Help*. Said I should come see you, but first, I really wanted to see you. Know what I mean?"

Abigail just whimpered.

"Saw you on one of them morning news shows, talking about your book. Didn't quite catch what it was about, cause I couldn't take my eyes off your legs. Had dreams about doing you. You know the kind I'm talking about." Mayer licked his lips and glared, "Wondering what it would be like." Mayer reached out with one hand, grabbed a handful of hair and pulled Abigail onto the desk. Ripping her panties down, he unbuckled his pants with his free hand.

Trembling, Abigail shook her head, "No!" she shouted.

"That's okay, you just keep fighting. I like a fighter."

The attack continued until Mayer peeked at his watch. "Only five minutes left in my session. Whad ya think, Doc? Time for one more go-round?"

The helpless psychologist just groaned.

"I thought so. Let's trip the light fantastic one last time."

Finished, Mayer yanked the cord from the floor lamp. Tying one end around Abigail's neck and the other around the inside bathroom door knob, he hoisted the doctor up and closed the door.

Relaxing in the executive chair, while Abigail flailed, Mayer rummaged through her files until he found exactly what he needed. "Just so you know Doc, some of us really are beyond all help."

CHAPTER

54

MARK TWAIN ONCE SAID that the number of people that show up to your funeral depends on the weather. That's not entirely accurate. There is an exception for those truly unique, selfless individuals that have such a profound impact on every one they touch, that elements be damned, they're there. Joe Mink had that effect as evidenced by a half-mile long string of cars that tied up traffic for two hours along the processional route. Mother Nature wreaked havoc with spine bending wind gusts and torrential rains as three thousand mourners, the vast majority under the age of twenty-five, stood in a soggy, silent vigil. The type of inclement day a Brit would describe as "balmy".

Goodson watched from the sidelines, surveying the crowd with the intensity of a Secret Service agent during the Inaugural Day Parade. Father Clarence Vaughn exhibited his unfamiliarity with the dearly departed by delivering an antiseptic eulogy, completely devoid of personal antidotes. As the somber gathering dissipated, the detective worked his way toward Michaels and Garvey, confronting them on a gentle slope that put the coeds an entire head taller than the five-foot eight-inch cop.

"Sorry for your loss."

"Just nail the bastard that did this," Sarah piped up with an uncharacteristic vehemence as she bowed her head and dabbed her nose with a white lace kerchief.

Jack eased her in tighter to his side, while his eyes darted in every direction to avoid direct contact. "Thank you," the soft, choked reply.

"Can you think of anything that might help us to catch the killer?"

Jack paused, giving the matter serious thought. "Go back to where the trouble started."

"Where would that be?"

"The Packard Industrial Complex. Someone was shooting at us."

"You said that was probably some kid with a BB gun."

"And you were trying to pin Mink's murder on me."

"Still might if you don't come clean." The tough cop routine difficult for Goodson; he was just too nice a guy. The kind a wild girl marries when she decides to settle down. But he decided to push; the kid was holding back. "*Look at him shuffling his feet; head bopping like the toy dogs you see in the rear window of an old Chevy. The needle would fly right off the lie detector. He's up to something. I've got to keep at him.*" "What's going on?"

"I honestly don't know, but we've decided that whoever shot at us must have something to do with it, so we're going back with surveillance equipment to try and find out who we're dealing with."

"Whose we?"

"The two of us."

"What kind of gear?"

"Motion sensitive night vision video cams and a voice activated audio system that makes a mouse fart through a concrete wall sound like a sonic boom a football field away."

"Where would you get stuff like that? I don't think we would have that kind of equipment."

"Julio, at the *I Spy Shop* out on Orchard Lake Road in Keego Harbor. He had Mink as an undergrad a few years back. He didn't even hesitate."

"People surprise you, detective," Sarah piped up.

Intrigued, Goodson pursued the remark, thinking the brilliant blond may finally divulge some details. "Who for instance?"

"Take that little weasel, Rasmussen, for example. The other day in class, the simpering wimp jumps up on his desk, assumes the lotus position, hikes his entire torso up with only his fists resting on the table top and swings back and forth like a chase lounge. Can you imagine the strength that took? I wouldn't have guessed that old geezer could do something like that in a million years."

Disappointed at the obvious snit, Goodson took a second to allow Garvey additional time to vent, chalking up her off the wall comment to her tender mental state. With her silence, the cop redirected his attention to Michaels. "When you going?"

"Tomorrow morning, around eleven."

"Mind if I tag along?"

"You think we might be on to something?"

"Can't hurt to check it out. Meet you at the main gate."

CHAPTER

55

THE LONG ABANDONED, SIXTY-ACRE, four-story edifice cast an imposing pall over the future revival of the city. Allowing a parcel of such magnitude, only two miles north of the city center, visible to one-hundred fifty-thousand daily I-75 commuters, to virtually rot, displayed a total lack of foresight, leadership and direction on the part of government and the private sector. The main entrance appeared as a horror movie scene lifted from the cutting room floor, with a cobweb infested, dilapidated guard shanty and broken down, rusted gates. Sarah and Jack's apprehension could easily provide the mental stimulus to imagine a skeleton wearing a security uniform waving them through the entrance.

"Where the heck is he?" Michaels huffed. "If I were a smoker, I'd have a pile of butts ass deep outside the car door." His left leg shot back and forth as though he lost all lateral control and his fingers tapped on the steering wheel with a rapid beat Gene Krupa would envy.

"We've waited forty minutes. That should be long enough. Let's go." Relieved, Jack whipped the candy apple red Vette around the lot and sped toward the driveway. "Where you going?"

"Following orders and getting the heck out of Dodge, sir."

"Stop the car!" Sarah gave her man 'the look'. "I meant, let's go in and set up the equipment."

"Surely you jest mon cheri?" Jack's flippant routine quickly faded as he caught her determined stare. "You've got to be kidding? The last time we went in this place, someone tried to kill us. Tell me you're pulling my leg?"

"We're here; let's get the job done."

"I don't like this one bit." Michaels threw the four-speed stick in reverse, smoking the ten-inch wide, v rated tires. "You'd make a great dominatrix." The half assed smile telegraphed his ambivalence, as he thrust the shifter into first gear and roared to the back of the building. "You ever think about it?"

"What?"

"The domination thing."

"Men are such dogs." Sarah appreciated the levity. She had no idea what possessed her to follow through with such a harebrained scheme. Especially when her instincts sensed serious trouble. "Grab the gear. Let's get this done."

The equipment fit nicely into a small tote bag Sarah stowed in the trunk, except for an unusual shaped object Jack held with both hands.

"What is that thing?"

"This here is a three-million candle power Husky model portable search light. This baby would illuminate the entire mighty Mississippi from Minnesota to Louisiana in fog as thick as pea soup. Arrr! Arrr! Arrr!"

"Are you through? What is it with guys and tools?"

Regaining his composure, Michaels shrugged, nodded and followed Sarah like a rebounding scolded pup. A rusted steel door with an obvious punched out lock, required the strength of both to pry open. Facing a black hole, Jack ordered Sarah to stand back. Firing up the lantern, a blinding beam shot a hundred yards into the cavern, providing the equivalent of daylight.

"I'm impressed," the adventuresome coed admitted and confirmed with a slight bob of her head. "But I do think you've watched entirely too many episodes of *This Old House*."

Assuming the alpha male role, Jack plowed ahead, approximately forty feet before stopping. Turning the light to his right, then to his left, the young explorer resembled an advertising searchlight commonly found in front of car dealership grand opening ceremonies.

"We'll leave the recorder here and put one of the cameras over there," pointing to a section of intersecting girders.

"How does it work?"

"The recorder has a continuous seven-day loop, triggered by the camera's motion detector. Theoretically, with as little movement as we anticipate in here, it could last months.

"Impressive."

"It is pretty cool, isn't it?"

"I meant you, Mr. Gadget."

"Oh, well then, let's hustle this up."

"It amazes me how we allow men to run the world. Guys think with their little heads ninety percent of the time."

"We're really productive with the remaining ten percent."

"Right!" As they approached the camera perch, Sarah balked.

"What was that?"

"I didn't hear anything."

"Some sort of low hum."

"Probably the wind. This place is more like a tunnel than a building." The site selection turned out to be much higher than anticipated. "I'm gonna have to boost you up." Jack handed Sarah the mini-cam. "After you set it in place, flip up this little antenna." Cupping his hands for a makeshift step, he hoisted the six-foot blond up four feet.

"Wait a sec!" Sarah forcefully whispered, grabbing hold of the girder with one hand to stall her ascent.

"What is it?"

"I heard something. Sounded like a cat purring."

"Just set the camera up so we can get a move on." Sarah reached up as Jack leaned his shoulder into her wobbly leg, struggling to maintain his balance.

"Almost got it. I…" An ear-piercing squall caused a shiver of terror to rip through Sarah. A claw swiped at subliminal speed, shredding the sleeve of her Nike jacket as she jerked back her hand, losing her footing and fell backward. Jack bent down to assist, but the leggy coed was already scrambling to run. "It's a fucking lion!" Sarah screamed as she bolted in a world record hundred-yard dash.

Jack grabbed the flood and aimed it at the beam, trapping two glowing yellow eyes. "Holy crap! He shrieked. The echo rang throughout the warehouse. Arriving at what she perceived a safe distance, Sarah paused to catch a breath. Glancing back, her panicked beau reminded her of an African bearer laden with gear, fleeing a herd of stampeding elephants in a 1930's Johnny Weissmuller *Tarzan* movie. The equipment satchel swung with every step, while the lantern beamed haphazard rays throughout the maze with a disco strobe ball effect. Reaching his companion, J.Z. stopped, bent forward, rested his palms on his knees and heaved for air. The musty atmosphere instantly clogged his sinuses.

"Let's blow this place. I don't know exactly where we are, but it looks like we can get out over there." The resilience of youth slowing his heart rate, allowing him semi-rational thought. Taking Sarah's hand, they inched toward the light, as Jack fumbled to adjust the top-heavy Husky with the other. Their third step launched a tirade of cackling, flappy winged beasts directly at them. The duo dove to the dust encrusted concrete floor, while bellowing stereo screams reverberated in distinct base and soprano tones. A four second flight later, the disturbed flock of nesting pigeons roosted comfortably on a support brace. Realizing their jittery condition, Jack and

Sarah brushed themselves off, cleared their throats and bravely strode to daylight.

"Oh man, I think I swallowed my uvula," Jack coughed, inflicting a mild judo chop to his Adam's apple.

"What?"

"It's that oval shaped thing hanging…"

"I know what it is, Jack. Let's just find the car." They rotated left and rounded the corner. Sarah let out a sigh of relief at the sight of the intact, glistening, sleek Vette, a mere fifty feet away. "Jack, did you hear something?"

"Very funny. You're a regular Gilda Radner."

"Stop, just a second. Can you hear it? It's like a real low growl."

"Yeah, right. You've got the keys, so you drive. I'm a wreck."

"Jack, shut up and listen, would you?" Sarah insisted, violating a personal code by uttering the disgusting phrase. She held him back with both hands by the upper arm. "I think it's coming from the direction of the car."

"Well, that's the only thing in this entire crud infested lot. If it is a monster, how big could it be? It's only a little car."

"Wait a second." Sarah raised the remote entry and pressed the panic button. As the horn wailed, a pack of mangy dogs nervously scattered. Heads hung low, the strays moved in closer, alternatively snarling and sniffing; then jumping back a step or two. Cautiously advancing, then retreating; surrounding the vehicle as though a Native American war party circling a wagon train.

"What in the heck is this place, some kind of wild animal sanctuary? Blimey mate, look at the teeth on that one," Jack scoffed in a terrible Aussie accent.

"Jack, now would be a good time for a plan."

"What do you want me to do, sit down and talk with them?"

"They're dogs---you're a guy; you should be able to communicate with them." Under ordinary circumstances, the comment would have garnered hysterical laughter. This time, Jack darted his eyes in disbelief. "Jack, do something now, before I pee my pants." One of the dogs sensed their presence and froze, startling the rest of the pack. One by one, they glanced, then growled, displaying various sizes of teeth.

"Okay. Okay. Babe, listen to me. You back up real slow and get back around the corner. I'm going to get their attention, then draw them away."

"Your plan is to outrun them?" Sarah's fear held her gaze on the largest canine. His slow, deliberate approach rated him the alpha male.

"The plan is to divert them so you can get to the car. Then come pick me up." The pack continued their cautious progress toward the frozen couple.

"Or, what's left of you. Think of something else. I'm not going to allow you to be a Beggin' Strip for a rabid pack of hounds."

The pack lingered two car lengths away, swaying their heads, bobbing back and forth, some raising their lips, bearing an evil grin; others, snouts in the air, searching for the scent of their next meal, revving up into a frenzy.

"Sarah, get moving now!"

A quick reactionary glance to Jack acknowledged the uncharacteristic tone. She slowly back peddled. Jack stood his ground. The urban dingoes warily moved forward, chuffing, sniffing and growling. Sarah continued her slow-motion retreat. Relieved at bumping into the building corner, she edged her body around the rough-edged masonry, all the while staring at Jack's backside; equidistant between her and the dogs. Announcing her arrival in a soothing tone, Jack slowly moved to his left, keeping a keen eye on the horde, taking fifteen second baby steps, and at the same time, desperately searching for an escape. High ground the ideal; only a pipe dream in the barren lot. Disintegrating concrete and weeds, coupled with an occasional worn tire, or pile of illegally dumped debris, transformed the area into an obstacle course. The creatures cut the distance to Jack in half in what seemed only seconds. Two of the stalking beasts moved in a circular pattern in an effort to cut off his egress. Jack decided it was time. He burst into a dead run on a diagonal toward the building. It took the dogs less than a second to pursue, instantly hitting full stride, simultaneously lifting all four legs off the ground; rabid greyhounds in a mad chase for the elusive rabbit. Jack searched furiously for an entry point into the building. There was none in sight. A glance back and to the side; he guessed four to five seconds at most before the pack caught up. Frantic, he noticed a security grate covering a broken window, head high. Knowing his time was up, he ran straight at it, separating his fingers as he lunged forward, striking the wall with one foot for an additional boost. Several digits smashed directly into the thick wire mesh, bending and ricocheting from the force of impact and sliding into the openings, providing a tenuous grip. His legs flailed as he struggled to climb. The frenzied dogs jumped, their teeth snapping, inches from Jack's feet.

Sarah fired up the sports car, jammed it into first gear and stomped on the accelerator, squealing the tires and raising a cloud that smelled of burning rubber. Whipping around in a circle to align the passenger side with the building, ripping the stick shift, she initially thought to lay on the horn to scatter the pack. Anger prevailed as the Vette hit 60 mph in 4.6 seconds and tore through the horde. One animal hit dead center and fell. The low-slung vehicle bounced over the carcass. Another impacted with the right front corner, smashing the headlight and bouncing up onto the upper windshield frame, before deflecting off into the building. The remainder scattered. Sarah slammed on the brakes, yanked up the emergency lever and swung the wheel a hard left. The Bear reacted with all the aplomb of a thoroughbred, rotating one hundred eighty degrees and shooting straight ahead, stopping for Jack.

Sarah lowered her window. "You can come down now, Spiderman."

Massaging his fingers as he walked around the car, Jack allowed himself to drop into the seat. "Been a long day and I still have to go to work. Home James."

Sarah moved ahead slowly, keeping a sharp eye for glass and debris to avoid further damage to the coupe as they searched for the exit. A chocolate brown Ford approached on the diagonal. Jack shook his head. "Now he shows up?" The Fairlane looped around to the rear of the Corvette and stopped. Michaels clicked the latch to undo his seatbelt just as the rear hatch window exploded. Sarah and Jack both screamed and instinctively bent forward covering their heads. The gunman fired another round, his pistol packed with a 410 load of buckshot that ripped off the driver's side headrest and blew out the windshield. "Get us out of here now!"

Sarah shook her raised hands in hysterics. "I can't see!"

"Just hit the gas now, or we're gonna die!" A third burst exploded the center console instrument panel just as Sarah reached for the shift lever. "Oh my god!"

"Go! Go! Go!" Michaels yelled, as he leaned over in the tight quarters and forced Sarah's foot down on the accelerator. Another shot rang out, peppering the bumper and shattering the brake lights as the Bear rocketed through the lot, the engine screeching at redline for second gear. Plowing through waist high weeds and bouncing over debris, the sports car collided with one of the few remaining sections of cyclone fence, ripping the chain link from its posts, shredding the fiberglass fenders, as it fishtailed onto the expressway service drive.

CHAPTER

56

Unlike the majority of his coworkers, Eric's heart pounded in anticipation of hearing Angie's voice, no matter the mundane discussion. Picking up the telephone to dial his soul mate, the office secretary slid a note in front of him instructing him to respond immediately to a situation at Grand Circus Park and Washington Street. Hanging up on the third ring, he glanced at his watch; 9:15 a.m., plenty of time to still meet the college students at eleven. Eric motioned for his partner to join him as he grabbed his sport coat and double-timed it out of the station house.

Twisting the key in the ignition to just shy of its breaking point, Eric and Quentin exchanged arched brows while they waited the requisite three "rrr-rrr-rrr's" until the old Pontiac's motor kicked in. Pulling out of the parking lot, the morning sun hit that aggravating sweet spot directly atop the windshield post, rendering the visor totally ineffective, no matter if you flipped it down, or, to the side window. As Eric made the adjustment, Quentin caught a yellow post-it note fluttering toward the floor.

Glancing at the missive, Quentin chuckled, "Now this one is going to require some explaining, partner."

"What?"

"Another love reminder from the Mrs."

"What's it say?"

"You are the wind beneath my sheets, accented with a smiley face and what appears to be ears, or, little horns on its head."

Eric broke out belly laughing. As he struggled to lift his hip under the strain of the seatbelt to pull his handkerchief from his right rear pocket to dab the tears, he explained.

"Last night, Angie tried to recreate her Grandmother's split pea with ham soup. The recipe called for four cloves of garlic. Well, the head of garlic that she picked up from Farmer Jack's was probably the biggest either of us had ever seen. Adding four of those beauties apparently was a bit too much. By 2 a.m., we both woke up to an awful odor. When Angie yanked the covers up over her head to escape the smell, she immediately realized her mistake. She jumped out of bed quicker than a jet jockey exploding from the cockpit after pulling his ejection seat lever."

The simultaneous laughter went on until Quentin asked, "So, how was the soup?"

Another round of raucous cackling, until Eric pulled himself together enough to respond, "Great." His mid-section heaving, "But I think we both realized the left-overs were something you could only eat outdoors."

"I gotta tell ya, Eric, I think it's way too early in your relationship for a farting episode. Isn't that like a seven or eight-year experience?"

"So, we got it out of the way early. I'm telling you, I've never laughed so hard in my life. She is so damned gorgeous, I can't imagine what she sees in me. But she's so down to earth, I can't imagine my life without her."

"You're a lucky guy. Don't look a gift horse in the mouth," Quentin commented as they pulled up to the accident scene.

CHAPTER

57

MINDLESS REPETITION DISPLAYING LIP service to the manners engrained in him as a child, Eric muscled his way through the horde of macabre gawkers to the yellow tape outlining a gruesome sight; five mangled vehicles of various descriptions crunched together as though haphazardly welded in place as a modern sculpture entitled, "Traffic Accident". An overwhelming assortment of emergency carriages clustered in a glittering multi-colored light show lent an almost carnival atmosphere to the ghastly scene.

"What the hell happened here?" Eric shouted to a uniformed officer while holding up his badge.

"A trash hauler lost control and slammed head on into a line of cars waiting in the left turn lane. We've got four bodies already and plenty more trapped in their vehicles. We sure could use your help in directing traffic."

"You got it," Eric replied as he and his partner headed for the intersection, exercising caution to avoid the slippery mixture of oil, antifreeze and gas seeping from the wreckage, covering an ever-expanding area.

Fighting the urge to inspect the carnage and at the same time inexplicably drawn to the tragedy as a Muslim to his prayer mat at sundown, Eric stole a quick glimpse, sensing a familiarity with the third car in line. Although damaged beyond recognition, the distinctive royal blue color, coupled with its apparent extra length in comparison to the other four vehicles, triggered an instinctive response to take a closer look. As he hesitantly stepped by rescue workers struggling with the Jaws of Life to pry open the driver's side door, a wave of panic overtook him as he envisioned a glistening mound of auburn hair resting on the windowsill.

"It's a station wagon. That's why it's longer." Eric blurted as he moved in for a closer look.

"What's that Eric?" His partner asked, now several steps ahead of the curious cop.

"Just like the Blue Beast," Eric mumbled as he realized the critical nature of his observation. The five-year-old Chevy Impala station wagon was purchased as much for its protective bulk as its excellent mechanical condition and low mileage. A spontaneous furious lunge, propelling the straining firemen out of way, allowed the unnerved public servant to stick his head in the window, inches from where he expected to find his unconscious love.

"This can't be Angie's car… she never leaves the office. What would she be doing here?" Eric concluded, a sense of relief racing through his nervous system, until he noticed the glint of a brushed nickel charm bracelet lying on the front seat.

"Oh no, God! Please God, no!" Eric screamed as he dashed across the top of the wreckage to the shattered passenger window to retrieve the trinket.

"Eric, what the hell's going on?" The flabbergasted partner hollered, standing next to the rescue workers thinking the level-headed Eric finally snapped.

"It's Angie's car… the blue wagon. I've got to find her."

"Get a hold of yourself, Eric. You can't be sure that's her car. There's so much destruction, you can't be sure of anything," the frustrated partner concluded after glancing in the crushed metal cube.

"It's Angie. I can feel it," the senses ravaged cop blubbered while lowering his head until his lips touched the tops of his clenched fists, "I've got to find her; she would never forgive me if I didn't. Where is she?" Eric screamed. "Where could she be?" Then the distraught lover glanced at the ambulances. "Oh no. Please God, no." Recognizing an E.M.T. technician, Eric called out, "How many ambulances have left the scene?"

"None, sir. The first is set to go now."

Bile shot up his throat; his chest heaved; his muscled legs felt as though encased in the concrete slabs beneath his feet as he turned and ran to the meat wagons, quickly scanning the four black zippered plastic bags divided between the trucks emblazoned, "Medical Examiner".

Moving with the hesitation of a cautious buck in deer season, Eric finally reached the first vehicle. Mustering the courage, he unzipped the first bag disclosing the surprisingly unscathed remains of a middle-aged woman; the second, the mangled body of an elderly male. Eric's hands quivered as he moved on to the second truck, realizing the odds stacked against him in this morbid Russian roulette. A horrified teen occupied the third container, his exposed iron clad teeth a frozen final shriek of terror. Eric knew the content of the fourth bag before he touched the zipper; a young woman, her beauty unmistakable, even in death. Each metallic rip powered a bullet of pain through Eric's brain, interrupting all motor control, sending the grieving lover to the pavement. Forcing himself to continue his macabre inquiry, Eric cried as he struggled to remove the polyurethane death shroud. "Angie! My God! Angie." Fighting to regain his footing, the distraught cop pictured himself caressing his backhand across Angie's ashen cheek one last time. Now accompanied by his silent partner, Eric collapsed to the ground, his body heaving in sobs of grief as the exposed corpse lay in front of them.

"Eric, it's not her!" The partner screeched in astonishment.

"What?" Eric muttered, unable to grasp the remark through the cloud of grief.

"I've only met her twice, but I'm telling you, this isn't Angie."

"What are you talking…"

"Need some help over here," the emergency tech yelled. "We got us a live one, boys. White, adult, female."

Every available rescue worker scrambled to respond to the plea.

"Let's do this one strictly by the book," the senior med tech instructed. "She's unconscious, so we'll assume the worse. Stabilize the body completely before we move her an inch."

As they removed the woman from the rear seat on the inflatable back brace, Eric pushed his way up to the stretcher, "Angie, my God, it's you," Eric sobbed, reaching for her hand.

A pock marked faced med tech knocked Eric's arm down with a swipe, "Sorry sir, but we can't chance moving her an inch. We don't know the extent of her injuries. It's a miracle she's actually alive."

"But how could she have been in the back seat?" Eric mumbled to himself, the tears streaming down his face. "I don't understand."

"We've seen a lot stranger than this, I'll tell ya. How it happens is anybody's guess. Just be thankful she's breathing."

"I am. Believe me, I am," Eric admitted, another burst of tears cascading across his face, as he stood alone in the center of the destruction.

CHAPTER

58

Eric refused to leave Angie's side for the few remaining days of her life. Unable to terminate the artificial support systems, he savored every moment, simply holding the hand of his only true partner. Politely refusing the repeated requests of hospital personal to leave, the staff eventually acquiesced, even assisting Eric's morbid vigil by providing meals and a cot.

Any sacrifice an acceptable price for one additional stroke on the motionless limb. Abandonment of the woman who nursed him from the depths of despair out of the question: her inexhaustible patience, listening to near incoherent ramblings of a haunted mind, no matter the hour; the indefatigable soft, soothing voice of reassurance to quell the anxiety of recurrence; the gentle caress of a rhythmic palm, calming a quivering cheek to return to the peace of an uneventful slumber.

Resurrecting Eric's psyche from the bizarre and horrific flashbacks of the '67 race riots' ghastly events reward enough, but then to bless his fledgling stability with her undying devotion and constant support, affording the recovering public servant the opportunity to experience an unconditional hat trick of love. No, he would stay. If for no other reason than his selfish desire to cling to what little sanity remained.

The date, time and circumstances a confusing blur, but the bone-chilling screech of the alarm indelibly etched in a disintegrating memory, now devoid of its only failsafe.

The comforting arms reaching out from behind to guide the grieving husband away from the room amplified into the constriction of a straight jacket enshrouding Eric's thought process.

"Mr. Goodson," the soothing, but morbid tone of a funeral home director, "It's time for you to go."

"No, I can't. I won't. She'll be okay. You have to do something."

"We've done everything we could. It's her time."

"No, you don't understand. She's all I have," Eric pleaded, frantically groping beyond the doctor who somehow placed himself between Eric and the bed. "You've got to do something. Please."

"There's nothing we can do. Her mind gave out at the accident scene. It's only now her heart finally caught up."

"Please," Eric implored, "Do something to bring her back."

"No one can do that, Eric," the calm voice confided.

"You don't understand. We were supposed to be together forever. She promised. We promised each other. I can't go on without her. She's my strength."

"I wish I had some magic words for you, Eric. Is there someone we can call?"

"No," Eric cried as he moved around the doctor, leaned over Angie and gently kissed her on the cheek, dripping tears that pooled under her eye and ran down the side of her face as though sharing in one last touching episode.

"No, now there's no one."

CHAPTER

59

A SELF-IMPOSED EXILE TO A roach infested rented room in a Cass Corridor boarding house where the bizarre elevated to normalcy, Eric hid the unwieldy crescendo of a vicious cycle: crying jags; revulsion at the mere sight of food; dry heaves wracking his frail body while braced against the wall on those rare occasions when he visited the communal shower to eradicate the foul stench, warding off the pesky biting black flies; and the futile exercise in pain management by the daily pickling of his mind in alcohol.

The routine perfected over the blurred days to a systems management ideal eliminating even the slightest wasted motion: a quart of Mohawk vodka delivered to his chair each day by the horny old hag next door hoping for possibly the last hump of her life; urination accomplished without a muscle twitch; defecation all but irrelevant. Withered to a mere one hundred five pounds, hoisting a full bottle to his lips required all of Eric's concentration, willing his atrophied muscles to move.

CHAPTER

60

THE IMPOSING STONE EDIFICE seemed an architectural enigma for a blue-collar town, but the Detroit Public Library always bustled with activity, anchoring the easternmost boundary of campus. Jack usually crossed the colorful Pewabic tiled foyer floor, admiring the craftsmanship, but this time concentrated all his energy on completing the mission of a lost friend. Turning left to the microfilm room help desk, he approached the cramped workstation of the librarian.

"I'd like to see everything you have on microfilm from *The Detroit News* and *The Detroit Free Press* for July 23, 1967 to August 10, 1967."

"That would be the time during the riots and two weeks thereafter."

"Yes ma'am."

"I'm sorry, but that material is currently out of circulation."

"When will it be available?"

"I'm not sure. Perhaps you could ask the gentleman over there using the microfiche processor," the librarian nudging her head behind and to Jack's left.

In mid turn, Jack immediately recognized Mamoud. "What the heck are you doing here?" The days coincidences initiating borderline panic.

"If it's karma, it's all bad," the preoccupied reporter replied in a serious tone, without lifting his head.

"What interests you about the riots?"

"None of your concern."

"And I thought we'd given up on the hostility."

"Look man, I don't want you anywhere around me. We clear on that?"

"What's your problem now?"

"It's not my problem. It's yours. They think you killed Mink and they're not shy about sharing their opinions."

A wave of bile gushed up Jack's throat. The burning sensation caused him to place a hand atop the microfiche machine to steady himself. "If you mean the police, I already talked to them. I've got a rock-solid alibi."

"If it's so tight, why they on you?"

"What are you talking about?"

"Just turn real casual like, laughing and shaking your head like we're funnin' around."

"Damn," Jack mumbled under his breath as a shadow ducked behind a stack. His heart raced and nausea now accompanied the sour mash taste in his mouth as he struggled to maintain a clear thought.

Sarah appeared, heaving to catch her breath, "Jack, the tests came back. It's real blood. Damn, I think we're in way over our heads."

"What she sayin'?" Mamoud demanded.

"We found a shoe and some goop in a heating duct of an old abandoned factory two weekends ago. People were shooting at us and now Mink is dead," Sarah rambled, tears streaming down her cheeks.

"Look, this all has something to do with police activities during the riots. I don't have any idea what, but I need to know as much as I can so I can try to figure this mess out. Can I please have the microfilm? Or, better yet, will you help us?"

"Maybe we help each other. As I told you before, my Father disappeared during the riots. I'm sure he's dead, or he would have come home. What I don't know is, how or where he died."

"Man, I'm sorry."

"I think we should contact the police," Sarah whimpered.

"Ordinarily I'd agree, but it's the cops who might be involved in a cover up."

"How about that Goodson guy who questioned you. He seemed genuinely convinced you had nothing to do with it," Sarah reasoned.

"Your Corvette is sitting in the body shop riddled with bullets from our last scheduled meeting with Goodson."

"Say what?"

"We agreed to meet him and instead got bushwhacked."

The reporter licked, then bit his bottom lip. "Ditch your tail."

Jack nonchalantly strolled into the stacks. A middle aged, potbellied, pale complexioned male in a green plaid Walmart sport coat, eased out from behind a pillar and moved toward a parallel aisle. Jack broke for the rear exit.

Mamoud scraped together all the curled-up microfiche copies and grabbed Sarah's hand. "I must be crazy messin' with you two."

CHAPTER

61

Mamoud and Sarah scoured the scratchy photocopies of the microfiche news articles, ignoring the constant metal screech emanating from the reporter's high back leather executive chair.

"Whoa! Allah be praised!" Mamoud screamed, jumping up and pulling a handful of Kleenex from a box on the adjacent desk.

"You okay?" Sarah inquired, marveling at the gentle stroke Mamoud used to wipe up the hot coffee from the creamy leather.

"Doin' fine, for almost poaching my gonads," the usually militant newsman chuckled. Then losing the smile quicker than a Greek Tragedy, Mamoud reminisced. "It's just that this chair is the only real memory I have of my Father."

"That explains it."

'What?"

"Why it's so out of place. Everything else in here is clearly second hand. But that chair is spectacular."

"After Papa disappeared, the firm he worked for bought all his furniture off Momma, except for this chair. She stored it in the basement for years. All that time, she'd spit fire every time his name was mentioned, but she always made an excuse when it came time to getting rid of this chair. When I was a boy, I would occasionally catch her in the basement, standing behind it, with both hands resting on the back, silently crying. There were a couple of times, I thought I could hear her talking to him."

Sarah backhanded the tears streaking down her cheeks. "I can't see anything that would help, do you?"

"I was hoping to find a clue about my Dad, but you're right, there's nothing concrete. Not even a sidebar on missing persons. But I can smell a good story developing. Check this out. There are significantly more obituaries between Tuesday July 25, and Friday July 28, 1967, than the prior and subsequent weeks. It's too difficult to tell how many were actually killed, since no cause of death is generally listed."

"Let's file a Freedom of Information request for missing persons reports. It would take time, but we could track down how many blacks are unaccounted for compared to prior weeks. Can you think of anything else?"

"Maybe we should ask the guys who've been following us."

"What are you talking about?"

"I think they're cops. Not the same guys from the library, but they're bulls, no doubt about it. No one can sit and drink coffee all day without taking a leak, except a cop. They have some sort of kidney control class at the academy."

"Where?"

"Across the street. But why would they follow us back here? Your boyfriend is their suspect."

"We should tell someone."

"Who? They're the man. Ain't no one else to go to."

"The papers," Sarah reasoned. "No offense."

"None taken. If we put this together, the dailies will pick it up." Mamoud's confident tone, accented with an affirmative head bob reassured Sarah. His lingering blank stare slowly eroded her nerve. His mumbled, trailing off comment sent her reeling.

"What do you mean, if we live that long?"

CHAPTER

62

Self-sufficient since the age of fourteen and unable to afford time off from work, Jack struggled to subdue an overwhelming grief over Mink's death, forcing himself to continue his daily routine. Pulling into the parking lot at the rear of the warehouse, Michaels noticed rail cars backed up three-deep. He dreaded an entire shift of unloading boxcars. Michigan's Indian summer pushed the thermometer to eighty-six; the temp would hit a minimum fifteen degrees higher in the steel box.

As Roy Blue delivered the manual hand jack on the forks of his hi-lo, Michaels worked with pliers to twist off the metal certification band wrapped around the lock at the brewery. As the wire snapped, the circular tag popped off, bouncing on the track and ricocheting under the freight car. After lifting and flipping the levers on each side of the mammoth steel door, Jack bent down to retrieve the tag, taking a hunched step under the railcar. A deafening reverberating boom released a rapidly expanding dust cloud as the four-ton steel door crashed to the ground.

"Jack!" Roy Blue screamed, stricken with terror as he jumped off his machine. The cloud obscuring his view as he bounded back and forth, Roy yelled, "Jack!"

Coughing and spewing phlegm, J.Z. rolled out from under the train, stood upright and slapped the dirt off his jeans. "I can't believe it takes a near death experience for you to call me by my actual name," Jack wailed, his ashen complexion an outward manifestation of his confused state.

"God, you're okay. I don't believe it. I thought you were toe jam," Roy Blue rattled with a sense of relief.

"What the heck happened?"

"Damn door fell right off."

"Jeez, how often does something like this happen?" Jack questioned, actually feeling the quiver in his voice.

"Never seen anything like it before. Those doors are on rollers that fit into a track that's welded directly to the side of the car. I can't image why it would have done that," Roy Blue explained, clearly puzzled, lifting his baseball cap and scratching his head with the same hand. "The railroad guys were just here this morning, checking things out."

"Did they have leader dogs with them?" Jack scoffed, trying to shake off the fright.

CHAPTER

63

JACK WELCOMED THE MID-WEEK evening meeting; the close call earlier unleashed a torrent of suppressed feeling since Mink's death. During the introductory reading, the leader clutched his hands around his steaming Styrofoam cup of coffee to squelch a nagging cold shiver.

"I haven't seen anyone fidget like that since my late husband had to give the birds and bees speech to my son, Nikki," Rose commented while gently patting Jack's forearm.

"I am experiencing quite the internal struggle. Would anyone mind if I gave the first example?" Jack asked and proceeded while the surprised group continued to nod affirmatively. "After a mishap at work, we shook off the incident and finished the shift. When I got to the locker room, it hit me; I could have been killed. It brought back a flood of memories of a friend of mine who died unexpectedly just a bit ago."

"Jack, can you keep it in the Recovery format?" Rose smirked, the gentle humorous rebuke eliciting a smile from everyone, but Gene.

"My entire body felt heavy, but empty. I was overcome with a sense of sadness. I experienced a crying jag, then anger. I jumped up and started slamming locker doors and screaming. It wasn't until I ran out of lockers that I started spotting. Then I realized that if it were a bigger locker room, I probably would have continued. Then I began to sabotage. The only reason I'm practicing the method was because I ran out of doors to slam. Here I am, a Recovery leader and I can't appropriately handle the situation."

"What did you spot?" John asked.

"I told myself that it was a normal reaction. It was an average response. That the feelings would pass without serious consequence and that I had the will to bear the discomfort. I thought of my friend and knew he would want me to see the humor in life, not the gloom."

Neil, the perfectly groomed maintenance supervisor, chimed in, "Your anger is something I deal with every day. You correctly spotted it as average. What you should work on, is not to hold yourself to a higher standard because you're a leader."

Gloria, a frumpy housewife, squeaked, "Grieving is average. It's a normal process that everyone goes through when you have a serious loss."

"You should endorse yourself, or, as you like to say, pat yourself on the back for practicing the method," Tracey added, cradling her useless arm against her midriff.

"And you controlled your muscles once you ran out of lockers," Abbot offered as he braced his glasses against the bridge of his nose and bent over to slurp an overfilled coffee cup. Completing the maneuver, the hypochondriac continued, "Doctor Low teaches us that with every setback, we become stronger."

"And how would you have handled the situation before your Recovery training?" Rose inquired with all the mastery of a true leader.

"I honestly don't know. Unlike most of you, I grew up with the system every day. I saw the dramatic improvement in my Mom. She made me practice the method as a young child. It was weird; I didn't even know what most of the words meant, but she'd keep telling me to repeat them and someday I'd understand."

"Now you do," Rose whispered, tapping the back of Jack's hand.

Everyone in attendance eagerly participated in helping their young leader analyze his example, except Gene; a troubling issue for Jack, since the heavy set, bearded young man reached his third week without the slightest peep. Since participation remained completely voluntary, the stymied guide refused to pry, although the urge gnawed at him.

"*You can always tell by the eyes,*" Jack thought to himself as they concluded the session. "*And that young man's torment makes my life a cakewalk.*"

CHAPTER

64

A solid rap at the door failed to interrupt the continuing Olympian attempt at self-pity. A second, more vigorous knock, likewise unanswered.

"Erie, I know you're in there. Come open the door, Son," the low, comforting voice commanded. The awkward silence failed to diminish the old man's resolve. "I've been searching all over the city for you. I can't believe I finally found you." No response. "Erie, it's time to come home with your family," the familiar friendly salesman tone persisted.

"Family," Eric mumbled in a stupor, slumping further down in the tattered, lice infested, over-stuffed chair, whimpering.

"Erie, it's me, Uncle Lenny. I've come to take you home."

"Home?" Eric questioned as if fumbling to recall the meaning, but sensing a familiarity with the concept.

"Yes Son, home to your family."

The howl of the severely wounded resonated through the desolate hall, prompting Leonard to shoulder the flimsy door. Unprepared for the ghastly sight of his nephew, the normally unflappable personal injury lawyer reached out as a tear trickled down his liver spotted cheek, stumbling to find the resonating voice that so eloquently persuaded thousands of jurors.

"Erie, time to return to the people who love you," Leonard remarked, placing his fingertips on his nephew's shoulder.

The course whisper such a departure from the normally confident tone, Eric raised his head not only to respond, but also to double check the intruder's identity.

"I've lost the only person I care about."

"But you still have an awful lot of people who need you."

"Who really gives a damn about what happens to me?"

"Your Aunt Mims and I do. We've scoured every tenement in the city since the funeral searching for you. We were never able to have children of our own. You are the closest to a son we will ever have. Angie is gone, God keep her beautiful soul close by, but we can't afford to lose you too. Please Erie, come home with me."

As the elderly counselor accompanied his despondent nephew out of the weekly rental dive, he tried to imagine the depth of despair that led the formerly vibrant young lad to this den of degradation; the demons of death forever skewered the delicate personality that brought he and his wife untold happiness, stranding two souls to drape the interned casket hermetically sealed under an avalanche of incalculable pain; the remaining hulk a useless corporeal vessel devoid of the inane instinct to survive.

CHAPTER

65

Aнві scrubbed the sink with the enthusiasm of a qualifying round for the *Guinness Book of World Records* on spotlessness. His intense concentration allowed him a reprieve from a constant stream of delusional episodes. The look of surprise each day on the faces of the employees at the spiffed-up facilities boosted an ego dormant for decades. He now yearns for a return to a near normal life that a lack of memory must have stolen from him. *"Scour the sink and think,"* he hummed to himself wearing his fingertips raw. *"Scour the sink and think,"* he repeated for the umpteenth time when the image flashed in his mind; the bloated suit with the flashy wrist gyrating and shaking reminiscent of a twisting and shouting Chubby Checker whacked on speed. *"God, please help me. What does it mean?"* Ahbi cried as he heard another soft whimper from outside the locker room. Intrigued at the unusual occurrence even for him, he decided to follow the sound to the conference room. The janitor slowly opened the door just far enough to peek in. The buxom young secretary who had shared a portion of her roach coach tomato soup with him the day before was pinned against the dark oak paneled wall by the weight of her enormous employer. Her skirt hiked above her waist, panties pulled down, blouse torn open, arms extended overhead and restrained by a tree trunk forearm;

her mouth covered by his other hand; her head jerking back and forth in a futile attempt to avoid full facial licks from a monster.

Distraction his hasty plan, Ahbi gently tapped on the door and inquired in his difficult to understand dialect, "Mister Harrold, do you need anything else done today?"

No reply. Only the high-pitched muffled groans and rhythmic bounce against the interior wall.

Continuing to push after another faint knock, Ahbi edged in the top of his head. "Sir, I just checkin' to see you okay."

The heaving breaths of an exhausting workout the only sound.

The trembling hands executed a final thrust, with the custodian losing his balance and landing three steps into the room. Quickly turning away from the ghastly scene directly ahead, Ahbi blurted, "Oh, excuse me, sir, I didn't know you was busy."

"Get out of here, asshole," Mayer hollered, his acrid eyes penetrating to the maintenance man's soul.

"I just thought you two might need somethin'," Ahbi sensing a delay may help the young lass.

"You want another beating, don't you?" The maniacal boss reasoned, his turn toward Ahbi restricted by his crumpled pants and shorts clinging to his ankles. "Yeah, I really think you need another lesson, don't you boy?" The crazed rapist now squared off, directly facing Ahbi, displaying a rock-hard penis without a tinge of embarrassment. "Well, school is in session, so polish up an apple for old teach," the sociopath instructed as he inched toward the trembling janitor.

The shivering secretary slowly bent down, yanked up her panties, grabbed the edges of her torn blouse to cover up her bare breasts and shot out of the room like a jack rabbit with a fox inches off her tail.

Mayer's slow hobble appeared almost comical, but elicited a bizarre smirk of intense fear. It was the eyes; cold, steely, ripped directly from the Devil's sockets in hell and transplanted, moving toward Ahbi, demanding a loss of bowel control supplicating terror. *"Oh Lord, what do I do now,"* Ahbi wondered, a tremor slicing through his deformed body. *"I don't think I can move."* The demon reincarnate shuffled closer; a few additional steps would put him within reach of the paralyzed janitor.

"Can you smell it, piss ant?" Mayer asked in an almost polite manner.

"Sir," all that Ahbi managed to squeak out.

"Death," Mayer said softly, tilting up his nose as though savoring the delectable aroma in a gourmet kitchen.

"Mr. Harrold, you can't be doin this now, hear," Ahbi pleaded, then slipping into a haze as the wide girth with the glint on the wrist approached. The dream would protect Ahbi from the pain as it had always done in the past. The terrified prey succumbed to his fate. "The vibration is new. What could that be?" the daydreamer thought out loud.

Roy Blue's hi-lo screeched to a halt in the doorway, directly behind Ahbi. The foreman stood up, gripping the suicide knob on the steering wheel with one hand and kicking the door open. "Now there's a sight no one should ever have to see in their lifetime," Roy scoffed.

"Get the fuck out of here, Blue, or I'll take care of you after I finish here with the street puke," Mayer threatened, still fixated on Ahbi.

"You think that little thing can handle two burly guys like us? I wouldn't bet my life savings on it."

"That's it, Blue. I'm gonna hurt you bad," the demonic tone causing Ahbi to flinch.

"You should be ashamed to wave that little pecker around, Butchie. You look like needle dick the butt fucker," Roy taunted, jumping down from the forklift and stepping in front of the trembling janitor.

"Why you …" Mayer screamed as he lunged for Roy, tangled in his drawers, losing his balance, stumbling to the side into a stack of folding chairs, crashing to the floor.

Roy stared down at the sorry excuse for a man. "All temper and no brains," the foreman commented, pushing a second pile of steel chairs onto Mayer.

"Tha, tha, thank you Mr. Blue," Ahbi stuttered, staring at Mayer under the pile of rubble. "Why he always doing stuff like that?"

"Just mean spirited, I guess."

"How did you know to come help?"

"It's not every day I see a naked woman running through the warehouse. Come on, let's go."

The dissipation of fear allowed Ahbi to feel the dampness, causing him to glance down at the puddle around his feet. His head hung, suspended in embarrassment.

Roy gently touch Ahbi's shoulder, "It's okay. He scares the piss out of me, too."

CHAPTER

66

Aₗₜₕₒᵤgₕ ₜₕₑ ₒₗᵈ Vᵢcₜₒᵣᵢₐₙ house stood empty for the past several weeks with the entrance roped off with yellow crime scene tape, Jack thought it best to wait until Saturday morning to execute a B & E. A turn of the handle revealing an unlocked front door simplified matters, requiring a combination step over and duck to circumvent the plastic barrier.

"Damn, this is creepy," Mamoud whispered as Jack stopped at the bathroom door, inches from where the body was discovered.

"I can't believe he's gone. You'd think a vibrant force like Mink would be around forever. God, I miss him," Jack lamented.

"No time for that now. Just hush up and get this done before anyone finds out," Mamoud on the verge of panic and experiencing pangs of regret for allowing Michaels to talk him into this foolish foray.

"We're fine, Mikey," J.Z. teased, attempting to relieve his own anxiety.

"Don't call me that!"

"Sorry." Rather than dwell on a mea culpa, Jack immediately refocused on the mission. "No one's ever around Monteith on the weekend."

"Tell that to Mink," Mamoud scoffed, immediately wishing he could take the statement back.

Jack froze at the remark, overwhelmed with a wave of grief. Taking a moment to regain his composure, he opened the door to Mink's office. "Look, if anyone catches us, we'll tell them we're looking for research papers. After all, I was his assistant."

"That works for you, but what about me? It's the black guy they always shoot," Mamoud reasoned, half serious about his remark.

As Jack reached for a volume on the bookshelf, he suspended the motion in midair, reflecting on the laughs and lively discussions he and Sarah experienced building the shelves with Joe three years ago as freshman. Mink advertised the project at the end of a lecture as a brainstorming session for research ideas to be held in his office on a Saturday morning. The only two students to fall for the ruse, Mink introduced Sarah and Jack to each other, as well as "carpentry 101" as he jokingly referred to the office improvement project.

"It's got to be here somewhere," J.Z. reasoned.

"Exactly what are we looking for?"

"I don't really know," Jack responded, "But it should include police records and a cop's personal notebook on things that happened during the riots."

"Where in the hell would he get something like that?" Mamoud asked incredulously.

"He would have copped it from the police archives. No pun intended."

"He stole them?"

"It's just a guess on my part, but yes, I believe he would have. They were too important a piece in the puzzle he was trying to put together," Jack surmised. "Besides, the way he talked about stumbling on them, it's a miracle he found them in the first place. Someone like Sarah would say, "It was meant to be." Jack took a second to recoup, feeling guilty about referring to Joe in the past tense.

Mamoud rifled through the desk drawers, while Jack continued the library inventory.

"*The Oxford Dictionary, American Edition,*" Jack mumbled. "That's strange."

"What's so unusual about a college professor having a dictionary?"

"Well, look over there," Michaels instructed. "There's an unabridged edition of *Webster's* the size of an entire set of encyclopedias sitting on the pedestal. Why would he need a second dictionary? It's a pocket size, comparatively speaking," Jack pulled the volume from the shelf with much more ease than anticipated. "No damned weight to it," J.Z. commented as he opened it up. "Well, I'll be!" The super sleuth lamented while stuffing the contents down the front of his Dockers.

"You a regular Dan Tanna," Mamoud remarked, slipping in and out of his ghetto dialect as smooth as the gearbox on a ninety-thousand-dollar Porsche Boxster. "Now let's get out of here."

"You're right Mikey, time to go."

"Don't dis me less you wanna be picking your teeth up off da ground," Mamoud smirked as he relayed the threat.

"Sometimes it's hard to believe you're a magna cum laude English Lit major."

"We gonna hang here all day just so's you can hear yourself rag on?"

67

Huddled on the floor of the tiny studio apartment with the stolen reports spread out on the coffee table, Mamoud and Sarah examined every scrap of paper, while Michaels paced incessantly.

"Jack, will you calm down and get over here to help? We've got to figure this thing out," Sarah ordered, resuming the focus of an experienced gem cutter about to make the first stroke on the Hope Diamond.

Ignoring the command, J.Z. continued the clipped limited strides of a lifer in his first thirty days of confinement. His short-circuited mental synapses reverberated through his entire system, triggering an effect similar to countless amphetamine induced sleepless hours.

"There's no question that Mink was on to something. I can't believe how he correlated the mileage logs with the incident and miscellaneous reports to arrive at the Packard Industrial Complex as a potential site," Sarah remarked with the reverence and respect her mentor so richly deserved, while readjusting her legs to a comfortable position.

"It was a real long shot," Mamoud reasoned. "But to make it pay off, we've got to figure out if the shoe and the blood have anything to do with a death, or if it was just some heating contractor who years ago lost one of his high top Keds and cut himself climbing out of the duct work."

"What we really have to determine is the identity of 'C'," Sarah commented, clasping her hands behind her neck and bending her head back and forth. Without breaking her concentration, the modern-day Emma Peele ordered, "Jack, you've got to get a grip. Yesterday you were doing B&E's and ducking a tail. And today you're as jittery as a human resources director at a laid off postal workers' convention. Why don't you practice your Recovery training?"

Jack's heart pounded against his ribcage; sweat rained from his armpits, soiling the sides of his black cotton tee shirt; he sucked in exaggerated breaths to relieve his air hunger. The rote phrases of Recovery not even a distant memory. He reacted with all the aplomb of a first-year psych student researching case studies in the DSM III Manuel.

"A clear-cut case of, do as I say, not as I do," Mamoud chided. "He's wasted. Forget about him for now."

For three and a half hours the duo meticulously noted dates, times, locations and players; assembling the evidence as though concentrating on a five-thousand-piece puzzle entitled, *San Francisco by Night*.

"I'll guaran-damn-tee you there were no Canadians out for a stroll in that neighborhood," Jack proffered. "Especially during the riots, unless it was some wayward reporter. No offense Mamoud."

"He's alive!" Sarah rang out.

"Mink already confirmed the borders were closed," Mamoud mentioned with a yawn, forcing the discussion back on track.

"If 'C' doesn't stand for Canadian, how about 'Colored'?" Sarah surmised, "considering the year 1967."

"That occurred to me, too," Mamoud injected. "But then why talk about the border? It's got to be some kind of code. Do either of you know a cop well enough to ask?" The reporter inquired, first glancing across the table at Sarah, then up to Jack.

Sarah turned her head and exchanged bewildered glances with J.Z., shrugged their shoulders in unison and responded in stereo, "No."

As the night wore on, Michaels settled down, convincing himself that working to solve the mystery would change his thoughts and help alleviate his nervous symptoms. Stale coffee and a couple of doobies inspired wild conjecture. "What if 'C' is code for a black and 'back to the border' refers to getting rid of him?"

Mamoud waved off a hit on the joint. Jack passed the doobie to Sarah. She sucked in a deep breath. "The dispatcher reports confirm that a Sergeant Dolan and an officer Reichert escorted a Canadian to the border. That implies the personnel manning the precinct house understood what the patrol cops meant."

"You're talking major conspiracy, Jack."

"I'm Mamoud; you're jacked, Jack," the reporter chuckled.

"Oh, that's it. You have to get him stoned on second hand smoke to show a sense of humor," Jack kidded.

"Knock it off for a second. Mamoud has a point. If he's right, we're in way over our heads," Sarah said, the concern in her voice chalked up to cannabis paranoia.

CHAPTER

68

THE SCREAMING MATCH ONLY lasted four minutes. The ruthless exchange an occasional acceptable teenage outburst, but unforgivable for a mother. The rotten remarks spewed in anger, drove her only child away in tears. Ten minutes later, Arlene admitted to herself that the makeup really didn't look that bad, especially for a first attempt. She decided to prepare her little girl's favorite dinner to smooth things over.

Marlee hitched a ride just outside Smiths Ferry on Highway 55 from a log hauler. Her smeared mascara and eyeliner lent a punk rock look, but fortunately, the driver being the father of three teens, recognized the ruse. They sat in silence the entire two and a half hour, sixty-eight miles to Boise. As the fifteen-year old climbed down the rig, the operator leaned forward, resting his left forearm on the steering wheel and pushed up the brim of his cap with the right hand. "You can always go home, you know."

The bus station consisted of a bench in front of a dingy Citgo station. The $14.95 special for a cross country ticket sounded reasonable, leaving her with enough to buy two fast food meals; one now, and the other when she reached California. As the coach headed down I-84 and the driver called out, "Twin Falls," the independent lass marveled at the prospect of traveling farther in a day, than she had her entire life. Staring out the window for hours and fighting off hunger pangs, she decided to disembark at an I-80 rest stop outside Cheyenne, Wyoming for a bite. Using the remainder of her funds, she returned to her seat, curled up and slept until the announcement, "Cedar Rapids". Several hours later, her gurgling stomach settled at the familiar call "Chicago". Convincing herself she must be close, another half day found her biting her cuticles for sustenance.

Arriving in Detroit, she approached the driver. "How much longer to California?"

Perplexed, the company veteran remarked, "Darlin', this here is the Motor City. You're a long way from the West Coast."

"This will have to do." Marlee exited onto the grime imbedded sidewalk and looked ahead, studying the revolving door into the station. Littered with trash and vagrants, the innocent child from Smiths Ferry, Idaho collapsed into a green fiberglass chair, pulled her knees up to her chest, dropped her head forward and sobbed.

"Hey sweet thang! You look like you could use a friend." The predator scooped the lower half of his full-length leather coat and sat down. Fascinated by her golden locks, he gently reached out, sticking his index finger in one of her natural curls and twisted. "I'll bet you're hungry. What say I buys you a good hot meal?"

Listed for eighteen months as a runaway on a national registry with two million other missing children, she endured the despicable acts of Raydon and his clients; acting on urges that surely rise from some dark place, unfathomable to a tender teen raised in a sleepy Rocky Mountain town. The anticlimactic gagging and hurling eventually morphed into total insensitivity; survival at any cost. With the instinct for self-preservation paramount, Marlee bolted from her captor at the first opportunity, making her way to the Eight Mile strip. Searching desperately until she found a working pay phone, the seasoned whore dumped her purse on the metal shelf, scrambling to assemble her change. Nervously punching in the ten digits, she felt instant relief as it rang, then ambivalence. As Marlee extended her index finger to quash the receiver, a familiar voice answered.

"Hello." The three seconds of silence prompted a second inquiry. "Hello? Is anybody there?"

Another short pause, then a weepy voice, "Momma, can I please come home?"

"Marlee? Is that you? Oh baby, it's so good to hear from you."

"Please, Momma. I swear I'll do anything you want. Just let me come home."

"Oh sweetie, I dreamed of hearing from you. I knew this day just had to come. Where are you? Can I come get you?"

"No, Momma. I'm in Detroit. I can earn enough tonight to get a bus ticket back. I wasn't sure you would want me."

"I've been worried sick. I'm glad you're okay."

"I'll see you in a few days. I love you, Momma." Click.

Attempting to primp in a dark phone booth with the benefit of intermittent passing headlight glare a complete failure, Marlee scraped her belongings back into her purse. Besides, she learned long ago that her tight young body earned her keep. Adjusting her ample boobs within the sheer cotton tank top and sliding her hands down her shapely hips to reaffirm the snug fit of her Lycra bicycle shorts, Marlee pranced to the curb.

A freshly washed black Ford Explorer cut across three lanes of traffic and whipped to the curb. Filled with salivating young white suburbanites stumbling over each other to view the merchandise.

"Want to go to a frat party?" The blond, blue-eyed front passenger inquired as the other three giggled in anticipation.

Marlee leaned forward, resting her forearms on the base of the window, checking out her perspective clients.

"Fifty dollars up front per person; blowjobs only."

"Two hundred dollars! You've got to be kidding? No way, man," the passenger blurted as the S.U.V. peeled from the curb.

The young hooker straightened up, arched a brow and rendered a condescending, "Hmph!" Glancing back to oncoming traffic, a slow rolling clunker coasted to a stop. Marlee approached the car. "Looking for a date Pops?"

"How much?"

"Depends on what you want to do…" Marlee responded, the open mouth gum chewing triggering a smile along with well-rehearsed snaps. "…And how many times you want to do it?"

"I want it all."

"Well, this is your lucky night 'cause I'm running a sale. The usual hundred-dollar job is yours for fifty."

"What are you, seventeen?"

"Sixteen pops. Fresh meat. Just like I know you like it."

"You don't know a thing about me. Get in."

As the streetwalker piled in, she unexpectedly slid across the seat. Glancing about, she noticed the same plastic on the door panel and dashboard. With several holes drilled into the floor, it reminded Marlee of a checker board.

"I like to keep everything neat," the john remarked, noticing her reaction.

Wrapping a hug around her client's right arm and leaning her head into his shoulder, she directed him around the block to the driveway of a burned-out abandoned home. "Pull up there."

Entering the back yard with lights out, he cut the engine. Marlee reached over and squeezed her hand into his pants, massaging his joint. "That'll be fifty bucks." The mark purred in pleasure as he passed her the bill. "About time we wrapped him up, don't you think?"

"Do we have to?"

"Well, I know I'm clean. You strike me as a nice guy. Promise me you are too!"

"Yeah, yeah, yeah. I'm clean."

"Okay, but I'm still taking a big risk. For another fifty, I can forget about it."

"Done," the john squealed, digging into his shirt pocket for the money.

Taking a moment before stuffing the bill in her ankle high boot, she held it to her lips and kissed it. *"This is my ticket home."* Lifting the tank top up over her breasts exposed a stainless-steel nipple ring and simulated diamond navel stud. Sliding the exercise shorts to mid-calf, she mounted the john from a kneeling position with her back braced against the dash. "I'm gonna give you my final ride, baby."

As the john nuzzled his bald head between her tits, Marlee wrapped her arms around his dome and bounced her ass in rapid fire motion. Crying out in ecstasy, at no additional charge, the retiring whore decided to go the extra mile for her last professional gig. She grabbed his ears, pulling back his head and repeatedly licked his face.

"Oh yeah, baby! That's it! Just like that!" The middle-aged lecher bellowed as he thrust forward and gripped a nipple in his teeth.

"Easy baby, those are irreplaceable."

The force of the bite increased dramatically. "Ow! Ow! Ow! Ow! Please baby, that really hurts," Marlee screamed, tears streaming down her cheeks. The john clamped his teeth together, severing the tip of her breast, while at same time, shoving a sharpened pencil in her neck and up into her skull. "But I'm supposed to go home…" Marlee mumbled as she collapsed forward.

Shoving his victim aside, the killer arched to zip his pants. Settling back, he leaned over, grabbed the body just under the armpits and hoisted it over the back of the seat. As it plopped to the smooth aluminum floor, the Professor reached to flick an under the dash switch. The whir of an electric motor signaled the activation of a mechanism that slowly slid the body into the trunk.

Relishing the anticipation of arranging his victim in exactly the right spot occupied his thoughts, as he started the thirty-minute trip to his lair. He envisioned dragging the corpse as though a rag doll, descending into the northwest corner of the basement and prying open the old vault door. As always, he would pause to admire his handiwork; an entire classroom of corpses in various stages of decomposition, all neatly arranged as though awaiting the teacher.

"Hi-ho! Hi-ho! It's off to school we go!"

CHAPTER

69

Cruising the center lane on eastbound Eight Mile Road, just west of Livernois Avenue, oblivious to the never-ending stream of heralding hucksters soliciting patrons for the myriad of strip clubs and topless bars, the Professor smiled as he churned the memory of his latest conquest. Constant review of every detail allowed a refinement in technique; the secret to avoiding detection. Overworked, underpaid and average intellect investigators lacked the time, skills and fortitude to corral a master craftsman. There was no thrill in the chase, because there was no chase. The Professor operated with impunity; plucking his prey at will.

While stopped at the red light at Livernois, his concentration was fractured from a low vibration originating in the glovebox. Reaching across to the passenger side of the dash, the driver pressed the button releasing the drawer. The incessant buzz crescendoed. Fidgeting with the bulky gray plastic Motorola Dynatax 8000x phone, the Professor fumbled to raise the aerial, then answered in a low timbre, "Yes?"

"That all you got is a yes." The gravelly voice grumbled. "I would have thought a man with your intelligence and fine upbringing would be more gracious in his salutations," the caller taunted. "How'd you like that 'salutations' remark? That's a real million-dollar word, ain't it, Professor?"

"Who is this?"

"I'm the guy who knows everything about you."

"How did you get this number?"

"Ain't you listening, Professor? I already told you, I'm the guy who knows it all. What you got going in your little classroom and all."

The blare of a horn jolted the Professor, prompting him to look in the rearview mirror, then glance up at the green light. Pinching the phone between his right shoulder and cheek, the Professor slammed the floor shift of the old Nova into first gear, revved the 327cu, 350 HP engine to four-thousand rpm's and dumped the clutch. The ferocious torque squealed the tires and forced a cloud of burning rubber across all three lanes. In a totally uncharacteristic move, the driver flipped the bird to the vehicle behind.

"My, my, but ain't you losing it now," the caller taunted.

"Who the hell is this?" The driver demanded, while busting through the gears.

"Better slow down, my friend. You don't want to get stopped now, do you? What with a body and all in the trunk. That's the kind of stupid mistake your competition makes." The voice breathing heavy. "How you gonna dress this one up? I liked the wedding party look you got going."

The driver quickly removed his foot from the accelerator. Flicking on his right signal, he turned onto the next side street, then immediately into the first alleyway, behind a row of single-story commercial buildings and quickly killed the engine and lights.

"What the fuck is going on? This is not like me. Everything is so well thought out. Did I slip up? Da! Of course, you did. But how did…"

"Professor! Oh, Professor! Right about now you're saying to yourself, 'I must have fucked up.' You sure did. Or, maybe you're just not quite as smart as you think you are."

"What? What do you want? The Professor stumbled.

"What I want is for you to pay attention. Pull your shit together. We have business to take care of."

"What sort of business?" Sweat streaked down his brow, causing a burning sensation in his eyes.

"The same kind that you enjoy in that little basement classroom of yours."

"My God, he knows about the…"

"Have I lost you again, Professor?" The agitation clearly visible. "Pull it together! I own you! I'll agree to keep your little private school private, if you agree to lend me a helping hand with no questions asked."

"I, I don't…"

"Would you like me to drop a dime on your little soirée? My goodness," the voice chuckled. "There's another one of them cutesy words."

"No," the Professor floundered, "I'll do as you ask."

The gravelly voice chuckled, then sang, "Hi-ho! Hi-ho! It's off to school we go!"

The Professor sat stunned; the dial tone blaring in his ear.

CHAPTER

70

Seated behind a repurposed pressed board secretarial desk with a rusted three-pound Maxwell House coffee can as a fourth leg, Miriam Mayer punched the blinking middle light of the five-line rotary phone. Although her deceased husband repeatedly proselytized that the secret to success in any business is to keep the overhead as low as possible, the condition of his office was deplorable. In every visit to the distributorship before his demise, she would beg him to let her remodel his office. His response never deviated, "I just got it broke in." Then he would suck in a deep drag on his La Aurora Cameroon and smother her in smoke that in a modernized office would have set off the fire suppression system. After his death, she couldn't bear to change a thing; it reeked of her David. That man's ferocious love for her even offset the constant odor of burnt tobacco. If kissing him was like kissing a dirty ashtray, it was her ashtray. The only dark cloud in their marriage had been her son, but David overlooked every transgression for her sake.

"Hello, this is Miriam Mayer."

"Ms. Mayer, my name is Leonard Goodson and I'm an attorney in downtown Detroit."

"Yes, Mr. Goodson, what can I do for you?"

"Well, I've written you two letters that have gone unanswered, so…"

"Excuse me, Mr. Goodson, but I don't recall seeing any letters from you. Could you hold just a few seconds so I can speak to my secretary? In the meantime, could you give me your number there so I can call you back if we get disconnected? Our system here is undergoing a renovation and I'm not quite used to it, yet."

"Yes, of course."

Mariam pressed the hold button, then yelled, "Alice, can you come in here, please?"

Within seconds, the scarred hollow-core wood door opened approximately eighteen inches and a mid-fifties bespectacled head appeared.

"Yes, Mrs. Mayer?"

"Alice, have we gotten any letters in the last while from an attorney Goodson?"

Alice closed her eyes and whispered, "Yes, Ma'am."

"Why haven't I seen them?"

Mariam's perplexed look prompted Alice to clear her throat and continue in a whisper, "Because your son took them from me."

"Why didn't you tell me?"

"Ma'am?"

"C'mon Alice, what's going on?"

"He threatened me."

"You poor dear. Enough said. Don't worry, I'll take care of everything. Thank you, Alice."

"Mr. Goodson, sorry to keep you waiting. What is this about?"

"I represent one of your former employees who was seriously injured at work."

"Well, let me give you the information on our work comp carrier and I'm sure they will handle everything."

"The problem is, work comp will not cover this matter, since it was an intentional act. I wanted to give you the opportunity to resolve this matter before I file suit in Wayne Circuit Court."

Beads of sweat formed on Mariam's forehead. "What kind of incident are we talking about?" She fidgeted in the antique chair.

"Your son, Butchie I believe they call him, brutally raped and sodomized one of your support staff." The long silence prompted Leonard to ask, "Ms. Mayer, are you still there?"

Holding her hand over the speaker portion of the phone while sucking in a deep breath, Miriam responded, "Yes, I'm here. Why don't you give me a couple of days to look into this matter and then I'll call you back. Please hold off on the suit in the meantime."

"That'll be fine. I'll wait to hear from you."

Mariam erupted from her chair, flipping it back. The wheels slid across the plastic carpet protector, rotating it sideways, slamming it into the wall and crashing it to the floor. Her left hip caught the straight edge corner of the desk, prompting a, "Dammit!" A quick rub with her finger tips, she bolted across the room in four large strides. Grabbing the tarnished imitation brass door knob, she yanked inward and let go, slamming it into the spring mounted baseboard doorstop, permanently crumpling the safety device. Stomping into the secretarial bullpen, Mariam abruptly stopped, scanning the room. Eyeing her target, she blasted across the floor and burst into the manager's office. Reaching out, she ripped the short-based microphone from Jimmy Pepatino's hand, tugging it in a direct line to her mouth, stopping millimeters from fracturing her perfect teeth. "Butchie! Butchie!" She screamed, startling one staff member to knock her coffee to the floor. "Dammit, what's wrong with this fucking thing," Mariam yelled.

A scarlet red faced Pepatino flicked his index finger upward, "You have to push the button."

Marian depressed the switch and in a piercing cry, bellowed, "Butchie, in my office now!" Then slammed the device back onto Pepatino's desk, retreating in a chuff to her office.

"Momma, you wanted to see me?" The contrite sociopath sheepishly inquired after two gentle knocks on the door.

"Don't Momma me, you fucking turd. This is the last fucking straw, do you understand me," Mariam hollered.

"What is it, Momma?"

"I can't fucking believe it!" Mariam shouted, violently shaking her head.

"Believe what, Momma?" The behemoth questioned.

"Will you quit with the momma bullshit already? It's as phony as it gets."

Butchie hung his head and contritely replied, "I'm sure it can't be that bad, Mo…" cutting himself off for fear of escalating her rage.

"I just got a call from an attorney who says you raped and sodomized one of our former staff."

"If that's true, why haven't the police contacted me?" The smirk clearly visible.

"You know damned well why you wouldn't have been contacted. You and your high and mighty friends on the force. I still find it incredulous that they stay so loyal to you. You really must have some serious dirt on them."

"So, who is this former employee?"

"He didn't mention a name, but I assume it's a woman."

Harrold burst a snicker.

"My god, that's really not a safe assumption, is it?"

Mariam collapsed back, slamming her butt onto the desk, dropping her head into her open palms.

"Your Father, I mean your real Father, tried to warn me time and time again that you were not all there. But I kept defending you; one excuse after another. At five, you would swat a fly, tear one wing off, drop him to the ground and delight in his spiral spin on the floor. I wrote it off as a phase you were going through, even while your Father commented on your facial expressions of pleasure. Taking you fishing for the first time, you were more interested in pulling the minnows out of the bucket and watching them flail until they suffocated. Then when you buried the neighbor's pet Chihuahua alive, your Dad insisted we have you examined. When diagnosed as a sociopath, I threatened to sue the psychologist. Finally, when your Father disappeared, I just assumed he abandoned us over a nasty argument we had about his nickname for you, Butcher, which, over time became Butchie. Something nagged at me for years, but I wrote it off as paranoia."

Tired of her rant, Harrold finally blurted, "Your point?"

"Don't you smart mouth me. This is the last straw. When I clean this mess up, it will be the last time I bail you out."

"Yada, yada, yada." "*When I take over this place, things will be a lot different. I'll have the money to do whatever the fuck I want.*"

"I don't know where you drift off to, but I've learned what it means. And no, even though David agreed to your asinine idea of adopting you as an adult and you taking his name, we both agreed that you would never have the run of this place. We have set everything up in a trust and it gets sold with all the proceeds going to Focus Hope. David has the utmost respect for Father William Cunningham, the Founder. So, don't get any ideas!"

"*You fucking whore; you bitch! I'll take care of you just like I did to that prick of a Father, and oh yes, your loving David.*" Butchie's eyes belied his anger; the dark pools of hell itself. "If that's what you think is best."

"Go on, get out of here. You make me sick."

As Butchie turned to leave, his Mother halted his advance, "One more thing. You ever threaten one of our employees again, I'll have you banned from the premises. Got that?"

Butchie just waved his hand without turning.

CHAPTER

71

THE ENDLESS VILE BLEND of uncontrolled bodily fluids and hallucinatory induced repulsive rantings of outrageous accusations failed to deter the warm, loving spirit of Aunt Mims. Her demeanor remained a constant soothing salve of salvation temporarily assuaging the physical and mental demons racking Eric's fragile body. No matter the disgusting display, Auntie Mims maintained her composure on her loving vigil, as though a night shift nurse comforting wounded soldiers in a World War I post-op unit under enemy fire.

"Oh god, I can't believe I did this again. I thought I was past this. I'm so sorry," Eric whimpered, scrambling to distance himself from the soiled sheets and curling up in disgrace.

"Now, now, it's alright. We'll get you cleaned up in no time," the kindly attendant relayed without a tinge of malice, reaching out for Eric's trembling hand and gently pulling him up to a sitting position.

"Let me help you out of these wet pajamas," the elderly matron requested.

Eric winced, clutching his chest.

"Now you get modest?" Mims smiled. "I've been married for forty-one years. Believe me, I've seen more than my share of naked men. It used to be quite exciting, but the last twenty years gravity has taken its toll. So, come on, off with the PJs."

"I feel so helpless," Eric cried while Aunt Mims peeled the nightshirt off, revealing his chalky rail thin torso.

"Nonsense, you're family. That's what family members do. They take care of one another. There is no shame in being dependent; only in staying that way when you have the opportunity to improve." Mims gripped her nephew by the upper arm, surprising Eric with her strength. "Let me help you to the shower. Your Uncle Lenny had handicapped bars and a seat installed yesterday, so you should be able to manage for yourself."

"Ugh, Aunt Mims, you shouldn't…" the patient shrugged, feeling the remorse of a convicted killer moments before execution.

"Nonsense," Mims interrupted, "Your uncle and I are getting older. It was something we should have done anyway. I'll be out here taking care of the bedding. If you have any problems, just call out."

As he shuffled the few feet to the shower, Eric whispered, "I love you, Aunt Mims."

A first tear tugged on a second, eventually causing a steady stream to cascade down her portly cheeks as she gathered the sullied linens. "I know you do, Erie. I know you do."

As Eric plunked his bare bottom on the newly installed ceramic ledge, his body shivered from contact with the cold stone. Leaning forward, he gripped the shower control and twisted, bracing for the onslaught of frigid water.

"Ugh!'" The recovering derelict yelled as he furiously yanked his legs up out of the way of the chilled droplets that sprouted goose bumps across his extremities. Withstanding the initial shock, Eric cranked the dial toward hot. With a rush of warmth, he reached out for the side rail and exerted every ounce of strength available, pulling himself up under the flow. "What am I doing? I'm nothing but trouble. Aunt Mim doesn't need this," Eric lamented as the water pounded on his face. A wave of nausea suddenly doubled him over with dry heaves. As his gaunt body torqued from the spasms, memories of Angie flooded his mind. "Why God? You could have taken me. She never hurt a soul," Eric wept, allowing himself to wallow in self-pity. The shower continued to pound, the sound now amplified to distressing levels in his head. "I miss you so much," Eric sobbed. The once soothing flow now a torture chamber. "I'm nothing without you. I can't possibly go on. I'm sorry darling. I know you'd never approve, but you were always so much stronger than me," Eric cried, grabbing hold of the back scrubber and sinking down the sidewall to the floor. Bawling uncontrollably, Eric snapped the thick plastic handle, creating a jagged edge. Digging the pointed end into his left wrist like a chef shucking oysters, he ripped through the skin and tore open the artery. The pulsating spurts of blood immediately diluted as it flowed in a snaking river trail toward the drain.

CHAPTER

72

THE TAN FORD SEDAN sat across the street from Jack's apartment in front of the fire hydrant on the north side of Palmer. The occasional red glare from the drags on cigarettes, providing the illusion of a trapped fire fly, the only evidence of occupancy in the darkness.

A larger vehicle, but darker in color, sandwiched illegally in the small private lot of the printing company next to Jack's, moved cautiously, without headlights, as Mamoud left the building, following him down Cass Avenue, back to the *Southern Edge* offices.

CHAPTER

73

T HE DOOR OPENED WHILE Jack still fumbled with the deadbolt.

"Needed a place to study. Hope you don't mind," the leggy seductress notified in her usual throaty voice.

"The library's always open for a beautiful woman," Jack teased.

"For any gorgeous female, or just me?"

"A man has to keep his options open."

"Well, I hope you and your options have a lovely evening," Sarah playfully huffed, as she pushed Jack aside to exit, the excitement of an entire evening with the lanky stud preventing the slightest thought of actually crossing the threshold.

"Forgetting your books, aren't you?"

"They're overdue and in your name, so you pay the fine."

"How about a late candle lit dinner for two?"

"Ewh! That just might do it. What do you suggest?"

"How about a Palmer burger with everything and a bag of grease dripping fries?"

"You sure know the way to a woman's heart. Hold the ptomaine?"

"Only for you."

While Jack double-timed it to the tavern across the street, a car door silently opened, the telltale interior light purposefully disconnected. Dressed in a dark cheap suit and crocheted tie reminiscent of an elementary school uniform, the oversized occupant moved with surprising speed, catching the building door before it automatically closed. Jimmying the ill fitted deadbolt of apartment 1-C with a credit card, the intruder panicked as the door swung completely open, slamming against the wall.

"Back already, Big Boy?" Sarah called from the bathroom with the water running. "I'm just going to take a quick bath."

No response as the intruder stood completely still.

"I know you're a shower man, so don't give me that disgusting line about soaking in my own dirty water. I'm just making the best out of what you've got --- no pun intended. Would you care to join me?"

The studio remained oddly silent as the extra-large figure moved about in the glow of two candles.

"If that failed to get a rise out of you, again no pun intended, I'm really losing my touch," Sarah chuckled, confident that her man stood salivating outside the door.

A slight clank echoed through the cramped room as the intruder ripped the eighteen-inch antiquated gas stove from its connection, allowing one of the two cast iron burner grates to fall to the floor.

The linoleum thud puzzled Sarah for a moment. "Oh, I get it. You're setting a romantic table."

The door closed quietly, the credit card easing the bolt back into locked position.

"The strong silent type really does turn me on. I like my men dumb and compliant. My goodness, could that have been another pun? I'm so naughty," the seductress admitted, slipping her lithe frame into the antique lion's claw cast iron tub. Her length required her to bend her knees above water level to fit. "I've got more bubbles than I can handle. Any volunteers to pop a few?"

The silence rapidly leaning to a lack of attention. "I'm going to slip under water and hold my breath until you give me the right answer."

Jack juggled the soda cans, burgers and keys. "What's that, Babe?"

The key finally inserted, J.Z. dropped a pop can, watching it roll down the hall. As the door opened on its own inertia, Jack scurried after the Dr. Pepper. The bolt skidded across the strike plate, the insignificant spark igniting the free flow of gas. The explosion ripped through the apartment, obliterating all interior and exterior walls. Jack slammed sideways into the wall across the hall, penetrating both panels of sheetrock and bouncing into the back of his neighbor's living room couch.

Sarah felt the vibration of an earthquake and watched from underwater as the ceiling crashed down onto the tub. The force of the blast accelerated through the water, rupturing both her eardrums. The violent ringing in her ears caused her to scream, emitting a rash of almost comical bubbles. As she inhaled, her lungs sucked in volumes of water. Gripping the sides of the tub, Sarah propped herself up, bursting through the layer of drywall, coughing and gagging.

Jack shook off the plaster remnants and smacked the side of his head with his palm to stop the incessant ringing.

"Sarah!" Jack screamed, darting into his gutted apartment, now reminiscent of a war zone. "Sarah!"

Blinded by the haze, Jack dropped to his knees rummaging through every inch of the debris. Reaching in the corner by the bed, Jack quickly withdrew his hand as the smoldering mattress scorched his arm. Moving farther into the room, J.Z. continually called out, "Sarah! Sarah! Oh, please God, let her answer."

A loud screech rang out, "Help me! Somebody, anybody, please help me!"

Jack clawed his way to what used to be the bathroom, "Babe? Are you here? Sarah?"

"Anybody there?" The panicked voice continued to call out.

"Is that you, Sarah? Oh God, please let her be okay," Jack beseeched, smearing tear moistened dust across his cheeks with a backhand move to wipe his face.

"Someone please help me!" The panicked woman's voice rang out.

Jack rose to his feet as the air cleared, stumbling over the rubble, desperately scrambling in the dim lit moonlight emanating through the gaping hole once an exterior wall. In the midst of the debris floating in the indestructible lion clawed tub, bobbed a strange figure; an albino head screaming as though a scratched forty-five record stuck on the refrain, "Anybody there? Someone please help me!"

Jack cupped her white plastered cheeks, "Oh Baby, are you okay?"

"What? Jack is that you? Who's there? Would you answer me please?"

"Babe, it's me, Jack."

What? Did you say something?"

Jack reached down in the polluted mess and grabbed Sarah under the arms, assisting her from the tub. Rummaging through the debris, he located a towel and wrapped it around her white powder caked torso. He lifted her ample frame, carrying her outside to the narrow strip of front lawn. Blood trickled from her nose and ears.

"Would someone get a blanket, please?"

"What did you say?" Sarah screeched in ear splitting tones.

"It's okay, Babe," Jack consoled, hugging Sarah's head in his lap.

"I can't understand you. All I hear is this terrible ringing," Sarah yelled.

"Shush," J.Z. whispered, stroking her hair.

"What happened?" Sarah wailed.

"That's not important now."

"Guess you were right about taking baths," Sarah yelled with a frightened smile.

"You really did wind up sitting in your own dirty water," Jack whispering the altered punch line they discussed on so many previous occasions, knowing she couldn't hear, but understood he would revert to humor.

The EMS technicians transferred Sarah onto a stretcher and into the ambulance.

Jack surveyed the damage. "Damn," was all he could think to say when he came so close to losing the only person he ever loved. As the emergency vehicle tripped its siren and sped off, humor faded into reality as the pillar of strength crumpled, pounding his fists on his thighs as his knees hit the ground, gasping to catch a breath in between heaving sobs.

CHAPTER

74

Mᴀᴍᴏᴜᴅ ʟɪꜰᴛᴇᴅ ʜɪꜱ ʜᴇᴇʟꜱ off the sticky tiled floor, forcing his soft leather executive chair to lean back while he mulled over possible outlines for a story. "Too many damn holes," he whispered aloud as he began a gentle rock with his tiptoes. "We need confirmation of the code by a cop and a body. Damn, talk about impossible. Mink's theory is nuts and Michaels is absolutely certifiable. What the hell am I doing hanging with these honkies?"

The 4x4 rolled through the alley without headlights, stopping at the rear of the *Southern Edge* offices. A hooded figure approached the back door, forcing entry with one swift jerk of a pry bar.

"Gwenda leave that damn cat here again?" Mamoud ranted at the muffled crack emanating from the file room. A squeaky hinge mistaken for a purr prompted Mamoud to track down the pesky varmint before he sprayed the entire offices out of boredom over the weekend. "That's it! God knows I hate memos, but effective immediately, no more pets at work," Mamoud ordered while engaging the pursuit. Neglecting to turn on lights, other than his reading lamp, the irritated sleuth stumbled through the narrow row of desks, halting at the storage/kitchenette doorway, grabbing onto the frame and poking his head in.

"Surprise!" The melodic tone from the darkened room sang out as a fist crashed into the confused reporter's face, exploding his nose and propelling him backward over a desk. "Ain't you an animal lover, shit face?" The voice teased, leaning over the disabled reporter, grabbing him by the shirt with two powerful hands, interrupting Mamoud's efforts to shake his head and clear his thoughts. "With that Brillo head, it's a wonder you don't get mistaken for one of them Chia pets," the assailant chided, pounding Mamoud's head back to the floor, cracking the back of his skull.

"Who are you?" Mamoud mumbled in a daze.

"I'm the boogey man your Momma told you about as a kid," the attacker responded, as he stood up and repeatedly stomped his boot directly into the side of Mamoud's head.

"What do you want?" Mamoud tried to ask, floating in and out of consciousness.

"I want to learn to dance, so I'm starting with the Motown stomp. How am I doing so far?"

"Please!" Mamoud whispered in labored breaths, "You can take whatever you want."

"Now ain't you just the most accommodating son of a bitch alive? What say, you see if you can fly, eh boy?" The monster decided, hoisting Mamoud into the air.

Battling to maintain consciousness, Mamoud's arms flailed. His knuckles wrapped on a desktop as he felt his body rise higher. The back of his hand bumped across a familiar shape. The tortured newsman concentrated all his energy, flipping his hand over to snag the object. Gripping the instrument in his numbed left hand as his body continued its ascent, he let the appendage drop, sticking the plastic letter opener deep into the side of the assailant's neck.

"Augh! You lousy bastard," the intruder screamed, tossing Mamoud ten feet across the room, landing on his own desktop, smashing his lamp and out basket, then flopping onto the floor.

Waddling to the rear door, the assailant picked up a two-gallon gas can and returned, generously slopping the accelerant throughout the building.

"I likes mine extra crispy," the arsonist chuckled as he flicked the match and closed the door behind him.

Mamoud lay motionless as a strange whoosh whipped through the office. The intense heat from the raging inferno singed his bare feet, shocking him to consciousness.

"Oh God!" Mamoud sighed, fire surrounding him on all sides. The blood from his head wound fried on the side of his face and scorched his light chocolate skin. The maimed newsman coughed and gagged from the thick smoke and toxic fumes, while he struggled to stand. "One last barbeque," Mamoud quipped, remembering Sarah's puns with fondness. *"It's funny what you recall before the end,"* he thought.

CHAPTER

75

Mesmerized by the flashing lights of the ambulance as it weaved around haphazardly parked emergency vehicles along Palmer, the gravity of his predicament finally dawned on him, jolting him back to reality.

"Mamoud!" Jack screamed as he turned and bolted around the corner onto southbound Cass in a full sprint through the center of campus, reminiscent of a marathon runner in sight of the finish line. Straining to maintain his furious pace over the nine-block dash, Michaels eked out every ounce of additional energy as he noticed smoke rise from the general area of Mamoud's office. *"God, give me the strength to make it,"* Jack prayed. Two short blocks away, flames shot through the roof. Jack screeched to a halt, crouching over, resting his palms on his knees while he heaved to catch his breath. "No!" He cried, "This can't be happening. What have I done?"

As he looked up, the front window exploded, expelling what appeared to be the bizarre sight of a man flying through the air with his head stuck in a piece of furniture.

"Mamoud, please tell me you decided to take off early," Jack whimpered in desperation, while approaching the carnage. Searching through the debris, Jack kicked aside a scorched Malcolm X poster leaning against a battered copy machine, exposing a bloodied torso.

"Help me, please," Mamoud whispered as he strained to remain conscious. "Is anyone here? Please, I need help."

"Well, I never thought I'd see the day when Mamoud Shaloub asked anyone for help, much less me," Jack kidded, fighting back the nausea at the gruesome sight. "What the heck happened?"

"Some wild ass honky tried to shake and bake me."

"Can you identify him?"

"Looked like a big fist."

"You just take it easy. Help should be here shortly."

"Jack, watch yourself man. This guy was just plain mean. He enjoyed every punch. It must be the dude who was following us."

"But I thought we agreed they were cops?"

"For a white boy, you dumb as dirt," Mamoud sniffled.

"Anything I can do?"

"Save the chair, Jack," Mamoud whispered just before he passed out.

"What the hell does that mean? I've heard of saving whales, accounts, the environment, but who the heck ever heard of saving a chair?" Michaels questioned, gently placing his friend's head on his rolled-up jacket.

CHAPTER

76

SURROUNDED BY A GAGGLE of med techs feverishly experimenting with every available instrument from a metal case the size of a small ocean cargo container, Jack nervously checked his dust encrusted Fossil watch. Irritated at the forty minutes spent stabilizing the patient with the hospital a comfortable six blocks away, Michaels finally unloaded, "Guys, excuse me, but he's gonna be dead if you don't get a move on."

The largest of the four medics stood up and confronted the interfering gawker. "Sir, you'll have to step back."

"I don't think so. Get him in the ambulance now, or you'll be talking to my lawyer in the morning."

The technicians exchanged glances and finally worked in one fluid motion, transferring Mamoud onto a stretcher and into the wagon, with J.Z. right behind. "Sir, you'll have to get out."

Regretting his reluctance to strong arm the attendant and jump into the ambulance transporting Sarah, Jack vowed to accompany Mamoud, no matter what it took. "I don't think so. He's my brother." Taking advantage of their confused state, Jack added, "We're twins."

Although difficult over the din of blaring sirens, Jack attempted to comfort his cohort.

Shivering from the burns, Mamoud managed to eek out, "Got him real good in the neck. Think he'll need medical treatment."

"Just save your strength. We'll talk later."

Sitting on a steel bench next to the med-tech, Jack unexpectedly slid toward the double rear doors as the driver flicked on the flashing lights and siren, then mashed on the accelerator, heading south on Cass Avenue. Zigzagging around cars reluctant to move aside, the driver seemed to use the solid yellow double centerline more as a guide than a restriction. Slowing dramatically as they approached the red light at West Warren Avenue, the paramedic riding shot gun yelled, "Clear!" Cautiously crossing the four westbound lanes, then the boulevard strip, the driver rapidly increased speed while turning left onto W. Warren. Straddling the two northernmost lanes as vehicles ahead peeled to the southernmost curb, the driver slowed to repeat his careful advance at Woodward Avenue, creeping across the nine-lane wide thoroughfare.

"Clear!" The passenger called out, as the ambulance shot ahead another half-mile to turn right onto southbound St. Antoine Street. Jack braced his feet on the floor, trying to shift his weight each time the emergency vehicle lurched or turned, silently praying for a quick arrival.

As they pulled into the crowded hospital lot, an armed guard directed them to stop twenty-feet short of the entry doors. A trauma team arrived within seconds to assist the paramedics unloading the gurney.

Jack bent forward to take a deep breath.

"You okay?" A paramedic inquired.

"Just peachy," Jack replied. "Just haven't been on a wild mouse ride since the fourth grade."

"I know what you mean. Most of us can't handle the ride in back. We do rock, paper, scissors before each shift to see who gets the pleasure." Extending a hand, "Here, let's get you out of there. Fresh air will clear your head in no time."

"Thanks."

"Hope your friend is alright."

"Yeah, me too."

As the attendants unloaded the gurney and entered the mad house of an emergency room, yelling for assistance, Jack stepped back, bumping into one of the numerous stretchers lined against the wall. Turning to excuse himself, he reared back in astonishment at the unconscious patient, "Detective Goodson?"

77

Fumbling with a jumble of thoughts, Jack just stood and stared at the site before him: a two-inch wide leather strap cinched snugly across Goodson's chest; his left hand tightly wrapped with what appeared to be a white bath towel, secured in place with one-inch wide surgical tape; ankles bound with lamb skin lined leather cuffs attached to the stretcher's metal frame; a "T" type metal hanger supporting a clear drip IV attached to the right upper arm, next to a pint of blood flowing down into the left arm; and, an oxygen mask covering his nose and mouth. Just as Jack turned to get someone's attention, an attendant appeared. He checked the chart tucked between the pencil thin mattress and the side rail, then snapped off the litter foot brake.

"Excuse me! Where are you taking him?" Jack inquired.

"He's scheduled for emergency surgery."

"What's wrong with him?"

"Can't say. You'll have to talk to his doctor."

Jack just shook his head and thought, *Well, the gangs all here.*

CHAPTER

78

MICHAELS PULLED ASIDE THE sliding curtain to find the emergency room cubicle empty. Catching the first available practitioner, Jack inquired, "My friend that was in here, can you tell me where they took him?"

"That was the burn victim, right?"

"Yes."

"Took him to radiology for some head x-rays, then he's off to the burn unit."

"How do I get there?"

"I'm not sure they would allow you in. You'd have to gown up since those patients are so prone to infection, but you can always give it a try. Just go straight across the building, down that hall, to the lobby. They'll give you the easiest way."

Peering down a dull beige endless corridor, Jack hiked past a myriad of identical doorways, except for the cheap dark brown plastic signs with gold stick-on lettering identifying nephrology, urology, endocrinology, rheumatology, immunology, pulmonology, and hematology. Jack added an extra bounce to his step passing by the door marked nuclear medicine. A stainless-steel wall-mounted water fountain drew his attention. As he simultaneously bent his head down and reached to grip the handle, he paused. Mulling over his circumstance, Jack decided drinking from a hospital dispenser was a risk, much less one installed immediately adjacent to the nuclear medicine department.

Continuing his trek, he felt a sense of relief when the bland crème colored asbestos floor squares morphed into beautiful sandstone tiles, rimmed with ten-inch-wide limestone slabs. The claustrophobic hallway ceiling transformed into a four-story high atrium with enough retail shops to rival a high-end mall. A steel framed multi-colored map with a red arrow depicting "YOU ARE HERE" stood in the center. Jack surmised the lobby help desk to be no more than two-hundred feet to his left, adjacent to the gift shop.

As he approached, a crinkled voice, accompanied with a wide smile, called out, "How can I assist you, young man?"

"I just came from the emergency room…"

The elderly candy striper interrupted, "Looking back on it, I bet you wished you would have packed a lunch."

Jack hesitated for a moment, then joined her in a chuckle. "You got that right." Clearing his throat, Jack continued his inquiry, "How do I get to the burn unit?"

"Good golly, that's a tough one. Let me check here just a minute," as she shuffled several pages around. "And you thought getting here from the ER was difficult." The look on Jack's face prompted, "You have to understand, twenty years ago, there was Detroit Receiving Hospital, Children's Hospital, Harper Hospital and Hutzel Women's Hospital, all within walking distance. When they merged, this is the confusing end result."

"Don't tell me, I can't get there from here," Jack smiled.

"Oh, you can, dear, but the odds are you'll get lost along the way." Glancing up at Jack, she continued, "But you look young and strong, so there's a good chance you'll survive." Reaching for a piece of note paper, the information clerk rattled off, "Go down the hallway to your left to the second set of elevators on your right. Make sure it's the second set, not the first. The first set takes you to the old Harper Hospital complex, and you don't want to end up there. The second set has one marked freight. Press B-2 and that takes you to the tunnels. Once you get off, you'll see several different colored lines painted on the floor. Follow the dark red line, not the burnt orange. Take the red line past all the boilers, janitor quarters and the loading dock. Watch out for the hi-lo drivers; they tend to be a little crazy."

"Pretty much a universal opinion," Jack interjected, nodding his head.

Peering over the top of her wire-rimmed glasses, the candy striper continued, "After a couple more minutes, you should see a door marked "Maintenance" on your right. Immediately adjacent to that is one elevator marked South Tower. Take that to the mezzanine floor. There should be a manned desk there. They can direct you to his room."

Handing the slip of paper to Jack, she offered, "Good luck".

Jack perused the notes, then responded, "Piece of cake. Thanks for all your help."

As Jack turned away, the candy striper called out, "Sir!"

Michaels stopped and turned, "Yes ma'am."

"Do you mind leaving your next of kin info in case we lose you?" The woman chuckled.

CHAPTER

79

EㅌxITING THE BASEMENT LIFT, Jack instinctively ducked as the ceiling height shrunk to approximately six-feet. The wall to his left supported seven horizontally mounted eight-inch diameter asbestos wrapped steam ducts, painted with the identical institutional off-white as the other major hallways. The natural concrete floor sported a four-colored rainbow of six-inch wide stripes, with red immediately adjacent to the wall. A claustrophobic sensation washed over him as he felt his pulse increase, pushing out excess perspiration. Twenty-feet from the elevator door, Jack followed the red stripe in a ninety-degree bend. Within two-feet of the turn, Jack ducked, narrowly avoiding a nose-high cast iron valve, the size of a car steering wheel, sticking out an additional four-inches beyond the pipes. Looking back, Jack wondered, *"Jeez, talk about dangerous. I wonder how many visitors wound up in the emergency room after smacking that bad boy."*

Half-way into the football field long corridor, Jack heard a faint scream. Glancing around, *"Hmph! Nothing around here. Must be the wind whistling through the pipes."*

Within ten seconds, he caught another high-pitched shriek. Stopping, he looked about, when a third scream rang out. *"Seems to be coming from up ahead somewhere,"* Jack thought. Cautiously continuing his trek another thirty-feet, Jack found himself immediately adjacent to a solid metal door on his left marked, "Boiler Room," when another screech rang out. A quick brisk yank propelled the door handle against the concrete wall, as Jack hustled into the room. Twelve-feet ahead, Max Torpo twisted a waist-high large red valve. Five-feet in front of the discharge tube, Rodeo squatted. Bent at the waist with his right hand set on his kneecap and his left hand supporting his fourteen-inch package. His pants and underwear were down around his ankles. As the pent-up steam escaped, it struck Rodeo's bare bum, sizzling as it engulfed the chalk-white flesh.

"Arrrrrrgh!" Rodeo yelled, as he let his member drop and grabbed his pants with both hands, jumping out of the path of the scorching vapor.

Twisting the valve closed, Max chuckled as he yelled out, "Four seconds. That's your best time yet!"

"What are you guys doing here?" Jack yelled over the clamor.

"Jack, you're okay?" Max cried out, as he ran over to hug his buddy.

Successfully re-hitching his pants, Rodeo bolted toward Jack.

"No, no. That's close enough!" Jack exclaimed, extending his arm with a flat open palm. "What are you guys doing here?"

Max cleared his throat. "Well, we heard about what happened, so we came to make sure you was alright."

"So, you naturally wound up in the hospital boiler room?"

"Well now, see that's Jimmy's fault," Rodeo proffered. "He went off to make sure Sarah was okay."

"That still doesn't explain why you're in the boiler room trying to scald your buns."

Staring at the concrete floor and shuffling his feet, Max explained, "We got sidetracked." With his head still tucked down, Max arched his brows, "We was suppose to find you. The lady at the desk didn't have a clue where you could be, so we came looking for you."

Rodeo chimed in, "See there, it all worked out. But what I can't figure out, is how y'all knew we'd be here?"

Jack just shook his head and ignored Rodeo. Glancing at his watch, "Max, visiting hours are just about over. I'm gonna try and find Sarah's room. You guys do me a favor and head up to the burn unit and look up a patient named Mamoud Shaloub. Here are the directions they gave me."

"Anything for our College Boy," Max offered. "We just need a few minutes for me to try and beat Rodeo's time," as the hi-lo driver dropped trou and squatted in front of the discharge pipe. "Let her rip, Rodeo!"

CHAPTER

80

His mind fogged from anesthesia, Eric strained for a clear view of the face peering down at him.

"I'm Doctor Nichols, your vascular surgeon, Mr. Goodson."

"Wha..."

"You're still feeling the effects of the gas. It'll take a few more hours for you to see and think clearly."

I can't..."

"Try to relax. You really did a number on your wrist. Usually, people prefer a quick clean cut. Makes our job that much easier. You, on the other hand, look like you used a chain saw. Had to call in a neurosurgeon to make sure you didn't permanently damage your ulnar nerve."

The doctor requested Eric wiggle his fingers on his left hand, then pricked each finger with a pin.

"Everything looks good so far. Tomorrow we'll transfer you to the psych ward." Glancing at the chart, "Says here you're a police officer. Real unusual for you to have injured yourself this way. Usually cops eat their gun. You must have missed that lecture in the academy, eh?"

Eric just stared.

"My bad. Just an attempt at humor."

Eric tried to raise his right arm.

"No can do, Mr. Goodson. We've got to keep you restrained until you've had one or two sessions with the psychiatrist. Don't want you screwing up all our good work, now do we?"

CHAPTER

81

THE WATER SPOTTED CEILING tile surrounding the bright white light tipped off the ruse. The leather wrist straps and foot restraints confirmed the failure.

"Hello! Is anybody here?" Eric called out. The silence he often found comforting now agitated him. "Can someone please answer me?"

The lack of response triggered an angry attempt to break the shackles. As the distraught patient torqued and twisted, the door swung open. A black face mounted atop a heavily starched white uniform filled the doorway. Waddling toward the bed, the nurse scolded, "Dat will only tear dem stitches, young man. It took a vascular surgeon four hours to straighten out da mess you made."

"You should have a call button on this bed," Eric admonished.

"You mean one dem clicker things on the end of a thick plastic-coated cord?"

"Yeah. I've been yelling for ten minutes before you came in."

"What a great idea! I'll have to let my supervisor know. We get a twenty-five-dollar bonus for each idea they use. Don't expect I'm gonna split that with y'all. Can't believe no one, in all these years, never thought of that."

Eric just laid there, staring, mouth agape.

"You think, maybe they don't want you wrappin' that cord around your skinny assed neck? Den you and me wouldn't be wastin' our time chitchattin', 'cause you'd be dangling from the side da bed, dead."

"Who are you?"

"I'm Nurse Ratched."

Struck by the familiarity of the name, Eric hesitantly inquired, "Do I know you?"

"You been here before?"

"I don't think so."

"You don't think so? Wouldn't you know? Just a few seconds ago, you was yammerin' on, demonstratin' what a real thinkin' man you was. Now, youse just can't recollect being here before?"

"Where is here?"

"Well, if you don't know, it ain't my place to tell y'all."

"Please, where am I?" Goodson pleaded, his exaggerated exhale evidence of giving up the struggle.

"Well, I'll bet you're sure dis ain't heaven, 'cause if all the angels looked like me, I wouldn't want to be here either."

"What do you call this place?"

"About ten yards north of Hell."

"Can you quit with the games, please? I'm really not in the mood."

"You're in Detroit Receiving Hospital psych ward. All things considered, you'd probably be better off in Hell, but then again, I'm only a highly trained professional."

"Are you nuts?"

"Hey, look around. I'm not the one tied down," the nurse smirked. "Not the sharpest pencil in the box, are ya?"

"Are insults part of the therapy?"

"No, but motivatin' your skinny ass sure is. How'm I doing so far? Bet you've talked to me more than anyone else in months."

"Don't plan on making this a career," Eric huffed, confused at the strange, but effective manner.

As Nurse Ratched opened the door, she paused, then turned to face Goodson. "Don't forgets to pee."

"What's that?"

"You don't know what peeing is? Y'all really is crazy," Ratched chuckled.

"Of course, I know what it is. I just didn't understand what you meant."

"If you can't pee, they's gonna come in here and turn you into one 'dem geldings."

As the door closed behind her, Eric swore he heard her laughing all the way down the hall.

CHAPTER

82

JACK EXITED THE TUNNELS at the sign for Harper Hospital and took the elevator up to the fifth floor. Sarah's room was easy to spot; it's not often you see an old man wearing roller blades and a number 9 Red Wing's jersey, while caressing a hockey stick, sitting outside a hospital room.

Pepatino jumped up when Jack approached. "College Boy!" He called out, while extending his arms for a hug. "You're still in one piece?"

"Pretty much. Got a terrible headache and my ears are ringing the *Vatican Rag*, but otherwise I'm okay."

"You actually made it through that maze of tunnels? Even most rats would have given up running around down there," Jimmy laughed.

"How's Sarah?"

"The doc says she'll ultimately be okay. She has a concussion and total hearing loss. The guess is the hearing loss is not permanent, but could last up to three weeks."

Changing his tone, Pepatino inquired, "You didn't happen to…"

Jack cut him off, "Ran into Darrell and Darrell in the boiler room, backing their bare asses up to a steam spigot."

Jimmy chuckled, turned beet red and allowed the spittle to fly, "You got to admit, those boys always keep you on your toes." Ending the comment with a fake jab to Jack's shoulder.

"Jimmy, those boys are a danger to themselves and anyone around them. They're just fucking nuts."

"Can't argue that!" Pepatino responded, shaking his head. "God, I love those guys. It's like teaching my own little special ed class. But when the shit hits the fan, they'll be right there fighting to their last breath. Hell, Max considers you the little brother he never had."

As Jack raised his arm to push open the door, Jimmy stopped him with a hand on the shoulder. "Jack, before you go in there, keep in mind all the normal things she'll be struggling with. My Mom was deaf. The silence most of us consider calming and take for granted, the hearing impaired find frustrating and even, frightening. The everyday sounds of a telephone, doorbell, oven timer, clothes dryer, or, god forbid, a smoke alarm, require constant vigilance, monitoring a substitute flashing light for a blazing siren. I guess what I'm trying to say is, take it easy. There are adjustments both of you will have to make, at least for a while."

"Thanks Jimmy. I'll keep that in mind."

"I know you will, kid. You're one of the good ones."

CHAPTER

83

SARAH LAY WITH HER hospital bed cranked up full tilt and her eyes closed, wondering if her lover could adjust. Unlike the lechers who paw you with their leering glare, Jack exuded the confidence that allowed him to be a considerate lover: gentle when required; firm to dominating when requested; always allowing her to finish whether naturally or mechanically.

Jack approached, gently touching his soul mate on the shoulder and whispering, "Hey there, gorgeous!" Sarah's body jumped in one massive convulsion. Startled, J.Z. lurched back, visibly shaken. "You okay?"

A tear trickled down her cheek. "I can't hear a thing you're saying," she yelled, believing her remark within normal conversational tones.

"I'm so sorry for what happened."

"What did you say?"

Jack turned and pulled the visitors chair next to the bed, then reached out for Sarah's hand. He bent forward and stroked her hair. They sat in silence for the better part of an hour.

Sarah finally broke the vigil. "Darling, I have something I've got to tell you." As Jack increased his stroke across her forehead, attempting to hush the impending confession, she pushed his forearm away. "Listen to me. I'm not who you think I am."

"Shhhh!"

Failing to understand, but realizing she was interrupted, Sarah leaned forward, grabbing Jack by the shirt. "Please let me finish. I want you to hear this from me. If this is going to work between us, we can't have secrets. I've kept one that has been bothering me since we became serious."

"You've got to calm down Babe. You've been through a terrible trauma."

Shaking her head in frustration, she yelled, "I'm fine. I just can't hear. Now shut up and listen. I know you've wondered how I can afford the Corvette, a fancy house and the designer clothes substitute teaching kindergarten a day or two a week." Jack arched his brow, curious where this was leading. "No, I don't have family money."

"You're a cat burglar. I knew it the first time you showed me your unusual talent for touching your nose with the tip of your tongue. Only a true feline could pull off that stunt."

Sarah waited till his lips stopped moving, but realized the nature of his remark when he chortled. "*You could always depend on Jack to laugh at his own joke.*" "I'm not ashamed of what I do. I just never thought it was anybody's business, but my own." Sarah took a deep breath. "I'm an exotic dancer." Jack's eyes bugged out like Barney Google and his head lurched back. She now had his undivided attention. "That's right, I'm a stripper. I dance three to four nights a week at the Booby Trap Lounge." Although his mouth hung open, the normally gregarious student found himself at a loss for words. "I do lap dances, but nothing more. During an average shift, I make four to five-hundred dollars tax free; on a night where the high rollers come in, I clear a thousand dollars." Sarah paused, clearing her throat and released a deep sigh. Since I got hurt, I realized how much I want you. If you feel the same way, you deserve to know the truth."

The room fell silent for Jack. Stunned, his blank stare told Sarah she had made a serious error. She momentarily closed her eyes, providing the man she loved a graceful exit.

CHAPTER

84

Exhausted by the exchange with Nurse Ratched, Eric repeated her name several times, finally drifting off into a deep sleep.

"Mr. Goodson," a quiet melodic voice asked. "Mr. Goodson, we need you to wake up," the nurse accompanied the request with a slight shrug of the shoulder. "Come on now, I know you can hear me." The attendant reached down for the hand crank. Raising Eric to just shy of a sitting position, the practitioner again inquired, "Mr. Goodson, wake up." Eric struggled to open his eyes. She continued, "Time to take your medications," as she lifted the tiny paper cup with four different colored pills to his lips. "Open up." She followed up with a larger cone-shaped cup full of water pulled from the wall-mounted dispenser. "Take a good-sized gulp. It's important you drink plenty of fluids to flush out the anesthesia. Have you urinated since arriving in your room?"

"No Ma'am, but you could bet your life savings I'm going to."

"My, aren't we the eager one. Well then, we'll just have to get you up, won't we?"

"I really don't feel the urge to go, but it would be nice to get these cuffs off me."

"Before I do that, you've got to promise me you won't try anything stupid."

"Yes, Ma'am."

"Yes, you will, or, yes, you won't," she smiled. "No matter. By the time we get back from the restroom, your medications will have kicked in."

After returning to bed, Eric commented, "Thank you for all your help. You certainly have the bedside manner one expects from a nurse."

"Why thank you, Mr. Goodson. That's so nice to hear."

"Yeah, not like the first nurse."

"The first nurse?" She questioned, while perusing the chart. "I'm the only one who's been in here."

"No, you're not."

The nurse just arched her brow.

"There was a heavy set, bowlegged black woman in here. She sure could use a refresher course on dealing with vulnerable patients. Had me convinced if I didn't pee, they would castrate me."

"Oh my, I see you've met Crazy Agnes. She's actually been a patient here for ages. Harmless, really. No one on the staff can figure out how she gets ahold of uniforms, especially ones that fit a woman of her size. She times her visits around shift changes. Actually, she has saved the life of more than one patient, as I hear it." The nurse's face turned beet red and a mild snicker escaped, "We don't do castrations. At the worst, we'd run a catheter up to the bladder. Most men find that possibility more than enough motivation."

CHAPTER

85

Drawing the occasional out of towner duped by the royal moniker visible from I-94, the Imperial Motor Lodge primarily catered to an hourly rental clientele. Owned for years by a socially elite investment group shrouded in a maze of shell corporations, the vibrant neighborhood flesh trade insured an enviable cash flow that outweighed the potential embarrassment of exposure as slumlords. Michaels reluctantly selected the dive for its proximity to campus.

Tap dancing around the trash-strewn parking lot to the office required the adept training and agility of an Olympic gymnast. Prescreened on his relatively clean-cut Caucasian appearance, the clerk buzzed Jack in without benefit of pressing the bell. The grit encrusted postage-stamp sized lobby reminded Michaels of the *Southern Edge* headquarters, sans the security: two wall mounted cameras; three-inch thick bullet proof glass; an intercom system; triple horned ceiling sirens; and, enough bright yellow warning stickers to paper the entire room; all in all, reminiscent of your typical self-serve Mobile station.

Although the manager sat less than three feet away, Jack uncomfortably leaned into the crud coated speaker, estimating a distance of an inch or two still within CDC safety recommendations. "I'm gonna need a room for a couple of weeks." The goofy smile on the clerk's bronze skinned face prompted Jack to go on the defensive. "It's not like that! I'm a student at Wayne State."

"Many of your colleagues frequent our establishment as well. They come and go. But not one of them stay such a long time," the Indian chortled, bowing his head with his hands in a prayer mode.

"Just give me a room where you're certain the stains are dry."

86

THE MILNER HOTEL OFFERED permanent residence to an eclectic mix of misfits trapped in a purgatory of failed relationships, economic stasis, moral degradation, or physical frailties. Once a five-star bastion of upper crust urban living, the pentagram of luxury chiseled off tips quicker than a diamond cutter on amphetamines, as the white flight to the suburbs accelerated through the seventies.

The two-tone green and tan Suburban coasted to the curb in front of the decaying ten-story brick and stone edifice. As the driver exited, his attention quickly diverted to safely negotiating the potholes from missing Pewabic tiles in the front walkway that once epitomized the excesses of a formerly vibrant downtown.

"I'm here for the game," Roy announced as he approached the bellhop, slouched on a folding metal chair next to the tarnished brass door.

"412," the doorman replied, dragging his ragged uniform sleeve under his nose, exposing a flying dragon tattoo on his backhand.

"Thanks. Don't bother getting up," Roy remarked.

"Up yours," the nonchalant retort.

The slightest contact with Harrold Mayer considered revolting, Roy instantly dismissed his disdain upon the extension of an invitation to a monthly poker game. The thought of passing up an opportunity to fillet a bunch of amateurs never entered Blue's mind. He ignored the chugging elevator as he viewed his distorted image in the opposite mirrored wall partially obscured by the quick-silver backing protruding through the glass. The dim lit hallway disguised the once elegant thread bare woolen tapestry. Roy stepped through the heavily painted ornate wooden door frame into a room that would look great in an out of focus photo. A quick survey of his opponents confirmed his theory.

"Mr. Blue, I presume. Glad you could make it. If you're packing, throw it over there on the table; otherwise take a seat," Dolan instructed.

"I'm traveling light tonight."

"We run a friendly game. Anyone gets their ass in a snit, we toss him. We're here to enjoy ourselves and get away from our old ladies for a weekend. I'm Dolan. The piss ant dealing is Marzoli, slippery just like the oil. And the guy here with the pile in front of him is O'Hara."

Blue acknowledged each with a slight nod. "The name's Roy. I appreciate the invite. House rules?"

"Stakes are $50/$100; minimum two grand buy in; grays are fifty and the blacks are a hundred; only chips on the table play; and, everyone seated kicks in twenty bucks at the top of the hour to cover the cost of drinks and eats. Questions?"

"What's your poison?"

"Seven card stud," Marzoli replied, flipping the cards with the apparent ease of a Vegas dealer to a novice, but floating the stack long enough for a seasoned veteran like Roy to read each hand while dealt. "Jacks or better to open, progressive; one-hundred-dollar house limit."

Roy executed a slight nod of his head. Within three hands, he pegged the tell on each player, significantly increasing his odds that he conservatively estimated at seven out of ten hands with reasonably decent cards.

"Four, possible straight for the Commish," Marzoli narrated.

Roy snickered privately, *"Straight my ass. He's an odds-on favorite for the flush."*

"Six to His Honor; makes him King of the Hill with his pair."

"Jesus, you dolt, the Judge can't wait to push his entire stack on the table and you can't figure he locked in trips already?"

"Oh, an eight to our guest. No help. So sorry."

"Yeah, you go ahead and feel for me as much as you can, schmuck. Pay no attention to my Queen-Jack in the hole and a ten face up."

"And the dealer takes a five. Dammit."

Dolan rapped his knuckles on the table, "Check to the pair." Leaning back and craning his neck toward the wet bar, the Commissioner called out, "Can I get another bourbon over here? I'm dry as the Mojave fucking Desert."

"Jeez Dolan, can you squeeze those cards any tighter," Roy chuckled to himself.

"Raise you a hundred," O'Hara placing the chips with authority, the plastic clink a warning to stay away from his pot.

"I'll see your hundred and raise you fifty," Roy stated matter-of-factly.

"You're pretty fucking cool for a guy who's got squat," the Judge commented, perplexed at Roy's nonchalance.

"It's only money," Blue responded without the slightest chink in his cool demeanor.

"That's a hundred fifty to me," Marzoli computed. "Guess I'll just have to…"

The alcohol flooded the tabletop as the elderly gent caught his foot on the Judge's chair leg, propelling the glass directly at the pot.

"Why you stupid son of a bitch," Dolan screamed, "You can't even carry a lousy glass over here without screwing up?"

"Sorry, sir. I didn't mean…"

"Yeah, yeah, yeah. And you people complain about being second class citizens."

"Don't let it ruin your fun. It was just an accident," Judge O'Hara offered. "It could happen to anybody."

Silently backing out of his chair, Roy slapped down his hand, hustled to the sink and grabbed a washrag and a platter to clear the mess. "Count the pot," Roy instructed as he wiped the table, then raked the sticky chips off and replaced them.

"Goddamned Canooks," Dolan muttered, "They're overrunning the country. We ought to deport the lot of them."

"*Man, is he over the edge, or what?*" Roy thought. "*This is too good to be true. Somebody pinch me.*" "The pot's square, gentlemen," Blue announced, taking the lead to diffuse an uncomfortable situation. "Marzoli, it's a hundred fifty to you."

"Guess you guys are just gonna have to put up with old Oil Can for one more round," Marzoli teased as he flipped the chips to center table.

"It's to you Commissioner," Blue remarked.

Dolan continued his mental tirade, occasionally slipping with a muffled slur, unable to concentrate on the game.

"Looks like the Commish folds," O'Hara remarked as Dolan continued to ramble.

"I'll tell you when I'm out. I don't need you assholes playing my hand for me. What I need is for somebody to get this stumble bum out of my sight for good so I can enjoy my weekend."

"Take it easy," Marzoli directed, gently pumping his palms.

Blue sat still, awaiting a response to the well-intentioned gesture.

Dolan's face reddened to imminent stroke level. "You come into my fucking house and tell me what to do?" The irate Commissioner bolted upright, crashing his chair backward to the floor, and slamming his cards on the table. "I can snuff your ass and no one here would care. I'm the fucking Police Commissioner, for Christ fucking sakes. You work for me! You speak when you're fucking spoken to and not a moment sooner. Do you understand me?"

"Don't you just love it when he gets like this?" Marzoli laughed, leaning over to Roy.

Blue held his breath, hoping for a lull.

"Are you through?" The Judge asked calmly. "Because if you are, I'd like to get back to my winning hand."

"What I want is for someone to get that asshole waiter out of my fucking sight. Is that too fucking much to ask?"

"He's the only guy we have. You want to be jumping up the whole damned weekend getting your own crap? I sure as hell don't," Marzoli concluded.

"Hey bud," O'Hara called, leaning back to the kitchenette. "Hit the road." As the nervous bellhop skirted by, the Judge held out a hundred-dollar bill. "Take this. It's the least we could do for you putting up with our crap." Glancing at Dolan, the Judge remarked, "So what are we gonna do now, Your Highness? You've managed to piss off just about everybody in this place over the last months. Any suggestions?"

"I've got a guy who might be interested," Roy offered cautiously.

"When you're ready for a break, call him over," Marzoli instructed.

"He can't be any fucking dumber than the Canadian," Dolan surmised.

Four hours into the game, Roy held steady, up a few hundred, down two or three. "*No sense sending them home early,*" Roy thought to himself. He loved the action too much. "*And besides, the Mrs. didn't expect him back until late Sunday night.*" The free flow of liquor guaranteed he could make his move at any time. "*Chumps,*" the pro concluded.

"Gentlemen, I need to take a break. I've got an errand to run. It will only take me a couple of hours. I should be back no later than midnight if all goes well," Blue announced, collecting his cash and stuffing it inside his jacket pocket.

CHAPTER

87

Aʜʙɪ ᴡᴀᴛᴄʜᴇᴅ ꜰʀᴏᴍ ᴀ distance as Harrold Mayer chatted it up with the occupants of the four-door black Chrysler Imperial that rolled into the rear of the warehouse. Appearing as though he assumed the position, the sociopath leaned against the sedan with his hands on the roof and feet spread, exposing his twenty-four-carat gold wristwatch. Ahbi found it difficult to concentrate on anything else and within seconds, the flashbacks: the overstuffed suit dancing in front of him with the rhythmic flash of gold while he floated aimlessly. "*My God, what does it mean? Am I really crazy,*" Ahbi cried.

Collecting his jumbled thoughts and returning to reality, he noticed the driver loading several cases of beer into the trunk and slamming the lid. Within a minute, Mayer pounded twice on the rear quarter panel as the vehicle slowly cruised out of the building.

Paralyzed in fear, a bone-chilling shiver coursed through Ahbi as he struggled with the mental commands necessary to move his legs, allowing him to slip further behind a protective pallet of beer, as Mayer walked by on the way back to his office. The trauma triggered another delusional episode, this time the cadenced glitter inflicted pain with each flash. "*Oh, sweet Jesus, please tell me what it all means,*" the janitor pleaded as he shuffled to the comfort of the locker room. Sitting on the edge of his cot, Ahbi dropped his face into his hands. *"Please let me remember. This can't be? I can't go on like this. Think! Think, damn it,"* he commanded, smacking his fist to his left temple, jarring a fleeting vision of a small child hoisted in the air. Startled, Ahbi stiffened his torso to an upright position as the apparition disappeared. *"Who was that?"* The confused janitor asked himself. *"Come back to me, please,"* Ahbi begged, but his mind remained blank.

CHAPTER

88

T HE THREE DETECTIVES PULLED up to the Milner Hotel, instructing their driver to haul the beer up to room 412.

"Everything go okay?" Marzoli inquired.

"Like a fine piece of ass sliding across silk sheets on payday," his henchman replied.

"Quit your cutesy act with me, asshole, or I'll string you up by your balls with piano wire. You got me."

"Yes sir. It all went down without a hitch, sir."

"That's better. Now get the fuck out of here."

"What did I miss?" Roy Blue asked as he sauntered through the door, with Ahbi in tow.

"Nothing. Every once in a while, you've got to give your employees an ass chewing and it happened to be their time." Marzoli glanced toward Ahbi. "Who's this?"

Roy Blue reached to move Ahbi around to his side, "Gentlemen, this here is our new bartender, Ahbi. He doesn't talk much, but he's a hard-working son-of-a-bitch. He's a friend of mine, so I expect he'll be treated with the same respect as you've treated me."

Abhi bowed his head, as Roy took his seat.

Roy arched an eyebrow, "Deal me in."

"What happened to your neck," O'Hara inquired.

"Nothing really," Roy answered, reflexively stroking his hand over the area.

"That's an awfully big fucking bandage for nothing," Dolan piped in.

"Just a sympathy ploy so you guys will let me win a hand now and then."

CHAPTER

89

Accompanied by an attendant, Eric was now allowed to line up for his medications at the nurse's station. Sticking his tongue out at the dispenser to show he swallowed the pills proved the high point of his day. Returned to his room after a dose of ten milligrams of Valium kept Eric depressed, but he didn't care. Curled up in a fetal position, he entertained himself by quietly singing the same tune for hours; avoiding the crying jags, emptiness and dark thoughts, but simply masking symptoms for a four hour stretch.

A slight knock at his door presaged the nurse sticking her head in, announcing, "Mr. Goodson, you have a visitor."

The interruption fractured his repetitive song, but failed to elicit a response.

"Mr. Goodson, time to make yourself presentable. You have a visitor."

"Go away!"

"That's not going to happen. The gentleman here to see you says he's your attorney."

Eric searched his fogged memory. "Uncle Lenny?"

"That's right. And he told me to tell you, if you refuse to see him, he'll sue."

Ignoring the nurse's instruction to wait, Leonard Goodson sidestepped the practitioner and pushed the door all the way open.

"Nephew, it's time to get your head out of your ass," Leonard announced as he stopped and stood at the foot of the bed.

Eric had difficulty lifting and rotating his head upward. His eyes felt as though they were filled with sand. "Uncle Leonard?"

"We've already crossed that bridge, Erie. Time for you to get your act together. Your Auntie Mims can't sleep. Every time she closes her eyes, she sees you slumped in the shower, then bursts into tears."

"I didn't mean…" Eric drawled.

"Of course, you didn't. But you did."

"I'm so ashamed."

"As you should be, but that's all in the past. Time to pull yourself together and get on with your life."

"That's easy for you to say," Eric whimpered.

"Easy! You think what you've experienced just affected you? Both your Auntie Mims and I lost our parents in the camps when we were just kids. Both of us smuggled out by friends, leaving everything we knew and loved behind. You never hear us bitching about it. You move on. Look ahead, not behind."

"I didn't know."

"No one knows. It's not something we advertise. Now it's time for you to get it together, as you young people say."

"But I can't live without her."

"Yes, you can. That beautiful person is looking down right now, shaking her head, not believing what she is seeing. She would want you to be strong and move on."

"I can't."

"You mean, you care not to." Leonard reached out, took hold of Eric's shoulders and lifted him to a sitting position. "I need you to promise me, for my sake and that of your Auntie Mims, that you're going to work at getting better."

"I don't..."

"Not good enough, Nephew. I need you to promise me."

"I promise," Eric whispered.

Leonard cupped Eric's cheeks in his palms, tilting his head back, leaned over and kissed his nephew on the forehead. "If you backslide, I hear a Nurse Ratched has taken a liking to you." Leonard snickered as he exited the room.

CHAPTER

90

After two non-sensical psychiatric visits in which Eric remained quiet, while trying to interpret heavily accented foreigners, he was deemed no longer an imminent threat to himself, or others. Freed from his constraints, Eric found his surroundings more reminiscent of a prison ward than a mental hospital: locked rooms; restricted access hallways; and, perpetual eggshell semi-gloss that would emasculate the strongest constitution.

Goodson did a slow-motion shuffle to the activities room. Standing in the entryway, he surveyed the sparsely furnished thirty x twenty-four-foot space. The west windowed wall to his left allowed diamond pattern filtered sunlight through commercial grade metal grates, hinged on one side and secured in place on the other by a Schlage heavy duty keyed lock. An identical set of three forty-eight-inch diameter oak tables with a single pedestal support surrounded by four high backed wood chairs lined the west and east walls.

A quiet threesome sat on a couch mesmerized by *Gilligan's Island* reruns on the north wall-mounted twenty-four inch black and white Mitsubishi television encased in a clear Plexiglas.

In the center of the room, a tall, thin, balding, white, male sporting a hospital smock and paper slippers slid across the scarred foot square cream and mint green asbestos tiled floor, reaching up toward the two x four-foot off-white acoustical ceiling as though picking fruit, taking one bite and discarding the remainder. Every reach revealing pale cheeks, given a jaundice glow from the overhead fluorescent lights.

Eric marveled as a muscular black man with an over-sized Afro, sitting at the center east wall table, face planted into a container of orange clay. Holding his position for a full minute, he lifted his head with the clay still attached, furiously trying to suck in air. In what appeared to Eric as almost slow-motion, the lone attendant rose from his stool in the southeast corner and ambled across the room. Reaching the now flailing patient, the attendant reached up with his right hand, extended his index finger mouth high and poked a hole through the clay. He casually strolled back to his perch.

A bespectacled gray-haired woman in a yellow terry-cloth robe jumped up from the westernmost table and accused herself of cheating at checkers. She jutted around to the other side of the table before responding to her own remark. The back and forth continued until the attendant called out in a stern voice, "Lillian!" The woman sat down and contemplated her next move.

Dumbfounded, Eric half expected to see his favorite actor, Jack Nicholson reappear in his role in *One Flew Over the Cuckoo's Nest*, when he jumped and squealed from a pinch on the butt.

"Well Mr. Goodson, I see you mus'ta peed."

Glancing over his shoulder, "Why Nurse Ratched, or, should I say Crazy Agnes?" But she was gone.

CHAPTER

91

Squeezed between a gas station and a welding shop prior to the strict enforcement of zoning codes, the thirteen-stool diner's blue plate special always included enough grease to lube and oil a Checker Cab. With the comfortable feel of a few greenbacks in his uniform pant pocket, Ahbi enjoyed the ambiance of Lou's with the enthusiasm of a Wall Street investment banker dining on the Chicken Etouffee at the Rockefeller Center's Rainbow Room.

"That's about the best burger I've ever ate," Ahbi mumbled through his permanently stiffened jaw."

"You eat the same thing here every night, you old fool," Eleanor chuckled, sticking her pencil back into her bleach blond bouffant hairdo.

"Yes sir," Ahbi nodded, "And I do believe that it's still the best."

"And I think you're a half bubble off plumb."

"Ain't no arguing with that, but I be a damned satisfied crazy man," Ahbi smiled, balancing a toothpick on his bottom left side molars.

"See you the same time tomorrow, handsome," the waitress giggled as she scooped up the fifty-two-cent tip."

"Won't be here tomorrow. Helpin' out a friend."

"Must be a good friend. You're our best customer. Hate to lose you, even for a day." Eleanor smiled.

"You keep my seat warm now, hear. Cause I be back, unless the Good Lord tells me my time is up."

The pounding on the overhead warehouse front door to announce his return drowned out the engine noise of the patrol car whipping up the driveway.

"You people breaking and entering in broad daylight on a busy street now?"

Ahbi turned, startled at the interruption. "What's that you say?"

The officer mistook Ahbi's muttering. "Oh, you've been drinking, have you?" The uniformed cop now inches from the custodian's face.

"No sir, ain't been doing that for a long time now," the skittish janitor replied.

"Turn around and spread 'em," the burly officer ordered.

"But, but..."

The policeman grabbed Ahbi's right shoulder, spun him around and shoved him into the overhead door with enough force to rattle the four glass panes. "Now you gone and done it. You have failed to follow the detailed instructions of a bona fide officer of the law. You're in a world of hurt now, boy. Any more of your sass and I can clearly see your face repeatedly smashing into my fist."

Ahbi drifted off into his private world of horror, the flashbacks striking with subliminal speed. The rotund figure punched Ahbi, the phantom blow causing him to shake his head. "*What was that?*" Ahbi questioned to himself with a whiff of terror. A second jab revealed a face on the monster. "*No, it can't be! God help me! It can't be!*" Ahbi wailed, but the image was unmistakable.

"Hey, what the hell is going on here?" Michaels screamed as he ducked under the rising door, jolting Ahbi back to reality.

"Caught this brother trying to break into the building."

"Oh, is that a fact. I suppose he stole one of our uniform shirts on a previous B&E? Did it ever occur to you morons that he works here?"

"You watch your mouth or you'll be getting hauled in with him."

"You're not taking anyone anywhere, other than your dumb asses out of here."

"One more smart-aleck remark out of you and it's all over."

"And any further attempts by you two to roust someone simply because they're black and you'll think cleaning up horse shit behind the Mounties in the Thanksgiving Day Parade is the highlight of your careers. Now leave this man alone and get a move on before I go wake your supervisor in the back lot."

Taking hold of Ahbi's arm, Michaels pulled him backward into the building and pressed the down button on the overhead door. "What are you doing here? I heard you were at Roy Blues' weekend poker game."

"He told me to take a break. Get some food, clean up and get his bag from his locker."

Jack checked his watch. "They've been playing for about twenty hours now, so I guess things probably slow down a bit. How's Roy Blue doing?"

"I think he's just funnin' with them."

"Sounds like Blue." Jack wrapped his arm around Ahbi's shoulder as they headed to the locker room.

"You always savin' my neck. Thank you."

"No thanks necessary. Cops like that give our city a bad rap. They're the same assholes who sleep out back every night. I think tonight we'll give them a little surprise."

"Please, no trouble on my account. Hard to believe, but they seemed to have helped me remember."

"Ahbi, how in the world could those clowns have helped you?"

"You knows how I always fade away somewheres?"

"The nightmares, or probably flashbacks?"

"Yeah, that's it. The huge figure beating on me has a face."

"Did you recognize it?"
"Yeah, it's Mr. Mayer."
"Now, that is scary."

CHAPTER

92

A MISHMASH OF BOOKS AND periodicals cluttered the claustrophobic office, allowing barely enough room for one client chair, much less the proverbial couch. Dr. Mirmashami, a Pakistani immigrant completing his psychiatric residency, sat quietly, framed in by stacks of journals, hands clasped on his desk, awaiting his 4:00 p.m. appointment.

Eric Goodson plodded through the ammonia-scented corridor, dreading the seemingly endless interviews with unintelligible foreign doctors, each sharing the same office, general appearance and mannerisms.

"Ah, here is my case # 3178 now. You are Mr. Goodson? It is so good to see you on this glorious day. Please, come sit. I have studied the file with great interest. You are a most unusual case. Cutting your wrist with such a crude instrument. You must excuse my curiosity; in my country, a man endures his suffering."

"They worship cows too."

"No, no, no. That is India. I am Pakistani," the doctor smiled.

"Big difference."

"For what reason do you do this thing?"

"I just didn't want to live anymore."

"And now do you feel the same thing?"

"Nothing's changed, other than I wasn't even good at trying to kill myself."

"Perhaps it was not meant to be."

"But it's meant for me to feel like this?"

"Sorrow takes many forms. To be free from sorrow, you must be very, very strong. If you truly meant to take your life, I think you are smart enough to have done a better job of it. You are a policeman? A weapon is at your disposal, is it not?"

"I happened to be naked at the time and staying in my aunt's house. I wouldn't do that to her."

"So, respect for others is not a problem. It is the respect for your own wellbeing that is of concern."

"I guess. I really don't know."

"The will to live is beyond all comprehension. In my country a man will squat for eighteen hours a day in a space no more than the size of this magazine; he will eat what little crumbs he may have; relieve himself with others all around; endure endless heat; because that is his square; his hope for the future. There is nothing wrong with a little sorrow. There is nothing that cannot be fixed with you. Accept it. Continue to live because that is all you can do. Seek the help of others if it is required. Our time is up. Go now, Mr. Goodson, your little square of life awaits you."

CHAPTER

93

Muttering, a common occurrence among the schizophrenic patients, but new to Eric's list of symptoms, accompanied his chain gang shuffle down the hall. Each movement an obvious effort, requiring the energy necessary to rip out a tree stump with the roots still intact.

"What the hell was that? That guy can't be licensed to practice psychiatry in this country. What do I care about some chump in India, or Pakistan, or who gives a tinker's damn where, sitting his ass down in the middle of some godforsaken street?" Eric's stride increased simultaneously with his mumble elevating to a grumble. "Who does he think he is to minimize my suffering? I'm really hurting. Not like some third world dolt who doesn't know any better." Passing the nurses station, Eric hit a full, hard charging, rumble mode back to his room. "Make fun of my pain!" Eric roared, "I'll show him."

"Mr. Goodson, is everything alright?" A concerned aide inquired, jumping up from her seat.

"Fine," Eric shouted. "Just fine," as he huffed back to his quarters, kicking open the door.

"Now he is ready to fight to get his life back," Dr. Mirmashami predicted, standing in the office doorway with his hands clasped behind his pudgy frame, twiddling his thumbs.

CHAPTER

94

ERIC CONTINUED HIS TIRADE, while he ripped the sheet from his bed. Hospital corners thwarted his effort to completely throw off the cover. His body shaking uncontrollably and his mind consumed with rage, Eric's exaggerated movements to bunch the fabric looked like a paratrooper attempting to gather his chute in a wind-swept field. He hurled the flimsy wad to the floor. Grabbing his pillow and rapidly punching it with three or four quick blows, he then tossed it back onto the mattress. Exhausted from his temper tantrum, he plopped into bed. As he curled up in a fetal position, his mind raced, zipping through a myriad of songs, none of which brought the calmness of past efforts. Minutes that seemed like hours, Eric finally drifted off to sleep.

Awakened by a chill, Eric recalled his assault on the linens. Rising to a sitting position, then swinging his bare legs off the edge of the bed, he hopped down. The cold tile floor sent an instant reflexive shiver up his torso. Glancing at the battered sheet crumpled at the foot of the bed, he immediately lamented his tantrum. *"God, that was stupid."*

Eric climbed back into bed, this time pulling the sheet up to his chin. He drifted off to a quick slumber.

"I be bettin' there's a hunk of man under dat sheet," Nurse Ratched squealed as she ripped the cloth covering her patient.

A quick head shake, then Goodson dove out the other side of the bed.

"Ewh! You a fast little sucker," Nurse Ratched remarked, while extending her neck to glance down at her patient.

"You're no nurse."

"Tellin' y'all a secret, I ain't crazy neither."

"Sure could've fooled me. If you aren't crazy, what are you doing here?"

"Beats livin' in a cardboard box, scroungin' for food in a dumpster. Leastwise, dis way, I gots a roof over my head, three squares a day and all the crazy ass men I can chase," Agnes remarked as she crawled up into the bed.

"Hey, come on now, what are you doing?"

"Oh, come now, sugar. Nurse Ratched gonna show you a real good time before you go."

"Where am I going?"

"You about to be discharged."

"How would you know that?"

"I can always tell when deys ready to leave."

CHAPTER

95

Aʜʙɪ ᴊᴜsᴛ ᴄᴏᴍᴩʟᴇᴛᴇᴅ sᴇʀᴠɪɴɢ a fresh round of drinks, so he decided to catch a cat nap on the bartender's cot, squeezed in along-side the kitchenette counter. He tossed in his sleep, unable to shake the horrible vision of Harrold Mayer's face mounted atop the monster. The image pursued the battered janitor with a vengeance, pummeling him at every opportunity. Ahbi cowered at every blow, pleading with the demon for mercy. Golden splashes, coupled with unusual ping sounds, formed the rhythmic basis of the macabre vision.

"*The name,*" Ahbi called out in his nightmare. "*There's something about a name. What name? Whose name?*"

Suddenly, Ahbi realized the beast had disappeared.

"*Something's just not right. Think! Try to concentrate. You use to think real hard before. Before? There must be a before. It couldn't always have been like this. Who am I? How did I get like this?*"

The frustration eased as the perplexed custodian abandoned the struggle of sleep and delved into his familiar tempo, "*Scrub the sink and think! Scrub the sink and think!*"

The worn enamel whimpered in silence as it fought to wear down the scrub pad with every twist. "*Think! Think! Think!*" Ahbi commanded as he bore down on the sink. Just as he decided to surrender to the futility, a random image of a long corridor with countless doors on each side raced through his mind. *"Doors? Why doors? Where do they go? What are they for? Where are they? I think I am going crazy. God, please tell me what it all means. I can't go on like this. I just don't have the strength. Just take me God. Quit your fooling around and end this, please?"* Ahbi cried, backhanding tears and snorting up a mucous plug to clear his head.

Falling back onto the cot, the custodian once again broke with reality. The rotund figure of Harrold Mayer pummeled the defenseless cripple. *"No! You can't do this no more,"* Ahbi screamed in his delirium. *"You go on and get, you hear?"* The admonition changed the image. The fat bastard now appeared encased in a blue shroud. A series of doors continued to race around the background of the assailant. *"So many doors. What do they mean?"* Ahbi moaned as he drifted off to sleep.

CHAPTER

96

As the sedation subsided, the mildly irritating incessant ear ringing built to a crescendo of nerve-wracking mania, blasting Sarah from her king bed with the identical force required to launch an Intercontinental Ballistic Missile. Shaking her fists overhead in a fit of rage as she paced in her living room, the statuesque vision couldn't believe her ironic epiphany; repeating one of Jack's cutesy ad nauseam precepts to change her thoughts.

"Reading is out of the question; I can't concentrate," Sarah surmised, not really knowing if she just mouthed the words, or if sound actually accompanied her lip movement. "The wash! That's it. The mindless waste of time spent listening to that damned machine drone on in the god-awful basement is the perfect solution. What a terrific Saturday night?" Sarah shook her head in disgust and hollered out loud, her overcompensation resulting from the lack of hearing almost comical.

Toting the torn plastic dime store white mesh laundry basket under one arm, with detergent, coins and keys in her other hand, Sarah carefully trekked down the squeaky, wooden, dim lit stairway to the dingy laundromat.

The thirty-one townhouses were built upon the salvaged foundation of a long-abandoned manufacturing plant. Renovated to provide tenant storage and a common laundry room with a bank of fifteen coin-operated commercial washing machines along the east wall and a like amount of heavy-duty dryers on the west wall. A center table top extended the length of the room, with scattered fiberglass bucket chairs throughout.

"God, I hate this place. It gives me the creeps. They spend all that money refurbishing these places and forget about the basements. I just don't get it. You wonder where landlords actually find bulbs that don't really light anything up. I'll bet the walls set world records on mold production."

Wiping a portion of the slimy tabletop, Sarah winced at the despicable layer of grime now coating her bath towel. Quickly separating the loads, the laundress held up a pair of men's knee-high argyle socks, "Incredible that a grown man can forget his socks," Sarah chuckled. "I must have really rocked his world," she roared, lowering her head in feigned embarrassment, but pleased at her accomplishment. The laughter morphed into heaves of regret as she realized her honesty drove him out of her life. Twenty minutes passed before she deposited the coins and studied the dial. "What are you doing? You do this every time. You really expect to find a delicate cycle on this piece of crap? Get a grip, girl." She tossed her undergarments into the machine.

Her peripheral vision caught commotion across the room. Turning for a better look, Sarah squinted in the poor lighting. An elderly man in a Red Wings jersey stood, resting his chin on the heel of a hockey stick. Moving around the table, she could see he was on skates. "Pepatino, is that you?" Sarah hesitantly called out, having only met him one previous time.

Cognizant of her hearing disability, Jimmy smiled and hollered, "How did you know it was me?"

Sarah approached cautiously, as she stated, "not many grown men going around on skates wearing a number 9 jersey and carrying a hockey stick."

"Point taken," Jimmy chuckled.

"What are you doing here?"

"Roy Blue wanted us to keep tabs on you."

"You mean, Jack wanted you to look out for me?" Sarah yelled. Jimmy cringed at the volume. "Sorry, I just can't tell how loud I am."

"It's okay," Jimmy mouthed, then added, "You know, the guys like a lost puppy without you. There's a full moon out. Nothing good happens with a full moon. When the moon changes, everything will work out fine."

Sarah failed to decipher every word, as tears streamed down her cheeks. Picking up on Jack's mantra about changing her thoughts, Sarah bellowed, "You said, 'us'. Who else is here?"

Pepatino raised his hockey stick and pointed to the two operating dryers, "Darryl and Darryl."

Sarah's eyes bugged out, "My God, they'll get killed in there!"

"Are you kidding? Look at those two mooks! They're having the time of their lives. Best fifty cents I ever spent."

Sarah just shook her head, then leaned in and hugged Jimmy, "Thank you for looking after me."

"My pleasure," Pepatino grinned, "Besides, where else could I find this kind of entertainment. It's priceless."

Sarah returned to her wash, while Pepatino opened the respective dryer doors. Rodeo fell head first, slamming his noggin on the concrete floor, then moaning, "Ah man, I think I'm gonna be sick."

Jimmy belly laughed, "You are sick, you crazy bastard."

Max exhibited a bit more finesse, managing to turn himself around and exit feet first. His whirling and howling akin to a madcap swirling dervish, Pepatino roared as Max bounced off one obstacle after another.

Sarah watched the antics from afar. It reminded her of the slap stick comedy in the old silent movies. She just shook her head, as a subtle shadow crossed over the bank of battered white enamel washing machines, startling her and prompting her to turn. Standing within a foot of her stood an imposing figure, his head above the illumination of the swaying bare bulb. Sarah screamed as the intruder reached his black hands toward her. Instinctively stepping back, the terror-stricken coed lunged her foot forward driving into the shadowy figure's groin with the enthusiasm of a place kicker attempting to tip the balance in a sudden death playoff on Super Bowl Sunday. As the interloper hunched over in pain, Sarah moved in closer, thrusting her knee into his face, propelling him backward into the wall mounted soap dispenser.

Alerted by the scream, Pepatino pushed off with his left foot and zipped across the room as if a Zamboni had just cleared the ice. Turning sideways and screeching to a halt, he smacked his stick on the side of the recovering assailants head.

Scrambling around the opposite end of the table, Sarah dashed for the steps, bounding them two at a time. Mid-flight, her toe slipped off the riser, pounding her shin into the edge and scrapping it from just below the knee to the top of the ankle.

"Damn!" Sarah screamed, ignoring the pain and regaining her footing. Racing through the hallway, the terror-stricken lass realized she forgot her keys in the basement. "Shit!" The adrenaline-soaked Amazon thrust her foot into the door, splintering the wood frame and springing the door backward. Bolting through the dark to the telephone on the opposite side of the room, Sarah collided with a large masked figure who instantly wrapped his arms around the beauty.

"Well, ain't this a pretty sight. The fair maiden runs right into my arms. Sure saves me a lot of trouble."

"Who the hell are you?" Sarah gasped, her heart heaving as though trying to bust the corporeal barrier.

"I'm your new little lover boy. Ain't that why you're here?"

The tinnitus obscuring the reply, the terrified coed screamed. "Get your hands off me, you pig."

"Now you shouldn't talk like that to your betrothed."

Sarah pounded on her captive's chest, surprised at the amount of bulk. "Let go of me, you bastard," she screamed, but couldn't hear.

"I think we have time to have us a little fun, darlin'. Whada ya say? You wanna feel the ecstasy one more time before you die?"

Sarah, sensed his motive from the rhythmic heat of his foul breath. "You'll have to kill me first, asshole," she screamed as the heel of her hand slammed into the area she perceived as her attacker's nose.

With the aplomb of a choreographed dance step, the assailant pushed Sarah back, retaining a grip on her blouse with one hand and viciously backhanding her with the other. Dazed, Sarah reflexively flailed her arms without the benefit of neurologic control. The attacker tore off her blouse and bra with one lightning move and punched her face, knocking her backward to the floor.

"I like my women bruised and compliant," the rapist relayed in an almost friendly tone as he started to kneel while ripping down his zipper. "I'd like you to meet Anaconda. He's a big old snake that's gonna hurt you bad, bitch."

The assailant straddled Sarah, poking his oversized tongue out of the mask and leaning down to lick her face. As she struggled to avoid the disgusting contact, the perpetrator stopped inches away, his liquored breath lingering like the putrid after taste of a diet cola.

"What the…" Sarah thought, quickly reviewing the unfolding scene as her restraints loosened.

Jimmy hustled up the stairs and into the apartment. Quickly surveying the room, he noticed a solid glass ashtray on the coffee table. Winding up, he smacked it directly into the middle of the assailant's back. The attacker landed a vicious punch to Sarah's jaw and let her drop. He turned his attention to Pepatino, who rapidly closed the distance and was winding up for a direct blow with his stick. The intruder deflected the blow with one arm and caught Jimmy's jaw with a short, hard right. The Italian collapsed to the floor, reminiscent of a first round Ali vs Liston knockout.

Returning his attention to Sarah, a brutal slam to the side of the head with the hallway fire extinguisher, lethal to a normal mortal, definitely distracted the attacker. Unable to hear the impact, Sarah swore she felt a vibration.

The assailant turned and looked at Mamoud, "So you wanna play again, eh boy! I can't believe you lived through our little barbeque. Or are you his brother. Oh, that's right, you're all brothers, ain't ya? You all look alike anyway. So, let's finish our little soiree," the monster grinned.

As he rose, Sarah lunged, grabbing his ski mask. His own motion pulled the cover from his face. The sick smile and realization that a serious whack with a metal canister failed to jostle the attacker, shook Mamoud.

"Time to tango, Canook!" The intruder joshed as sirens blared in the background.

Mamoud wound up with the CO2 tank for another shot as the attacker shoved him aside and hustled out the door in an off cantor hip-hop while attempting to zip up.

"Sarah," Mamoud called out, tearing the sheet off the bed to cover her chest and leaning over her, clearing her hair from her face. "Sarah, are you okay."

"I can't hear you. The ringing is still too bad in my ears," Sarah yelled. "Be careful. There's another one in the basement."

"Not exactly," Mamoud smirked. "I thought getting beat up and fried hurt, until I experienced your self-defense moves. Jack ever gets out of line with you and he'll be one sorry ass mother."

"I can't understand anything you're saying. Do you think we're okay?"

Mamoud shook his head affirmatively, smiled and caressed his friend's cheek. "We're just fine."

Pepatino moaned, while opening his eyes. Mamoud inquired, loud enough for Sarah to understand, "Who's he?"

"Jack's boss. He was here to protect me too."

"Do all of Jack's friends wind up getting beat to crap?"

Sarah smiled, "Just the close ones."

Torpo and Rodeo burst into the room. Huffing, Max asked, "Wha'd we miss?"

CHAPTER

97

RATHER THAN DETER A true player's enthusiasm, the stench of forty hours of stale cigar smoke and cramped muscles invigorates the participants to push their war of endurance to its limit. The dedicated hard-core place more significance in the stamina of their opponent than the cards he draws. The first day and a half of a weekend marathon is a sizing up period. The fatigue factor is the real test: a steady infusion of booze to cloud an already precarious judgment; sleep deprivation's psychological impact altering the delicate balance of personalities on the precipice of crisis; the stress of frantically stemming mounting financial losses; the punishing blow to fragile egos facing repeated failure; and, the rewards, both tangible and abstract, to the lone survivor who exhibited the grit and determination to simply outlast his opponents, much the same as the odds ultimately favoring the house.

"All those chips blocking your view of the table, Blue?" Marzoli's smirk meager camouflage for his sarcasm.

"No," Roy deadpanned as he bumped the pot another five-hundred.

"Your raise is nothing more than another contribution to the judicial retirement fund," O'Hara grinned, upping the bet another three-hundred.

"That's eight hundred to you, Mr. Commissioner," Marzoli relayed, a touch of deference evident to Blue.

Dolan's face wrenched in a self-induced anguish. "What are you, my fucking C.P.A.? I don't need you to tell me where the pot stands. You got that? Why don't everybody just shut the fuck up so I can enjoy the game?" Dolan ranted, throwing his cards on the table as he bolted from his chair to the makeshift bar. "Another bourbon! Neat this time; not that watered-down crap you've been serving."

"Yes sir," the accommodating waiter replied, tipping up the fifth in a ten second free pour.

"Don't you dare touch it with an ice cube…"

"No sir."

"Cause I'd have to kick your ass."

"I just be filling it with the whiskey likes you like it, sir," Ahbi kowtowed.

Blue glanced over Marzoli's head to keep his eye on the exchange in the kitchenette.

"Surly bastard, isn't he?" Marzoli commented. "You oughta hear some of the old war stories of his tour on the streets. He'd get in a mood and God help you if you were the next person he met. Made Dirty Harry look like an altar boy."

"Those are nothing more than precinct house rumors," the Judge remarked. "Best to concentrate your thoughts on raising my pot."

"Raise you four-hundred," Blue stated matter-of-factly.

"Must be a week's pay for, what is it, a hi-lo driver?" Marzoli remarked.

"No need for your snide remarks when Mr. Blue has kindly ponied up," O'Hara jumped in.

"It's his tell. Ever notice how his mouth flaps like a whippoorwill's ass when he's bluffing?" Roy winked at O'Hara, who immediately picked up on the ruse.

"How do you think I've nailed him the last two hands," the Judge taunted.

"Bullshit! My mouth runs whether I'm bluffing or not," Marzoli chuckled, his admission ending the derision, allowing him to toss his chips with confidence.

"What do you figure, Roy, about eight-grand sitting there?" The Judge inquired.

"Seventy-eight hundred," Roy instantly replied without so much as a twitch.

"Well, time to test your mettle. I call," O'Hara exclaimed, laying open three kings.

"Can you fucking believe that?" Marzoli cried, slamming his cards face down on the table.

"Yeah, I can," Roy remarked softly, smoothly fanning out a flush. "Sorry Judge, I know you had your name on that one."

"It's not as brutal when you're cleaned out by a gentleman," O'Hara smirked.

"You're a long way from a house cleaning, Judge," Marzoli chaffed. "You want to see tabletop, just look this way."

O'Hara and Marzoli marveled at Blue's shuffling skills, captivated by each crisp snap as the card flipped from his hand, face down onto the tabletop. As the last hole card landed, the hotel room door burst open, slamming against the wainscot.

"Holy crap! What the hell's going on?" Marzoli screamed, ducking on impact as though anticipating an attack.

"Son of a bitch!" Dolan cried, jumping up and brushing off his pants. "How many fucking times does a guy have to endure this shit? Did I tell anybody here my last name was Martinizer? Do I really look like I operate a fucking laundromat?" The Commissioner wailed, glaring at the players. "Well, do I?"

O'Hara immediately lost interest in the bizarre episode, instead concentrating his gaze on Roy Blue with the intrigue of a budding scientist witnessing his first cell division through an electron microscope.

With all the excitement, the forklift operator failed to so much as twitch. *"Unbelievable,"* the Judge thought. *"No one could stay that cool."*

With everyone but Blue concentrating on the doorway, a young black bombshell bursting out of an outfit comprised of less material than the average handkerchief, scooched in at the unceremonious nudge of the towering beast behind her.

"This here is Yolanda," the gargantuan figure announced as he squeezed his hand around the back of her neck, causing the hooker to wince. "She has graciously agreed to relieve your tensions from the grueling sport of poker for the remainder of the weekend."

"From the size of the bandage on your neck, it looks like she already relieved some of your tension. Covering up the worlds' biggest hickey?" Marzoli chuckled. "Or, did you and Blue get a two for one deal on tattoo removal?" Glancing at Yolanda, "Damn Butch, she can't be more than sixteen," Marzoli complained. "Why do you keep fooling around with jail bait?"

"Cause I like the edge," Mayer snickered. "And besides, who she gonna complain to?" The sadistic slob reasoned as he shoved her toward the bedroom. "Us?"

"Stupid bastard's gonna bury us all one day," Marzoli prophesized.

"The kid just needs to blow off a little steam," Dolan remarked.

"Aren't you getting tired of covering for that asshole?" Marzoli asked, his frustration evident.

"We got history."

"Yeah, and all of it gives the Dark Ages a new luster."

"Now gentlemen," the Judge interceded. "No need to air our dirty laundry in front of Mr. Blue. Lest we forget why we're here. I think it's to you, Marzoli."

With only the quick dart of an eye, Roy checked on Ahbi. The bartender slipped into a catatonic state at the first sound of Mayer's voice.

"Ahbi, can you bring me a soda, please?" Blue requested.

"What you askin'?"

"A Coca Cola, please."

"Yes sir, coming right directly," the shaken porter replied.

The loud smack and sharp cry internally jolted Blue, but he refused to exhibit any outward sign.

"He just loves to tune up his women," Dolan quipped.

"The guy needs help," Marzoli griped. "His idea of foreplay is gonna kill someone someday, if it hasn't already."

The second slap propelled the teenage prostitute into the nightstand, knocking off the lamp.

Blue telegraphed his intent by the unobtrusive move of setting down his cards.

"Ah! So the man of steel finally cracks," O'Hara thought to himself while he cupped Roy's backhand. "Best to stay out of things that don't concern you," O'Hara advised softly.

"Besides, she's nothing but a black whore. City's full of 'em. It's getting so you can't cross a street without bumping into one. Fucking assholes have ruined this town," Dolan ranted.

Another vicious thwack and Blue bolted from his chair. Restrained by a combination choke hold and hammer lock before he crashed through the door. Marzoli's lightning speed surprised Blue. The dominating detective turned his guest around to face the table. "You're here to play. Now sit down."

Blue's inability to assist ate at him as the beating continued and he folded nine straight hands, regardless of his openers.

"I've had enough. I'm out of here," Roy announced. "Ahbi, let's scoot."

"I don't mind you leaving with your queasy stomach and all, but you can't take our bartender. I just got him broke in," Dolan bitched.

"He goes with me," Blue biting his lip, holding back from voicing his true fear of what could happen to Ahbi.

"It's a shame we didn't discover this weakness yesterday. It would have saved me a lot of money," Marzoli scoffed.

"Mr. Blue, please," the Judge implored. "Mayer will be finished in a second or two." O'Hara naughtily glanced at his snickering comrades.

"Yeah, he's a regular revolutionary. We call him the minute man," Marzoli scoffed.

"I apologize for my crass partners, but you did come here to play cards, just as we did. Sit, please," the Judge implored.

As Roy's indecision stalled movement, the bedroom door ripped open.

"Next?" The barbarian called out, buckling up his belt under his flabby midriff. Raising his head, Mayer instantly zeroed in on his employee. "Well, looky here. If it ain't the great Roy Blue; professional card shark and hi-lo driver, all in one. We gonna play some poker, Roy?"

A shiver of ambivalence momentarily coursed through Blue, until the overwhelming desire to teach the fat bastard a lesson won out. "You got it!"

"Let's rock and roll."

"One condition; you say one harsh word to Ahbi and I'm gonna kick your ass."

"Who the hell you talking about?"

"Our janitor is bartending. He serves drinks without abuse. You got that?"

"Just deal the fucking cards, would you?"

The next twelve hours cost Mayer roughly twenty-eight thousand dollars.

"Gee Harrold, looks like you're out of this one."

"My credits good here."

"Not with me. House rule: you play only what's in front of you."

Harrold Mayer held two aces with a third on the flop, accented with a pair of deuces; the full house meant bet the farm.

"This here is a genuine solid twenty-four carat gold Omega, inlaid with twelve diamond chips. Retails for fifteen thousand," Harrold related, twisting the watch off his wrist.

"May I?"

As Blue examined the timepiece, he flipped it over and read the inscription out loud. "To my favorite C.P.A., all my love, L.T." Without taking his eyes off the Omega, Roy matter-of-factly inquired, "You a bookkeeper, Fat Boy?"

"What are you running your mouth about now, hi-lo driver?"

"The inscription."

"Damn, he said he was an accountant; I never believed him. Ain't life a bitch?" Mayer recalled out loud. "I took it for collateral on a loan."

"Yeah, right!"

"Hey, I escorted a Canadian back home. Even gave him a ride in the tunnel," Mayer smiled, as Dolan choked on his Scotch.

"You're still light. A pawn shop would only give ten percent of the value. What else you got?" Roy inquired.

Butchie struggled to lift his ample frame from the table. "Hold on a sec!" Disappearing into the bedroom, Roy heard a zipper ripped open, then a rustling noise. Butchie waggled to the table. Raising a midnight blue wad of material, Butchie announced, "This here is a genuine Detroit Police Department bullet proof vest. What'd ya say, Roy?"

"Now wait just a goddamn minute, Butch," Marzoli yelled. "You can't go around giving city property to civilians."

"No worries. He ain't got a chance in hell of winning."

"What would I do with a bullet proof vest?"

"I'd wear it around me, if I were you," Butchie threatened.

Roy Blue shook his head in disbelief, "Pfst."

"You gonna let me call, or just weasel the pot?"

"Go for it."

"Full house; aces over deuces," Butchie laughed, reaching for the pot.

"Go figure. And all I have are two little pair of twos," Roy scoffed.

"He cleaned you fair and square," O'Hara commented.

"He took us all. We should have let him go when he wanted to hours ago. I guess that'll teach us," Marzoli lamented.

"Ahbi, let's blow this pop stand."

"Yeah, you and your boy vamoose," Mayer instructed.

While sliding through the room with outstretched arms and his back to the wall, reminiscent of a damsel in distress tentatively negotiating the narrow 30th floor precipice of a New York high-rise in a 1930's style big budget film to escape her attacker, Ahbi instinctively reached forward with his hand as Roy tossed him the Omega while he cashed out his chips. "Guard that with your life," Roy instructed with a smile.

Zigzagging through the inner city on the way back to Dearborn Beer, Roy observed Ahbi rotating the gold band in his hand with the familiarity of a nun fingering her favorite rosary beads.

"Remind you of something?"

"Can't remember. Trying, but it won't come."

"Why don't you hang onto it for me?" The cool card shark sensed the comfort of his usually conflicted companion.

Ahbi continued to stare at the watch, rotating the band between his thumb and forefinger, breaking all contact with reality.

"I'll take that as a yes."

CHAPTER

98

OPTING TO MAINTAIN THE comfort of her routine and forsaking the lure of supermarkets, Mims Goodson usually enjoyed her daily excursion to Levine's corner store, but found herself fretting over her nephew's deepening despair. Pulling her two-wheeled wire grocery cart to the side door of the modest three-bedroom ranch in Oak Park, a blue-collar suburb on Detroit's northwest border, Mims created enough racket to attract the attention of a hearing-impaired pet. Schlepping the bags up onto the kitchen counter, she caught a glimpse of Eric slouched on the living room couch.

"I found some of your favorites today, Erie. Why don't you come see?" Mims cheerily suggested, while straining to reach the top cupboard.

No response; only the background noise of a daytime soap theme.

"Hostess Cup Cakes, fresh off the truck. The driver promised me he picked them up not more than an hour before from the bakery. You can't get any better than that."

The blank stare and listlessness troubled Mims more than the grief induced alcoholism and attempted suicide. Standing in the kitchen doorway, the concerned aunt shook her head as she watched her favorite nephew.

"Erie, there's more to life for a young man than watching television."

The lack of response frustrated Mims.

"If you insist on exposing yourself to that bunk, your brain will eventually turn to mush and leak out of your ears."

Eric popped the top off the Seconal and swallowed another ten-milligram tablet without the benefit of water. Unable to tolerate the sight, the petite matron shuffled to the kitchen table, plopped down in a chair and dropped her hands into her lap as her chin slumped to her chest.

"I promised your father I'd look after you. I don't think I've done a very good job when I see you like this," Mims rambled while tears streamed down her cheeks. "The doctor told us you had rediscovered your will to live. What happened to change that? Or was he wrong? I guess everybody makes mistakes, even professionals, except for your Uncle Lenny. God forbid he should error. No matter what it was, I'd surely get blamed. Men, they just can't seem to cope alone," Mims sniffled while smearing the tears with the back of her hand. "From the day you were born, I felt you were mine. I think I even experienced false labor pains when your Mother carried you. I couldn't love my own child more than I feel for you. Now I know why God didn't allow me to have children. He knew you were coming into my life, so why not pass my allotment onto someone really in need. I understand all that now. Lenny and I feel all the fulfillment of any parent, because of you. I would give my own life to get you back." Mims pulled the handkerchief from her sleeve and wiped her eyes. "Listen to me ramble like a yenta," Mims moaned, startled as the arms wrapped around her neck in a gentle hug, Eric leaning down cheek to cheek.

"I love you Aunt Mims," Eric slurred. "Please don't give up on me."

Mims reached up and cupped Erie's upper arms, lightly tapping her fingers against his withered muscles. Each silently sobbed, ignoring the depressing background dialogue of the afternoon soap.

Touched by the tender scene, Leonard stood quiet, knowing he stumbled on a once in a lifetime moment; the kind trial lawyers dream of staging in a courtroom with an impromptu effect. Allowing the vision to wane, the brilliant wordsmith fumbled with a docile knock on the doorframe, "Well, this is an unexpected treat. Mind if I join in?" Leonard bent over, wrapping his long arms around Mims and Eric, stifling a cry, but failing to hold back the tears. "Son, I think it's time you went to see that young man you spoke so highly of at the meetings with the nervous patients."

"I'm gonna do whatever it takes," Eric remarked, fighting to pronounce each word succinctly.

CHAPTER

99

THE FIRST TIME IT happened, it caught Detective Goodson by complete surprise; a Monday morning rehash of a ref's bad call against the Detroit Lions in a Sunday afternoon football game. The second time, while erasing a mistake while filling out his monthly expense report. The most recent, while paying for a Chicken Shack four-piece lunch special. He can't explain it; can't control it; and it has been happening with more and more frequency.

"Sir, are you alright," the septuagenarian counter clerk inquired with a crackling voice.

His vision blurred by the unexpected tears, Eric rubbed his right eye with the back of his hand, while responding, "I just didn't expect such a good deal."

"Well now," the cashier responded while wiping her hands on her yellow apron before reaching up to adjust her matching nursing cap, "You have a good one, hear!"

Goodson hoisted the sack with his left arm, twisted and reached with his right hand to the condiment counter behind him, swiping a handful of napkins from the dispenser and hustled out to his car.

"Loretta," the fry cook called out, while hunched over a vat of hot oil, "What was that all about?"

"Darndest thing I ever saw," Loretta replied, shaking her head. "A grown man crying cause our chicken was so cheap."

"Wait'll he tastes it," the cook deadpanned.

Detective Goodson wheeled his unmarked car behind a vacant Great Scott supermarket, backing up against the six-foot high brick wall that separated the store from the adjacent subdivision. Throwing his head forward onto the back of his hands gripping the top of the steering wheel, he yelled out, "Why am I feeling this way? The weepiness; this loss of self-confidence. Pull yourself together Eric." Hoping to avoid a chatty operator, Goodson reached for his radio and called in that he was taking a lunch break, while fighting an uncontrollable urge to cry. "I keep thinking I'm over my head in everything. I can't keep doing this. I need help, but that would damage my permanent record. What can I do?" Eric talked calmly to himself as though he would to a potential suicide victim. Realizing the frightening side to his predicament, he mumbled, "I am a possible suicide." Mulling over his thoughts, he shook his head. With a review of each symptom, his head shake intensified into a dire crescendo straining his vertebral limits of elasticity, coupled with rapid steering wheel fist pounds providing an onlooker the impression of a Mick Fleetwood manic drum rehearsal.

Reaching across the bench seat in his not yet classic Pontiac Grand Prix for his bag of chicken, Eric's peripheral vision detected the distinctive blue with yellow trim cover of Dr. Low's book lying on the back seat. Disregarding his lunch, he reached for the volume and opened to a random middle section. A woman was describing her fears facing a trip to her in-laws for Thanksgiving Dinner. Although unable to empathize with her exact circumstance, the similarity in her feelings were uncanny. As Dr. Low led her through his method, not only did the patient find relief, but Eric experienced his crying jag slowly dissolve.

"God, maybe there really is something to this," Eric thought. "I know Angie would have wanted me to do everything humanly possible to fight my way back."

CHAPTER

100

THE PLAINCLOTHES COP CAUGHT Jack's attention as he approached the table. Excusing himself from the group, Jack confronted Officer Goodson, grabbing his arm and leading him off to the side, next to the coffee urn.

"You can't come in here and disturb our meeting. These are vulnerable people. Your presence could set some of them back months. You'll have to wait outside until I'm through. I'll cooperate with anything you need. Just don't disturb the meeting, please."

"I'd just like to sit in," Eric stated with a quiet hesitancy.

"I can't allow that. These people need help. For some, this is their only lifeline to normalcy."

"I need your help."

"The last time you were going to help, Sarah and I were almost killed."

"What are you talking about?"

"The meeting at the old Packard plant. You never showed, but some of your buddies did and almost killed us."

"I'm sorry to hear that, but I had nothing to do with it. I got called out just before we were to meet and..." Tears raced down Eric's cheeks. "...and, and..." The detective stammered, "I've got to do something," Eric answered as he hung his head and quietly cried.

"My God, you're serious. I'm so sorry. Of course, you're welcome, just as anyone else would be," Jack reassured, placing his hand on Eric's shoulder. "Take a moment to pull yourself together and then come join the group."

As they approached the table, Jack held out his hand, "Sit anywhere you like. This is Eric. Some of you remember he visited us a while back. Now he's decided to join us."

The entire group introduced themselves with the exception of Gene, who sat fidgeting, reminiscent of an elementary school child awaiting discipline outside the principal's office, but more movement than he displayed in the last several weeks.

"*I can't be this bad off,*" Eric commented to himself, as he tugged on his left shirt sleeve to cover his bandaged wrist.

"Ca, ca, ca, can I s, s, say som, som, some th, th, thing now?" Gene stuttered in a soft tone, his head hung down avoiding eye contact.

The members scanned the table for the origin of the unfamiliar utterance, aligning their sights on the heavy set, bearded member.

"*Unbelievable,*" Jack whispered under his breath. "Please, go ahead," Jack instructed.

"I, I, I re, re, really do, do, don't know wh, wh, where to, to s, s, s, start," the timid reply.

"Begin wherever you are comfortable."

"I ge, ge, ge, guess that's af, af, af, af-ter my ca, ca, car wre, wre, wreck. I do, do, don't know."

"You're doing fine," Jack coached.

"I se, se, seem to, to, to have lo, lo, lost my se, se, self c, c, c, confiiiii-dence."

"Tell us how you recognize that?"

"We, we, well, I, I, I'll be s, s, sitting dow, dow, down eh, eh, and all of a s, s, s, sudden g, g, get we, we, weepy."

"*God, this sounds just like me,*" Eric thought, dumbfounded.

"Are you able to make decisions?" The leader gently prodded.

"I, I, I'm, I'm a, a, a, frai, frai, fraid to, to, to, g, g, g, go out," Gene stuttered. "I, I, I'm a, a, frai, frai, fraid to, to, d, d, drive; my wa, wa, wife ha, ha, has to br, br, bring me to, to, to ma, ma, ma, meetings."

"We'll take that as a 'no' on decision making," Rose chimed in with a smile on her face.

"Gene, can you give us a specific example of when you experienced nervous symptoms?"

"Tha, tha, tha, that's j, j, just it! I ha, ha, have th, th, th, them all the t, t, time. I fe, fe, fe-el li, li, like I'm so, so, so ma, ma, ma, much wor, wor, worse off than th, th, the re, re, rest of you. I fe, fe, feel like I, I, I'm go, go, go, going to, to, to die."

"No one has ever died from nervous symptoms, Gene. Make no mistake, they are uncomfortable, but with experience in handling them, you will improve," Jack reassured the hesitant participant. "Believe me, we all started out feeling like you do. We take small steps and build on them to become stronger. Let's talk about one thing today that triggered symptoms."

"Wh, wh, when the me, me, mee-ting wa, wa, wa, was in, in, inter, interr-up, up, up-ted by thi, thi, this guy," Gene reluctantly nodded his head in Eric's direction, "I, I, I wa, wa, was st, st, st, still tr, tr, tr, try-ing to, to, to de, de, decide if, if, if I, I, I wa, wa, was go, go, going to sa, sa, say som, som, som-th, th, thing.

"Describe your feelings at the time," Jack asked softly.

"I, I, I ga, ga, ga, got fla, fla, flus-tered."

"Anything else?"

"I, I, I've b, b, been a, a, a, a-frai, frai, fraid t, t, to spe, spe, spe, speak out; my st, st, st, stom-ach st, st, st, starts tur, tur, turning in na, na, knots; I fe, fe, feel like I, I, I, I'm g, g, g, going to, to, to dr, dr, dry he, he, he, heave; I g, g, g, get li, li, li, light hea, hea, headed and g, g, get a, a, a, frai, frai-d th, th, that I'm g, g, g, going to, to, to, p, p, p, pass ou, ou, out. I wa, wa, wa, want to, to, to, gra, gra, gra, grab one of my p, p, p, pills to, to, to, ca, ca, calm dow, dow, down."

"Have you been examined by a doctor?"

"So, so, so, m, m, m, man-y t, t, t, times, I, I, I c, c, c, can't t, t, tell you."

"Has he run tests on you for the light headedness?"

"Ye, ye, yeah. He, he, he, he h, h, h, hooked up, a, a, a, all th, th, these wa, wa, wa, wires a, a, and squi, squi, squi-ggly li, li, li, lines sh, sh, sh, shot ou, ou, out of th, th, th, this ma, ma, ma, ma-chi-chi-chine."

"What did the doctor tell you about the results?"

"He, he, he, sa, sa, sa, said ev, ev, ev, eve-ry, ry, ry, thi, thi, thi, thing tur, tur, turned out n, n, n, norm-al."

"Have you ever passed out before?"

"No, no, no."

"Did the doctor know about all your symptoms?"

"Ye, ye, yeah. He, he, he sa, sa, sa, said I wa, wa, wa, was o, o, o, okay. It wa, wa, was all in my, my, my h, h, h, head. He, he, he g, g, gave me t, t, t, the pr, pr, pr, pre-scrip, scrip-tion to ca, ca, ca, calm d, d, d, down."

"Does it work?"

"I g, g, g, guess, ba, ba, ba, but it m, m, m, makes me goo, goo, goo, goo-fy."

"Does anyone care to join in?"

"Recovery does teach us to believe in our doctors. When every disease has been ruled out, we pretty much can guarantee it's a nervous symptom," Neil, the meticulous custodian, offered while adjusting his book exactly parallel to the table edge.

"Anyone else?"

"Dr. Low also tells us to take any prescribed medications according to the doctor's orders," Tracey added, coddling her useless arm as though hugging a baby.

"Did you spot any of your symptoms?"

"Ya, ya, yes, wa, wa, wa, while I wa, wa, wa, was s, s, s, sit-ting here. I t, t, t, told my, my, my, my-se, se, self that I h, h, h, have ne, ne, ne, ne-ver fa, fa, fa, fain-ted; tha, tha, tha, that my fe, fe, fe, feel-ings were di, di, di, di-stres, stress-sing, ba, ba, ba, but not d, d, d, dan-ger, ger-ous to, to, to me; I to, to, to, told my, my, my-self re, re, repea, pea-tedly, ly that I, I, I ha, ha, had the wi, wi, wi, will to b, b, b, bear the di, di, di, discom-com-fort br, br, brought on b, b, by my, my, my st, st, st, stom-ach do, do, doing ba, ba, back f, f, flips."

"And how would you have reacted before your Recovery training?"

"I wou, wou, wou, wouldn't even b, b, b, be h, h, here. He, he, he, heck, if it wa, wa, wa, wasn't fo, fo, for my wi, wi, wife in-sis, sis, sis-ting tha, tha, that I at-te, te, tend the me, me, meet-ings, I pr, pr, pro-ba, ba, bly wou, wou, wouldn't s, s, show up. I'd b, b, be in bed, h, h, h, hid-ing fr, fr, from the wo, wo, world. I'm a-frai, frai, fraid to d, d, do or s, s, s, say any-th, th, th, thing. I've ga, ga, ga, got wha, wha, what you g, g, g, guys k, k, k, keep ca, ca, call-ing s, s, symp-toms r, r, right now."

"The important thing is you recognize them and work at controlling them instead of letting them control you," Rose contributed with an efficiency as though reading from a text, avoiding her usual rambling.

"You controlled your muscles, commanding them to do your bidding," Gloria chimed in, adjusting her outdated cat's-eye black rimmed glasses back onto the bridge of her nose with her index finger.

"Don't forget to pat yourself on the back for finally speaking up today," Abbot jumped in. "It's called endorsing yourself. Dr. Low considers it a critical part of your recovery."

"Any other comments, suggestions, or assistance to offer Gene?"

The attendants looked at each other and exchanged satisfied glances.

"I think this is an excellent point to call it a day. Thank you all for one of the best meetings I have ever attended."

"*Maybe this can help me,*" Eric concluded.

"And Eric, you have a book as well as the guidelines. I hope to see you here again," Jack offered.

"I think you can help."

"I know we can."

On the way to his car, Eric spotted Gene waiting on the corner for his wife. "Gene," Goodson called out, "I just wanted to apologize for interrupting the meeting. I hope I didn't cause you too many symptoms," Eric smiled.

"Th, th, th, ats o, o, okay. My, my, my life's be, be, been a me, me, mess since tha, tha, that damned fif, fif, five car pi, pi, pi, pileup an, an, anyway. So, so, so ma, ma, ma, many pep, pep, people di, di, died. I dr, dr, dr, dream about tha, tha, that garbage tra, tra, tra, truck all th, th, the time." Gene's thoughts drifted.

"The quadruple fatality in Grand Circus Park?" Eric instinctively switched to an interrogation mode.

Gene shook his head affirmatively while clearing his throat. "I, I, I'll ne, ne, ne, never un, un, un, under, under, sta, sta, stand wh, wh, why the ca, ca, ca, cop wi, wi, wi, with the wa, wa, walkie ta, ta, talkie he, he, helped the, the, the tr, tr, truck driver an, an, and na, na, na, not me. He lo, lo, looked right a, a, a, at me, me."

"The police arrived after the accident and chased down the driver," Eric recited.

"N, n, n, no. H, h, h, he was pa, pa, parked ri, ri, ri, right there, wa, wa, wait, wait, waiting," Gene relayed as he turned and got into his wife's car.

As she sped off, Eric yelled out, "Where are you going? We've got to talk. You can't leave now. This is important."

Eric failed to notice the non-descript Ford sedan pull away from the side-street curb.

CHAPTER

101

FRAMED IN THE FLIMSY aluminum storm door as though a Norman Rockwell original entitled, *The Elderly Immigrant*, Albert sensed despair as he waited to greet his grandson. Lacking the rhythmic bounce of his usual gait, his suspicions were confirmed as the young man lumbered up the stairs, abandoning his energetic two at a time bound. Timing his last step, the old man swung open the door. "Come!" As Jack entered, Albert sandwiched his grandson's face between his sturdy palms, rose up on his tiptoes and planted a kiss on his forehead. "Mongo! You so good to remember Papa." The greeting accented with a welcoming wave as the elder Michaels slipped around Jack in the cramped foyer, following him into the living room.

"Sit!"

J.Z. dropped into Albert's charcoal gray velour Lazy Boy recliner. Gramps disappeared for two minutes, returning with two long neck bottled beers. Handing one to Jack, they clanked the containers together. "Nostrovia!"

After a healthy swig, Albert decided to pry. "Crazy people no make you feel like this. You say they good for you. Only one thing do this to young man---woman. Tell Papa."

Jack squirmed. The beer dangled over the armrest. "I left Sarah."

"Where you leave her?"

"No, no. We split up." Gramps knelt down, peering up to force Jack to look at him. "Actually, I broke it off."

"Why you do such a thing?"

"She's not the person I thought she was."

Albert scrunched his face. "A beautiful, caring, woman, no?"

"Not quite." Jack refused to raise his head.

"She no fool me. Eyes say she love you."

"She lied to me."

"Everyone have secret. No need to tell." The aging sage patted his grandson's knee.

"I wish she wouldn't have."

Albert waited as Jack struggled with embarrassment. "What so bad?"

"Ugh Gramps, she's a stripper."

The old codger's eyes lit up as he mumbled some unintelligible Russian phrase. "I come to this country for freedom. At same age you, Cossacks raid village and take away my Katrina. Do terrible things. Throw her out with trash when finished. No need talk. Hold her through night. Feel good she alive. Never away again." Albert extended his arm and lifted up Jack's chin. "You go!" He took the dangling beer from his grandson's hand and set it on the coffee table.

Wired from the startling revelation, Eric burst through the doors of the fatal squad and headed straight for the closed file cabinets, disregarding his medical leave status. Locating the manila folder entitled "Goodson, Angie" the stressed detective commandeered the nearest desk and began the tedious task of reexamining each scrap of paper.

"There is no record of an officer witnessing the accident," Eric exclaimed to the empty room. *"No one assisted the truck driver. They arrested him an hour later sitting in a bar. Either Gene is stark raving crazy, or someone is hiding something."* A resolve not felt for months, Eric decided to retrace all the investigative steps.

Goodson hustled up Woodward Avenue to the Elwood bar, releasing the door handle as he entered and instinctively rubbing his thumb across the inside of his fingers on his left hand, wondering quietly about the composition of the sticky goop.

Flashing his badge to the tee shirted, tattooed bartender, Eric inquired, "Were you on duty last spring when the cops came in and busted the sawed-off prick that killed the four people with the runaway garbage truck?"

"Whoa! Slow down there, partner."

"Well?"

"Yeah. But I heard he pled out. You're a little behind on your caseload, ain't you sport? You one of them mentally challenged hires the government makes to beef up their stats?" The bartender snickered.

Eric sucked in a deep breath to quell his rising nausea. "You can give me all the guff you want as long as you can help me out, but if you're just jerking me off for your own personal amusement, I'm gonna douse your ass with your finest screw cap blend and turn you into a gigantic smartass flambé. Have we succeeded in establishing a pleasant repartee?"

"Hey look man, I was just funning with you," the repentant waiter replied, defensively holding up his hands. "What can I do for you?"

A tiny white bubble in the barkeep's goatee distracted the detective until he concluded its origin as spittle. The bizarre observation had an equally strange calming effect on Eric. "Tell me what you know."

"The guy came in, sat down right about where you're standing and ordered a draft. Five minutes later you guys came in and busted him."

"That's it?"

"I asked the cop what he did. He said the guy killed several people in an accident down in Grand Circus Park and fled the scene a few minutes earlier. Then he told me to mind my own friggin' business."

"Something strike you as unusual?"

"Didn't smell like a garbage collector. It looked like he was out for a casual stroll. Not our usual clientele, if you get my drift."

Eric scanned the tavern, "Yeah, I see. Anything else?"

"No sweat."

"What?"

"The guy was a freshly powered baby's ass. What did he do, take a friggin' cab? That accident was over a mile away. He's scrambling from the scene and he hasn't broken a sweat?"

Eric scribbled his name and number on a napkin. "It's a get out of jail free card. Thanks."

CHAPTER

103

Eric's mind raced with scattered thoughts, accented by the backdrop of a persistent pounding in his ears. Normally interpreting his feelings as an exploding aneurysm, or, the onset of a stroke inciting fear of imminent physical danger and touching off a vicious cycle of nervous symptoms, the energized detective ignored his frailties and decided to re-canvass the scene. His first choice, the Deputy Dog Coney Island, a landmark storefront restaurant on the southeast corner of Grand Circus Park. A hotbed of around the clock activity transcending every social strata, Eric approached the counter, "Excuse me, I would like to ask you a few questions?"

"What's to question? We got hot dogs, coney dogs, fries and Coke," the strong voice of an obvious foreigner responded as he slapped down a plate with two coneys and walked away.

"But I just…"

"Two on one with, and a single loose," the counter clerk yelled to the grill man over the din of rambling customers.

Following the waiter to the soda dispenser, Eric asked, "Could you give me a minute? I…"

Sliding the Coke down the counter, the waiter stopped briefly to take another order and bellowed, "A deuce loose light."

Eric zipped around the counter as the waiter turned away, "Just a goddamned minute. I need to ask you some questions and I need to do it now."

"Sit," the waiter commanded.

"I don't have time…"

"I fix it to go."

"All right then."

"Two in the yellow tubes and a fry," the immigrant shouted.

"I didn't order French fries."

"Then maybe I can't answer questions."

"Jeez. Alright already," Goodson scowled as the waiter snickered. "Do you recall the five-car pileup with the garbage truck last spring?"

"Yes. I call you several times and no one does nothing."

"You mean you telephoned the police at the time of the accident."

"Certainly. But I call many times for several days before, and you don't care."

"What are you talking about?"

"The garbage truck. It sits in the alleyway for three days blocking my deliveries. I call, but nobody cares. The driver just sits there, smoking his cigarettes and tells me to mind my own business. He talks in a box to somebody."

"A box?" Goodson pondered. "You mean a walkie-talkie?"

"I don't know how you say it. All I can tell you, he race out the back and into the cars…boom!"

"Thanks." Eric left his order sitting.

"Tip! No tip?" The waiter called out.

"Oh, sorry about that," Eric responded, tossing a five on the counter.

CHAPTER

104

Reeking of booze and attempting to primp his disheveled preppy attire in the distorted image of the leaded glass side panel, Jack leaned on the buzzer to the townhouse. Still tucking in his shirttail, the door opened. Stunning in a skintight, two-piece, royal blue with white trim, Nike exercise outfit and sporting one-carat diamond earrings, Sarah silently ran her eyes across Jack.

The half in the bag contrite stud stumbled for the appropriate opening. "Gramps said we were made to be together. Something about Cossacks raping and pillaging. I never quite understand him, but he is, barring none, the wisest person I know."

"Look at you? I leave you alone for a couple of weeks and you fall apart on me. Do you want to come in?"

Jack nodded and reached out for her hand. They moved to the couch without a word. Jack laid down as Sarah guided his head to her lap. She placed one hand in the center of his chest and stroked his hair with the other.

"I can't imagine my life without you," Jack whispered.

Tears streamed down her cheeks. "I love you too." They rested quietly for an hour. Sarah peered down at Jack. "I really am good."

"What are we talking about?"

"The dancing."

"I can't wait to see you."

"You already have, once."

Jack, eyes scrunched, "I don't recall."

"Maybe an encore will refresh your memory." In one fluid movement, the lithe vixen got up from the couch and led the wide-eyed pup into the bedroom.

CHAPTER

105

Detective Goodson secured the address through the DMV and abruptly shot from the far-left lane to the I-75 exit on the right, heading to the bedroom community of Royal Oak, approximately thirty minutes north of Detroit. The lack of trash strewn grassy berms alerted Eric to his arrival in the suburbs. Slowly cruising along a row of recently renovated 1920's style Georgian row houses on Main Street, Goodson hunched his head over the wheel and squinted to make out the address.

"Where are you, you little rascal?" Sleep deprivation clouding clear thought with taunting mind games, tricking Eric into borderline absurd conduct. "Hah! Gotcha," Goodson yelled as though finally discovering the elusive piece of a puzzle as he whipped to the curb.

Ornate cast iron street lamps lined a brick paved public walk that branched off to the stone step entrance of each townhouse, encasing an impeccably trimmed postage stamp of lawn. Goodson bounded up the steps, his toes slipping off the third of five stairs, lunging him forward onto his right shin.

"Son-of-a-bitch!" Eric screamed, immediately bending over to rub the injury. *"Pull yourself together, Eric. You're a professional, remember?"*

The solid rap at the door jolted Jack from a deep sleep and propelled him to his feet.

"What is it? What's going on?" Jack fumbled with his under shorts, managing to clear one leg while trapping the other in the seat, losing his balance and crashing to the floor. Exasperated, he took a moment to regroup. Reflexively reaching down to his crotch to investigate a strange sensation, the groggy flounder realized he neglected to discard his used prophylactic. "*Ewh! This could be a problem.*" He gently picked at the plastic. "*Three years into a relationship and she still makes me wear these things. Unbelievable!*" Another series of mind-numbing pounds interrupted his delicate endeavor. Flailing around in a second frenzied attempt to adjust his shorts in a scene reminiscent of a Dick Vandyke slapstick episode, Jack finally triumphed.

"Jack, what are you doing down there?" The sultry vixen inquired, shaking off her dream state.

"I'm in the final of two out of three falls with my boxers."

"Are you okay?"

"I think I broke Little Louie," Jack lamented, peeking down his shorts. "How would they fix him, anyway?"

"Jack, would you just answer the door?"

"At the very least, I de-laminated him."

"Quit your mumbling and get the door, please. But be careful. It can't be anyone we know at this hour," Sarah managed while torquing to sit up.

"Boy, I guess the honeymoon really is over."

The relentless pounding continued as Jack traversed the kitchenette to the living room.

"Alright already! Couldn't you just ring the bell like a normal person?" Jack muttered as he peered through the leaded glass side panel at the distorted image. "Detective Goodson? What the heck are you doing here? It's the middle of the night, isn't it?" Jack asked, rummaging his hand through his hair. "Don't tell me it's the Mink case again?"

"Jack, can you open the door please?"

"Oh yeah, right."

Stepping into the tiny, but elegant foyer, the combination of sleep deprivation and personal loss exploded into a barrage of desperation, "You've got to give me Gene's address right now."

"What? Gene?" Jack inquired, scratching his head. "Gene who?"

"You know. The quiet guy from the group."

"How did you even find me here?" The semiconscious suspect inquired.

"Your girl's address was in my file. I stopped by the apartment, but the building was vacated; some kind of gas leak, or something. I figured you'd most likely be staying over with her."

"*My girl,*" Jack thought. "*A secretary? But I don't have... oh, okay.*"

"Why would you need to contact him?" Jack asked, now back on track.

"It's personal. Just tell me where he lives, would you?"

"I can't give you that."

Alarmed at the intensity and volume of the unfamiliar voice, Sarah called out, "Jack, who's there?"

"It's okay, babe. It's nothing, really. I'll be back in a minute. Go back to sleep."

Visibly agitated by the interruption, Eric jumped in, "Don't give me that privileged crap. You're not a licensed therapist. I checked."

"No, you don't understand."

"I need to find him now."

"I don't know his address, or his telephone number. Several of the group have my number in case they have a setback, but I don't have anything on them. It's a totally anonymous system."

"You don't understand how important this is," Goodson pleaded.

"I really don't have any information on him other than what he has revealed during the sessions. I really can't help. You'll just have to wait until the next meeting; that is, if he shows."

"But what if he doesn't?"

"I don't know what to tell you."

"It can't wait. There must be another way."

"Maybe if you tell me what's going on, we can figure something out."

Eric's confrontational mood swung to borderline depression. "It turns out he was in same auto accident that killed my wife."

"You promised me you wouldn't take advantage of the group. You're not a cop at a meeting."

Sarah slipped into a white terrycloth bathrobe and struggled to find the sash, while stepping into fuzzy eared bunny flip-flops. Making her way in a half-dazed saunter to the bedroom doorway, she leaned against the jam, listening to the exchange.

"I didn't break my word," Goodson responded softly. "He mentioned it in casual conversation while he was waiting for his ride."

Jack quietly exhaled while unclenching his fists. "Don't you have records on it, then?"

"I checked and rechecked them. On routine traffic accidents, files are incomplete. Cops consider them a pain in the ass. They leave it to the insurance companies to sort out the mess. But when the fatal squad gets involved, they're always thorough; measurements, photos, interviews, IDs and narrative reports. This case is slop. It doesn't make sense. The investigators should have been raked over the coals."

Recalling Goodson's reaction to mentioning his wife's death, Jack uncharacteristically searched for tactful phrasing. "Would there be a criminal charge in a fatality?"

"The guy responsible immediately copped a plea. There was no need to tie up loose ends."

"What about Mamoud?" Sarah's raspy voice caught both Jack and Eric by surprise.

"What does he have to do with anything?" Jack's remark clearly meant to deflect an intrusion.

Sarah allowed a second for J.Z.'s brain to catch up to his mouth, then interrupted the contrite stud's anticipated apology. "He's a newspaper reporter; they're all part bloodhound. I'll bet he could help find Gene."

"Who's she talking about?"

"Mamoud Shaloub. He works for Wayne State's paper, *The Southern Edge*."

"What can he do that could help?"

"Maybe nothing, but another body couldn't hurt," Sarah shrugging off Eric's attitude.

"He's quite a resourceful guy," Jack offered, shaking his head in agreement with Sarah's suggestion. "We met him when Mink got us involved in his harebrained scheme to track down unreported police killings during the '67 riots. Turns out his Father disappeared during that time. Since we hooked up, so much weird crap has happened you could write a book."

A searing pain shot through Eric's head, triggering a momentary extended blink, coupled with a noxious heave as he groped to catch a breath.

Recognizing the onset of symptoms, J.Z. reached out, taking hold of Goodson's upper arm, "You okay?"

Struggling to regain his composure, Eric stammered, "Tell me exactly what's been going on."

Sarah stood erect, "I better put on a pot of coffee; this could take all night."

"All night? What the hell have you gotten into?"

"That's what we'd like to know," Jack snickered.

The litany of freakish events spanned the spectrum of the police felony handbook and flabbergasted Eric. Silently retracing his own steps while Jack and Sarah continued the discourse, Goodson shuddered at the realization of police involvement and his own inadequacies as an investigator.

Completing the tale, Jack and Sarah stared at Eric. Snapping out of the mental lapse, Eric ordered, "Call your friend. We're gonna need all the help we can get."

CHAPTER

106

THE UNMARKED TAN FORD sedan swerved from the center lane of westbound Congress Street into the southernmost curb lane, just behind the City County Building, cutting off a SEMTA bus. As he jumped out of the vehicle, Marzoli raised his middle finger in response to the blaring horn, abandoning the car in a no parking zone, with the right rear corner still blocking the path of the bus.

Hustling up the walkway, the Detective gripped the aluminum framed exterior door and pulled with the fury of an Olympic Discus athlete going for the gold. At the sound of crashing glass, a young lawyer following behind dove three feet to his left to avoid the ricochet. Approaching a packed elevator, an elderly clerk noticed the look on Marzoli's face and voluntarily stepped off. As the door re-closed, the Chief of D's shoved his arm in front of two cramped riders and pressed the button for the fourteenth floor. With each stop, Marzoli swore under his breath. The lone occupant to the top floor, the detective shot out of the lift and headed for Prosecutor Evans' office, ignoring the hail of the receptionist.

Bursting through the intricately carved mahogany double doors, Marzoli commanded, "Evans, we need to talk!"

"Why certainly, Chief," Evans calm response caught Marzoli by surprise. Shifting his gaze to his three department heads, he instructed,

"That's all for now. We'll continue this discussion during lunch at the Caucus Club. I'm buying." Riley glided two short steps to the floor to ceiling windows, admiring the view of a five-hundred seventy-five-foot freighter sauntering up the Detroit River.

As the door closed behind them, Marzoli commented, "How magnanimous of you." The lack of response brought further comment to a halt, while Marzoli realized his guffaw and considered his next move.

Swallowing hard, Tony's stutter cut short from a rapid turn and Evans outburst, "Who the fuck do you think you are?" Riley raged, a barrage of spittle flying with every syllable. "Barging in here while I'm in the middle of a meeting with my key people." The prominence of a bulging vein on the left side of Evan's head a clear indicator this would be the brow beating of the century. "Nothing in that thick Italian head of yours could be important enough for you to interrupt me."

As Riley pulled out the pocket square of his thousand-dollar custom suit to swipe across his mouth, Marzoli mistakenly thought it the appropriate time to apologize. "You're not listening, asshole!" Riley screamed, while simultaneously drawing a nine-millimeter from a quick release shoulder holster. "I could drop your ass right here and the three people you saw me dismiss earlier would all testify under oath that I drew in self-defense. That's loyalty; and not one of them would ever consider interrupting me the way you did."

Marzoli fidgeted with a slight foot shuffle and glanced to a wall of exquisite paintings, while the rant continued. "I've known you since eighth grade. You were a low-life fuck then, selling twenty-five cent cop a feels on Lucy Nordell's tits in the vegetable isle of Vince's Party Store at Vinton and Georgia. Come to think of it, you married that bitch."

"Okay, okay. You made your point. Will you quit waving that thing around? I was pissed. I'm sorry, okay?"

"It ever happens again, I put a nine mill right in your head. It would be a terrible waste of an asset after all the time I put in mentoring you, but, by god, I'll do it."

"I know, I know, I know. I'm sorry and it will never happen again."

"I know it won't!" Evans declared. "Now what was so fucking important that you had to spoil my morning? Lucy refusing to put out?"

"C'mon Riley, I already apologized."

"Okay, okay. Now spit it out!"

"Goodson has been trying to talk to one of the accident victims. The guy is so fucked up he can't even talk; stutters like a jack hammer. Can't imagine he could get anything out of him."

"That's why you burst into my office and screwed up my morning? That's something you could easily take care of yourself. Just off the son of a bitch."

"I know, I know. I guess Goodson is getting to me. It seems that no matter what we do, he just keeps on coming, like that fucking energizer bunny."

Got to be more than that!"

"Sorry. Had a fight with the wife. She's been humping some fuck who bought her a twenty-thousand-dollar necklace."

"What are you complaining about? That's a hell of a profit increase from the twenty-five cents a throw to feel her up in eighth grade."

"Well, when you put it like that," Marzoli chuckled.

"Now get the hell out of here. I'll talk to O'Hara, but you know how reluctant he'll be about offing a cop."

CHAPTER

107

THE BREAKFAST DISCUSSION STARTED innocently enough, but soon escalated in to a full-blown shouting match.

"Dad, it's casual Friday. No one wears their uniform," the perky sixteen-year old calmly explained.

"You're my daughter and I will not have you appear in public in that outfit," her Father insisted.

"It's my volleyball uniform. I wear it every day after school for practice. I don't see the problem," the teen pleaded. "Everyone wears their sport uniforms on casual Friday."

"That is not appropriate attire for private school. Everything hanging out everywhere. That's the sort of thing you expect at public school."

"But Dad…"

"Don't but Dad me. Up to your room immediately and don't come down until you have an appropriate uniform on. I'll speak to your Headmaster later."

"Oh, great! I'll be the only one in uniform today. Everyone will think I'm a dweeb."

"Up to your room." Glancing at his solid gold Rolex, he said, "Two minutes!"

"I hate you," the young lass screamed, storming off to her room.

The staff could tell by the look on his face, this was going to be a trying day. His clerk pursued the all-business approach. Dispensing with niceties, the summa cum laude Michigan Law School graduate placed the day's docket in front of the Judge. "Your Honor, your first case is The State of Michigan-vs- Alonzo Thorton. If you recall, Thorton is the eighteen-year-old male with a full ride basketball scholarship to Tulane who allegedly, along with his cousin, assaulted a fifteen-year old on her way to school."

Their discussion was interrupted by the Judges private line. In response to the low chime, the clerk collected an arm full of files and backed out of the room.

"Yes," the Judge's abbreviated response.

"We have a problem," District Attorney Riley Evans relayed.

"Which is?"

"Leonard Goodson, an old classmate of yours, is appearing before you today in the Thorton case. He is the uncle of Detective Eric Goodson, the cop looking into the riots."

"Killing his wife didn't deter him?"

"No. Marzoli's convinced he's the Energizer Bunny."

"Hard to believe that didn't stop him. What a waste of a gorgeous woman. I officiated at their wedding. Did I ever mention that?"

"I'm touched."

"I'm sure you are."

"No matter what we've done, he keeps digging. Time to mess with the rest of his family."

"Your point!"

"Leonard is the personal guru for his nephew. Think maybe, you should put him in his place?"

"Looking forward to it."

The District Attorney just stared at his telephone receiver, relieved at the absence of the usual thirty-minute argument to convince the conservative Judge to adhere to his idea. *"Now, why in the world would he jump at the chance to purposefully tube a case?"*

The Court Clerk announced, "All rise: The Third Circuit Court in the State of Michigan is now in session. The Honorable James O'Hara presiding."

Judge O'Hara, "You may be seated."

The Clerk, "The Court calls case number FH-45872-87, The State of Michigan-vs-Alonzo Thorton, one count aggravated rape and one count of statutory rape.

"Your Honor, James O'Toole for the State."

"Leonard Goodson for the defense, Your Honor."

The Court, "Gentlemen, we are here for jury selection; are there any pre-trial motions you would like to entertain?"

"Yes, Your Honor," the assistant prosecutor proffered while rising out of his chair. "The prosecution would move to have defense council sanctioned for intimidating the complainant and her neighbors."

An indignant Judge, "In my chambers immediately, gentlemen."

"It has come to the prosecutor's attention that Mr. Goodson visited all the complaining witness' neighbors, as well as, the complaining witness' residence itself. In doing so…"

The Judge raised his arm, palm extended, to the prosecutor, "I've heard enough counsellor." Turning to the defense lawyer, "Mr. Goodson, care to explain, because if you don't have an iron-clad excuse, I'm going to toss your well attired torso in jail and then have your license pulled. Is that clear?" The Judge's voice bouncing off the cherry wood paneled office walls, as he threw himself back in his chair and cupped his hands behind his head.

The old warhorse faced many a cantankerous Judge throughout his multi-decade career. In his early years, a similar threat would have precipitated numerous immediate nervous symptoms, but a forty-year career of demanding judges immunized Leonard Goodson. Standing his ground, but in a respectful tone, "Your Honor, I took the time to thoroughly investigate this case, just as I have any of the thousands of cases I have handled over the years. Did I canvass the neighborhood for witnesses? I certainly did. Did I stop at the complaining witness' house? Yes, I did."

"You see, Your Honor, he admits it," the assistant prosecutor jumped in, akin to a second grader squealing on his classmate.

"If I could continue, Your Honor?"

Judge O'Hara swung his high-backed dark cherry leather executive chair forward, slamming his forearms on the desktop, "You've got sixty seconds!"

With the demeanor of a priest listening to a litany of sins from a penitent during confession, Attorney Goodson continued, "The complainant resides in a residential neighborhood comprised of two-family flats and four-plex units. She lives in the southwest quadrant of a four-unit building. I avoided any contact with the victim, but I did personally knock on the other three doors, one of which happened to be the grandmother. When I introduced myself and handed her a card, she informed me, in no uncertain terms, that the prosecutor instructed her not to speak to anyone. I thanked her and left. I assume she called the prosecutor's office. No harm, no foul."

"He had no business there, in the first place. He knew his presence would scare the victim," the prosecutor chuffed, a spray of fine spittle arching to the judge's desk.

"I'm inclined to agree with you, Mr. O'Toole," the Judge's conciliatory tone deeply concerned Goodson.

Jumping in, before the Judge could continue, Goodson questioned, "Your Honor doesn't believe I have a duty to thoroughly investigate a case on behalf of my client?"

"There can be a thin line between investigate and intimidate," Mr. Goodson.

"Your Honor, I have six witnesses sitting in the hallway, awaiting the bailiff's call. Each of them discovered by my neighborhood canvass and each will testify that the victim approached and pursued my client willingly. There was no rape."

"Great! Then this case is resolved," The Judge boomed. "Maybe no forcible rape, but we are still left with statutory rape, since the victim was only fifteen at the time. Let's go out and put this on the record, then call it a day."

"But, Your Honor, in order to prove statutory rape, there has to have been sexual intercourse. We're not admitting that."

Playing off the Judges sentiment, O'Toole chimed in, "Seems pretty clear to me."

"Really, Mr. O'Toole? There is absolutely no physical evidence to support your claim; no rape kit; no clothing; nothing at all to indicate a sexual act took place. If she's lying about the rape, and she is, you think the jury will believe her about the sex?"

"Seems you gentlemen should be able to work out some sort of plea on this," the Judge reasoned. "In the meantime, I'm putting this matter over thirty days and remanding the defendant to the Wayne County Jail."

The Judge caught the first chink in Goodson's armor, a mild flutter of his left eye along with profuse sweating.

"But, Your Honor, this is a one-day trial. The investigating police officer is already in the courtroom and all my witnesses, who are all elderly, are out in the hall. Surely, we can conclude this matter today."

"You heard my ruling, Mr. Goodson."

"But, Judge, my client is an eighteen-year old who will lose a full-ride scholarship to college. Can't we…"

"That's it! Twenty-five hundred dollar fine for contempt. One more word out of you and you'll be joining your client in the adjacent cell."

Goodson turned and while storming out of the office, declared, "See you in the Court of Appeals, gentlemen."

Observing the assistant prosecutor's awkward backward shuffle out of his chambers reminded the Judge of a medieval court jester's move to placate a maniacal king. Picking up his private line and pressing number 2 on his direct dial, Prosecutor Evans answered, "Yeah, Evans here."

"Gave Goodson something more to think about," the Judge relayed.

"Really?"

"You should have seen the look on his face. Pretty much knocked his dick in the dirt."

"Outstanding. You're getting more like me every day."

"Now why did you have to go and spoil it like that?" The Judge griped, slamming the receiver into the headset.

CHAPTER

108

By 5:00 A.M., JACKED on adrenaline, Eric decided to travel the one hundred twenty miles to Jackson State Prison. The drive on Westbound I-94 seemed only minutes as Goodson ignored the monotonous string of strip malls and fast-food outlets interspersed every five miles at easy on-easy off ramps between cornfields, repeatedly reviewing the accident events. Pulling up to the ice-cold monolith surrounded by twenty-foot-high barbed wire topped blood red brick walls always piqued a disturbing nerve in Eric. Home to several thousand hard-core felons, Jackson State harbors a national reputation as a shit hole. With only minimal updates for computerization, the Spartan structure retains all its original 1930's design; depressing for the inmates, as well as, the guards. Lacking any pretense of reform, death, generally vicious and swift, the only variable thwarting a one hundred percent recidivism rate.

Eric checked his weapon and incurred a full body search prior to log in. An overwhelming stench reminiscent of his high school locker room and the earsplitting cacophony of thousands of frustrated inmates reverberated through the corridor as security led Goodson to an interview room. He tossed an opened pack of Winston's on the table as a shackled prisoner entered.

"Melig?" Goodson asked as the blotchy faced skinflint collapsed into the metal folding chair.

"Yeah, who wants to know?" The rough edge an obvious ploy from the frail con.

"I'm Detective Goodson from the Detroit P.D."

"Whoop de fucking do."

"Are you okay? You look like ten miles of bad road," the regrettable remark slipping out.

"You Mary fucking Kay and my sadistic cellmates are bitching about my lack of foundation, or something? I ain't heard them complain when they ram it up the Hershey highway every chance they get. Now speak your mind, or get the fuck out of here and leave me be," the agitated inmate railed, the taint of self-disgust evident in his body English.

"My name doesn't ring a bell?"

"You some kind of asshole game show host now? Why don't you give it up and quit messing with me, or, get lost?"

"Sorry. I'm looking into the accident that put you here."

"Tell somebody who gives a shit."

"My wife was killed in that accident."

The inmate sat silent, twittling his thumbs.

"I'd like to hear your version of what happened."

"Go read the Court transcript. I said the brakes failed and they said I was drunk. Who cares?"

"I do. So many things don't add up."

"Nothing's perfect."

"But this is so far off the mark that I'm surprised it didn't raise all kinds of questions."

Lonnie Melig refused eye contact, but his nonchalant mannerism of clutching his open necked shirt now abandoned for outright fidgety movement.

"Help me out here, please," Eric pleaded, bending over and placing his left palm on the con's shoulder. Melig visibly tensed. Goodson, sensing he crossed the line to intrusion, pulled back. "Anything. Anything at all that might help. C'mon, I'll do what I can for you."

"The last time I helped the police, look where it got me; a two-bit whore for any con with a hard on and twenty pounds over me."

"What can I do to help?"

"You can get me the fuck out of this pit!"

"That's not going to happen unless you've got something really good that I can use to prove your innocence."

"Well then, I guess we're both fucked, because I was driving that truck," Lonnie conceded, turning away with a dead stare, an almost imperceptible trace of moisture trailing down his cheek, collecting at the jawbone.

Goodson allowed Melig a moment, as much for himself as for the con. An uncontrollable urge to burst into tears consumed the cop. "*Can I really be empathizing with this pathetic creature trapped in this cesspool, or, is something still terribly wrong with me? Pull yourself together and get the info you need out of this scumbag.*" "Why were you sitting behind the coney island for three days before the accident?"

"Who says I was?" Lonnie shot back, with a fractured inflection in his voice.

"An eye witness saw you there several times."

"Just taking a break, I guess."

"How did you get to a bar over a mile from the scene so fast?"

"Always quick on my feet," the smartass con regaining his prison composure.

"But you didn't even break a sweat?"

"Strong gene pool."

"Who was the cop that helped you out of the truck before all the other emergency vehicles arrived?"

Lonnie subtly stiffened, pausing a few seconds before answering. "Don't have any recollection of that."

"Did you have a walkie-talkie on you?"

"Yeah. I like to keep in touch with my kids," Melig's conspicuous twist just shy of a squirm.

"Speaking of your boys, how do you afford to keep them in that fancy private school up in Beverly Hills? Kind of hoity-toity at twenty plus grand a year per kid, wouldn't you say?"

"My parents were a product of the Depression; they taught me to save."

"By my calculations, your Mom would have given birth at roughly, age fifty. I don't think so."

"Okay, so my grandparents. So what?"

"Even if you stashed every cent you made, you couldn't pay the freight. And besides, didn't you just start that job the week of the accident?"

"Lucky day at the track, I guess."

"Quit jerking me around. I didn't come up here to yank your chain. Short of getting you out of here, is there anything I can do to help you out?"

"Kill me," Lonnie whimpered, a tear now flowing down his cheek.

"Get serious."

"Do I look like I'm fucking kidding?"

"Give me something, anything!"

"And what? You're just going to dump on me like your buddies."

"How did they screw you?"

"I'm in here, aren't I asshole?"

"But you killed four people, including my wife. I'm supposed to feel sorry for you?"

"I was supposed to be segregated from all the other prisoners."

"But why? You're no obvious threat."

"Because the last time I was in here, somewhere between the first and nine hundredth gang rape, I tested positive for HIV. Now, I'm a twenty-four hour in call bitch service spreading my own little epidemic. Do you have any idea what this place is like for a guy my size?"

Goodson reared back, stunned as much by the brutal honesty as the admission, but his training triggered skepticism. "But they test prisoners on a regular basis, then separate the AIDS cases from the general population."

"Yeah, but somehow my tests always come out negative. Go figure."

"If I get you solitaire, what can you tell me?"

"They paid me to hit that line of cars and take the fall."

"Who did?"

"Some animal. Never saw him before; haven't seen him since."

"But why?"

"I'm not really sure, but I've heard things since."

"Like?"

"You sure you can get me segregated?" The wretched death for stoolies a clear picture in Lonnie's mind.

"No promises, but I'll do everything I can, including getting a lawyer for you if I have to."

"They wanted to whack some cop's wife," Lonnie relayed softly, glancing at Goodson for the first time. "Sound familiar?" The tough con act too engrained to let go.

Eric staggered, gasping to catch his breath while the room spun uncontrollably around him. "Why? Why would they want to kill Angie?"

"You must have seriously pissed somebody off."

"Why would you do it? You don't have a violent history."

"I already had a death sentence from the last stretch and they knew it. I wanted to make sure my boys would be taken care of. I'm sorry."

"My God! She's dead because of me," Eric mumbled as he turned and instinctively waived for the guard to open the door.

CHAPTER

109

THE DISLODGED TRIO NESTLED in a back booth at the Traffic Jam, petrified with fear, further muddling their predicament with steady massive infusions of caffeine. The jukebox blared with Janis Joplin praying for a *Mercedes Benz* while a well-intentioned jean clad waitress' efficiency spoiled J.Z.'s perfectly cream-colored coffee.

"Don't be staring at her ass like that. It's not that great," an accusatory Sarah unloaded on Jack.

"What? I wasn't checking her out, I was glaring."

"Do you drool when you stare?"

"I said 'glare'; she ruined my coffee. You know how long it took to get that delicate balance of cream and sweetener? She snuck up on me and destroyed it before I had a chance to wave her off."

"You were ogling her ass. You don't think I know when a guy is ogling? You can feel it right through your buns as you walk by them. Men are such dogs."

"Look kids, can we call a truce here," Mamoud pleaded, as he scratched at his peeling skin. "If we don't figure something out quick, we can all kiss our cute butts goodbye. There are people out there trying to kill us. We need help. We're in way over our heads."

"I wish Mink were here. He'd figure something out," Sarah lamented. "God, he loved this place."

"I actually try not to think about him because I always get choked up," Jack confessed.

"I'd give anything to have him back just for a day," Sarah whimpered.

"Look, if you two don't pull yourselves together, we'll all be doing the Shirley Temple stairway to Heaven tap dance on the six o'clock news and seeing a lot more of Mink than you could ever imagine. He's the one who got us into this mess to begin with, so don't be shedding too many tears," Mamoud raved. "We're on someone's serious shit list of people and things to eliminate. Now get a grip! You two have been going at it recently like two pit bulls."

Embarrassed, their exchanged glances acknowledged a truce.

"Since detective Goodson is looking into it, shouldn't we be okay?" The statement uncharacteristically naïve for Sarah, but the return to her naturally sultry voice once again commanding the undivided attention of the most disinterested of the male species.

"Someone almost killed us and it's a good bet he's a cop, just like your friend."

"He's also a wreck. I'm really not sure how much help he could be if he really wanted to," Jack shaking his head in doubt. "The guy tried to off himself by slashing his wrist."

Sarah got up to go to the ladies' room, but paused with a thought, resting her right hand on her hip, thirty-eight inches above the floor. "What about Roy Blue at work? You always speak so highly of him. How he seems so well connected and resourceful."

"He could be with them. When Mamoud told me about stabbing the guy, he shows up at work the following Monday with a bandage on his neck the size of my wallet. Gives me some cock-and-bull story about having a boil lanced. I know for a fact he was at a card game all weekend with the cops."

"We've got to put this thing together and give it to the papers. It's the only safe way for us," Mamoud reasoned.

"What about you publishing it?" Jack quipped. "You're the one always pressing me to give you a good story, aren't you?"

"If you've paid attention to what's been happening the past several weeks, Sherlock, you would have deduced that: a) my offices have disappeared in a blaze of gory, pun intended; b) I wanted to write a story, not my own obituary."

"Point taken."

"We've got to piece this thing together and we need help doing it," Sarah concluded. "The pig who attacked us isn't giving up."

"But he did confirm one important point by calling me a Canook. It's got to mean a black man. If we're right about that, taking 'C' to the border has got to mean they kill him."

The room fell silent. Racking their brains to form a strategy, or, entertaining the idea of just giving up, Sarah finally got the discussion back on track.

"What is it that got us in to this mess in the first place? If we know that, maybe we can flush these guys out somehow."

Brenda strutted up to the table, pot in hand, ready to pour. "We're all fine. Bring us the bill when you get a chance," Sarah ordered, darting her eyes for a peek at Jack. A quick learner, Jack retained his focus on Mamoud. His friend propped his elbow on the table with his chin resting on his thumb, gently shaking his head and smiling at the display.

"The article on Mink's lecture," Mamoud bellowed, scrambling to list the incidents on an imaginary sheet of paper.

"That could be it!" Jack chimed in, scooting around in his seat reminiscent of a tike during a preacher's Sunday sermon.

"Alright then, let's put together enough for a follow up story. Maybe we can make them nervous and take the pressure off of us," Jack reasoned.

"I don't think that will be enough," Sarah commented.

"Why not? You may have scared him off, especially since you can identify him now," Jack offered.

"No, not him. Sarah's right," Mamoud chimed in.

"How the heck do you know that?"

"He enjoyed it too much," Mamoud stated. "He literally tried to pound my head through a concrete floor. I've even got the stitches to prove it."

"You could see it in his eyes. Scary, sadistic, demented eyes," Sarah relayed in a cold drone, staring straight ahead.

CHAPTER

110

DETECTIVE GOODSON PACED UP and down the sidewalk outside the old church for a full thirty minutes, awaiting Gene's arrival.

"Damn, what if he doesn't show? What am I gonna do then?" Goodson muttered to himself.

"What's that you say, young man? Eric, isn't it?"

"Oh, sorry. I just need to talk to one of the group and I'm hoping he comes today."

"And that would be?"

"Gene, Ma'am."

"Well, he's been quite fastidious about coming. And after his breakthrough last week, I can't image him not making it. And my name is Rose."

"Yes Ma'am." The elderly woman dipped her head and arched her brows, giving the look. "Thank you, Ma'am; I mean, Rose."

"You have a look that reminds me of my Edward."

"What's that?"

"Determined. If it involves Gene, tread cautiously; he's in a delicate state. Patience is a virtue, you know."

"I will Ma'am." A quick partial glance called attention to the error. "Er, Rose."

Rose moved to Eric's side and slipped her arm under his, patting the back of his hand.

"Time to go inside. You have to settle down some before you do whatever it is you have to do."

Eric melodically tapped his fingertips on the table, pausing every ten seconds to glance at his watch and then, scan the entrance. Passing on the introductory reading, he excused himself to get a coffee. Returning to the table, it struck Eric that everyone seemed to be waiting on him.

"What?"

"I think it might be a good time to give your first example," Jack coached.

"I really can't think of anything to say," Eric responded, as he unconsciously rubbed the healing scar on his left wrist.

"Sometimes, the simplest little things make the best examples."

"Such as?"

"Well, what about your feelings right now?"

"Nothing special."

"Really. You think that's why the entire group is focused on you? You've been as antsy as a terrorist in a kennel of bomb sniffing dogs. Besides the physical manifestations we've witnessed, I'm sure you're experiencing nervous symptoms. Do you care to share them with us?"

"I'm waiting on Gene. Everybody tells me he's always here and I have something important to discuss with him, and, as you can see, he's not here."

"Does that produce any discomfort?"

"I'm a wreck!"

"Try to avoid interpretations. Just tell us what you're experiencing."

"I don't know what's racing faster; my brain or my heart. I'm fearful that he won't show and it's making me nauseous. I'm starting to think he's purposefully late and I'm angry. I'm showing temper at him for his tardiness and at myself for not being able to locate him on my own."

Have you attempted to spot your symptoms?"

"Not until you put me on the spot."

"No pun intended, I'm sure," Rose smirked.

"But I can see now that I've worked myself up into a vicious cycle when it's a situation over which I have no control. There is no right and wrong in what's happened. My expectations for him to be on time were unreasonable."

"My, but you've been paying attention," Jack kidded.

"Angie always said if I put my mind to it and studied, there was no one better. I guess she was right about that."

"Remember that your feelings are distressing, but not dangerous," Tracey offered, cuddling her useless arm.

"To go along with Tracey's comment, you must convince yourself that you have the will to bear the discomfort," John contributed in his distinctive Bavarian tone.

"Although you didn't take the time to endorse your efforts, it's never too late," Rose relayed with her matronly charm.

"Eric, you've really taken the time to learn the language of Recovery; now you've got to continually practice. Eventually, you will control your symptoms instead of allowing them to control you," Jack commented, genuinely impressed by Eric's display.

The meeting continued on with a second example as Gene meekly slid in, head down, whispering, "sa, sa, sa, sorry", as he took a seat next to Eric.

"No apologies necessary, Gene. We're all just glad to see you," the leader stated.

Eric's mind raced; his concentration on the group lost. He found himself rattling off the Recovery sayings one after the other. Eventually, he found himself regaining his composure and actually listening to the presentation. *"I'll be darned. There may really be something to this system."*

Adjourning for cookies and coffee, Eric corralled Gene.

"My wife died in the accident you were involved in."

"Sa, sa, sa, sorry,"

Eric tried to hide his impatience as he waited for Gene to finish. "Thank you. There are so many things about that day that don't make sense; I was hoping you could help me."

"I, I, I'll d, d, d, do wa, wa, wa, what I ca, ca, ca, can."

"You said the cop was sitting there waiting."

Gene nodded.

"What kind of car was he in?"

"Ta, ta, tan fo, fo, fo, Ford se, se, se, sedan."

"Can you describe the officer for me?"

"Ta, ta, ta, tall, da, da, da, dark ca, ca, ca, comple, ple, plexioned, eh, eh, eh, ta, ta, talian, shar, shar, sharp dre, dre, dress ser, mi, mi, mid thri, thri, thirties, ha, ha, ha, hand, sa, sa, sa, some, li, li, like an ac, ac, actor."

"Did he say anything?"

"Ta, ta, told the, the, the d, d, d, dri, dri-ver to ge, ge, get hi, hi, his ass mo, mo, mo, moving."

"Anything else you can remember, strike you as curious, or unusual?"

"He, he, he ha, ha, had one wa, wa, walkie ta, ta, talkie wa, wa, when he g, g, got out of, of, of the ca, ca, car and ha, ha, had t, t, two wh, wh, when he, he ga, ga, ga, got out of, of, of the tr, tr, truck."

"You're certain?"

Gene nodded.

"My God," Eric mumbled, "The whole thing was staged. But why?"

Tears streamed down Gene's cheeks, "Ple, ple, ple, please fi, fi, find out who, who, who di, di, did thi, thi, this to, to, to, me."

"I will."

"Promise?"

"I promise," Eric stared squarely into Gene's eyes, as he shook his hand.

As the detective approached the stairway, Jack commented, "Get what you needed from Gene?"

"I did."

"You sure don't look happy about it."

"I may be in way over my head. Now, I think I might have endangered Gene."

"Well, you're a cop right?"

Eric nodded.

"Then get him protection."

"That's the problem. I think it's the police who caused his accident. I don't know who I can trust."

"Don't sweat it. I've got just the guys."

CHAPTER

111

Rodeo laid on the horn as he wheeled the bright orange 1978 Ford F-100 4x4 pickup from the northbound Schoenherr Road center turn lane onto westbound Canal Road.

"Lord God Almighty, you trying to kill us, you crazy hillbilly," Pepatino screamed from the passenger side as he hoisted his hockey stick to slash Rodeo.

"Whoa! Whoa! Whoa!" Torpo yelled from the center seat, attempting to block the blows.

"What?" Rodeo questioned. "Anyone could see it was a late yellow."

"Late yellow, my ass. That light was red for at least five seconds. Cars were already in the intersection. You just don't have the slightest idea what a brake is for. You've been zipping around like you're the only one on the road."

"Almost never get stopped. Cops always assume from the color, it's a road commission vehicle."

"Or, they don't want to deal with a jackass that would buy a truck this butt ugly."

"Ladies, ladies, please," Max pleaded. "We should be coming up on it any minute now. Jack said to look for the white clapboard house with a big old red barn behind it."

"All I'm seein' is subdivisions," Rodeo commented.

"There it is, up there on the left." Jimmy smiled, "Look at the old Mail Pouch Tobacco ad painted on the barn. Haven't seen one of those since I was a kid."

"Wow, that was back in the olden days, huh?" Max chuckled, as Pepatino started to raise his stick.

As the trio climbed the seven concrete steps to the front porch, the door opened, emitting a waft of smoke.

"Well, looky here? A hockey player, a cowboy and a what, beer salesman? You boys a might early and a little old for tricker-treaters, ain't ya?" The figure filled the doorway in a colorful Hawaiian themed moo-moo, with her head wrapped in a matching babushka, tied with a knot in front.

Max swallowed hard, "We're here to protect Gene, Ma'am."

"That's rich! Whad ya, weigh? Bout the same as a loaf of white bread. And you call me Ma'am one more time, you better be wearin' a helmet, cause I'll pound you into the ground like a fence post. Name's Bernice."

"Bernice it is." Max responded as though apologizing to his first-grade teacher. "I'm Max. This here's Rodeo and number nine is Jimmy Pepatino."

As she pushed open the screen door, Rodeo leaned into Pepatino and whispered, "Man, she's scary. Maybe they don't need our help."

"Sure they do. They just don't understand what they're up against."

As the group assembled in the living room, Gene suddenly appeared, extending his right arm up and around Bernice's waist. "I, I, I s, s, s, see yu, yu, you me, me, me, met my li, li, li, little angel." Glancing about, Gene continued, "Wo, wo, wo, wow, y, y, y, you re, re, really are on s, s, s, skates."

Jimmy smiled, "Have been all my life. Played semi-pro hockey for fifteen years. Just couldn't hang 'em up. Helps me keep in shape."

"Well, you picked the perfect number for this area. Howe's a saint in Macomb County," Bernice conveyed.

"Taught him everything he knows," Jimmy laughed. "He just had a hell of a lot more natural talent than I ever did." Everyone chuckled, then Pepatino continued, "Well, we better get busy. We've got about six-hours to prepare. Jack tells me these guys move real quick, so they'll probably show up tonight, or, tomorrow at the latest."

"Shouldn't we be calling the police?" Bernice asked.

"Wouldn't do any good to call now," Pepatino related. "Cops side with cops. It's after they fuck up and can't explain what they were doing that'll get the locals to question them."

"Okey-dokey, but if you get my man hurt, I'll be puttin' the hurt on you. Understood?"

"We're gonna do the best we can."

As Bernice turned to leave, Jimmy sheepishly asked, "Say Bernice, are those rum soaked you're smoking."

"Sure are. Still get these babies for ten cents apiece."

"We packed up in such a hurry, I forgot all about my cigars."

"Whole jar of 'em out on the kitchen counter. Feel free."

"You're a life saver."

"That's what I'm expecting you to be too." Bernice raised her right eyebrow, turned and sashayed into the kitchen, her flip-flops clacking with each step.

CHAPTER

112

Arriving just minutes after sundown, a series of red cones blocking the drive prompted the four-door sedan, lights out, to coast to a stop within inches of the rear bumper of Rodeo's truck. Three of the four occupants jumped out, 9mm pistols in one hand and walkie-talkies in the other. Moving around the pickup, the assailants glanced in, then two hustled to cover the front and rear entrances to the house and the third to the barn.

"No lights on in either building and it's not that late," one intruder cautiously conveyed.

"But that's their truck in the drive," the second assault team member assumed.

"Guy is supposed to be a basket case. Probably turns in early," the driver chimed in. "You guys smell anything strange?"

"It's a farm, asshole. Now get your head screwed on straight and let's get this job done. I want to catch the rest of the game tonight," the attacker waiting outside the barn barked.

"On my mark!" The leader's voice squawked over the handhelds. "Remember, no one comes out alive. It's a home invasion gone wrong."

After shoving the antique pine kitchen table aside, Pepatino surveyed the line of sight to the rear door. Nodding in satisfaction, he instructed Max, "Grab that six-pack out of the freezer. Set the first can down right here," pointing to the dimple in the linoleum from a table leg. "If it takes more than one, which I highly doubt, toss a second one on the same spot."

Racing to the living room, they repeated the procedure, creating a clear line of sight on the diagonal to the front door.

"Remember Gene, pull the cord soon as you hear somebody fiddlin' with the door," Max instructed. "I've lined it up the best I can. It'd be a million to one shot you actually hit somebody, but it sure will scare the crap out of 'em."

Bernice paced incessantly, with the fingertips of one hand gently tapping on her upper chest and fanning herself with the other. "Max honey, you sure that little toy is gonna stop some maniacs hell bent on killin' us? When y'all first said you was here to protect us, I had my doubts. But this …," vigorously shaking her head, "…This is just plum loco."

"It's just to stall him long enough until we can get to you. Believe me, this little beauty really packs a punch. When I was a kid, my uncle brought one over and shot it off in the basement. Put a spike eight inches into a solid brick wall."

"We're dependin' on y'all. My Geney can't take no more pain."

"Everyone set?" The lead assailant whispered into the microphone. "Two?"

"Two is a go."

"Barn is quiet."

"We're good at the road."

"Go, go, go!" the detective ordered.

Charging up the seven stone steps two at a time, the intruder instinctively prepped to kick the door. As his foot hit the thin plastic mat, it plunged five-feet onto a pile of prearranged jagged rocks, followed a millisecond later by a two-hundred twenty-pound body. As his right foot caught between two rocks, his remaining weight in freefall snapped and compressed the three ankle bones. His left leg struck a broken glass gallon jug Max had added at the last minute to remind him of his glory days in the tunnels. It shaved the kneecap off with the precision of a skilled surgeon.

The rear villain stealthily worked his way up the back stairs, slowly turned the knob, opening the unlocked door. Taking one step into the dark kitchen, a loud smack froze the invader. A split-second later, he clutched his neck and sunk to his knees; dead, but still struggling to overcome. The perfect execution of a Stanley Cup game winning shot on goal. Pepatino giggled like a middle schooler.

"Never heard an Adam's Apple crunch like that," Max cringed.

"Get a move on!" Jimmy yelled.

The slight jar of the metal clasp triggered Gene to yank the string. The miniature canon exploded, propelling a marble-sized steel ball-bearing at super-sonic speed, while lifting itself a foot off the ground. While Bernice scooted over to Gene, gripping him in a bear hug, the projectile penetrated the half-inch thick, weathered oak plank siding.

Rodeo threw off the tattered and stained painter's canvass tarp and scrambled up to the driver's seat. Pumping the gas pedal with the fury of the lead cyclist in an uphill battle to the finish line at the Tour de France, he turned the key. The raw fuel ignited as it shot past a live spark plug expertly installed at the end of the tailpipe. Fire engulfed the sedan, reminiscent of a World War II maneuver clearing an enemy bunker with a flame thrower.

The driver relaxed, allowing himself to drop his head back and close his eyes, leaving the details of the mission to his capable confederates. Coterminous ungodly screams, a canon blast and the truck in front of him seemingly bursting into a ball of fire, jolted him. Fumbling for the two-way radio lying on the bench seat next to him, while bulging eyes stared at the blaze ahead, he screamed into the radio, "They got a fucking bazooka, or somethin'! What the hell is going on? They blew up the fucking truck."

Instinctively rushing to the aid of his associates, he threw open his door and attempted to jump out. Restrained by his seatbelt, flames charred the interior upholstery and scorched his upper torso, while he struggled to release the clasp. Recognizing his predicament, he grabbed hold of the interior handle and pulled the door shut. Before he could start the car, the conflagration rapidly spread through the four-inch-deep straw, dusted with a light mist of kerosene, scattered from the road to the rear of the truck.

The front door opened. The assailant gave a full tooth smile at his turn of fortune. As he struggled to climb out of the hole, he pointed his weapon directly at Torpo.

Max jumped back and yelled, "Gun!"

Simultaneously, Pepatino wound up and let loose with a vicious slapshot six-inches off the floor. The sound of crackling enamel brought shivers to Torpo. The makeshift puck struck dead center in the transgressor's mouth.

"Score!" Max cried. "You're two for two, Jimmy."

Rodeo ran the Ford up to the barn, while the straw fire raged. Jumping out, he checked on a body lying prone in the dirt, fifteen-feet from the door. "Damn." Within seconds, Torpo and Pepatino caught up. "Was just gonna check on Gene," Rodeo stated.

Bending down to inspect the victim, Max exclaimed, "What a lucky fuckin' shot. Right in the eyeball and out the back of his head. Jeez, that had to hurt."

"He wouldn't have felt a thing. Now the guy on the front porch, he's in some serious pain. Think I knocked out every tooth in his mouth. He's gonna wind up looking like me," as the retired center popped out his false teeth. "Hope the city has a good dental plan." Pepatino gummed.

Wiping a tear from his eye, Jimmy remembered, "Hey, what about their driver?"

"If his car is still there, he's shish-kabobbed," Rodeo announced, shaking his head.

The explosion rocked the ground beneath them and induced a group duck.

"Ewh! He's done like dinner, Boss," Max chortled.

"Okay then. The local bulls should be here shortly. Max, get Bernice and Gene out of the barn. Have Bernice help you locate anything to make a quick sign for the front porch stating, 'Keep Off'. Get my travel bag and pull out the roll of caution tape and run a piece across the stairway. Rodeo, hook up a hose and try to put that fire out. Make sure to pick up the driveway cones."

Rodeo raised his arm and twirled his index finger.

"Maybe he's improving. Usually wants to twirl something else," Jimmy commented, then immediately walked it back, "Naw."

"Whada you gonna do, Boss?" Max inquired.

"I'm gonna see if this guy could have made it in my old league," Pepatino's sinister look raised everyone's eyebrows.

CHAPTER

113

PEPATINO RUMMAGED THROUGH THE kitchen drawers until he located the aluminum foil. He quickly ripped off a two-foot-long section, crumpled it up into a ball and skated to the front door. Squatting down, he slapped the intruder's face.

"Wake up, douchebag! Time to see if you're as tough as you've always thought." The unresponsive assailant angered Jimmy. A vicious smack to the multiple fractured jaw drew an exaggerated groan and a plea, "No more."

Pepatino grabbed a handful of hair, jerking his head back. "No más, no más, won't do it. You would have killed all five of us. When you were done, you and your little band of wannabe desperados would've hit the nearest bar to celebrate. So, I'm gonna show ya how we use to do it in my day."

Jimmy grabbed hold of the assassin's nose with one hand and his chin with the other, prying open the fractured jaws and shoved the ball of metal foil into his mouth. Amid the muffled screams, Pepatino explained, "When I played semi-pro hockey, the guys were real animals. Not like these wimps today. We played with broken bones and concussions. You could tell how many years a guy's been playing, by how many teeth were missing. Thing was, we had a routine we went through every time we spit out a tooth. We'd chew on tin foil to see if we had any raw nerve endings, cause that would mean the fifty bucks a game we got paid was gonna go to the dentist instead. Used to give me the heebie-jeebies, know what I mean?"

Simultaneously, pushing down on his head and up on the chin, the executioner's head turned purple, tears streamed down his face. The screams faded to gurgles and then, nothing.

Sirens in the background sidelined the interrogation. "You're one lucky asshole," Pepatino remarked, while gripping a handful of hair, forcing the assailant to look at him.

Multiple police, EMS and fire trucks arrived on the scene, as the five survivors stood in a group alongside the house. Firemen peeled off and immediately tackled the ground fire and smoldering car.

"Jeez, there's a body in the car," one firefighter called out.

A tall, white, uniformed Sterling Heights officer approached, "What happened here?"

"It's a long story," Jimmy sighed.

"Well, give me the Cliff's Notes version."

Max scratched his head, "Who's Cliff Notes?"

"Don't worry about it, Max. I'll explain later," Jimmy smiled.

"Better start explaining real quick, cause there's apparently a body in that burned out car," the officer demanded.

Pepatino leaned in and noticed the shoulder stripes, "Well, Sergeant, is it?"

"Yeah, Sergeant Orlowski, SHPD."

"We better take you on a tour, because there are two more bodies and one survivor."

"Just a second, I better call this in," Orlowski instructed, then walked back to his car. After informing the dispatcher to get ahold of the chief, he yelled, "Listen up! You two, block off Canal Road a quarter mile in each direction. Nobody gets in or out, unless they are police personnel. Got it!" Directing his attention back to the group, "Take me to the survivor."

"This way," Jimmy pointed with his stick, while pushing off with one foot to get his momentum going. Ducking under the tape, he took the steps as easily as anyone in shoes.

"Get the paramedics up here," the sergeant called out, while he reached down and felt the carotid artery for a pulse. "Think he's gone too."

"Pity," Pepatino muttered.

"What's that you said?" Orlowski questioned.

"Nothing, sir."

"Musta swallowed one a dem poison things hid in his teeth," Rodeo commented.

Max, Jimmy and the Sergeant glanced at each other and just shook their heads.

"What?" Rodeo questioned. "You see it all da time on TV."

Returning to an upright position, Sergeant Orlowski stared at Pepatino, "Tell me something. Do you always run around on roller blades and carry a hockey stick?"

"Most of my life."

"Hmph. And you always hang with the cowboy and the beer man?"

"They're friends."

Pepatino, Max and Rodeo directed the officer to the kitchen, then on to the barn.

"All three guys in cheap suits, carrying walkie-talkies and packing 9mm's. If I didn't know better, I'd say these guys were cops."

"Really," Rodeo blurted.

"You gentlemen have any reason to think that."

All three shook their heads in unison and answered, "No, sir."

"At first glance it certainly looks like a home invasion gone bad, but we'll know more when the forensic team gets here. In the meantime, you want to tell me how you guys managed to pull this off?"

"Just lucky, I guess," Pepatino responded.

"Yeah, right. You clowns took out four professional killers with a fucking hockey stick and a toy canon," an astounded Orlowski stated.

"Well, it's late, but I want all of you to get checked out by the paramedics, then you can go. You're all so hopped up on adrenaline, probably won't do any good to get your statements tonight."

Orlowski called out to the officer that inspected the truck. "Find anything?"

"Nothing but an old painter's tarp, sir."

"No weapons, or anything?"

"No, sir."

Turning in the direction of the burned vehicle, "Any ID on the crispy critter?"

"Nothing yet, sir. But you better come over here and check out this plate."

"What's the problem?"

"I think it's a municipal plate, Sarge."

"Son-of-a-bitch. They were cops. This is gonna get real messy, real quick."

Walking back to the group of five, Bernice and Gene were hugging Max, Rodeo and Pepatino.

"Okay to leave, Sergeant?"

"We've got all your contact info and I'm sure our detective division will be contacting you for formal statements. So yeah, you can go."

"Thanks again."

"Anything for old Number 9. He's the greatest athlete of all time."

Bernice couldn't help herself, "Told ya, Jimmy."

CHAPTER

114

T HE EPITOME OF FINE dining in Detroit, the London Chop House, located in the Murphy Building at 155 W. Congress, was a comfortable stroll for both Judge O'Hara and Prosecutor Evans. The black uniformed doorman greeted the Judge with a full-face smile and vigorous handshake; a curt nod acknowledged Prosecutor Evans. Drawing the attention of the maître d', Ricardo scurried around the hand-carved black walnut dais, arms extended with an arched back, "Your Honor, what a pleasure to see you again."

The Judge easily slipped into the hug and returned the embrace, "Ricardo, you always brighten my day." As O'Hara stepped back, he inquired, "How are the wife and kids?"

"Fine, fine, fine, sir. Thank you for asking."

"Your oldest is staying on the straight and narrow?"

"He's been wonderful."

"Good. You tell him I'm rooting for him."

"Most certainly, Your Honor. Now, may I show you and Mr. Evans to your usual table?"

"That would be wonderful, Ricardo."

As they followed Ricardo to table number one, Evans leaned into O'Hara and whispered, "Jim, I'll never understand why you waste your time with the peons of the world."

"It makes me feel good to see people smile."

"I'll never understand that."

"No, I don't suppose you would."

As Ricardo motioned for them to enter the U-shaped maroon leather booth, he snapped two folded black linen cloth napkins open and placed them on their respective laps. "Will there be anyone else joining you today?"

O'Hara responded, "Two more."

"Ah, Commissioner Dolan and the Italian actor, no doubt," the maître d' smiled.

"Your memory always astounds me," O'Hara responded with a gentle shake of his head.

As Ricardo sashayed back to his station, Dolan and Marzoli blew by him without the slightest acknowledgement. Cramming into the booth, Dolan dispensed with the small talk, "We've got a serious problem."

"So nice to see you too." The Judge's mild rebuke went unnoticed.

"What now?" The Prosecutor demanded, as the waiter approached the table.

Before he could say a word, the Judge chimed in, "Jason, we've some business to tend to. Bring us a pitcher of water, please. Then give us about thirty minutes uninterrupted."

"Certainly, sir."

The foursome waited for the waiter to return with the water before continuing.

"We lost four of our best guys last night," Dolan relayed while wringing his hands.

The table clearly deferred to Evans. "Who is lost and how did you lose them?"

"They went out to take care of that guy, Gene. The witness that Goodson talked to."

"So, they got lost?"

"No, dead is what they got."

"All four of them?"

"Yeah."

"How in the hell did that happen?" Evans volume clearly escalating.

"Don't really know. The details are real sketchy." Dolan turned to Marzoli. "Fill him in."

Chief of Detectives, Marzoli cleared his throat, "Well, they headed out to Sterling Heights last night to take care of that witness, like we talked about earlier."

"Wait," the Judge instructed. "We were never told he lived out there. I think we all assumed he was a Detroit resident. I know I did."

"Whatever," the Prosecutor quipped. "What fucking difference does that make? We'd fucking kill him wherever he lived."

"It's a huge difference," the Judge argued. "We can control almost everything that happens in our jurisdiction. Macomb is a whole different story. But okay, give us the rest of it."

Marzoli shook his head, "Don't really know. Called a former DPD cop to sniff around and he was real hush, hush. So, I called the Macomb County Medical Examiner. No autopsies as yet, but the preliminaries show one guy got a crushed larynx; a second, some large round, like a fifty caliber, in the face; another burned to death; and the fourth, get this, choked on a ball of tin foil."

"Have they been identified as police officers?" O'Hara inquired, shaking his head.

"Not yet, but it's only a matter of time."

Evans left foot kept a private beat, while his grip tightened on the crystal water glass.

"This is a nightmare," the Judge commented to no one in particular. "The press is going to be all over this. And when they find out all four were Detroit police officers, it will make national news."

Dolan leaned in, setting his forearms on the table. "We'll stall, as long as we can, but their prints are on file. We've got maybe a day, two at most. We'll have to throw together a story about them being rogue cops and we have no idea what was going on. Marzoli, I'll need you to plant some drugs, or whatever."

"You got it."

The Judge's hand visibly shook as he raised his glass to take a sip, causing water to dribble down his chin. While he reached for his napkin, he calmly relayed, "I told you from the start, just let this thing die down on its' own. You guys wouldn't listen. Now the bodies are really piling up."

Riley Evans could feel the blood rushing to his head. His heart pounded so hard, he thought his chest would explode. His grip on the water glass tightened to the point of discoloring his fingers. "Enough!" He commanded. A final squeeze and the Waterford crystal shattered, slicing through several fingers and gouging the palm of his hand. "Son-of-a-bitch," the Prosecutor huffed as he quickly wrapped the injury with his napkin.

Jason hustled to the table with a clean chef's apron. "I'm so sorry sir. What can I do to help?"

Accepting the makeshift towel, Riley uncharacteristically responded, "Nothing. I'll be fine. Thank you for your concern," and calmly walked to the restroom.

O'Hara just arched a brow.

Jason replaced the table linens, cleaned up the debris and brushed off the bench seat."

Dolan, Marzoli and O'Hara exchanged glances. The Judge broke the silence. "At least he didn't throw it."

CHAPTER

115

Aʜʙɪ ꜱᴀᴛ ᴏɴ ᴛʜᴇ edge of his locker room cot, repeating the inscription on the back of the watch. Through his permanently clenched teeth he wondered aloud, *"She musta really, truly loved him. I wonder if a woman could ever feel like dat bout me? Course not, you broken down old fool. Ain't nothin' works no more, sep maybe dat; and it ain't no sure bet on dat neither --- been so long."* The melancholy janitor slipped the Omega onto his wrist, surprised at the instant comfort he derived, despite its loose fit. Allowing his body to fall to the side, he drifted off to a peaceful sleep.

Ahbi dreamed of wearing slick suits and dining at a fine restaurant, similar to places in downtown Detroit he passed in his days on the street. People greeted him with a smile and treated him with the respect deserving a pillar of the community. They all commented on the wristwatch.

"Got dat from a friend of mine; a Mister Roy Blue. He gave it to me, he surely did," Ahbi related to all those within earshot.

"My, must be some friend," a well coifed, shapely young woman without a face, remarked, *"That's a once in a lifetime kind of gift."*

Ahbi thought a second, *"Oh, it's nothing like dat. I just holdin' it for him. He a good friend."*

As the maître de seated Ahbi at a window table, the bellicose harangue of a familiar voice abruptly interrupted the enjoyable episode.

"What was that?" Ahbi shook his head and listened intently as he tried to decide whether he was still dreaming.

"I should have killed that son of a bitch when I had the chance," the ranting continued as it grew in ferocity and proximity.

"No, God please, no!" Ahbi cried, jumping from the makeshift bed and scrambling to reach the light switch. *"You've got to escape to the warehouse,"* the panicked custodian told himself.

As Ahbi hustled down the narrow, dim lit hallway separating the locker room from the conference area, the gargantuan figure of Harrold Mayer appeared, blocking his exit.

"Well, if this ain't my fuckin lucky day. I oughta hit the liquor store and buy a lotto ticket on the way home," the ogre calmly reasoned, although his bulging eyes and weird grimace exposed his true intentions.

Ahbi panicked, twisting to the right, then to the left; overwhelmed with fear, he took slow, deliberate steps back, silently praying for a miracle.

Snickering at the helpless little whimp's predicament, Mayer mirrored Ahbi's movement. "You're mine now, asshole."

Reaching the middle of the corridor, Ahbi extended his arms to the walls, ostensibly bracing himself for a beating.

"Why you little scumbag, you're wearing my watch. Give it back now and I won't mess you up too bad."

Ahbi stared at the Omega; a sense of serenity and strength urged him to resist. "Belongs to a friend. Wouldn't be right allowing you to steal it."

"You piece of shit. I'm gonna rip it off, along with your arm. Then I'm gonna beat you to death just like I did to your brother years ago."

"I have a brother," Ahbi murmured, momentarily halting his retreat.

Stunned at the perceived quandary, Mayer fell out of character, "Goddamn, you an ignorant bastard. I was speaking in one of them metaphor things. I can't believe we've put up with you people all these years."

Ahbi snuck in an additional step back, grasping a doorjamb with his right hand; a second step allowed him to grab the knob. In one blistering quick motion, the custodian disappeared.

"Why you sneaky prick. Now I'm gonna beat on you till I can't raise my fists one more time. Your own mother ain't gonna recognize ya," Mayer screamed, barreling down the snug hall with the velocity and intent of a bullet through the muzzle of a weapon of vindication aimed at a live target.

Ahbi dashed across the conference room to the main exit. Jerking open the door, he collided with a massive figure.

"Surprise!" Harrold roared, lifting Ahbi off his feet with one hand. "Move pretty quick for a big man, don't I puke?"

Ahbi squirmed, but Mayer twisted his fist and tightened his chokehold. Starving for air, Ahbi flailed his arms, the pad of his left index finger striking a soft, wet substance and eliciting a shriek out of Mayer. Instinctively, the struggling prey raised his arthritic finger and thrust forward, driving the craggy nail deep into Mayer's right eye.

Butchie dropped Ahbi, clasping both hands across his face as a gusher of blood seeped through his fingers. "You poked my eye out! I don't believe it! You dirty little prick; you blinded me. I'm gonna rip your shriveled little balls off and stuff them in your mouth. You bastard!" Butchie blared, as he tossed back and forth, doubled over in pain.

Ahbi scattered to the far corner of the complex, attributing his good fortune to the Omega. *"It just feels like it belongs."*

CHAPTER

116

Eric bounded up the precinct steps. His preoccupation prevented a negative comment on the depressing condition of the building.

"Got a message for you Detective," the desk clerk handed the pink telephone slip to Eric. "Said it was important."

"Yeah, thanks," Goodson replied, noting the call from the warden at Jackson State Prison regarding Lonnie Malig.

"Warden, Detective Goodson here. My boy finally wants to talk?"

"That would be difficult."

"I don't get it."

"Found him dead in the shower. Apparently slipped on a bar of soap."

"Yeah, right. Well, thanks for your call."

"Hold on, there is one more thing."

"You had video cams in the shower?"

"No, afraid not. Privacy laws and all that, you know. But a search of his cell turned up a letter from a lawyer regarding trust funds. Our inmates generally converse with their attorneys in person, or by phone to avoid a paper trail. You told me to keep an eye out for anything unusual, and this certainly qualifies from our point of view."

"Who's the lawyer?"

"A guy downtown in the Asner Building by the name of Lawrence Draw."

"Never heard of him. What firm is he with?"

"L.G. Draw Law."

Stunned, Eric froze; his mind blank, he struggled to remember what he was doing with the receiver in his hand. *"My God, that's the schlock Angie worked for."*

"Detective Goodson? Are you still there?"

"Yes," Eric cleared his throat, "I'm here."

"I thought we got disconnected there for a minute."

"Can you fax that over to me?" Eric responded in a soft whisper.

"Glad to. Hope it helps."

Eric plopped back into his chair, trying to regain his composure. The trite Recovery sayings popped into his head: "*Distressing, but not dangerous; I have the will to bear the discomfort; the way to shed your fears is to give firm directions to your muscles.*" He found himself calming down and deciding his next move.

CHAPTER

117

"Uncle Leonard, its Erie."

"It's been so long, a vindictive person might respond 'Erie who?' But it's always so good to hear your voice, I can't help but be elated."

"Always talking to the jury, aren't you?"

"It's a living. Now, my son, to what do I owe the pleasure."

Eric brought his uncle up to speed on his investigation.

"Have you ever heard of a lawyer named L.G. Draw?"

"In the Asner Building?"

"That's the one."

"Isn't that the firm Angie worked for?"

"I never put it together before, but yeah, she was a file clerk. She never really talked about it. Whenever I asked, she just said, 'same old, same old'. I just assumed she was bored. So, what's the skinny?"

"Just rumors mostly; real shady character; a professional liability carrier's nightmare from a legal malpractice standpoint. I do recall him being disbarred several years ago. I think it involved him forging a Circuit Judge's name to a court order. The attorney defending him before the bar association died under mysterious circumstances the morning of the hearing, if I'm not mistaken. Allegedly took his own life while walking across his front lawn on the way to his car at 5:00 a.m."

"That is peculiar."

"Two of his former partners met premature deaths as well. He's a real schlock."

"Would he have any contact with the Detroit P.D.?"

"Not directly, but I do believe one of the partners has represented the police union for years."

"That's it! Thanks Unc."

"Let this be a life lesson for you."

"What's that?"

"Never trust anyone who uses an initial instead of their real first name; they're hiding something."

"Okay, Unc."

"Erie, if these guys hurt my little Angie, just let me know what I can do to help."

"You've done more than enough already, Uncle Lenny."

CHAPTER

118

Goodson's fingers blazed across the antiquated keyboard, ignoring the tacky keys splashed with untold cups of coffee and stained from years of second-hand smoke. Another achievement he attributed to Angie. "*It's as if she's looking over my shoulder, smiling. Remembering all those nights I cursed my head off while learning the Mavis Beacon typing program she surprised me with on my birthday. The howling belly laugh when I complained about Mavis' foul mouth; unbecoming conduct for a teacher. God I miss her so much! Concentrate! She would want you to push on.*"

The internet search of the Police Union failed to turn up a lead, but Eric refused to give up. Scanning every word of the website, he caught a reference to the Police Benevolent Association. Under the heading 'Charitable Programs', sub category 'Scholarships', the money was awarded to the Melig brothers for their academic achievements by the Chairman, Police Commissioner Dolan. A link to the Board of Directors listed Prosecutor Evans, Judge O'Hara and Chief of Detectives Marzoli.

"*Pretty Boy Marzoli! Son of a bitch! That's who Gene saw at the scene.*"

CHAPTER

119

In no mood for traffic signals, Goodson raced four blocks east to southbound I-75, rather than follow a straight shot on Woodward Avenue to Downtown Detroit. Violating procedure, Eric flipped on his dash mounted red strobe light and zigzagged through traffic, reminiscent of a stock car driver charging to the checkered flag. Momentarily distracted by a constant loud thump, Eric finally recognized the sound as the beating of his own heart.

"The feeling is distressing, but not dangerous; I have the will...bullshit! Maybe this feeling is distressing, but wait until I get my hands on that shyster lawyer; he's gonna find out how dangerous I am. And we'll see if he has the will to bear all the discomfort I'm gonna bring his way. I'm gonna move my muscles all over his face. We'll see what Dr. Low thinks about that!"

Eric took the Madison Avenue exit, which dumped him onto Grand Circus Park, the site of Angie's accident. Too intent on interrogating L. G. Draw to dwell on the unpleasantries of the collision site, Eric whipped left onto Washington Boulevard. Blowing past the hoard of abandoned retail and office buildings, occasionally interspersed with a yuppie loft renovation, in excess of thirty miles per hour over the posted limit, Goodson arrived at the corner of Michigan Avenue in twenty seconds. Abandoning his vehicle at the curb on an angle facing oncoming traffic,

Eric bounded toward the office tower. Years from rejuvenation and a considerable distance from the courthouse, Eric failed to notice the unusual location for a law firm. Pacing while awaiting the elevator in the refurbished neoclassic meets cheap chic lobby, he elected to run up the stairs to the third floor. Glancing at the bronze nameplate on the fake stone background, he burst through the door.

"Police! Which way to Draw's office?"

"Down the hall to the right, but you can't just go down there; he's in conference."

The irate cop hoofed down the aisle yelling, "He's gonna be in the morgue by the time I get through with him."

Within seconds, the loud speaker announced, "Security to third floor," just as Goodson threw open the door.

The startled attorney yelled, "What's the meaning of this?" While he arched his back to pull up his pants, hidden from view by a precariously balanced two-foot-high stack of manila folders.

Eric bolted around the desk. Glancing down, he smirked. "Everyone said you were a snake. I always try to see the best in people, but apparently, you have no good side." Motioning to the secretary squatting before him, Eric ordered, "Beat it, honey. And on your way out, try to find a little self-respect." Turning back to Draw, "And as for you, you prick," Goodson ranted, while he grabbed the lawyer by the lapels and hoisted him out of his chair, tossing him back atop his credenza and into the window. "You son of a bitch! What kind of deal did you make that cost my wife her life?"

"What's this all about?" The attorney shrieked. After wading through the fear, Draw asked, "Do I know you from somewhere?"

"You sent my wife on some mindless errand so Marzoli and his buddies could kill her and I want to know why? If you don't tell me everything you know, I'm gonna break every part of your body imaginable, so you'll think quadriplegia would be an enormous step up."

"You got this all wrong!"

"Is that right? You set up the trust for Melig through the Police Benevolent Association. You sent Angie on bullshit errands three days in a row. I'll bet they wiped out the evidence against you in the Dan August death. You're going to tell me right now, or your own mother won't recognize you when I'm done."

"Okay! Okay! I tell you whatever you want."

"Damn straight, you will."

120

WITH HIS RIGHT ELBOW planted on the desktop, the Professor twirled his blue Bic pen, rotating it through his fingers akin to a professional gambler toying with a chip, while gazing at the blank yellow legal pad. Rather than experiencing the frustration of most creative types as they struggled to compose, he purposefully withheld a flurry of ideas to test the limits of his students' patience. Nary a one broke their blank stare. *"Ah yes, the perfect class; once again, hanging on my every word."* The contemplative moment shattered by the annoying buzz of his Motorola phone. "What the… excuse me class, but I must take this call," the Professor declared, while extending his left index finger in the air. "No one would knowingly disturb us, unless it was of the utmost importance," he relayed as he fumbled to extend the antenna, while turning his back and strolling toward the steel framed security door.

"Who is this?" The Professor demanded in a whispered tone.

"It's your best bud!" The baritone grumble swelling into a taunted laugh.

"I don't have time for you, now. I'm right in the middle of something."

"Giving one of them great lectures to your class, are ya? What're you talking about, the Dead Sea Scrolls?" The voice chuckled.

"I've told you, I don't have time for you."

"Oh, having second thoughts, are we? Well, let me just tell you an interesting little story about a bastard son born to a nun at the Dominican Girls School on Cadieux on Detroit's eastside. Are you still with me Professor?"

The Professor's mind swirled. "*No living sole knows about this; there is not even a birth certificate. He's got to be bluffing.*" "I don't have time for this horseshit," he finally responded.

"Well, excuse me all to hell. I guess you don't want to hear some of the best parts. Like how Mom easily hid the pregnancy, what with all the nun robes and such. Or, how she grew your hair so long and dressed you in those cute plaid uniforms, so you'd fit in with all the other little girls. The only thing I haven't figured out is how you hid your thing all through grade school. Must be a tiny little sucker."

"You're making all this up!" The Professor responded, desperately trying to squelch his rapid breathing.

"Oh, that's right, how could I possibly know you were raised in a convent with a sadistic House Mother who whacked you on the head with her roll of keys, or scrubbed your filthy hands raw with a metal tined brush? Well, let me check my notes here because I had to write it down… it's here somewhere; ah, here it is… because I'm the Omnipotent Omniscient One. Now ain't those a couple of million-dollar words? I swear, I could be one of your, what do you call 'em, colleagues! Wow, there's another one!"

Slumped in complete surrender, his thoughts racing with no discernible pattern, he responded, "What would you have me do?"

"Now that's the old college spirit! Grab yourself a pen, because hi-ho, hi-ho, it's off to school we go!"

CHAPTER

121

Logistically, the Booby Trap Lounge provided the perfect site: located at the heavily trafficked intersection of Eight Mile and Dequindre; quick access to I-75 a few short blocks away; and, the robust nightlife allowing him to blend, either on foot, or by car. A cheap toupee, fake eyebrows and a mustache purchased from a theatrical supply provided him a look similar to the caricature on the side of a bus of local radio personality, Dick Purtain. Unlike the perverts frequenting adult bookstores and peep shows, camouflaging their raging emotions with trench coats and sunglasses, his disguise protected a distinguished position, as well as, his sacred mission. As the Chosen One, he tolerated the aberrant behavior of the masses; scantily clad young tarts with a yard of kite string barely covering critical spots, gyrating perky flesh under blinding strobes, freeze framing their lewd gymnastics; their total disdain for simple laws of physics, ignoring the narcotic effect of their cum hither scent wafting through animal nostrils, igniting the urge and inducing copulation fever; the overt seduction of in your face bump and grind, lap dance, table dance, sucker can you buy me a drink of champagne at two-hundred dollars a pop. No, his role as shepherd imparted to him the divine inspiration to rise above the compulsion. He sits alone in the same dark corner booth every Thursday night, observing;

never allowing himself to partake in such a tawdry public display. Some things are meant to be private.

The announcer introduced Trish the Dish, mild mannered elementary school teacher by day…stripper extraordinaire by night, as the jukebox pounded out the beat of Rod Stewart's *Do You Think I'm Sexy?* The lithe frame sashayed onto the stage, wrapping her taut legs around the aluminum pole in a sensual caress, sliding up and down, while staring directly at him.

"My god, it's her!" The discovery unnerved him. He shook so bad, it was impossible to extinguish a cigarette without steadying the ashtray. His Gray Goose slopped down his chin as though drinking from a dribble glass. Fighting his instincts to rush the stage, he reminded himself of his objective; securing the final piece for his recreation. *"Restraint. Without control you are no more than common riffraff. Your time is at hand. Patience."*

Trish threw on a flimsy wrap she grabbed off the backstage rack and hustled down the stairs to the disc jockey booth. Howard leaned forward, holding back the hoard of gold neck chains nestled in his web of black curly chest hairs, preventing them from swinging into the Plexiglas.

"You ever do that to me again and I'll cut your balls off and serve them to you as olives in your next martini. Got it!"

"Oh, come on, toots. I was just funnin' with ya."

"You keep my personal life out of this trash heap. Understood?"

"Hey, nobody's the wiser. It's just between you and me. What say we go for coffee after your shift?"

"Drop dead."

Exhausted by the 2:00 a.m. close, Trish mindlessly wandered through the parking lot filled with every conceivable brand of luxury vehicle. As she clicked the remote door opener to her Vette from five paces away, a gloved hand suddenly gripped her mouth, abruptly yanking her head back to rest on the point of a sharp instrument. Her scream muffled, a hot foul breath whispered in her ear, "Shush! Not a word until we get there. You understand?" Rapidly nodding her head, the assailant continued, "Smart girl. You get to go to the head of the class. Now move."

Several disoriented businessmen, reeking of booze and searching for their misplaced cars, casually commented on the attacker's luck as he and Trish strolled off the lot to the dark side street. Pleading into the rank smelling leather, the kidnapper stopped, digging his fingers into her cheeks.

"No talking. If you fail to abide by the rules, you will be punished. Is that understood?" The terrified dancer once again nodded. "I've been searching for you since you left the eighth grade. I loved you. I followed you home and watched you undress every night, not just the one time you caught me. You betrayed me. Mother beat me with a leather strap until the welts tore open. Now, I'm going to hurt you." Tightening his vice grip, Trish winced, but the gag stifled her squeal. "Now that we understand one another, we can continue."

A half block down into the residential area, the attacker pushed Trish against a dark colored sedan. "Get in!" He commanded as the creaky door squeaked open. As she turned to line up her torso, a tremendous force slammed her from behind, propelling her into the doorframe face first, knocking her unconscious.

The rescuer rousted the assailant with a series of kicks. "You gonna abduct someone, you should have you a real weapon. What kind of moron uses a lead pencil? You some kind of freaky geek?"

"But we had a deal," the Professor cried out.

"Oh, we did, did we?"

"You said she was mine."

"I lied. Go on and scram, before I change my mind."

"But she's my…"

"But, but, but. Now scoot, you little piss ant, or I'll squish you like the little bug you are."

Trish awoke just as her abductor rolled on the ground and stood up. A cockeyed hairpiece lent him an almost comical appearance. *"He looks so familiar. Do I know him from somewhere?"* Her savior lifted her up from behind. "You okay, Miss?"

I think so."

"Good."

"I can't thank you enough!"

"Oh, you got that right!"

CHAPTER

122

Sᴀʀᴀʜ ꜰᴇʟᴛ ᴀ ᴘᴜɴɪꜱʜɪɴɢ blow to the left side of her head, accompanied by a loud crack just prior to blacking out. A ticklish sensation on her nose awakened her, but darkness remained. A sticky substance matted her hair to her chin and the side of her face. A severe migraine interrupted a clear assessment of her predicament, although she felt a wide band of tape across her mouth, hands bound behind her back and leg restraints. A rough material rubbed against her face, hands and ankles. *"What the heck? I must still be dreaming. What is this thing? Am I in some kind of bag?"* Instinctively controlling her breathing, Sarah fought to maintain her composure. *"Think! What is this place? How did I get here? This has got to be a dream! What's that constant hum? Am I in a car? Dear God, what's going on?"* An extended distorted muffled howl, *"Jack!"* strained her vocal cords and triggered uncontrollable sobbing heaves. *"No, that's not the way. Maintain your cool. You're stronger than that. Breathe easy. Focus."* Sarah laid quiet for a moment. *"What's that vibration? Are we moving? Yes, that's it, we're moving. I must be in a car."* Sarah attempted to roll over. The weight of her torso crushed her wrists, but she continued to wriggle until she found her movement restricted to inches each way. Although unable to straighten her legs, she surmised the bag as much a culprit as the container. *"Think this through! I've got to find out what's going on. If I am in a car, maybe I can talk to them if I can get them to stop. But how?"* Sarah reasoned, forcing back tears and talking up her self-confidence. *"That's it!"* She screamed into the tape as she thrust her legs repeatedly at what she perceived as the side of the vehicle. Within minutes the motion ceased, a car door slammed, faint footsteps and the click of a lock.

"You need it again already, bitch? You're one horny little whore. Okay then, but remember, same as last time. I love when you beg."

Sarah cringed, recognizing the awful voice as the assailant in her apartment. *"What does he mean, I need it again? Dear God, did the bastard rape me?"* Helpless, she whimpered as a powerful grip lifted her and slung her over a shoulder.

"Oh, that's right! You slept through our last encounter. I guess it couldn't have been as good for you. Well, we'll just have to remedy that little faux pas. That's French, you know; the language of romance. I can tell slick talk like that puts a fancy bitch like you in the mood."

"Relax; he's just playing you. Wait until you have an opportunity to talk with him," the half hysterical collegiate coached herself.

Sarah heard a car door open, and then experienced a backward free fall, followed by a minor bounce. The attacker pulled down the sack. A moonless night still allowed Sarah to discern shapes; they were under several large trees, inside the backseat of a full-sized sedan.

"Please don't hurt me. I won't say a thing, I promise. Just let me go," Sarah abandoning her skimpy mental cover and rambling a panicked plea through the tape in an unintelligible jumble. Tears free flowed while her eyes bugged out to burst point.

"Bet you wish your skinny assed black friend was here to help you again, don't ya? Well, he ain't, so we gonna have us another party," the kidnapper ranted as he flipped Sarah over.

"My God, what happened to my panties? The pig did rape me," Sarah rationalized, feeling hands spreading her bare cheeks.

Mounting her from behind, the first vicious thrust evoked a shrill reverberating through Sarah's brain, but again muffled to the outside world. The animal continued his relentless assault, driving into his victim with a total disregard for human sensibilities or anatomy. A merciful God allowed Sarah to black out, rather than endure the excruciating pain.

A teeth-reverberating shiver woke the sodomized coed to the same darkness; now in a sitting position on a cold hard surface. This time the bag clearly restricted leg movement. The sound of a metal latch and the creek of a door opening provided a sense of hope as Sarah leaned forward.

"Well, looky here! My little Cinder-fuckin-rella is ready for action again. I swear, Momma, you gonna wear me out. Don't you ever tire out?"

Sarah heaved to catch her breath as the monster lifted her straight up with one hand and pulled back the cloth bag with the ease of peeling a banana with the other. The delirious prisoner noticed her breath in the cold and stacks of shinning metal barrels as her body slammed face down onto a hard-rounded surface. The blow of the impact collapsed her rib cage inward, propelling a high velocity mixture of air, blood and phlegm through her nose. Large warm clamps gripped her hips.

The beast leaned over and licked her cheek, whispering in her ear, "You know, baby, I'm what you call one of them sexaholics. Even went to school for it. I figured what better way to meet great partners. Screwed every member: guys and girls; even the teacher. But none of them wanted it as much as you."

Within seconds, the god-awful routine tripped into instant replay. Her mind, numb from the pain and cold, prevented her the relief of unconsciousness. With each powerful lunge, the demented creature sent wave after agonizing wave of pain wafting through Sarah's battered body. Choking as the spittle blocked its only passage, she gave up all hope. As the hedonist maintained his rampage, a stupor relieved her pain. As the assault continued, despair turned to anger.

"I'm gonna kill this son of a bitch. I'm gonna survive and I'm gonna slit this bastard's throat," Sarah convinced herself.

"There now, wasn't that everything you anticipated and more," the ogre goaded. "If you're up to it, maybe we can do this a couple more times before I get your faggotty boyfriend here and cut off what little balls he has left. You'd like that wouldn't you?" The fiend inquired as he zipped up the bag and tossed Sarah against the wall.

CHAPTER

123

Aнbi scoured the warehouse after hours to kill time his first two weeks on the job, searching every nook and cranny. A curious knack of the homeless, who learn to scurry in the background of life, finding refuge in the most unusual places; reminiscent of that ingenious sparrow that builds his nest causing you to comment, *"Now how the heck did he get in there?"*

Accessed only by service men for monthly maintenance, or an emergency, the padlocked room adjacent to the cooler contained the refrigeration system. A poorly anchored floor level dust encrusted ventilation grate on the rear sidewall allows entry to Ahbi's secret hideaway. The constant low hum of the generators, coupled with the darkness, afforded the fleeing custodian a sense of security. Seated, with his back resting against an asbestos wrapped pipe, Ahbi gently tapped his index and middle fingers against the watch crystal, praising its comfortable feel with his newfound self-confidence. Ahbi took a job well done, stress relieving siesta. Settling back, he closed his eyes. "What's dat?" The startled janitor responded in a forced whisper, shuffling his legs to a get ready position.

"Eeeeeeeeee," the soft screech.

"Who dat?" Ahbi realizing the human quality of the sound. "Don't be funnin with me now, you hear?"

A few seconds elapsed, then a distinct sniffle.

"Please don't hurt me," the low, childlike voice pleaded.

"Where you at?"

"Here. Please."

"Oh God, I thought I was over hearing the voices," Ahbi remarked, on the verge of breaking down.

"I need help. Please don't let me die here."

"Who are you?"

"Sarah. Sarah Garvey."

"And where you say you at?"

"I must be right next to you."

"The Almighty playin' with me again."

"No, please. I'm in some sort of bag."

"Oh Lord, I be goin' crazy for sure."

"It's a tarp, or something. Please, I think I'm dying."

Ahbi involuntarily resumed the tap on the Omega. "*You a strong man now. You know you got to help this girl. Now get to it!*" Rotating to his knees, the reluctant Good Samaritan supported himself with one hand while waving his other in the darkness, similar to a blind man's use of a cane. The first sweep failed to make contact, but the voice urged him on.

"You've got to be close. I can hear you breathing."

Ahbi ignored the piercing pain in his arthritic knees and slid forward, waving his arm back and forth. "You sure you not playin' with me now?"

"Reach down lower. I'm on the ground. I can smell you."

"Honey, dat ain't nothing I'm apologizing for. I so scared, I drippin water worse than a shakin dog dat been swimming in the swamp to drown his fleas."

Ahbi felt a canvas material about twelve inches from the floor. He pushed down on his finger until the give ended. "You in there?"

"Yes, please get me out of here."

As Ahbi felt his way around the bag, a loud whelp stopped him cold. "Are you okay?"

"No, I'm hurt real bad. Please, we've got to go before he comes back."

"Who?"

"The monster. Now please, try to open this thing up."

"I'm hurrin', but it be difficult in the dark."

"I'm sorry. I have to get out of here because I know I'm not going to last long."

"Who did this to you?"

"I don't know who he is, but he's been trying to kill me. I just don't seem to die. Bet that really pisses him off."

Ahbi worked the cloth down to what he determined to be the woman's shoulders. "Somethin' sticky all over you." Raising his hands to his nose failed to identify a distinct smell.

"I think it's blood."

"Oh Lord!" The amount on his hands confirmed her dire straits. "I needs to get some help. I'm gonna sneak on out of here, but I promise, I'm comin' back."

"Where am I?"

"You in the refrigeration room."

"But what is this place?"

"A beer warehouse."

"What's it called?"

"Dearborn Beer."

"Unbelievable," she struggled to whisper, then fell silent.

Roy Blue strained to keep pace with the hobbling old coot as he zipped through the maze of inventory.

"You sure you haven't been sampling some off the breaker pile?"

"Now Mr. Blue, you knows I don't drink. Never cared to, even with all those years on the streets."

"You been hearing things again?"

"Well, you got me there. I still sometimes has those dreams dat seems so real. But I been good as of late, I don't mind tellin' ya."

"Where the hell are we going?"

"We almost there," Ahbi advised as he darted around the end of a double high row of pallets and squeezed against the cinder block wall.

Roy struggled to wriggle through the tight fit. *"How does he do it? Must be part rabbit; anything he can get his head through."*

"Here!" Ahbi pointed, reaching down to pull the grate off.

"Isn't this the refrigeration shack?"

"Yesim."

"I've got a key. I'll go around front."

As Roy turned on the light and looked down, the normally unflappable gambler gagged. "Jeez! What happened here?"

"She talkin' about a one-eyed monster. Only one of dem round here."

"Butchie?"

"Musta been. We got to call an ambulance."

Roy bent on one knee. "Pulse is erratic, shallow breathing; no time. Help me pick her up."

"Ain't spose to move dem when dey likes dat, is ya?"

"No, you're not. But I bet if you asked her, she'd want to get the hell out of here."

CHAPTER

124

PLEASANTLY SURPRISED THAT HIS few remaining worldly belongings were still intact, the exhausted warehouseman collapsed onto the stained floral print bedspread. His bellowing, wall-bending snore blended with the trifecta of banging headboards in the adjoining three rooms.

The telephone call jolted Jack out of a deep sleep. Fumbling around the nightstand, he picked up the sticky receiver. "No thanks, not interested," the groggy student relayed, reaching to replace the handset.

"Your bitch been cheatin' on you," the sick rhythmic tone greeted. "Can't take a punch as well as some broads, but she's got a fine ass."

"What? Who is this? How did you know I was even here?"

"I'm the man your woman's gonna be dreamin' about every time you stick it to her. And I know everything you do."

"Go play with yourself, you pervert," Jack huffed and slammed down the phone.

Thirty seconds later, a second call.

Jack grabbed the receiver, "Go screw yourself."

"You better be careful; I just love to hurt them. I may have second thoughts about trading her for you."

"What kind of creep are you?"

"I'm the scariest kind you could ever imagine and I've got your girl. Now, I can't deny I've hurt her, but she could heal, eventually."

"You have no idea what you're talking about. Now don't call again, or I'll have the police on your ass."

"Oh, ain't that excitin'. But it's not gonna help Sarah."

Jack scrambled to sit up. "How'd you know her name?"

"I know everything about her. Well, everything I want to know. You should thank me."

"For what?"

"She's much more adventuresome sexually, thanks to me."

"If you have her, let me talk to her."

"She's indisposed, to put it politely. My, I surprise myself. I don't believe I've ever been polite before. I don't think I like it."

"If I find out you do have her, I'll rip your head off your shoulders."

"My, aren't you the tough guy. Meet me in one hour at Dearborn Beer Distributors on Joy Road at Livernois."

"I know where it is," Jack replied in a clipped cadence. *"How the hell does he know where I work? They must be following me everywhere."*

"I'll leave the rear overhead door open and the light on for ya," the sleazy voice snickered. "We'll be in the cooler. You bring anybody else, I'll carve her up and deliver her to you on a deli party tray."

"You hurt her, you die."

"You're pretty fucking stupid for a college boy. I already told you I hurt her. I hurt her real bad. The only question is whether she's gonna live."

Jack frantically called Sarah at her apartment. The answering machine clicked on after four rings. "She's with the man of her dreams and that's not you, Jack," the sinister voice relayed. "Jack, I'd get my ass over here as soon as possible. Times a wastin'; tick, tock."

CHAPTER

125

Jack jumped out of bed and dressed in under ten seconds. Fumbling with the punch dial phone, he reached Mamoud on his car phone. "Mikey, I don't have time to explain…"

"Damn it Jack, I told you never to call me that…"

"Shut up and listen. Sarah's in trouble. They're holding her at Dearborn Beer. In the cooler."

"I'm already there."

"How could you know?"

"I'm literally right across the street at Orleans Poultry. Doing an exposé on…"

"Yeah, yeah. Scout it out for me, would you? I'm ten minutes away."

"You got it!"

Jack stomped the accelerator to the floor. The Le Car strained under the demand, but continued a steady acceleration. He laid on his horn, zigzagging through traffic and stop lights to Westbound I-94. His heart pounded against his chest wall with sledgehammer force. He swore he felt ribs crack, while cutting around motorists with the reckless indifference of a teen sensing his first foray into sex.

CHAPTER

126

Mamoud hobbled down the gravel alley, his old football injury rebelling against any youthful burst of speed with excruciating stabs of searing pain. Bordered on one side by the blistering pee yellow cinder block east wall of the warehouse and along the other by a row of dilapidated garages, their unusual list a modern-day excursion into the forest of Oz, the rapt reporter's concentration shattered at the unsuspecting lunge of a maniacal pit bull against a weed infested, rotted wood fence.

"Damn!" Mamoud screamed as he dove across the passageway, slamming against the building. Taking a moment to catch his breath, as well as, confirm the rattling of a chain, the dedicated scout stood to resume his reconnaissance. Keeping a watchful eye on the snarling dog, Mamoud's first step landed on the edge of a pothole, twisting his knee with an audible snap. "Augh!" The maimed newsman squealed, gripping the appendage with both hands and falling backward into a water filled chuckhole. Rocking back and forth, Mamoud's scathing howl triggered an almost comical cacophony of neighborhood animals yelping in unison. Pulling himself together, he struggled to regain his footing, his gait reduced to a slow limp.

Rounding the corner to the rear of the structure, he entered through the open overhead door. The non-drinking convert marveled at the seemingly unending stacks of beer to his left and the meticulously parked trucks on his right. Each step an exercise in pain management, Mamoud continued his trek, listening for any sign of activity. Not sure of the layout, he decided to follow a straight path toward the front, pausing to check each intersection. A loud crash startled him. Determining the noise to be ahead and to his left, Mamoud tottered in his finest Walter Brennan impression. Arriving at an imposing door with a thickness comparable to a bank vault and a height the equivalent of a basketball hoop, Mamoud slowed his approach.

"Anyone here?" No response.

Mamoud limped ahead two abbreviated paces.

"Excuse me? I'm looking for Sarah Garvey. Is anyone around?" Complete silence; too quiet for a building spread out over a half-acre square.

The college reporter continued his leery advance. Ten feet from the doorway, Mamoud collided with an invisible barrier of frigid air. A penetrating shiver stalled his momentum. "Is someone in here?" Dismissing his inner voice of reason, the curious investigator moved to the entrance of the cooler. Glancing about the four thousand refrigerated square feet with floor to ceiling stacks of four to a pallet one hundred sixty-five-pound stainless steel half barrels of beer, Mamoud eyed the back of a broad-shouldered man in a thousand-dollar fine woven wool blend suit.

"Excuse me, sir!" A quizzical expression registered as the enormous figure rotated, displaying an eye patch and neck bandage. "Don't I know you?" Mamoud inquired, racking his brain to place the face.

The well-dressed hulk inched forward.

"*That's unusual. Must be a real introvert.*" The almost imperceptible advance stymied Mamoud. "Sir, I'm looking for Sarah Garvey." Ignoring the overture, Mayer slid forward, keeping his head cocked at an unusual angle with his chin tucked into his shoulder. "Perhaps you didn't…"

A blistering kick lashed out, crushing Mamoud's kneecap, buckling him to a forced genuflection. The deep baritone voice bellowed, "Don't remember me, street puke? Shucks, my feelins' is hurt." Crashing down with the heel of his foot into the middle of Mamoud's back, forcing the newsman to the slick concrete floor, the monster railed, "I almost forgot! I ain't got no feelins'." Butchie shouldered a stack of kegs, toppling them onto Mamoud.

CHAPTER

127

"Ahbi, would you go see what's going on out there?"

"Ain't nothin', but rats."

"What are you talking about, rats? It sounds like World War III out there. No one's supposed to be in here at this hour."

Roy hoisted the battered girl in his arms and gently remarked, "I know this breaks all the rules of first aid, but I got the feeling if we wait for an ambulance, you're gonna crap out on me."

"Thank you," the strained whisper.

Roy struggled in the cramped quarters to move Sarah to the door of the mechanical room. Ahbi followed, commenting over Sarah's constant mild whimpers, "I'm tellin' ya, we got em."

"Got what?"

"Rats; as big as alley cats. When y'all leaves your pizza boxes laying out, it don't take but a minute for dem suckers to swarm all over 'em. Dey rats, I tell ya!"

"Would you get your head screwed on straight for once and go see what's out there?"

"Already knows. But I guess I gots to prove it to ya."

Roy Blue had pulled his '65 Chevy Bellaire into the warehouse, parking perpendicular to the loading dock, in anticipation of dropping off several cases of beer to a customer on his way home. He gently placed Sarah across the back seat. Popping the trunk, he dumped the contents of an old Windsor Casino swag bag. A wild striped beach towel plopped out on top. He spread the make-shift blanket over Sarah.

"Sorry, it's the best I could do on such short notice."

"Kay," Sarah whispered.

A rapid succession of thunderous clangors, alerted Roy to check on Ahbi.

"I'll be right back."

"Please don't go."

"It'll only take a minute. Promise."

Sarah trembled with each of four rapid shots.

"Please God, I don't want to die here."

Trying to calm herself, Sarah repeated the rote phrases of Recovery she had heard Jack use so many times. As she steadied her breathing, a tremendous crash, then screeching brakes halted her effort. Within seconds, a male voice called out, "Sarah!"

"Jack? Jack. I've got to warn Jack," Sarah cried as she threw off the blanket.

128

Aнви darted around the kegs bouncing out of the cooler. Requiring all his concentration to avoid getting crushed, he neglected to observe Mayer, standing just inside the door.

"Satan must have the upper hand today, cause I ain't never wasted a second on clean livin'," the devious voice bellowed.

"Oh, sweet Jesus!" Ahbi cried out, afraid to raise his head to confirm his suspicions.

"Come on in here, boy! Want to show you my new custom-made eye patch."

"Didn't mean to hurt you, sir." Abhi kowtowed. Glancing about, he shuddered at the sight of Mamoud on the floor.

"What evil you gone and done now?"

"What we have here is called a genuine industrial accident."

"Nothins an accident with y'all, sep maybe the Good Lord allowin' y'all to be born."

"Shucks! Your low opinion of me warms me down to my tippy toes. Now get your ass in here and help me rescue this poor nappy haired brother."

Ahbi moved closer with the hesitancy of a stray dog to a friendly handout. When he came within arms-reach, Butchie grabbed him by the neck and slammed him to the ground.

"A twofer. I can't fuckin' believe it," the monster railed as he hoisted a half barrel overhead to drop onto the whimpering janitor.

"Put it down, fat boy. Your Momma ain't here to protect you today," Roy Blue ordered.

"Well, looky here, Mr. Boy Scout, his own bad self," a glossy eyed Mayer snickered, tossing the hundred-and-a-half-pound container to the side.

Roy winced as the barrel hit the floor, then bounced and landed with a dull thud directly onto Ahbi.

"You sick fuck!"

"Why thank you. Coming from an observant card shark like yourself, I'm flattered," Mayer remarked, sliding his right hand into his pant pocket.

Checking out the eye patch, Roy calmly remarked, "I see you ran into someone who tired of your shit. Now, you're gonna step out here and I'm gonna finish what the other guy didn't."

"Sorry, but I ain't got the time. Got a date with Sarah, I do."

"Sarah? That girl you beat to a pulp is Jack's Sarah?" Roy asked incredulously, the stoic now suppressing reflexive anger.

The look on Butchie's face showed the same surprise. A split second later he added, "Don't forget raped and sodomized."

"I'll kill you!"

"Hey, what's all the fuss? They do incredible things now days with plastic surgery. She could have used bigger tits anyway. This way, once she's under the knife, they can fix it all."

Roy charged Mayer. He failed to hear the click of the gun hammer, as four deafening blasts stopped his advance. Glancing down at his chest, in stunned disbelief, Roy Blue's body deflected back and came to rest against the cooler door frame.

CHAPTER

129

Jack unexpectedly found himself repeating aloud, "I have the will to bear this discomfort. The way to shed my fears is to give firm command to my muscles. The circumstances I face are distressing, but not dangerous." Jack jerked his head in disbelief, "Who am I kidding? I'm probably gonna get killed," he scoffed, spittle spraying his windshield. The split second of humor triggered a mental clarity, spreading a sense of calm right down to his fingertips. *"He called me college boy. Roy Blue tagged me with that nickname the first time we met. Could it be? Can't be."* Exiting on Tireman for a straight shot of six blocks to the dead end at Joy Road, Michaels plowed ahead with the tunnel vision of a rookie cop in his first high speed chase. *"And that voice? I don't think it sounds familiar. Could easily be a disguise. How did he know where to call? I only left the number at the office."* It took a split second to register. Michaels grip on the wheel tightened until a bone cracked behind his right ring finger knuckle, snapping him back to reality as he sideswiped a glistening new Lincoln Navigator. *"Damn, he plays cards with a cop named Dolan, same as in the reports. He had the cut on his neck from Mamoud too. The box car door, remember it never happened before."* Whipping the steering column sharply left, he regained control. *"It couldn't be!"* His mind screamed. *"What kind of sick dog am I dealing with?"* The sense of betrayal dumping Jack into an abyss of despair; his head pounded with confusion. A hard left and his car skidded sideways, slamming into the far curb. Jack regained control for the short block to the front of the building, whipping up the drive and crashing through the warehouse door, halting forty feet from the rendezvous point. As he bolted from the demolished car, Jack raced through the warehouse as four shots rang out. Recognizing the shape of his colleague, he called out, "Roy Blue, you sick prick. What's the hell are you doing?"

The traitor robotically turned, a pale blank stare on his face.

"Where's Sarah? How could you do something like this?"

Roy stood motionless, his figure encased by the doorframe. Jack raced to within five feet of the entrance.

"What the...?" Michaels suddenly stopped as Roy mechanically raised his right hand. Blue eyed the appendage as though a first alien contact. A droplet of blood trickled from his palm. Glancing at Michaels, Roy collapsed to his knees, falling face forward to the freezing concrete floor, landing simultaneous with the spatter.

Stunned, Michaels momentarily froze, jolting back as he eyed a large figure on a hi-lo. *"It can't be! Why would that fat prick be involved in something like this? And where is Mamoud?"* Relieved for a split second, but immediately overcome with fear having witnessed Mayer's cruelty first hand, Jack tried to compose himself. He thought with only one point of entry, he better stay close to the door for quick egress in the event of a problem.

"My, my, my, such a dramatic lad," Butchie smirked, squinting to get a closer look at his victim. A hint of hesitation on the beast as he rallied a thought, "You!" Mayer screamed. "Why this is gonna be better than I could ever have imagined. I've wanted to pound your smug ass to a pulp the very first time I met you. I could never figure out what Roy Blue saw in you college boys. Must be some suppressed feelings for you sweet thangs."

"Enough of your crap!" Michaels ordered as he treated the doorway as a border crossing into hostile territory. "Where's Sarah? And what did you do to Roy Blue?"

"My, but aren't we testy? I'd cool my jets if I were you, College Boy. And, as you can see, the gambler finally crapped out; took four of a kind to the chest. Nice grouping. Now, you do what I say, or I'm gonna do your girlfriend again right here, so's you can watch. Do you get the picture?" The sick smile and glossy eyes penetrated to Jack's soul. "Revolting, ain't it? Now move your ass around here," Mayer commanded, jerking his head to the side.

"I'm not going anywhere until I see that Sarah's okay."

"How's a dumb ass like you ever make it in college. I thought all you pussies was supposed to be so smart. Didn't I already tell you twice? She's hurt real bad. You make me repeat myself again and you gonna really piss me off. Now get your ass in here!"

J. Z. cautiously moved into the cooler. Simultaneous with his fourth step, the hi-lo engine revved, startling Jack. An entire stack of half barrels lurched forward, propelled by the fork tip caught on the bottom pallet. Michaels gasp in horror as the free-falling steel drums crashed down. Diving to his left in a vain attempt to avoid the barrage, Jack experienced a tremendous expulsion of air as three left ribs snapped like the crack of kindling across a knee.

CHAPTER

130

The sociopath burnished his lurid smile with a quick swipe of his serpent sized tongue, as he hoisted Roy Blue's corpse.

"What? No fancy card left to pull out of the deck? I kept telling you not to fuck with me. Now all I gotta do is pin you to a hi-lo fork like the stuck pig you are, and it's been one terrible industrial accident. Momma's gonna be pissed at the increase in comp rates."

As Butchie lifted the limp torso to ram it forward onto the elevated metal sleeve, a non-descript male voice called out, "What's going on here?"

Mayer shook his head, "Is this some kind of fucking joke? Where are you people coming from? Am I on Candid fucking Camera?" He twisted at the waist to confront Goodson.

"Where's Jack Michaels?"

"Under the kegs. Been a fuckin' disaster here today. Gonna have the hangover of a lifetime, if he's alive."

"Who the hell are you?"

"I'm the owner."

"What's with him?" Eric nodding to Blue, while experiencing an escalating feeling of being overwhelmed at handling what was clearly his first real dangerous situation.

"Fork lift slipped out of gear is my guess. Stuck him pretty good. Kegs got the others."

Mayer allowed Roy to slide down in front of him and slowly moved toward the hi-lo.

"Stay where you are!" Goodson commanded, swallowing to force back a rising level of bile and hoping his eroding self-confidence remained hidden.

Mayer halted for a split second while staring into the detective's eyes, then smirked, sensing fear. He continued his cautious advance for two steps, and then mounted the forklift.

"Where's the girl?" Goodson asked, silently praying the crackle in his voice was nothing more than an imagined nervous symptom, but making the rookie mistake of wiping his brow.

Butchie bent forward, firing up the machine. His gaze glued to the tense cop. "What girl?"

"Sarah Garvey, Jack Michael's girlfriend," Eric replied, forcing all his concentration to maintain a normal professional tone.

"Don't have a clue," Mayer responded, jamming the forklift into gear and flooring it.

As the stunned detective jostled back to reality and fumbled for his right-side belt mounted .38, he reached into an empty holster. As he visually cocked his head down to check, a series of deafening blast rang out next to his right ear. Buckling over in pain, he wrapped his forearms around his head as a final shot exploded.

"I'm right here, you filthy prick," Sarah remarked, firmly gripping the smoking police special with both hands.

CHAPTER

131

Despite its unkempt appearance, Detroit Receiving Hospital held a national reputation as a distinguished urban trauma center. Eager young doctors initially fought for the limited resident openings, honing their craft and eventually blossoming into an outstanding professional, or, burning out on the unending stream of gunshot, drug overdose and motor vehicle accident cases.

Eric's first step onto the rubber mat triggered the horizontal sliding door, as well as, a barrage of long subdued emotion; the pronouncement of Angie's death and numerous subsequent emergency admissions for his own frailties. Dodging a helter-skelter assortment of gurneys and wheelchairs, Eric couldn't help but emote with all the people in similar positions to his own only weeks before. *"I hope their situation turns out a heck of a lot better."*

Flipping his badge at the well coifed retiree volunteer behind the Patient Information desk, Detective Goodson inquired, "Sarah Garvey's room please," as he continued a steady stride toward the elevator.

Running her arthritic index finger down a list and hoisting herself above counter level, "That would be 612, officer."

Detective Goodson slowed his approach as he noticed the group huddled in the semi-private room. He smiled as he passed through the extra wide doorway, "What is this, an Americans with disabilities conference?"

Jack halted the smooth stroke on his love's hair and twisted on his crutches. Mamoud maintained his delicate grip on his friend's right hand, just below the intravenous needle.

"Michaels, you're already up and around."

"Three broken ribs and a fractured leg. It's Ahbi we're worried about; internal injuries. They can't seem to stop the bleeding and there's a shortage of his blood type."

"I just wanted to give you some bad news in person."

"You've come to arrest me?" The frail blond whispered.

"Now why would I want to do that?"

"Because I killed him."

"I'll call the nurse in to check your meds. Do you suffer these hallucinations often?"

Her perplexed look prompted a smile from the cop.

"But I…"

"Look, he tried to run me over with a forklift. It was a righteous shoot. You were there. You saw it. If someone were to sneak up on me and take my gun and then shoot someone with it, I'd be in a heap of trouble. Probably lose my job and my pension. I certainly wouldn't want that, would you?"

"No, I guess not. Thank you."

"Don't thank me yet." Goodson broke eye contact. "He's not dead."

"Oh God!" The high-pitched screech.

"It's okay, he'll pay with a life sentence. Bastard's strong as an S.U.V. hyped on angel dust. He's got five holes in his chest big enough to see through and they expect him to pull through. Can you imagine that?"

"He's here? In the same building?" Sarah cried out.

"Don't worry, he's not going anywhere. He's restrained and has a twenty-four-hour police guard."

"That won't mean a thing. Look at me! Look what he's done to me! All the while he laughed that even if he's caught, the police won't do a thing to him."

"She's right. He said the same to me on the two occasions he tried to kill me," Mamoud recalled. "It's as if he were bragging about it."

"Roy Blue told me that Dolan and Mayer were partners years ago, during the riots," Goodson offered.

"His name never showed up on any of the records we found," Jack added.

"What records?" Goodson asked.

"Police records from the riots we, I mean Professor Mink, discovered in the basement of 1300 Beaubien."

"Mink was down there too?"

"Yeah, as part of his investigation into police atrocities during the riots, he figured it best to search their own records. Once he discovered what he considered incriminating evidence, he took it so he could verify his work later on, if it was questioned."

"You didn't say anything about hard evidence when we initially talked."

"I was already being investigated for a murder I didn't commit and top priority on a police hit list. You think I wanted to add a felony theft charge?"

"Besides, we weren't sure we could trust you," Mamoud added.

Goodson shook his head, then continued. "He took on his step father's name a few years back when his Mother married into the beer distributorship. Roy Blue always thought it strange that at his age he would do something like that. Always figured he had something to hide."

"Do you know his real name?" Jack inquired, while continually stroking Sarah's hair.

"Yeah, Blue mentioned it. Rich something; Rouch? Rouchet? Damn, I'd know it if I heard it," Goodson reassured, flustered at his inability to recall.

"Reichert?" Mamoud proffered.

"That's it!"

"Holy smokes. We've got 'em together at the old Packard plant, probably killing a black guy they refer to as a Canadian," Jack deduced. "You're a cop, you should know that."

"A lot of things are kept from you when they realize you won't play ball."

"No wonder they been tryin' to kill us," Mamoud concluded.

"Well, you don't have to worry anymore."

"Why's that detective," Mamoud asked.

"Because I've turned everything over to Internal Affairs. Marzoli should be packing for Jackson State right about now. I'll bet a month's pay that Dolan's scrambling to cover his ass along with O'Hara. The prosecutor has to be Evans. He came up with those guys."

"Thank God," Jack whispered.

"You can thank him when that prick is dead," Sarah screeched, straining under the restriction of several tubes, "And not a second before."

"Amen," Mamoud added quietly.

CHAPTER

132

By 2:00 P.M. THE hustle bustle of the Hart Plaza lunch crowd diminished to a few stragglers: a fortyish button down Brooks Brothers exec stealing an occasional glance at his giggling, barely legal secretary, while sharing carryout soup and salad on a bench facing the river; a brisk gaited vagrant in a hurry to nowhere in particular, clad in sufficient layers of tattered clothing to survive a two week artic expedition, nary breaking a sweat in the ninety degree heat; a roving band of truant pre-teen young toughs, testing the intimidation effect of their cookie cutter street hip dress of two hundred dollar sneakers, sagging jeans, three pound steel wallet chains with matching necklaces, doo-rags and unabashed bravado; and a meticulously manicured, anxious, prosecuting attorney, gripping the safety rail abutting the water with the ferocity of a strong man contestant in a telephone directory ripping event.

Judge O'Hara approached from Evan's left, mulling over his opening, hoping to escape the pent-up wrath of the perfectionist.

"I certainly hope you're not contemplating a jump, Riley?" The Judge opting for humor to diffuse the prosecutor's apparent anxiety.

"Cut the crap, Jim," Evans snapped, glancing around to make sure no one could overhear. "I find it incomprehensible that Dolan and Marzoli can't take out some dumb ass college kids and a basket case of a cop. What the hell's going on?"

"Now Riley, your blood pressure has to be off the charts. Calm down," the Judge reluctantly placing a hand on the prosecutor's shoulder.

Evan's eyes seethed with anger. He swiped his backhand against O'Hara's forearm, knocking the gesture of reassurance into freefall. "Don't tell me to take it easy. I want those teenage misfits gone. Do I make myself clear? We've blown up, burned out and shot up more of this city chasing these assholes than we did during the riots."

"Now that's a bit of an exaggeration."

"I'm not in the mood, Jim. Save your platitudes for someone who gives a shit."

"Riley, I was just…"

"Then, we're getting rid of Butchie Boy. I can't believe that upper crust wannabe sociopath got himself arrested. Make sure he doesn't have a chance to cut a deal."

"The guy kidnapped, raped and beat a girl to a pulp and attempted to kill three others, including a police officer. I don't think he's going anywhere," the Judge stated with assurance.

"You certainly are one dumb son of a bitch. Any asshole who watches the news on any given day can tell you, for what that psycho has to offer, he'll get a free walk."

"Who's going to believe him?"

"It doesn't matter if they do or not. The press from the investigation will ruin all of us. I don't know about you, but I'm not ready to retire. I have much larger political aspirations."

"No, really?" The Judge smiled.

Hunched with his forearm resting on the railing, staring out at the river, with the city of Windsor, Ontario on the horizon, Prosecutor Evans commiserated, "I'm sorry, but I think I've looked out for everyone quite well over the last twenty years, including myself. I'm just not ready to give this up for anyone at any cost." Turning to face the Judge, "Marzoli can take out Reichert, then we'll deal with Goodson and the kids once and for all."

CHAPTER

133

THE BEAT-UP TAN FORD Crown Vic whipped to the curb in front of Samir's Party Store on John R. The Chief of Detectives hopped out.

"Wait here, I'll be back in a sec," Marzoli instructed.

Stepping between two winos sharing a brown bag, a hail stopped Marzoli short of the ironclad entrance.

"Yo pig! You finally gonna bust the rag head today?" The young voice rang out.

Tony turned, "First off, how'd you know I'm a cop?"

"Ain't no one drive a piece of crap like dat, 'cept a cop. You white," the sawed-off street punk continued, "Wearing a cheap assed suit. Who else you gonna be but da Man?"

Marzoli chuckled, as he drew his left backhand down his right arm. "This here is a genuine custom-tailored work of art. So, get the hell out of here before I bust you for being a smart ass."

"Ain't no law gainst dat."

"Don't have to be. I'm the Man, remember? The law is what I say it is."

Marzoli jerked his head to the left in reaction to the putrid odor of rotting meat as he pushed open the solid steel security door. "I oughta haul your ass in for selling that crap."

"It no bad," the middle-aged Arab male responded from behind the bullet proof glass, shaking his finger. "Freezer out. No sell bad meat."

"Yeah, right," the detective nonchalantly remarked. Reaching over to a top shelf, Tony picked up a jar of baby food. Flipping it over, he read the date.

"Hey, asshole, this baby food is four years past its' expiration."

"No, no, no. Food is good. You read it wrong." The store owner argued.

"I oughta do you a favor and put a bullet in your head."

"No, no, please. I work hard. It like dealing with animals. I have family to support. Please, no shoot."

"Yeah, and I'll bet you don't feed your family this crap."

The Detective tossed the jar back on the shelf. The crash brought the owner out from behind his bullet proof glass to clean up.

"If there was another store around, believe me, I'd take you out."

Marzoli turned the corner to the rack of girlie magazines.

"What's this?" Marzoli inquired, holding up a sealed plastic wrapped issue of *Club* magazine."

"That is good deal. New issue. Just come in," the foreigner rallied at the possible five-dollar sale.

"They don't come like this?" Tony questioned, raising the package shoulder high, exposing the well-endowed blond wearing only high heels, a necklace and cum hither smile.

"Yes! Yes! Just arrived."

"Okay, I'll take it. But if I find you scammed me by tearing the cover off and putting in old guts, we'll have a score to settle later."

"That no happen here."

"Yeah right, when dikes fly," the grumbling detective snorted as he slipped a fin under the glass.

Tony bopped around the loitering derelicts on the sidewalk and sauntered around the front of his vehicle, opening the door and flipping the magazine to the center of the bench seat.

Glancing down, his partner inquired, "We have nothing better to do than stop for your whack off material?"

Shooting a frown, Tony responded, "Get a grip! You think that giant pervert would believe us if we showed up with flowers, or candy?"

Taking a moment to digest the statement, "I guess not."

"Damn straight. Now just shut the fuck up and get ready to take care of business when we get there."

CHAPTER

134

Mᴀʀᴢᴏʟɪ ᴢɪᴘᴘᴇᴅ ᴀʀᴏᴜɴᴅ ᴀɴ unloading ambulance and left his car tying up the fire lane. Blowing by the approaching security guard with a flip of his badge, he broke stride to avoid colliding with the automatic door. A quick jaunt down the packed hall to the elevators, the detectives commandeered the first empty lift, waving off an orderly pushing a gurney.

Marzoli gazed at the interior soiled fabric walls. "Why does this place always smell like piss?"

"That's pine scent."

"No, that's the crap they teach you in science class so you're not afraid of the great outdoors. It's really grizzly piss. How many people you think would go to Yellowstone if they knew. How do you think the place got its name?"

"Can't argue with genius."

"I agree," Marzoli concluded, stepping off the elevator and naturally veering to his right as though he'd visited the room a hundred times, while his associate paused to read the directive plaque.

"481 is right up here," Tony chimed.

"You a psychic now?"

"How do you think I rate Chief of Detectives? Using asshole logic like the piss story? Got my own hotline too. Just like that crazy black singer bitch." Marzoli continued his march, turning left at the end of the corridor.

"What the…?"

"What is it Chief?"

"It's what there isn't asshole," Marzoli sarcastically responded. "Where's the fucking guard?"

"Probably went to get a coffee."

"He'll be walking a beat tomorrow."

"Chief, we don't have enough guys to relieve him. Eight hours is a long time to be out here. It's supposed to be a two-man assignment."

"His orders were to sit out here and not let any unauthorized personnel in."

"Doesn't this make our job easier?"

"He'd be a witness after the fact. We'd all be in the clear. I find him, I'll kill him too," Marzoli seethed. "Wait out here," the detective commanded, pushing open the door.

A sheet covered half of the sleeping patient's face, but exposed the restraints on his legs. Marzoli grabbed a pillow from the empty bed to his right, tightly gripping the ends and jamming it over the slumbering victim. "Good riddance, you sick bastard." Anticipating a struggle, Marzoli pushed down with his entire upper body strength. Surprised after twenty to thirty seconds by the lack of resistance, the detective loosened his grip and moved the pillow aside. The eyes were still closed; no apparent breathing. Tony pulled down the sheet, exposing the guard; his neck obviously broken.

"Damn! Where could he be?" Marzoli screamed in exasperation. "Think! Think!" The detective taxed his deductive powers, pounding his fist on his forehead. "The girl! The crazy son of a bitch has gone after the girl."

CHAPTER

135

F INALLY LAPSING INTO THE R.E.M. sleep she so desperately sought, a nurse shook Sarah by the shoulder, "Miss, it's time for your medication."

Startled, Sarah felt her body flop on the bed, followed by a cold chill. Her eyes opened to a round black face outlined by a white uniform.

"I just fell asleep."

"Well, this will help you get back to sleep."

"Why would you wake me to give me a sleeping pill?"

"It's not just for sleep; there's also a pain pill."

"But I'm not in any pain when I'm sleeping."

"Doctor's orders," the nurse chimed, handing the plastic container of pills and tiny paper cup of water to the drowsy patient.

Attempting to lift her head off the pillow, Sarah retorted, "That's like the Church's final response of 'it's a mystery' when they can't explain something." Gulping the tablets, Sarah dropped her head back.

"Whatever you say, darling," the nurse responded, already half way out the door.

Sarah tossed and turned within the confines of I.V. drips, respiration monitors and alarm hookups. The twists of frustration and spontaneous contortions abruptly halted with the brief scent of an unusual odor. *"Where do I know that smell from? It's so distinctive."* The odiferous scent wafted through her subconscious, triggering the connection. "Oh God! Please no!" Sarah screamed, emitting a burst of perspiration equivalent to the ballast ejection of a nuclear submarine during an emergency float, as she sprang forward from the pillow, her eyes restrained from popping out by arterial connections.

"I knew you'd be glad to see me. They all were, eventually. Could never get enough of old Butchie."

"Nooooo!" Sarah screamed, grabbing for the call switch, frantically thumbing the button as the nightmarish apparition stood in the doorway, his white hospital smock sporting several distinct blotches of blood, chest high.

"You go ahead sweet thang, scream all you like. Had to keep my hand over the mouth of that chubby black bitch that gave you the pills to keep her quiet. Did her doggy style just to warm up for you. Ain't had no dark meat in a long time."

Sarah's mouth agape, but no sound emitted. Tears streamed down her cheeks, combining with the excessive sweat, producing a salty taste on her lips.

"You go ahead and scream now. Everyone on the graveyard shift is dead. No one left to hear you. Kind of apropos, ain't it?" The fiend reasoned, reaching his left hand under the smock to rub his member. "That's what you call a million-dollar word that I learned in one of them TV self-improvement courses. Bitchin' ain't it?"

"It can't be you! I'm dreaming. I know it. You're tied up and under police guard," Sarah ranted, reeling in her knees and pulling the sheet up tightly against her chin.

"Yeah, hard to believe, ain't it? You should have seen the look on that guard's face when I put his own gun to his head and made him munch on little Petey. Pussy pissed all over his self. Imagine that! A grown man; a cop, no less; that scared. He wasn't nearly as good as you though, sweet thang. I missed you baby," the beast declared, now rapidly stroking his erect penis.

"Please God, this can't be happening," Sarah cried, her entire body shivering.

"Ain't these the coolest," the sociopath remarked, raising up the front flap of the hospital gown, exposing his hard on. "Nothing to unzip, unbuckle or unbutton. Just great for that spur of the moment fuck," Mayer remarked as he moved forward toward the hysterical woman.

"No please! I'm dreaming. I know it. Wake up, Sarah! It's just a nightmare," she screamed, inching into an upright fetal position in the far corner of her bed.

Mayer took a steady stride forward.

"Aaaahhhhhh!" Sarah shrieked, slapping her palms against soaked cheeks and turning her face down and away from the approaching beast.

At that moment, the bathroom door flew open with the clang of a bed pan sliding out onto the tile floor. Pepatino skated out, wound up with his hockey stick and smacked it. The flying hunk of metal struck Butchie with the open end, directly between the eyes.

With the sound of impact, Jimmy chortled, "Man, that had to hurt."

The irate giant stopped, clearly flummoxed, as a sticky brown substance dripped from his face.

"God, what's that smell?" Pepatino queried.

Max stuck his head out around the bathroom door frame, "Well, Jack told us not to touch anything, but I really had to go."

"So, you took a dump in the bed pan?"

Torpo just hunched his shoulders, then chuckled, "Clean up on aisle nine."

Stunned, Sarah laid motionless in her bed until she heard the blood curdling scream. Pepatino raised his stick into checking position and charged.

"I gonna kill you all. I'm gonna rip..."

A deafening explosion rang out, echoing through the corridor. Mayer stopped his advance. A confused glance down, he noticed his smock fluttering back after ballooning out. The remnants of his chest, mixed with a sizeable portion of cloth, zipped over Pepatino's head and splattered on the eggshell wall beyond.

"Hmph," the nonchalant comment, as the alternative head controlled the demon's response. As he took a second step, Jimmy jumped aside, planting his back against the side wall. Another explosion rang out. The hollow tipped .357 magnum ripped through the spine, severing all lower body control. The fragments of nerve endings, tissue and blood blotted the paint, inches below the first mass. Mayer collapsed to his knees with a look of complete bewilderment. The remaining torso fell face first to the scuffed tile floor.

Sarah's frenzied screams met with the consoling arms of Detective Marzoli, "There, there now, Miss. It's all over."

An antsy partner paced within the confined room, finally pulling Marzoli aside, whispering, "I can't believe you did that?"

"The first shot should have stopped an elephant," Marzoli replied.

"No, you fool," the frustrated partner jumped in. "You should have let Mayer take them out first, then kill him."

"Just reflex, I guess."

"Your reflexes are gonna put us behind bars."

"There are some lines even I won't cross. That pig deserved what he got without hurting anyone else."

EPILOGUE

Sarah woke from two days of sedation to find herself surrounded by familiar faces: Mamoud's swollen head throbbed in unison with his fractured knee, while his healing second degree burns itched under their wraps; Detective Goodson wore a smile of satisfaction, his self-confidence definitely on the rise; Ahbi's humility and idiosyncrasies allowed him the opportunity to keep his head down and to use his gown to polish the chrome on his wheelchair handle without guilt; Jimmy Pepatino, in full hockey regalia, blocked the bathroom door; and, Jack Michaels, hunched on his crutches, stroking the golden locks of the woman of his dreams.

A loud commotion in the restroom drew everyone's attention to Pepatino.

Jimmy hung his head down and whispered, "Shit!"

"Jimmy, what's going on?" Sarah inquired.

Shaking his head, Pepatino responded, "It's Torpo and Rodeo."

"What are they doing in my bathroom?"

"Well, initially, they were here to keep an eye on you," Jimmy proffered.

"Then?" Sarah prompted.

"Then they found the enema bag hanging on the inside door hook. No telling what those clowns are doing."

"Ewh!" The collective response.

"I know. I know," Jimmy conceded. "Just let them be. No sense them spoiling our reunion."

Sarah shook her head, then gazed at her audience. "Detective, it looks as though you're finally pleased with yourself."

"Angie always told me I had it in me, but I never really believed her. She gave me the strength. I didn't think I could do it on my own until I met you guys. I couldn't believe what you were going through. I got better because of you."

"You improved because you wanted to and you worked hard at it," Jack rattled off matter-of-factly without taking his eyes off Sarah.

"Well, I realize all you guys are in no shape for a night on the town to help me celebrate, so we're all going to move into the lounge for a catered meal from Kozinski's. Best burgers in town."

"I must admit, this is more fun than usual," Jack chortled. "Usually, successful Recovery patients just quit coming to meetings. You generally don't get to celebrate with them."

"No, it's not that! Well, it is partly. But what we're really celebrating is the conclusion of the biggest police corruption case in the history of the department; the apprehension of a serial killer; and, my promotion to detective first grade."

"What police corruption?" Sarah asked.

"Prosecutor Evans, Circuit Judge O'Hara, Police Commissioner Dolan, Chief of Detectives Marzoli and Harrold Mayer were involved in a conspiracy to kill my wife, Angie, as well as, all of you."

"But why? What did we ever do to them?"

"The same thing I did. You started investigating police atrocities during the '67 riots. They were all beat cops then. They summarily murdered several innocent people, just because they were black."

"But we never proved that," Michaels insisted. "They had no reason..."

"Our similar troubles started when we went down to the tombs to look up old run sheets and logs. It doesn't matter that we couldn't pinpoint anything. No one realized what a jumbled mess all the old records would be. They just wanted to be notified in case someone snooped around."

"So, they killed your wife?" Sarah questioned incredulously.

"Yes," Goodson responded, his head held low and his tone instantly sinking to the verge of despair. Collecting his thoughts, Eric continued, "She was my weak spot. Kill a cop and all hell breaks loose, even if he was a schmuck. This way, they effectively eliminated me without all the hoopla; a tragic auto accident that seriously debilitated me from looking further into the records."

"God, that's sick!" Sarah commented, squeamish at the thought.

"And to reward themselves as they rose through the ranks and pulled off their brazen schemes, they looted the Police Benevolent Fund. With the help of a slime bag lawyer, they literally used it as a private piggy bank with absolutely no regard for covering their trail. That's how they could lose so much money on a cop's salary and not give it a second thought. Blue told me, usually, even when someone can afford to throw money away, they have regrets over a substantial loss, but not these guys."

"You make it sound like Blue and you were pretty tight," Mamoud inquired with the wrinkled brow of a serious reporter.

"How do you think I kept up with you kids? I needed someone on the inside to help me along. None of you would really open up to me after the parking lot incident."

"Roy Blue wouldn't snitch," Jack huffed in disbelief.

"Of course not. But he'd lay down his life to protect a friend." A somber pall shrouded the gathering, as if a Sunday preacher asked the congregation to bow their heads in prayer.

"Did I hear someone call my name?" Roy Blue inquired as he stuck his head through the door.

Jack stumbled back on his crutches in disbelief, his butt finding purchase on the floor mounted H-Vac system. "My god. We thought you were dead."

"No such luck. I'm just down the hall," Roy responded, as he ambled into the room.

"But the medics said you had no pulse."

"College Boy, I can't believe you could think that dirty fat rat bastard could get the better of me."

"But how…?"

"Oh, make no mistake. He put me down, hard. Took three hits on the paddles on the way to this place to bring me around."

"But you were shot four times."

"Yeah, and each one would have been fatal had it not been for my bullet proof vest."

"What vest?"

"As luck would have it, it was Butchie's. Won it in the last hand at our weekend game. Ironic huh?" Roy smiled. "I'd like to say I was smart enough to wear it as a defensive measure, but really I had just tried it on as a lark when Ahbi called me for help."

"You could have let us know you were alive." Jack growled, shaking his head.

"It was Goodson's idea for me to lay low in here to see how things played out."

An awkward silence was broken by the reporter's inquisitive nature.

"Detective Goodson, with Mayer dead and Marzoli a hero for saving Sarah, how are you going to prove a case against them?" Mamoud asked, his crunched face flagging his doubt.

"Internal Affairs recorded a recent meeting between O'Hara and Evans. They have everything they need on tape."

"So, they killed Professor Mink?" Jack inquired, his face beet red at the remembrance.

"No, as strange as that seems. They would have killed him, but someone else beat them to it."

"Who else would possibly want to kill Joe Mink? He was one of the nicest and smartest people I knew," Jack offered, tears welling in his eyes.

"A serial killer we've been after for years. He's murdered and mutilated dozens of prostitutes across the county. A brilliant guy who never left so much as a trace fiber to track him until Mink's death."

"Why go after Mink?" Mamoud inquired.

"Jealously and rage," the detective replied. "Your little foray into the riots caused you to unknowingly stumble upon his lair. And because he's a fellow academic."

"Well, you just going to keep us guessing?"

"Because it's Professor Rasmussen."

"You've got to be kidding! That bald headed wimp!" Jack questioned, the bounds of logic stretched to the max.

"Alopecia; no body hair at all, generally associated with stress. A primary reason no connecting evidence existed. Over two dozen women, mostly prostitutes in Detroit, were murdered with a number two lead pencil, same as Mink. I remember Sarah's off the cuff remark about the brute strength it must have taken for Rasmussen to demonstrate his yoga move of propping himself up on the tabletop and swinging his torso back and forth. I couldn't do that if my life depended on it. So, I did some checking. Every time Rasmussen was out, dead whores started showing up. Generally, nobody cares. The cases are given such a low priority that some buffoon is assigned to investigate. This time... moi. When I started asking around, it was clear Mink's popularity with both fellow staff and students was off the charts and his prolific writings assured him publication several times a year. Rasmussen knew his department head status was in peril. For a tenured professor like him, the humiliation would be intolerable. He saw his chance and he took it."

"Unbelievable!" Mamoud sighed

"We'll still need a signed confession to convict him, but we found his lair two floors below ground and what appears to resemble an entire classroom of victims, thanks to your video cam. We can't specifically make him out, but we'll put some serious pressure on him. I can't tell you what he did, but rest assured that Rasmussen and Mayer have some despicable similarities. The ME is trying to ID the bodies."

"When did you realize I had nothing to do with it?"

"At the scene. Using a pencil for a weapon is such a distinctive signature, I knew the killer had slipped up; probably out of rage."

"Thanks for telling me."

Goodson shrugged his shoulders and flipped up his palms in one fluid motion.

"Wow! That's a lot to absorb. This is going to take an entire issue of the *Southern Edge,*" Mamoud declared, abandoning his ghetto dialect.

"You better get ready for a front-page sidebar," Goodson continued with a rare dramatic flair. "It struck me as peculiar that when the doctor informed us of Ahbi's extremely rare AB- blood type, you immediately offered to be a donor. What are the odds?"

"About 2.7 million to one, as Roy Blue would calculate faster than a computer chip," Sarah quipped, a smile finally gracing her battered face.

Roy Blue nodded and smiled.

Ahbi picked up his head and listened intently for the first time.

"You're probably closer than you know. I ran Ahbi's finger prints in the off chance he hit the system at some point."

"Don't tell me, another serial killer," Mamoud concluded.

"No, but somebody everyone had given up for dead. I even took liberties with the department's budget and ran his DNA so there would be no mistake about it."

Michaels reached down a hand to Ahbi's shoulder, preparing for the worst.

"Okay, so what do you have?"

"I present you with Robert Thayer a/k/a Bobbie. He disappeared during the riots and was never heard from again."

Tears swelled in Ahbi's eyes.

"Youse really knows who I am?" The janitor reached out to hold Goodson's hand.

Eric cupped his other palm over Ahbi's backhand, but concentrated his glistening eyes on Mamoud.

The reporter stood stunned, stammering to make sense of the revelation. "What kind of crap you shoveling?"

"No bull. Ahbi is really Robert Thayer, a C.P.A. who lived on Boston Boulevard and was reported missing by his wife, Lucinda on July 26, 1967. He worked with the firm of Preston Brown, who at the time occupied an entire floor in the Guardian Building in downtown Detroit. In their day, they were an accounting powerhouse. You could get your days exercise just by walking the long hallway. Before being awarded a certification, the Fitness and Character Committee performs a criminal background check that requires finger printing. That's why he was in the system. His DNA confirms that he is your father."

Jack turned to Ahbi. "No wonder you felt so comfortable with the Omega. I just thought you had good taste. The dead fat rat bastard must have taken it from you during the riots."

"Exactly my theory," Goodson reaffirmed. "Officer, if you would be so kind," Eric ordered, as the uniformed cop behind Goodson left the room.

"Bullshit!" Mamoud shouted. "This is complete bullshit!"

The uniformed officer returned, escorting Mamoud's Mother, clad in her Sunday best with a matching wide brimmed hat and veil. Goodson moved from Ahbi's view as the woman approached.

"Bobbie?" Lucinda inquired.

"I don't know. I really don't know," Ahbi cried. "I can't remember."

"Momma," Mamoud implored, "This can't be. You said Daddy was dead."

"I never really believed it. Somehow, I always knew he'd be back," Lucinda explained with a look of comfort to the child she had raised on her own. Then peering down at Ahbi, she reached out, encasing his cheeks, "I'd know you, sweet man, anywhere. You're my Bobbie."

"Oh, dear Lord. I wished I could remember."

Goodson squatted down next to the wheelchair.

"It's you. The dried blood on the tennis shoe that Mink found at the Packard plant also matches. Dolan and Mayer a/k/a Reichert beat you to a pulp, stuffed you down a ventilation shaft and left you for dead. By some miracle you survived, recovered as best you could and lived on the streets all these years until Michaels and Blue found you."

Mamoud stood speechless.

"Come on baby, let's go home," Lucinda commented, offering her hand.

As the uniformed officer wheeled out Bobbie Thayer with Lucinda at his side, Michaels turned to a stunned Mamoud.

"Now, that's a story!"